As Lord Wilderness touched the wound in his chest, it puckered and closed like a scar in living wood. Serenely his eyes sought Sturm's.

"It has come to this, young Brightblade. You have made your point and mine," Vertumnus announced, and the stones at his feet grew over with thick moss.

"The rest is your own foolishness. You have entered my game. Which, alas, you must now play to its end, as your injured shoulder will tell you daily and nightly.

"Meet me on the first day of spring," Vertumnus ordered, again with a strange smile. "In my stronghold amid the Southern Darkwoods. Come there alone, and we shall settle this—sword to sword, knight to knight, man to man. You have defended your father's honor, and now I challenge yours. For now I owe you a stroke, as you owe me a life. For it is written in your cherished Measure that *any man who returns a blow must stay the course of battle. . . .*"

THE DRAGONLANCE® SAGA

MEETINGS SEXTET
Volume Four

The Oath and the Measure

Michael Williams

DRAGONLANCE® Saga Meetings
Volume Four

The Oath and the Measure

Copyright ©1992 TSR, Inc.
All Rights Reserved.

First Printing: May 1992
Printed in the United States of America.
Library of Congress Catalog Card Number: 91-66507

9 8 7 6 5

T8343-620

ISBN: 1-56076-336-1

U.S., CANADA, ASIA,
PACIFIC, & LATIN AMERICA
Wizards of the Coast, Inc.
P.O. Box 707
Renton, WA 98057-0707
1-800-324-6496

EUROPEAN HEADQUARTERS
Wizards of the Coast, Belgium
P.B. 2031
2600 Berchem
Belgium
+32-70-23-32-77

Visit our website at **www.tsr.com**

For Margaret Weis

———

Palanthas
Mnts.
Vingaard River
High Clerist Tower
Verkhus Hills
Plains of Solamnia
Vingaard Keep
Vingaard
Solamnia
Mara's Grove
Solanthus
Dun Ringhill
Thelgaard Keep
Mountains
Southern Darkwoods
Garne
Kayolin
Lemish
Southlund
Garnet

Chapter 1

A Surprising Banquet

Lord Alfred MarKenin grew restless as he stood before his place at table. He shivered and rubbed his hands back to life and let his eyes wander through the council hall. Tonight it was a cold sea of banners.

The standards of the great Solamnic houses hung ghostly and strange in the wavering torchlight. The old fabric, once brilliant and thick, now gossamer with age, lifted slightly and floated as the winter wind trickled through the drafty hall. The sign of MarKenin was there, of course, and the farfetched signs of Kar-thon and of MarThasal, interwoven designs of suns, kingfishers, and stars. Among them hung proudly the intertwined roses of Uth Wistan and the phoenix of House Peres. The lesser houses—Inverno and Crownguard and Ledyard and Jeoffrey—were also represented, and their colors fluttered dimly across one another as the banners settled. The first solemnities were observed, and three hundred Knights of Solamnia seated themselves to wait out the death of the year.

For isn't this the beginning and end of the Yuletide? Lord Alfred asked himself as simple Jack, a transplanted gardener, awkwardly lit the candles on the table. The death of another year?

The powerful Knight, High Justice of the Solamnic Order, shifted uncomfortably in the high-backed mahogany chair at the head of the longest table. He dreaded the unexplainable, and the unexplainable was no doubt approaching as the candlelight swelled and lengthened. He looked about, into the faces of his cohorts and lieutenants. They were numerous and as varied as gemstones, and in their eyes, he saw their reflections on this ceremonial night.

Lord Gunthar Uth Wistan sat to his left, stocky and scarcely thirty, though his hair was already steely gray. After Lord Boniface Crownguard, whose honor was legendary, Gunthar was the most skillful swordsman at the banquet. Such men were always impatient with ceremonies like this, finding them somehow too settled and pretty. Lord Alfred sympathized and continued to watch his friend. Gunthar plainly wanted it over with—all of it, from meal to ritual to the grand disruptions. Uneasily he stared out across the vast armada of standards to where darkness swallowed the silk and linen and damask, to the place where Lord Boniface, his marginally friendly rival, also sat with an entourage of youthful admirers—squires who mimicked his attitude and envied the great man's swordsmanship.

No doubt a similar impatience rose from those shadows. Though Gunthar claimed that Boniface wore the waiting more gracefully in his ardor for Oath and Measure, there was something else to the big Knight's restlessness and silence, thought Alfred. To Gunthar's way of thinking, ceremony was the delay between battles, but to Boniface, it was the battle proper.

To Lord Alfred's right, Lord Stephan Peres, an ancient veteran on his last but extraordinarily durable legs, had seated himself with an audible creak and a quiet groan. Alfred leaned back, drumming his gloved fingers across the dark arms of the chair, then raised his right hand. At his signal, the music began. It was a ponderous march, slow and melancholy as befit the dirge for the year, the three hundred and forty-first since the Cataclysm.

Beside the High Justice, old Lord Stephan smiled faintly in his forest of a beard. He was a tall man and lean, having parried gracefully that tendency of the older Knights to sink into heaviness and dreams. They said it was eccentricity that had kept him healthy—that and the gift of being amused at just about anything that came to pass in the Tower and the Order.

Tonight, though, the old man's amusement was strained. The end of his eighty-fifth year approached, and with it, as always, this ceremony of memory where the halls were decked with banners. He was weary of it all: the pomp and the trumpetry, the abyss of winter, December's winds full bitter in the Vingaard Mountains.

Lord Stephan raised his glass, and with lowered eyes, Jack filled it once more with amber Kharolian wine. Through its glistening gold, Stephan watched the squires' table nearest that of Lord Boniface, focusing on a solitary wavering candle in the ceremonial darkness.

A young man sat by the flame, lost in thought. Sturm Brightblade, it was. A southerner from Solace, though his family was northern, ancient in the Order.

The image of Angriff Brightblade, Lord Stephan thought. Of Angriff Brightblade and of Emelin before him, and of Bayard and Helmar and every Brightblade all the way back to Bertel, to the founding of the line in the Age of Might.

Sturm would have been pleased with Stephan's thoughts, for after all, it was to find his place in that chain that he had returned to beleaguered Solamnia after six years of exile.

Smuggled from Castle Brightblade one winter's night in his eleventh year, he remembered his father in images and episodes, as a series of events rather than a living person. From the beginning, Angriff Brightblade had concerned himself with Solamnic duties, leaving the lad to the care of his mother and the servants.

Sturm, though, had fabled a father from scattered memories, from his mother's stories, and no doubt from sheer imagining. Angriff grew kinder and more courageous the longer the boy dreamed, and dreams became his refuge in Abanasinia, far away from the Solamnic courts, among indifferent southerners in a nondescript hamlet called Solace. There his mother, the Lady Ilys, raised him with more tutors than friends, schooling him in courtesy and lore and his heritage. . . .

And ruining him, Lord Stephan thought with a smile, for anything except Solamnic Knighthood.

Ilys had died of the plague. They said the boy had dismissed his few friends and grieved alone, in silence and with the proper vigils. That fall, Lords Gunthar and Boniface, who had been Angriff Brightblade's closest friends, arranged to have Sturm brought back to Thelgaard Keep, where he could be trained further in the ways of the Order.

Sturm hadn't taken to the North at first. He was smart, that was certain, and the years of genteel poverty had toughened him in ways that the northern boys secretly envied: He was knowledgeable in the woods and rode horseback like a seasoned Knight. But his southern ways and old Solamnic charm seemed like relics of the last generation to the urbane younger men, squires and Knights from prominent Solamnic families. They called him "Grandpa Sturm" and laughed at his accent, his storehouse of remembered poetry, his attempts to grow a mustache.

They once laughed at his father, too, Stephan mused. Some laughed right up until the night of the siege.

It was hard going at Sturm's table, this or any night.

"Where is *your* banner, Brightblade?" Derek Crownguard hissed mockingly over the boards. He was nephew to the great swordsman and exceeding proud of his family ties, though he hadn't yet proved whether he shared more than blood and a name with his legendary uncle.

Derek sneered, and his burly companions, all hangers-on to the Crownguards of Foghaven, stifled their laughter. Two of them looked nervously to the High Table, where the assembled lords sat lost in memory and ritual, from the oldest loremaster and counselor to the younger war leaders, such as Gunthar and Boniface. Assured that their masters' gazes rested elsewhere, the squires turned back like hyenas, grinning and eager to feast.

"Be still, Derek!" Sturm Brightblade muttered, his brown eyes averted. It was a weak retort, the lad knew, and yet it was all he could summon against the vicious teasing of the other squires. Derek was the worst, all puffed and proud at being Lord Boniface's chosen squire, but all were difficult, all scornful and superior. His friends Caramon and Raistlin had warned Sturm in long conversations over firelight and ale that talk at the Tower of the High Clerist was quick and sharp and often political. When Sturm's fellows turned upon him with their edged words and jests about his missing father, he felt rural and awkward and disinherited.

And in fact, was he not all those things?

Sturm flushed angrily, clenching his whitened fists under the table. Derek snorted in triumph and turned to the center of the hall, where the ceremonies continued, as they had for a thousand years in this very room. The harpist, a silver-haired elf in a plain blue tunic, had stepped out from the swirl of banners, and there in the red tilt of light cast by the encircling torches, had begun to play the time-honored Song of Huma, that old contraption of myth and high-blown heroics. "Out of the village," it began,

> . . . out of the thatched and clutching shires,
> Out of the grave and furrow, furrow and grave,
> Where his sword first tried the last cruel dances

> of childhood,
> And awoke to the shires forever retreating, his
> greatness a marshfire,
> The banked flight of the Kingfisher always
> above him. . . .

Quietly the Knights began to mouth the words, and slowly the song rose in the torchlit room—the tale of Huma's love and sacrifice and enshrinement. Sturm's anger subsided as he, like the rest of the young men who sat around him, entered the world of the story.

Sturm knew the tradition. If the song were sung perfectly and in unison on a night of special auspice, a night such as Yuletide or Midsummer, Lord Huma himself would return and be seated among the singers. That was why the foremost place at the foremost table was always left empty. Slowly the lad joined in, breathing the words as the room filled with the sound of a soft wind, of one clear elven voice raised in song and three hundred others whispering. Only the youngest still held out hope that extraordinary things would happen at this or at any Yuletide.

So they continued, chanting monotonously, until the outburst of the flute startled them all.

From the rafters, the harsh tune tumbled, frenzied and playful, and with the music a rain of light, green and golden, dispersed the shadows in the great hall and dazzled the astonished Knights. At once the whispering faded into silence along with the song of the bard as the new, discordant music rose and quickened and the chamber swelled with its notes. It was like the trilling of birds, or the droning of bees, or the whine of wind through the high evergreen branches. All of the Knights remembered it differently later, and whatever their description, they knew the song eluded it, for it was shifting and large and ever-changing.

Dumbstruck, Sturm braced himself heavily against the table. The wood shuddered beneath his stiffened hands, and the goblets chimed absurdly as they dropped to the stone floor and shattered. The sweet woodsmoke in the air turned suddenly to a sharp and watery perfume, the odor of spilt wine, then of fresh grapes and strawberries, then the sudden, pungent freshness of leaves. The torches around the tables extinguished, and suddenly, surprisingly, the great council hall was awash in moonlight, silver and red.

"Great Solin and Luin!" Sturm exclaimed under his breath, exchanging shocked glances with Derek Crownguard.

Then Lord Wilderness appeared in the rafters above them, bristling with music and green sparks.

* * * * *

Sturm had never seen the likes of him. The man's armor glistened with the waxy, depthless green of holly. Embossed roses, red and green, intertwined on his breastplate, and leaves and scarlet berries cascaded from his gauntlets and greaves, trailing behind him like a rumor of spring in the lifeless midwinter hall. About his face, more leaves flared and clustered like green flame, like a glory of grassy light, at the center of which his wide black eyes darted and glittered and laughed. He was a huge green bird or a dryad's consort, and again he raised the flute to his lips and again the music burst forth limitless, out of the dusk and cedars and pines. He leapt to the floor with astonishing lightness.

Slowly, their faces stern and forbidding, Lord Alfred, Lord Gunthar, and Lord Stephan rose to their feet, their hands riding lightly on the hilts of their swords. Sir Adamant Jeoffrey and Lord Boniface of Foghaven stepped from behind their tables, moving toward the center of the room, then suddenly stopped, their expressions uncharacteristically cautious. Servants scattered to the far corners of the hall as more crystal broke and silver jangled on the stone floor. The strange, leafy monstrosity ignored the commotion, crouching comically in the center of the hall as the elven minstrel picked up his harp and scrambled away in a flurry of oaths and twanging strings, his coat tangled in holly thorns.

"Who are you?" Lord Alfred asked, his voice thunderous. "How dare you disturb this most solemn of nights?"

The green man pivoted full circle, his flute vanishing somewhere in the jungle of leaf and armor that covered him. Faintly Sturm heard its music echoing up the stairwell, as echo doubled back upon echo until the melody finally traveled beyond his hearing.

"I am Vertumnus," said the intruder, in a voice mild and low. "I am the seasons turning, and I am the home of the past years."

"And the belfry for a thousand bats," Derek muttered, but an icy glance from Lord Gunthar silenced the young man.

"And what," Lord Alfred asked, "does . . . m'lord Vertumnus want of us this Yuletide?" The High Justice was tense, ceremonious, his fingers playing across the gold pommel of his sword.

"I wish to make a point near and dear to my heart," Vertumnus announced, seating himself unceremoniously on the floor.

He removed his helmet, and green fire danced at his temples.

Sturm frowned nervously. He knew that dark enchanters were wizards of merriment, urging their victims to be less somber, less gloomy. Finally less good. Then, when they had you lost in laughter and song, they would . . .

What they would do, he did not know. But it would destroy you.

"You Solamnics gather like owls in these halls in the dead of the year," Vertumnus said, "hooting of dark times and times past and how far the world has tumbled from ages of dream and might. Look around you—the Clerist's Tower is a hall of mirrors. You can see yourselves from all vantages and angles, preening and garnishing and admiring your own importance."

"By your leave, Lord Alfred," Lord Gunthar interrupted, his sword half drawn from its sheath. "By your leave, I shall show this . . . this *pasturage* the door, and perhaps the shortest way down the mountain."

Vertumnus smiled menacingly, his windburned face crinkling like the bark of an enormous vallenwood. The banners drifted in a warm, unseasonable breeze. "Never let it be said," he announced calmly, the faint rustle of his voice surprisingly audible even in the farthest corners of the enormous chamber, "that when there is sword or mace or lance available, Lord Gunthar will settle for words or wit or policy."

"Mild words will not avail you, Vertumnus," Gunthar menaced, oblivious to the insult.

Lord Wilderness only laughed. Rising with a creak of armor and a rustling of leaves, Vertumnus waggled his flute at the foremost table, at the empty chair. It was a clownish gesture, but unsettling, even obscene. The older Knights gasped, and several of the younger ones drew swords. Calm and unhurried, Vertumnus turned gracefully about, brandishing the flute like a saber. It whistled hauntingly as he waved it through the air, and Sturm watched him in fascination.

"To my point: There is a seat where no one sits," Vertumnus observed. "Nor guest nor beggar nor orphan nor foreigner—none whom you have sworn by the Oath to guard and to champion. And the chair is empty this night and all others, a seat for the parrot and popinjay."

Lord Alfred MarKenin glowered at Vertumnus, who continued serenely.

"For the Oath you swore in this nest of oaths," Vertumnus claimed, his wild eyes riveted to the empty chair, "is dark and grim and wise in the depths of the night. But you have no joy in following it. Even this festival shows so."

"Who are you, outlander, to tell us of our joys and our festivals?" Lord Alfred boomed. "A thing of leaf and patch and tatters, to speak of Huma's waiting chair?"

Gunthar and Stephan turned suddenly toward the shadows, then back again, their faces unreadable in the shifting light. Suddenly Lord Alfred stepped from behind the table and, pointing at the Green Man, addressed him in a voice usually reserved for horses and underlings and untrained or untrainable squires.

"Who are you to question our customs, the thousand year waiting of our dreams? You—you *walking, tooting salad!*"

"Old man!" Vertumnus retorted and lurched, stopping mere inches from the High Justice. "You empty, gilded breastplate! You vacant helmet and flapping banner! You mask of laws and absence of justice! You tally sheet! You plodding ass with a snout for letters, foraging honor in a barren plain! If a prophetic breeze passed by you, you would mistake it for the flatulence of your brothers!"

Sturm shook his head. The strange name-calling was too fanciful, almost silly, as though it were a duel of bards or, even worse, a quarrel of birds in the rafters. Lord Alfred MarKenin was the High Justice of the Solamnic Order, to be addressed in respect and deference and duty, but the Green Man rained words upon him, and, stunned and spellbound, the High Justice only staggered and fell silent.

All about Sturm, his comrades fidgeted and coughed, their eyes on the windows and rafters. For a band of lads who delighted in banter and wrangling, they, too, were strangely quiet. Occasionally a nervous laugh burst out of the shadows, but no squire dared to look at another, and certainly none dared to speak.

Now Lord Stephan stepped forth, his eyes bright with a sudden amusement. Sturm frowned apprehensively, for the old man was half wilderness himself, teasing the young knights from the strictest observance of the Oath and laughing at the far outreaches of the Measure, where grammar and table manners were set in stone for even the youngest Solamnics.

It was a head wound sixty years back, suffered in some

obscure Nerakan pass, that had rendered him oblique and irreverent. He seemed to be enjoying this shrill exchange, and Sturm realized, with rising embarrassment, that the old man was clearing his throat.

"What, Lord Vertumnus, would you have us do?" the old man asked, his voice still loud and firm after eighty-five years. "What would you have of us, if we are hypocrites and masks of justice? I see no widows, no orphans with you. What have *you* done for the poor and the outcast and the unfortunate?"

"I have made you ask that question," Vertumnus replied with a sly smile. "You are an old fox, Stephan, full of more wisdom than a bloodhound could find in the rest of this roomful of addleheads. And yet the old fox doubles back on his trail, turning on his own stink until he circles the woods and goes nowhere."

"Poetry instead of policy, Lord Wilderness?" Stephan asked, his white beard rising like spindrift as he settled himself with a grunt and creaking of knees directly in front of the Green Man, who neither flinched nor backed away.

"What I do for orphans is not your concern," Vertumnus answered calmly, "for it does not change the ruinous shires of Solamnia, the vanishing villages and the fires and the famines and the new, unspeakable dragons. No orphan here would question *me*. No, he would second my outcry."

He paused, his dark eyes searching the room.

"That is, if there were aught of orphans here."

You are wrong, Lord Wilderness, Sturm thought, shifting his feet, preparing to step forward.

But no. "Orphans," he had said.

"Besides," Vertumnus continued, "*I* have sworn no oaths to protect them."

A torch fluttered and gasped in a sconce near Sturm Brightblade, and Vertumnus raised the flute again to his lips.

His melody hovered, sad and haunted, and within it, Sturm thought he heard something of autumn and dying and an impossibly vanished time. It was a thin, melancholy music, and the dead leaves whirled about the hall like ghosts fleeing an enchanter, yellow and black and hectic red.

He *is* an enchanter, Sturm thought. He speaks in double-talk and riddles. Do not listen to him. Do not listen.

Vertumnus took another step forward. He stood face-to-face with the ancient Solamnic lord, and their eyes met without anger, and words passed between them, so hushed that even Lord Alfred, who stood not two strides away from Lord Stephan, swore later that he could not hear what was said. Then the Green Man rocked back on his heels and laughed, and Lord Stephan Peres unexplainably sprouted foliage.

Shoots and tendrils and branches flourished in the old man's armor, so that leaves intertwined with his beard and vines entangled his fingers. Vertumnus stepped back toward the center of the hall and again played his flute, this time a merry summer's air, and the elegant old man who had served long years as the steward for the missing High Clerist now blossomed sweetly with a hundred blue flowers, and a navy of yellow butterflies descended from somewhere out of the winter rafters and settled happily on Lord Stephan Peres.

" 'Tis enough!" Lord Gunthar exclaimed and stepped forward, his fists raised and doubled, but the legs of his table were sprouting, too, and corded roots snaked and tangled about his ankles, slowing his progress toward the center of the room. Stephan gestured, but his meaning was lost among the flowers. Vertumnus whirled from the charging Solamnic lord gracefully as Gunthar crashed into a table where the Jeoffrey brothers were seated, sending glassware and crockery and Jeoffreys scattering in all directions. Young Jack, who had apparently crawled beneath the table in search of better banquet leavings, scrambled to safety as the table collapsed and then began to take root in the floor, its dark boards branching and budding.

Someone pushed Sturm aside. "For the Oath and Measure!" Lord Boniface shouted, and surged rashly into the center of the room. His sword was drawn and his shield ready, his cold blue eyes as bright as tempered steel with the prospect of battle. Vertumnus spun about, winked at the Knight, then turned to face the onrush of one of the Jeoffrey brothers as Boniface fell facefirst onto the stone floor, his leggings mysteriously fallen about his ankles.

The Jeoffrey reconsidered, then fainted, and wordlessly Vertumnus leapt atop another table, hurdling the grasp of the other Jeoffrey, who suddenly found himself rooted to the floor like a sapling. The young Knight cried out, and the room fell to an ominous stillness, a dozen men poised for attack, their single adversary dancing on one foot atop the table, flute raised to play again.

It is an indignity! Sturm thought. An indignity past the telling and enduring. He caught Derek's eye as he stepped forward, scarcely thinking about what he was doing, and drew his shortsword. Aside from that of the thoroughly embarrassed Boniface, it was the only bare blade in the room. It had never even been blooded.

Vertumnus twirled to face the lad, then ceased his dance. A mournful shadow passed over his face, and he nodded. As though in reluctant agreement, he stepped down, set aside his flute, drew his own enormous sword, and moved to the center of the great hall. The Knights of Solamnia stood rooted and helpless amid the green thicket of broken tables. Peering through the leaves and shadows, they watched the swordsmen circle each other, Green Man and green lad.

Sturm knew at once and too late that he was overmatched. Vertumnus had the thoughtless grace of an expert swordsman, and the blade took life in his hand. He spoke to the lad as they circled each other, his words as soft and insinuating as the wind, his eyes locked on Sturm's.

"Set it aside, boy," Vertumnus whispered, the dark eyes flickering. "For you know not the forest you're bordering . . .

where the blade fails against darkness and thorn. . . ."

"Enough poetry!" Sturm muttered. "My sword for Brightblade and the Order!" He would at least make a good show of it.

But his thrust was tentative and slow. Vertumnus brushed it lightly away.

"For *Brightblade* and the Order?" the wild man hissed, suddenly behind the lad, who stumbled as he wheeled to face him. "For the Order gone bad in the teeth and botched? For a father . . . your father . . . who had no business with Solamnic honor?"

"No business?" Sturm's hand wavered with his voice. Vertumnus backed away from him, eyes on the main entrance to the council hall, to the stairway and the winter night. He thought he heard Derek snicker. "No business? Wh-what do you . . ."

Lord Wilderness's dark stare returned, fierce and almost predatory. With a swift turn of the wrist, as bright and elusive as summer lightning, Vertumnus's sword flashed by Sturm's uncertain guard and plunged deep into his left shoulder.

Dazed, breathless, Sturm fell to his knees. His shoulder, his chest, his heart blazed with green fire and lancing pain. The air hummed about his ears like a choir of insistent gnats, their song mournful and menacing.

So this is dying I am dying dying, his thoughts tumbled, and suddenly the pain subsided, no longer unbearable but dull and insistent as, to Sturm's consternation, the wound in his shoulder closed swiftly and cleanly, the fresh blood fading from his white ceremonial tunic. Yet the pain burrowed and seared, as insistent as the humming in the air.

"Look about you, boy," Vertumnus said scornfully. "Where is a place for a man like your father among the likes of these?"

Sturm forgot his wound at once. He shouted and surged to his feet, his young voice cracking with emotion. He rushed toward Vertumnus blindly, both hands bracing the shortsword. Calmly his opponent stepped aside, and the blade lodged deeply in an oaken limb, recently sprung from the heart of Huma's chair.

The lad tugged at the sword and tugged again, glancing frantically over his throbbing shoulder as Vertumnus stepped menacingly forward. Then slowly Vertumnus lowered his sword. He measured Sturm as the boy labored his blade from the hard wood and smiled when the young man whirled awkwardly to face him.

Vertumnus's grin was baffling, as unreadable as the edge of the wilderness. It angered Sturm even more than his words. With another cry, he lunged at his adversary, and Vertumnus's knees buckled as the lad's blade drove cleanly into his chest.

Chapter 2

The Call of the Measure

The flute clattered to the floor and lay still. Instantly the chill of winter returned and settled painfully about the Knights' feet. The hall lay silent, as if the air were frozen.

"Sturm . . ." Lord Stephan began in astonishment. The young man staggered, wrenched free the sword, and Vertumnus fell forward solidly and quite lifelessly. Gunthar rushed toward the Green Man, and Sturm winced as the strong hand of Lord Alfred clutched his shoulder.

The smear on Sturm's blade was clear and wet, and the resinous smell of evergreen rose from its blood gutter. He turned wildly, marking the puzzlement of Alfred, of Gunthar, Lord Stephan's strange wounded stare, and, by the sundered table, the anger of Lord Boniface, who glared incredulously and jealously at the lad, then stooped to wrench up his leggings.

"What have you done, lad?" Alfred bellowed. "*What have you . . .*" The question rang in the hall, again and again, the only sound in the abject, cavernous silence.

Then Vertumnus sprang up and pushed the astonished Lord Gunthar aside. Throughout the hall rushed an enormous intake of breath, as though the room itself had gasped. As Lord Wilderness touched the wound in his chest, it puckered and closed like a scar in living wood. Serenely his eyes sought Sturm's.

"It has come to this, young Brightblade. You have made your point and mine," Vertumnus announced, and the stones at his feet grew over with thick moss.

"The rest is your own foolishness. You have entered my game. Which, alas, you must now play to its end, as your shoulder will tell you daily and nightly."

Outside the window, the songbirds choired again. Wide-eyed, Sturm looked from the Green Man to his unwiped sword, from the sword back to Vertumnus. In great perplexity, with controlled focus, the young man touched his blade. It was dry and clean.

"Meet me on the first day of spring," Vertumnus ordered, again with a strange smile. "In my stronghold amid the Southern Darkwoods. Come there alone, and we shall settle this—sword to sword, knight to knight, man to man. You have defended your father's honor, and now I challenge yours. For now I owe you a stroke, as you owe me a life. For it is written in your cherished Measure that *any man who returns a blow must stay the course of battle.*"

Sturm looked about him in confusion. Gunthar and Alfred stood frozen on the dais, and Lord Stephan opened his mouth to speak, but no words came forth.

Hawk-eyed, expectant, Lord Boniface nodded. What Vertumnus said concerning returning blow was indeed enshrined in the Measure. Sturm was trapped in an ancient statute by his impulsive deed.

"I will lead you to that place when the time comes," Vertumnus announced. "And you might learn something of your father in that place and time. However, you must make your own way. If you fail to meet me at the appointed place, on the appointed night, your honor is forever forfeit.

"Nor is your honor alone in jeopardy," Lord Wilderness continued with a mysterious smile. "For indeed, you owe me a life, Sturm Brightblade, and you will pay it whether or not you arrive at the appointed time."

Dramatically he gestured at the lad's shoulder.

"You can come like a child of the Order and meet my challenge," he pronounced, "or you can cower in the halls of this fortress and await the greening of your wound. For the deeds of my sword bloom forth in the spring, and their blossoms are dreadful and fatal."

The hall filled with more leaves and vines and tendrils, with briars and roots and branches enough to take a week to clear. The Green Man closed his eyes, bowed his head, and vanished amid the rustle as the torches on the walls burst suddenly into a cold white flame. Astonished, Sturm squinted through the shadowy thicket, but Vertumnus was truly gone, leaving behind mist and woodsmoke and the watery, metallic smell of the woods after lightning.

"Of all the trouble you might have uprooted, lad," Lord Alfred proclaimed sorrowfully, "of all you might have done or left undone, this indeed was the worst of things."

"The worst of things?" Sturm asked. "I . . . I don't . . ."

Already, with their sober efficiency, the young knights were clearing the hall of foliage and brambles. Sturm stood in the midst of the razing and repair, looking up at the assembly of Knights who had gathered beside the empty throne of Huma. The young man shook his head, trying to banish the night as he would a confusing dream.

"Will you follow me, Sturm Brightblade?" Lord Alfred asked, this time in a softer voice. Gunthar and Stephan closed ranks behind him, their ceremonial armor glittering almost blindingly. From their places amid the wreckage of Vertumnus's visit, Lord Adamant and Lord Boniface joined the formidable triad.

Like suns, the lad thought. Like suns and meteors. I cannot approach them, and it is hard even to look at them.

"I thought . . ." Sturm began, but in the echoing hall, his voice was thin and weak. He couldn't say what he had thought. He could no longer think of it.

Alfred nodded, and Lord Gunthar stepped forward as Alfred gracefully took the younger man's place beside Stephan.

Behind him, the sawing and hacking died. Only the servants continued with their tasks—old Reza and the boy, Jack, sweeping up the last of the shattered crystal. The young men of the Order, reluctant to do a servant's work in the first place, had stopped to listen to the drama unfolding beside Huma's throne, delighting in the discomfort and possibly the punishment of one almost their age. For despite its devotion to the various honors of the Measure, the Clerist's Tower was home to gossip and to rivalry that was not always friendly.

Lord Stephan was a veteran of these wars, too. He stepped toward Sturm and, clutching the lad's arm in his gloved hand, led him past the craning necks and the sidelong glances, straight through the western door into the hush of the chapel. Lords Gunthar and Alfred followed closely behind, and behind them, the renowned Lord Boniface. Those left in the council hall returned to their business, no doubt imagining great mysteries and chastisements unfolding in the tinted light of the locked room.

There Lord Stephan seated the lad none too softly on an oaken bench by the window. Sturm clutched his shoulder and shivered as the wind crept through the old stone tracery behind him. But he shivered also at the ancient patterns in the stained glass: the rose, the horns of the bison, the yellow harp and the white sphere, the blue helix, all within the silver triangle of the great god Paladine, who contains all things yet transcends them. All were symbols of the old pantheon, which the Order still honored, despite dark times and the dangers of Ansalon.

The shelves sagged with thick, leather-bound volumes of mathematics, physics, architecture—studies the young man had shunned in the sparse days with his mother in Solace. "Sturm," she had warned him then, "it is the books for you now. Sword and Order and father have failed you. A scholar may not be a wealthy man, but a scholar eats, his house safe from fire and his head from the axe." Sturm frowned and shook his head: The Lady Ilys had called out these things from the centermost room of the cottage, a chamber away from the light and windows. He had pretended to listen, then set aside the books and scrambled to the thatched roof of the house. There, above his mother's admonishments, he fixed his eyes to the north, over the Plains of Abanasinia, where the horizon was nothing but light and plains, but a boy could imagine the turbulent Straits of Schallsea and north of that the southernmost coasts of Solamnia.

Now it seemed to Sturm that the chapel's books mocked him and his wasted years among thatch and squirrels and birds. He had traveled far from Solace, only to be brought to another dark room and these same books, on what he now realized to be most somber business.

"The fault is not entirely yours, lad," Lord Stephan began mildly, and yet Sturm heard a strange confusion in his voice as the old man paced before the altar, his eyes downcast. "Not entirely yours. This Vertumnus, it seemed, unsettled and surprised the lot of us."

"How *did* that happen, Lord Gunthar?" Boniface asked mockingly. "I assumed that the guardianship of the hall was under your . . . capable command, as is always the case on a banquet night."

Gunthar snorted angrily and leaned against the chapel door. There was no love lost between the two superlative swordsmen, the result of a generation's fierce rivalry.

" 'Tis being seen to, Boniface! No need for your damned gloating and delight!" he rumbled, his gray brows smoldering.

"Well . . ." Lord Stephan interrupted, his dry voice melodious and soothing. "Whatever the circumstance, we have no doubt finally met the fabled Lord Wilderness, and he's every bit as curious as the stories say."

"The stories!" Sturm exclaimed, half rising from his chair. "Do you mean to say you *knew* of this monstrosity, and . . . and . . ."

"We knew indeed," Alfred replied. "Lord Wilderness is the companion to a hundred rumors, and deaf is the Solamnic Knight who hasn't heard one of them. We knew of him but had never seen him. How could we have expected his visit? This chorus and burgeoning of vines?"

Gunthar glanced at Boniface angrily, and the four Knights settled into their private thoughts.

"The hour is late," Alfred replied after a long pause, "and our thoughts border on fancy. Perhaps we should address this in the morning, when sunlight shines on what has come to pass, rather than the curious double light of the moon."

"I agree with Lord Alfred," chimed in Lord Boniface, and Lord Gunthar nodded also.

"But wait. Who *is* Vertumnus?" Sturm asked.

Nervously the Knights exchanged glances.

"I have heard," Lord Alfred began, "that he is a renegade Knight whose path entangled with elves and all kinds of woodland foolishness. I have heard that he captains a band of Nerakan bandits down in his Southern Darkwoods."

"I have heard Vertumnus is a druid," Lord Gunthar declared. "A great pagan priest whose heart is as hard and knotted as oak. His sanctuary in the Darkwoods is a forbidden place, where birds whisper the last words of criminals and the dead hang like fruit from the limbs of trees."

Sturm frowned. *That* seemed even more fanciful than the renegade Knight.

"And I have heard," chimed in Lord Stephan, stirring up dust, "that the blood of the man is pure wizardry, that his dark eyes are fashioned from stone from the black moon Nuitari. I have heard that the Southern Darkwoods are all an illusion, born of the black moon and the sorcerer's dreams."

"And yet he visits us in the Yuletide?" Sturm asked. "And wizard or druid or bandit Knight, he gains our most listening ears? How . . . how did this happen? And why?"

"I expect," Lord Boniface observed dryly, "that Lord Gunthar will see to that answer shortly. How a single man could weave through vedettes of Solamnia's finest young men, leading that great boar after him . . .

"Great boar?" the four others exclaimed, turning in unison to Lord Boniface. The famous Knight frowned, and Alfred laid an uneasy hand on his shoulder.

"We . . . we saw no boar, Lord Boniface," the High Justice explained. "Perhaps the night's confusion . . . or the wine . . ."

"I tell you, 'twas a boar I saw!" Boniface insisted angrily. "And if I saw it, 'twas there, by Paladine and Majere and whatever good god you could name!"

"Be that as it may, we saw no boar," Alfred repeated patiently. "Only the flock of ravens in the rafters . . ."

He paused as the other Knights stared at him in puzzlement.

"You . . . you saw no ravens," he concluded bleakly. "None of you did."

"I did not look above me," Stephan soothed. "Though by Paladine and all the assembled gods, I remember the shrill and insulting dryads the Green Man brought with him."

It was his turn to be the curiosity. The Knights gazed at him in perplexity.

"Something also of corn and murmuring bees, it was," Stephan muttered, "and a great *bear*, not a *boar*, danced in our midst."

"No, no," Gunthar corrected. "It was Vertumnus alone. I'm positive."

"A hall of mirrors, this business," Stephan muttered.

"But the shedding of blood?" Sturm asked. "The sap flowing from a wound?"

"Sap?" Lord Boniface asked incredulously. Four pairs of Solamnic eyes turned toward the lad, as though he had suddenly announced that the moons had fallen.

Stephan chuckled, and then suddenly grew somber, his eyes on the shivering lad who sat uncomfortably on the bench before him. "The problem is, Sturm, that whatever we saw, we agree that you were wounded, that in rage you dropped Lord Wilderness, and we all heard the challenge afterward."

"The boy was wounded?" Gunthar asked in alarm. He stepped toward Sturm and extended his hand. "Where did he cut you, Sturm?"

"At my shoulder," the lad replied, pointing to the wound . . .

. . . which had vanished entirely. The pure white fabric of his ceremonial tunic, unstained and untorn, covered the spot where the wound throbbed faintly. In silent bafflement, Gunthar and Alfred examined Sturm's shoulder.

"Whatever you're feeling," Alfred pronounced quietly, "I see no wound. And yet a wound would make sense. Without it, the last threats of that green monstrosity would be ridiculous."

He looked at the other Knights, who nodded gravely.

"Whether you be wounded or whole, Sturm Brightblade," Lord Alfred continued, raising his index finger pontifically, like a scholar or lawyer, "there remains the problem at hand. Whatever we remember, this thing—this swordplay and killing and rising from death and . . . and *dripping sap*, for the gods' sake!—'tis more important than dryad or boar, or your wound, for that matter. For Vertumnus addressed *you*, and it was to you that his challenge descended."

"Indeed," Lord Boniface said, firmly but not unkindly. "And now we must decide what this means."

Sturm looked from face to face in the dimly lit library. Already the shadows in the room had shifted from the deepest blackness to a sort of foggy gray. Perhaps that, too, was a power of Vertumnus's music—to collapse a long night into a brief conversation. Or perhaps the time had passed so rapidly, like the years in Solace, merely because Sturm had not kept track of it.

Sturm was almost relieved when a soft rapping at the door signalled the entrance of the Tower sentries, or at least two of the company, whose honor or misfortune it was to speak for the threescore men assigned to guard the stronghold and the ceremonies therein. Shamefaced and shuffling, red to the ears and downcast of shoulder and eye, they stood in the doorway.

The sixty sentries were crack foot soldiers, gathered from all over Solamnia, schooled by the Order, and blooded in the Nerakan Wars. They were not the kind of men accustomed to nodding at their posts.

But out of their number, fifty had heard a soft, plaintive music rising out of the winter night. Some swore it was a folk song from northern Coastlund they heard on the brisk December wind; others thought it was something more refined and classical, the likes of which they had heard in the vaulted courts of Palanthas.

Some claimed it was a lullaby. But whatever the tune that reached the sentries who manned the walls from the Knight's Spur to the Wings of Habbakuk, it acted as a lullaby indeed, for they awoke hours later, tied to their stations by entanglements of vine and root, their comrades tugging frantically at the undergrowth that imprisoned them.

Lord Alfred listened in a fuming silence as the pair mumbled through their story. He scarcely looked at them as he dismissed them, his eyes on a tumbled stack of books that lay tilted and open on a lectern in the corner of the room. The door closed behind the sentries, and an enormous mutual sigh faded with their footsteps into the distant clamor of the hall.

"So he's as powerful as they say, this Vertumnus," Alfred said quietly in the restored silence of the room. "That is all the more troubling, especially when I consider what lies ahead for the boy."

All eyes returned to Sturm. He wished he could have joined the sentries in their retreat, but he held his breath and fought down the fear.

"I believe," the High Justice began, "that you have been singled out for a purpose."

"What kind of purpose?" Sturm asked.

"If you've been listening, lad, you've probably gathered that we're no closer to answering that than you are," Stephan explained with a smile. "All we know is that something in the music and the mockery and the flyting was such that it fell to you to bear sword against Lord Wilderness and to defeat him in combat, only to find that he is the victor while the game is not over. It's a riddle, to be certain."

"And the answer?" prompted Sturm.

"I believe he gave you the answer," Lord Alfred replied. "That on the first day of spring you—and you alone—are to meet him in his stronghold amid the Southern Darkwoods. There apparently the two of you shall settle this issue, as the Green Man said, 'sword to sword, knight to knight, man to man.' 'Tis written full clear that the Measure of the Sword lies 'in accepting the challenge of combat for the honor of the Knighthood.' "

Sturm swallowed hard and slipped his cold hands under his robe. The Knights regarded him grimly, uncertain whether a death warrant lay in Lord Alfred's pronouncements.

"One thing is certain, lad," Boniface said. "You've been called to a challenge."

"And I accept, Lord Boniface," Sturm said bravely. He stood, but his legs wobbled. Swiftly Lord Gunthar moved to steady him with a strong hand.

"But you are not a Knight, Sturm," Lord Stephan said. "Not yet, that is. And though the Oath and Measure run in your blood, perhaps you are not bound to them."

"And yet," Lord Boniface insisted softly, "you *are* a Brightblade." He leaned toward Sturm, his blue eyes searching and raking at the heart of the boy.

Sturm sat again, this time clumsily. He covered his face with his hands. Again the strange banquet played through his recollection, and the edges of his memory were blurred, uncertain. Vertumnus's face was vague when he tried to recall it, as were the melodies, the alien tunes that only an hour ago Sturm thought he would never forget.

What was certain in this? He remembered only the challenge clearly. That challenge was certain—as certain as the Oath and Measure, by which a Knight was bound to accept such challenges.

"Lord Stephan is right when he says I am not yet part of the Order," Sturm began, his eyes fixed on the library shelves beyond the Knights. The books seemed to dance in the dim light, green bound and mocking. "And yet I am tied to the Oath by heritage. It's . . . it's almost as if it *does* run in my blood. And if that's the case—if it's something that connects me to my father, like Vertumnus said, or I thought I heard him say—then I want to follow it."

Alfred nodded, the hint of a smile at the corner of his mouth. Gunthar and Stephan were silent and grave, while Lord Boniface Crownguard looked away.

Sturm cleared his throat. "I suppose things like rules and oaths are . . . even stronger when you can do otherwise but you choose to follow them because . . . because . . ."

He wasn't really sure why. He stood again, and then Lord Alfred slipped from the room, returning at once with the great sword Gabbatha, said once to grace the belt of Vinas Solamnus. It was the sword of justice, a shimmering, two-edged broadsword, its hilt carefully carved in the likeness of a kingfisher, the golden wings spread to form the crosspiece. So there, before the most powerful Knights of the Order, Sturm set his hand to Gabbatha and swore a binding oath that he would take up the challenge of Lord Vertumnus, the druid or wizard or renegade knight.

When the words were said and the oath was sealed, Lord Stephan, now abstract and pensive, stalked from the room at once, muttering something about impossible odds. As the old Knight opened the door, the room outside echoed with the sound of axe against wood.

Sturm shifted from foot to foot, looking up at the older men, awaiting advice, instruction, orders.

"Very well," Lord Alfred breathed. "Very . . . well." It was as if he had lost something.

"Go within a fortnight, Sturm," Lord Boniface urged. "Prompt departure will give you . . . time to travel unfamiliar country. If we are to believe Lord Wilderness, time is of the essence in this challenge."

"I remember," Sturm said bleakly. " 'Appointed place and appointed time.' "

"But you should prepare yourself first, Sturm," Gunthar urged indecisively.

"That is true," Alfred agreed eagerly. "Choose a horse from the liveries—that is, a horse *within reason*. You are, after all, a son of the Order, and we shall do our utmost to equip you and train you and ready you for the spring and the Southern Darkwoods."

Sturm nodded. The evening had dwindled to halfhearted promises. It was as though the Knights knew it, and knew that a still darker issue lurked beneath the promises.

The boy had been wounded, after all. Or so he maintained, and sharp-eyed old Stephan Peres confirmed it. And in spring, Lord Wilderness had threatened, the wound would come due.

It was all chaotic, this business before them, all grim and unforeseeable in its mystery.

Gunthar sidled to a shelf and thumbed through a book while Alfred recited the equipment Sturm would need, where it was available, and in what quantity or quality the Order was willing to provide it. Sturm continued to nod and thank the High Justice, but his eyes were distant and his thoughts elsewhere.

So they left him, still nodding and quietly thinking, standing in the midst of the library, all of Solamnic history surrounding him, leaning in on him from atop the dusty and indifferent shelves. Lord Boniface was the last out the door—Angriff's good friend, his rival in swordsmanship.

"I'm proud of you, lad," he said, and turned swiftly away, his face masked by the shadows of the dimly lit room.

"Thank you," Sturm breathed again, and the door closed behind all of them, leaving him alone with his fear and musing.

"How do you fight a mystery?" Sturm asked aloud. "How do you even *follow* one?" He turned and faced the darkened stained glass window.

Beyond the glass lay only the faintest of lights—the sunrise oblique in the east, scarcely visible because of the baffling mountains, the vaulting walls, and the simple fact that the window faced west. Behind the yellow of the harp and the white sphere of Solinari in the corner of the window, the lad could see sharp, wavering shadows. It was a sprig of holly, grown up against the wall outside, trembling in the breeze of the winter morning.

Chapter 3

INNS AND REMEMBRANCES

The twins had warned him, that autumn night at the Inn of the Last Home, in the week before he saddled Luin and rode away from Solace into the forbidden north.

It was a last night of reunions and farewells as the three of them sat over cold tea and guttering candles at the long table by the trunk of the enormous vallenwood tree that rose through the floor of the inn. Otik the innkeeper, solicitous as ever, cleared the last of the glass and crockery while the three companions drank absently, staring across the table at each other over the dodging lights.

Sturm felt ill-suited in his mourning gray cape and robes, especially among his old friends. He wondered if that was part of bereavement—that after the six months of gray and fasting and confinement, you were supposed to weary of it all, to yearn for setting aside the robes and moving to other things. Times were when he still missed his mother grievously, but already the face of Ilys Brightblade was blurred in his memory, and he had to tell himself the color of her eyes.

But the story she had told him was fresh in remembering, down to the smallest details. Recounted on her deathbed, before the fever gave way to delusions and unconsciousness, it was a tale that would send him from Solace.

Sturm shook his head, startled from memory by a loud, low voice. The dark imaginings of the clerical incense, of his mother's unnaturally pale face, vanished into light, and once again he was at the Inn of the Last Home, Caramon leaning across the table, questioning him above the glowing candles.

"Were you listening, Sturm? Here we are on the last night before you leave, your saddlebags packed full of provisions and letters and souvenirs. I wish you weren't so set on Solamnia and this banquet and staying there for good. . . ."

"I never said I would not return!" Sturm interrupted, rolling his eyes. "I've told you both before, Caramon. It's . . . it's a *pilgrimage* of sorts, and when I've learned a few things in the north and settled a few others, I'll be back."

Caramon clutched the sides of the table with his red, thick-fingered hands and smiled apologetically at his prim and serious friend. Raistlin, meanwhile, remained silent, his dark, attentive face turned toward the hearth and the last of the dwindling firelight.

"But all this questing and searching, Sturm," Caramon explained. "It *could* take you away forever. It does that with the *real* Solamnic Knights."

Sturm winced at the *real*.

"And if it did, we'd be none the wiser as to why you went in the first place."

"That, too, I've told you again and again, Caramon," Sturm repeated calmly, his voiced strained and brittle. " 'Tis the Oath and the Measure, and it is the Oath that binds the

Solamnic brotherhood. *That's* why I have to go north—into Solamnia . . . the Vingaard Mountains . . . the High Clerist's Tower."

"The Code again," Raistlin observed, quietly breaking the silence.

The two larger youths turned at once to their scrawny, dark comrade. Leaning back in a darkened nook in the vallenwood trunk, the young adept was half lost in shadows, almost as insubstantial as his own sleights and illusions.

Out of the gray flickering gloom, Raistlin spoke again, his voice melodious and thin, like the high notes of a viola. "The Code and the Measure," he said scornfully. "All of that smug behavior that the Solamnic Order swears by. And the thirty-five volumes of your Measure—"

"Thirty-seven," Sturm corrected. "There are thirty-seven volumes to the Measure."

Raistlin shrugged, wrapping his tattered red robe more closely around his shoulders. Quickly, with a birdlike grace, he leaned forward, stretching his thin hands toward the fading glow of the fire.

"Thirty-five or thirty-seven," he mused, his pale lips tightening to a smile, "or three thousand. All the same to me, in its foolishness and legalism. You aren't bound to obey a page of it, Sturm Brightblade. Your father, not you, was the Solamnic Knight."

"We've disagreed on this before, Raistlin," Sturm scolded. He stopped himself and leaned uncomfortably back in his chair. He sounded like a reproving old schoolmaster, and he knew it.

Raistlin nodded and swirled his tea in the cup, staring into the bottom as though he were reading omens in the cool dregs.

"There have been other years, Sturm," he whispered. "Other Yules."

Sturm cleared his throat.

"It's . . . it's because Mother's gone now, Raistlin," he replied tentatively, looking thoughtfully at the glittering pool of wax in the dark ceramic candle holder. The wick floated on the shimmering surface. Soon the candle would go out entirely.

"The Order is my last remaining family. There's nowhere else to go but north. But mostly it's because of what Mother told me . . . about what happened the night my father vanished."

The twins leaned forward, stunned by this sudden news.

"Then there was something more?" Raistlin asked. "More that your mother hadn't told you?"

"She . . . she was waiting for the proper time," Sturm replied, his hands unsteady on the table boards. "It was just that . . . the plague . . . then there was no other time . . ."

"Then when she told you was the proper time," Caramon soothed, resting his huge hand on Sturm's shoulder. "Tell us, in turn. Tell us of that night."

Sturm looked into the eager brown eyes of his young companion. "Very well, Caramon. Tonight I shall tell you that story. Remember that it is not easy in the telling."

And with the twins leaning toward him expectantly, the autumn night uneasy with the high wind and the rattle of leaves across the roof of the inn, Sturm began the story.

* * * * *

"First of all," Sturm began, his gaze fixed on the table, "Lord Angriff saw to me and the Lady Ilys. Smuggled us off on the western road, before the peasants' torches closed a full circle about the castle. Soren Vardis was our guide, and the snow swirled over the high road, or the peasants might well have found us. In their anger, they didn't remember what the Order had done for them."

The twins exchanged a curious glance, and Raistlin cleared his throat. Sturm continued, his gaze fixed on the dwindling fire.

"As to my father," he continued dreamily, abstractly, "when we were safely away, he turned his thoughts to the castle and its garrison. Alfred was there, and Gunthar and Boniface and a hundred men, of whom Father thought he could trust only the twenty Knights. For you see, the countryside went over to the peasants suddenly and swiftly, and the heart of many a foot soldier turned from the Order in the last weeks before the castle fell."

Sturm clenched his fists, his dark eyes smoldering.

"What would you expect, Sturm Brightblade?" Raistlin murmured. "What would you expect from peasants and brigands?" He rested his thin hand on the shoulder of the Solamnic lad. The mage's fingers were pale, almost transparent, and there was something unsettling in his touch.

Sturm shrugged and scooted his chair away from the table.

"Go on," Raistlin breathed. "Tell us your story."

"Father descended into the bailey, where his soldiers had been assembled. The men crowded together for warmth, shivering in threadbare blankets, in secondhand robes. All but a dozen were there, and those who were absent were trusted Knights, deployed by Father to man the walls while he held council.

"The courtyard was a sea of gray shapes and misted breath, and the snow fell mercilessly as the morning approached. Father paced confidently in front of the troops, stopping only to draw a line in the snow, a commander's gesture. I had seen him do it before myself, in the Nerakan Wars, but even to grown men it was still quite a show."

Sturm paused admiringly, a sad smile creasing his face. Outside the inn, the summer night swelled with music, the wild fluting call of the nightingale cascading over the slow, steady creaking of insects. Together the three lads listened to the sounds around them as weary Otik passed by the table, his arms heavy with half-filled tankards and dirty crockery.

Sturm looked up at the twins and resumed the story.

" 'Those who are with me,' Father said, 'stay your ground. For it shall come—snow and siege and insurgence.'

Then he pointed to the line at his feet, and they said that the mist dissolved above that troop of men, simply because not a one of them was breathing.

" 'Those who would go,' he said, 'whether to safety or to the ranks of the insurgents, may cross this line and travel hence with my blessings.' "

"With his *blessings?*" Caramon asked.

Sturm nodded. " 'Twas blessings he said, no matter who tells the story. And I cannot figure it for the life of me, though I suppose that if neither heart nor oath could hold their allegiance, 'twould have been a crime to send them to battle.

"But the real crime was what followed. When eighty of them crossed the line and walked from Castle Brightblade . . ." He clenched his fists, then blushed, surprised at his own feelings.

"Tell us the rest," Caramon said, lifting his hand as though to still his friend's torrent of anger.

"Father said not a word against those men," Sturm continued, red-faced and glaring. "Instead, he ordered the Knights down from the walls. Then there were but a score of them in the bailey, all of the Order, and the snow kept falling, falling upon those who stayed as well as those who left."

Raistlin stretched and rose from the table, leaning against the mantel. Sturm shifted in his chair, his young thoughts muddled and bitter.

"As to those who left, who joined the peasant army, the gods know what befell most of them. I have heard that many served their new allegiance bravely and well. But those who remained were still confident. For you see, my father had told them—told the Knights and the Knights only, his close group of followers sworn to the Oath and the Measure—that old Agion Pathwarden, in his seventies then but full of vigor and vinegar, was coming to lift the siege with fifty Knights, almost all the fighting garrison of Castle di Caela, just an afternoon's ride to the south. They could wait it out, of that they were certain.

"Certain until a messenger came from the peasant commander—an old druidess whose name my mother could not remember—that Lord Agion and his company had been betrayed. Someone in Father's garrison had sneaked word to the peasants as to the secret, roundabout road Lord Agion would take from Castle di Caela to Castle Brightblade. They were ambushed in the foothills, grievously outnumbered. Not a Knight survived, though they all died fighting. They say that Agion was among the first to fall."

Sturm closed his eyes.

"Did they ever find the traitor?" Caramon asked, always one for justice and retribution. Sturm nodded slowly.

"So they say. And the best were all on the hunt— Gunthar, Boniface, Alfred MarKenin. Father had told them to let it go, but they hounded until Boniface flushed the turncoat. The man was a new Knight—from Lemish, predictably. Lord Boniface accused him, the man denied and denied, and of course it was trial by combat next. But the coward slithered away that very night. It is said that the peasants hanged him themselves; Gunthar saw a body on the gibbet when he passed through their lines.

"Father sent word to the old druidess on the morrow. Despite the druidess's natural skills as a general and a strategist, the peasants maintained that she was just and fair—just and fair to a fault. Since those whom he had trusted had betrayed him, Father ventured his faith into other grounds. He told her, that druidess, that he wanted no further bloodshed between Solamnics, whether they were of the Order or against it. That if such were impossible, that the spilled blood be his alone. To assure such a warring peace, he handed himself over to the peasantry in exchange for their promise of safe passage for the Lords Alfred and Boniface, for Gunthar and for the remaining garrison of Castle Brightblade.

"Or so they say," Sturm muttered, his gaze angry on the

glistening shield. "For that night he walked into the blinding snow, and none who survived that time ever saw him again."

The common room of the inn fell into respectful silence. Otik paused in sweeping the hearth and leaned against his broom, and the young girl he had hired to spread fresh rushes on the floor ceased her midnight labor and crouched by the bar, knowing somehow that this pained, intimate talk demanded her stillness.

"Did I tell you that Lord Angriff went to his fate laughing?" Sturm asked with an odd smile. "That as easily as if he were disrobing for the night, he handed his shield and breastplate to his good friend Lord Boniface?"

Sturm closed his eyes. His voice cracked as he continued the story.

" 'They are no use to me where I go,' he said, 'these instruments of Knighthood. And why are you troubled?' he asked them. 'Why do dark thoughts arise in your hearts?' It was all they could do to keep from weeping, Mother said, for they knew that he went to his death and that they would never see the likes of him again.

"So he embraced his companions that afternoon and passed from their midst, soon lost in the swirling countryside beyond the walls of Castle Brightblade. Two men followed him into the blinding snow. They disobeyed my father's commands because of the love they bore him, and for a moment, the weeping men of the garrison saw my father and the two who followed him as a triad of dark spots in the depth of the blizzard, and then again at the very edge of sight, where the snow-shrouded torches of the peasants looked like low and distant stars, and the three of them seemed to enter the thin, dark ranks of the enemy, never falling, but as though they walked blindly into an impenetrable thicket."

Sturm shivered. "It is out of that thicket that the son of Angriff Brightblade has emerged, my friends. I shall find Lord Angriff Brightblade, or what has become of him, though the Jaws of Hiddukel stand in the way, full intending to undo me."

"Which they well may do, lad," Raistlin said quietly. "Which they well may do."

Sturm swallowed nervously. "Whether they do or no, 'tis time I should test them. Would that I had your wits in my service, Raistlin Majere. Or Caramon's strength. The High Clerist's Tower is a fierce place for a backwoods boy."

"You are no weakling, Sturm!" Caramon encouraged loudly, startling the little girl by the bar, who scurried into the shadows, trailing rushes. "You can ride, too, and use a sword far better than I can. It's just that . . . just . . ."

"I'm no swordsman," Sturm asserted. "Not really. Not like my father was, nor like they're accustomed to seeing in the north. Nor half as brave, nor nearly the horseman. Ask my mother. Ask our Solamnic friends, who travel south just to tell me these things."

Caramon opened his mouth as if to answer, then leaned back in his chair disgustedly. Words once again had mastered him. Somewhere below them, on the road that wound through the vallenwoods of Solace, the whicker of a horse rose out of the whistling night wind, and the harsh shout of a rider followed it.

"What we both are trying to say," Raistlin urged, turning away from his thoughts and regarding Sturm with a bright, unsettling stare, "is that if you hear such things in Solace, you'll hear worse in the Vingaards. This is too early, Sturm. The North is ravenous, and the Order . . . well, the Order is as you have told us."

"It must be now, Raistlin," Sturm argued, lifting the cup to his lips, tasting the tepid, smoky brew. "It must be now because, above the Code and Measure and my mother's last stories, I can stand it no longer."

"What's that?" Caramon asked, his mind already elsewhere. But the story continued in his thoughts: the incomparable Angriff Brightblade, master swordsman and hero and noble Knight, who had the nerve to vanish magnificently at the siege of Castle Brightblade.

Who had the nerve to leave behind a son and too many questions.

"I have to know," Sturm announced dramatically. "I have to find my father. Yes, yes, he may be dead. But up there, he's a memory instead of . . . well, instead of a legend."

Raistlin sighed. With a strange, broken smile, he turned back to the fire.

"Everything my father has done," Sturm explained, "in the lists, in the Nerakan Wars, in keeping castle and family—"

"Tramples on your young days," Raistlin interrupted. He coughed, no doubt a winter cold, and swirled the lukewarm tea in his cup. "This hunt for fathers," he observed ironically, "is a haunted thing. You have to put a face on the one who is killing you."

Caramon nodded slowly, though he did not really understand. His gaze followed that of his brother. The twins sat in silence, staring at the red embers.

Yes, it is haunted, Sturm thought angrily, looking at the two of them, content in their strangely balanced fellowship. But you will never understand. Neither of you. For no matter what befalls, you have each other to . . . to . . .

To show you who you are.

And no one is killing me.

Baffled in the thicket of his own thoughts, Sturm rose from the table. The twins scarcely noticed his departure as he walked into the bracing Abanasinian night. Caramon waved softly over his shoulder, and the last Sturm saw of his friends, they were sitting side by side, framed by firelight and yoked by shadows, each lost in his opposite dreams.

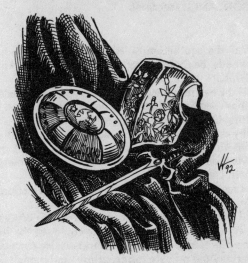

Chapter 4

A Parting Story

Now, with the journey north and a season in Solamnia behind him, all Sturm had kept of that moment was
its expectation and gloom.

As midwinter stormed toward the first blustery week of
February, and windswept snow dusted the dark inclines of
the Vingaard Mountains, Sturm spent the time in training,
schooled by Gunthar in riding and swordsmanship, by
Lord Adamant in the lessons of forest survival, and by all
most Solamnically in vigil and prayers and deep dread. In
the evening, after his instruction, he paced the battlements
of the Knight's Spur, squinting southward where the Wings
of Habbakuk sloped down to the Virkhus Hills, then even
farther down onto the Solamnic Plains. When the weather
was clear and windless, the lad imagined he saw a ridge of

green at the southernmost edge of sight. The Southern Darkwoods, he thought, and his shoulder ached. And Vertumnus. Late winter, and I am far from ready.

What he had in place of Raistlin's cryptic comments were questions more immediate. He asked them of himself nightly, setting his lantern on the crenellated wall.

"Why did the Green Man come to the Tower? And why was this Yule different from any other? Why was I chosen, and what does he want of me? What awaits me in the Southern Darkwoods?

And regardless of sword and horse and instruction, how can I prepare for a man of shadows and magic?

Lord Stephan Peres would watch from his offices with rising concern. Out his window, he could see the solitary wavering lantern in the morning darkness. He had watched Sturm train and prepare for departure, and though the lad was a quick study, he had started green and clumsy and would end not too far from where he started.

It was a clumsiness that might prove to be Sturm's undoing, the old Knight thought darkly.

There was the matter of the peasantry, for one thing. The common folk of the Solamnic countryside had never forgiven the Knights for their supposed role in the Cataclysm—the disastrous rending of the world by quake and fire over three centuries ago. Grudges endured among the peasants, and though hostility and rebellion would submerge for a long while—perhaps ten, twelve years on occasion—trouble would resurface sporadically, as it had in the uprising five years back.

As it had again, evidently, in the cold weeks following the Yule banquet.

The Wings of Habbakuk, those broad, muddy foothills that lay due south of the High Clerist's Tower and provided the easiest road into the mountains, had recently become a quagmire of snares and pits and crudely designed traps. Experienced Knights had no trouble recognizing the signs—a thickness of fallen vallenwood leaves over a well-traveled path, an unaccustomed play of shadow and light in the thickets that dotted the sloping plains. They were used to peasant trickery, as was even the greenest squire who had grown up within sight of the Tower.

But Stephan was worried about young Brightblade, who three times had narrowly averted disaster while roaming the Wings with his comrades. On the last occasion, the lad's sly old mare, Luin, had shown more wisdom than her skillful but incautious rider, hurdling a pit that would have killed the both of them while tossing Sturm from the saddle in the sudden leap. The lad's game shoulder had ached for days, but that troubled Lord Stephan less than the curious circumstances.

It was almost as though the traps had been set for Sturm alone.

Lord Stephan rested his weight on the stone sill of the window and mused over the fading events of the Yule banquet—the arrival of Vertumnus, the fight, and the mysterious challenge. They were all dim, fading in an old man's memory. Stephan thought of birds in autumn, how each morning there were two, or three, or four less on the battlements. Memory was like that, and you would look up at the first frost, and only the hardiest birds would remain.

Spring was a more puzzling matter. Throughout winter, the moons had shifted in the sky, appearing first in the west, then the northwest, then altogether low in the east as they were supposed to at midsummer. Red Lunitari and white Solinari changed places and phases, and the astronomers claimed that black Nuitari did so, too. At first it was alarming, for the same astronomers, the scientists and the scholars maintained that the shifting moons could signal a greater disruption to come. Perhaps the Cataclysm would return, bringing with it the rending of earth, the shifting of continents, and absolute destruction. Perhaps it was something even worse.

Soon, though, these fears had subsided. The moons weaved about the sky for several nights, and no crevasses opened in the ground beneath them. Greatly relieved, the folks in the Tower settled back into daily routine, and the foot soldiers even began to make bets as to where the moons would appear each evening. Finally even the most nocturnal inhabitants of the High Clerist's Tower—the astronomers, the sentries, and the ever-vigilant Sturm—ceased to pay attention to the uncertain show in the heavens.

Then the more subtle problems became apparent. Birds, accustomed to migrating by moonlight and using the position of the moons as a guide, became lost and confused. The robins and larks arrived early in the region, only to shiver amid the eaves and crenels as the winds and the snows returned.

One morning Lord Stephan had been surprised by three gulls at his chamber windows. Tricked by the dodging moons, they had wandered very far from any sea. Their feathers were ruffled, and the tips of their wings were iced.

Subject to the unsteady pull of Solinari, the Vingaard River first swelled, then receded, then swelled again, dangerously close to topping the old floodwalls built over a century ago by Sturm's Brightblade and di Caela ancestors. The plants accustomed to growing by moonlight, moonflower and aeterna, burgeoned wildly in the Tower gardens and topiaries, and out in the farmlands, asparagus and rhubarb and the sharp-tasting winter oleracea broke through the ground early, to the surprise of most gardeners and the dismay of most of their children.

The most disruption, however, came in more speculative realms. For magic, of course, revolved around the phases of the moons, and the strange, erratic alignments in the heavens disrupted the local spellcraft so that all but the most powerful divinations failed, the winds and the weather were as changeable as the moons, and wavering lights dotted the Wings of Habbakuk. Several enchanters appeared before Lord Stephan with sausages or lanterns or shoes attached to their faces or more hidden parts of their anatomies, since the constant feuding among wizards was as liable to twist and backfire as it was to succeed.

Lord Stephan had frowned at the complaining mages, doing his best to put on a face of outrage and sympathy, though he could hardly keep from laughing aloud. Finally, in the presence of one red-robed wizard from whose ears grapevines continued to grow noisily, he suggested that, if nothing else, by autumn the whine would turn into wine.

Still, the changes in young Sturm were less amusing. With his grimness and walks on the battlements, he taxed the patience of even the most Measured and diligent Knights. His long afternoons in the Chamber of Paladine raised all kinds of speculation.

"Praying, no doubt, for the Cataclysm to come again," Lord Alfred had muttered gruffly to Lord Stephan that morning on the stairs. "If the world would open up and swallow him, it would be just as he wishes. And the swallowing world is welcome to him."

"Now, Alfred," cautioned the older knight, his soothing tones unconvincing. "If you cannot find forbearance for the sake of the lad's lost father, then surely remember the burden. It is time to set aside thoughts bitter and hard, and help the boy in his final preparations."

Spring drew nigh in the Vingaard Mountains, despite the wanderings of the moons and the confusion of plant, bird, and mage. The days marched on, and though the calendar was the only reliable measurement that time was passing, indeed the time approached for the boy's departure.

* * * * *

Sturm was alone in his chambers, the early evening upon him. He had spent a long morning in the central courtyard, Lord Gunthar instructing him roughly in the particulars of swordsmanship. Still panting from the exertion, his shoulder swollen and heated, Sturm removed the heavy vambraces from his arms, wincing as the metal and padding rubbed over bruises due to the fall he had taken riding the Wings, but also those from more recent outrages, born of training in combat and his teacher Lord Gunthar's enthusiasm. It had been *arms courteous*, the wicker weapons padded and blunted to boot, but Gunthar was terribly strong, and the blows were telling, no matter the precautions.

Sturm groaned and tossed the vambraces to the floor. Leaning back on his hard bed, he stared at the ceiling, his face flushed with exertion and embarrassment. Exertion, because Lord Gunthar had worked him over. Embarrassment, because the older man had done it easily, almost effortlessly, in a calm voice lacing the rout with instructions.

"Raise your shield, Sturm!" Gunthar had railed. "You're shuffling and puffing like Lord Raphael!"

Sturm had winced. Lord Raphael was a hundred and twenty-three years old and babbled in senile rapture about the Cataclysm he really did not remember.

Slowly the two men circled each other, student and tutor. Gunthar's gray eyes never left the lad, fixed on the padded sword that bobbed in his right hand.

"Your guard is low, lad," Gunthar urged. "Vertumnus'll have a sword in amidst you before you raise it!"

Sturm had stumbled then, and Gunthar had pushed him back, seating him on the hard bailey ground. The Knight stood over him grimly and explained in a clipped, cold voice how Lord Wilderness would not wait politely for him to regain his footing.

For the Green Man is not of the Order. He cannot be expected to fight with dignity and according to the Measure. There is no Measure in the outlands, which is why there is a Measure here. You will be the Measure at that meeting!

Now Sturm closed his eyes, and the sudden knock on the door startled him. He must have been sleeping, he thought with dismay, and he struggled with the laces to his greaves as the door opened and Lord Boniface Crownguard of Foghaven stepped into the room, broadsword in hand, on his shoulder a large canvas bag, filled with something that rang and clattered as he closed the door behind him.

For a brief and nightmarish moment, the lad thought that instruction was about to resume with another sound thrashing at the hands of Lord Boniface. For a moment, he even thought something darker, even worse, was about to waylay him in the shadowy guests' chambers. But Boniface was quiet, even mild, setting down his burden and seating himself at the corner of Sturm's cot, the sword across his knees.

His boots were muddy, and vallenwood leaves clung to the soles.

"I saw you with Gunthar. You tire too easily," Lord Boniface said gruffly.

"And Gunthar tires not easily enough," Sturm answered with a weary smile, dismissing his bewilderment and fear. The older man chuckled.

"Angriff Brightblade's boy you are, though," Lord Boniface concluded, and Sturm looked at him hopefully. "Somewhere down in the cellars of yourself. Yes. It's just a matter of letting the Brightblade out to air. You see, Angriff would have stayed at Gunthar in the courtyard until he won—'tis as simple as that. Till death or Cataclysm come, Angriff used to match me sword on sword, and though I was the better swordsman . . ."

Boniface paused and cleared his throat.

"Though I was the better swordsman," he continued, "your father would have won on sheer mettle and daring and backbone."

Boniface paused again and looked curiously at the lad beside him. "There was also," he said thoughtfully, "an affinity with the sword itself, as though something in him could sense the thoughts and movements of metal. A good smith or armorer he might have made, had not the Order called him. But such things were subtle, almost unconscious, as though he received them as an inheritance of blood."

"None of which I am heir to," Sturm declared weakly. "Neither affinities nor mettle nor daring nor backbone."

"And yet you are off to face Lord Wilderness," Boniface

replied softly, "after considerable training and study. By what road will you travel?"

"They say the best way is always the most direct," Sturm replied. "I intend to ride straight toward the Vingaard Keep, then south down the river to the great ford. I shall cross the Vingaard there, then pick up its southern branch and follow along the banks straight into the Darkwoods themselves. Nothing more simple, no smoother road."

Lord Boniface's firm hand rested heavily on his shoulder.

"A brave plan, Sturm Brightblade, and worthy of your name," he pronounced. "I myself could have fashioned no better route."

"Thank you, Lord Boniface," Sturm replied with a puzzled frown. "Indeed your confidence assures me."

The older Knight smiled and moved closer to Sturm. "Did Angriff ever tell you," he asked, "the story of his feud with his own father?"

Sturm shook his head and smiled slowly. Since he had arrived at the High Clerist's Tower, it seemed that each Knight he met had a tale to tell of Lord Angriff Brightblade. Happily, eagerly, the lad learned forward, prepared for yet another story.

A slow smile creased the face of Lord Boniface, and he began the telling.

*　*　*　*　*

"Your grandfather, Lord Emelin Brightblade, was a good Knight and a good man, but he was known for neither patience or gentleness. Son of Bayard Brightblade and the Lady Enid di Caela, Lord Emelin was Brightblade tough and di Caela . . . haughty? Stubborn?"

Sturm glowered. He remembered absolutely nothing of his grandfather Emelin, but he wasn't sure that he liked the critical words. Still, Boniface was accustomed to speaking his mind to Brightblades, it seemed.

The older Knight continued, his eyes on the sword in his

lap. "Well, it has never been the easiest of bloodlines. An-griff feared his father as much as he respected him, and in the difficult years of his teens, he steered away from old Emelin at formalities, preferring to meet him only at the hunt. For it was there that their spirits usually blended, as the poems and histories tell us it should be with fathers and sons."

Boniface stretched back on the cot, linking his hands be-hind his head.

"Usually," said Sturm.

"I remember those hunts," Boniface continued. "The smell of woodsmoke on cold mornings like this, when we would ride after the boar. I remember best the winter of Lord Grim."

"Lord Grim, sir?" Sturm asked. Despite his love for So-lamnic history and lore, he remembered no Knight named Grim.

Boniface snorted. "A boar. Grim was a great-tusked boar who eluded the best of us in that winter of three seventeen, when your father and I were seventeen ourselves and ready for anything except that pig. Lord Grim lost us in the moun-tains, in the foothills, in the level, snow-covered plains where you could track for days.

"The Yuletide passed, and still we could not catch him. It was not until midwinter when we brought him to ground, not far from here, in the Wings of Habbakuk. I remember the day well. The hunt. The kill. But mostly what happened afterward."

Sturm set down the greaves carefully, his gaze locked on his father's old friend. Boniface closed his eyes and was si-lent so long that Sturm was afraid the Knight had fallen asleep. But then Lord Boniface spoke, and Sturm followed him into the story. It became twenty-five years ago and far south of the Tower.

"Lord Agion Pathwarden led us into the foothills. Your cousin. As burly a Pathwarden as ever arose from that now-vanished line. Named for a centaur friend of his eccentric father, Agion was. Your grandfather's best friend, and a great brawler, and many was the time that the two of them came to blows, scuffled cleanly, and parted friends. Like his namesake, Agion seemed half horse, a big man in the saddle, charging like the south wind over the slopes and inclines of the Wings.

"We had caught the trail right after dawn, the thick-necked alan dogs, our best hunting beasts, caterwauling at the mere smell of Grim and racing through the rocks like water rushing uphill, fanning wide and converging, pouring through a narrow pass into a stand of scrubby aeterna where the boar was waiting. It was all the huntsmen could do to restrain the pack. They bayed and bellowed and swirled around that narrow copse of evergreen. Grim was in there, everybody knew, but each of us was . . . reluctant to go in and greet him first."

Sturm nodded and shuddered, having survived his first boar hunt back in the fall.

"Finally four of us dismounted and entered the copse on foot: Agion and Emelin and your father and I. Angriff and I were along as squires, more or less. We were supposed to hold the spears, stand our ground and be silent. But Angriff wasn't the sort. When Agion crashed through the brush and chased the boar from cover, your father was on it like a panther, quick and menacing, striking the beast once, twice, a third time with spears. Grim was old and thick of hide, and your father's casts were those of a youth—swift and accurate, but lacking the muscle to pierce through gristle and bone."

"So it simply enraged the boar," Sturm observed, and Boniface nodded.

"Grim charged at Agion, who turned, ran, and scrambled out of the way through a thick aeterna, the boar skidding and stirring gravel just a step behind him. Meanwhile, your grandfather circled about the creature and waited for the chance at the delivering cast.

"That chance did not come, because Angriff was impatient. Through the brush he rousted old Grim, and time and again I lost him in the mist and the thicket. Finally I heard a shuffling, a cough, and I stumbled around a thick lattice-work of branches . . . and found myself face-to-face with old Grim himself."

Boniface paused. He stood and began to pace the room as Sturm held his breath, listening.

"He was as shaggy as the bison of Kiri-Jolith, dripping with dew and mud and half-hidden in mist and evergreen. He looked like something from the legends, out of the Age of Dreams and the bardic tales. I remember thinking, right before he charged, that if Nature were to take on flesh and form, it would be this beast before me, in its unruliness and terror and its strange hideous indifference."

Again the Knight paused, his hands clenching, grasping the air as though he were trying to clutch something or push something away.

"He . . . charged you, Lord Boniface?" Sturm asked finally. "The great boar charged you?"

Boniface nodded. "Had my sword out in a flash. But I never used it."

A strange shadow passed over the Knight's face. Sturm waited expectantly, sure that the man was remembering that moment, the horrible charge of the boar.

"I never used it," Boniface repeated. "Angriff's spear passed neatly between Grim's shoulder blades, and the boar staggered and rose and staggered again. Believe me, I was well out of the way by the second stagger, but I saw it all unfold—your grandfather and Agion burst into the clearing, and Lord Emelin's sword flashed silver in the winter sunlight as the blade rose and came slashing home.

"For a while, we all stood there above the boar. The alans were baying somewhere outside the circle of trees, so distant in our thoughts that it sounded like we were only remembering them.

"Then Lord Agion spoke. 'A fitting end to our adversary,' he said. 'To Lord Grim, whose trophy shall grace the hall of

Lord Emelin Brightblade, his slayer.'

"Your grandfather smiled and nodded, but your father stood pale and too quiet, and at that moment, I knew that something between them was about to unravel, perhaps beyond repair. 'But, Lord Agion,' Angriff protested, stepping into the matter as brashly and foolishly as he stepped into each hunt, each tournament. 'I expect that the history will show that I cast the first and telling spear.'

" 'Nonsense,' Lord Emelin protested. 'My sword struck the boar, and it died. There is no more to say in the matter.'

"Indeed there *was* no more to say. But I could see Angriff start to say it, nonetheless. He began to answer back and defend his honor. But Lord Emelin would have none of it."

Lord Boniface paused and regarded the lad before him. Sturm gaped at him, his fists doubled. Imagine the injustice of Lord Emelin! Sturm thought angrily. Why, 'tis against the Code and Measure entirely!

"Not at all, Sturm Brightblade," Lord Boniface corrected, as though he was reading the younger man's thoughts. "The rules of the hunt are simple, as simple as Lord Emelin set them forth that morning in the Wings of Habbakuk. Angriff, though, was livid. There was something in this, he felt, that passed beyond rule and protocol, but rule and protocol said that the rest was silence. He withdrew his spear . . ."

Boniface paused and shook his head, a little sadly.

"And I sheathed my sword, and we mounted our horses. I watched my friend ride and fume," he maintained, "from the Virkhus Hills back to Castle Brightblade. As mute as a sheep before the shearer, he was, and he spoke not a word that afternoon and into the evening. For you see, defiance of one's father was more against the Code and Measure than anything Lord Emelin had done by the rules in the clearing.

"Agion teased young Angriff all the way back to Castle Brightblade, calling him 'bush-beater' and 'lyam-hound' and 'alan,' as though the lad's part in the hunt were simply locating the beast. Angriff stewed further, and still he was silent. But I knew we had not seen the end of the matter.

"It was at the banquet that night for Lord Emelin's triumph. All the principal families were there—the MarKenins, the Jeoffreys, the Celestes—and the talk was of hunt and ceremony.

"When dinner had been served and the guests had settled into the lull of food and wine, Angriff approached his father's seat. Agion, at the left of Lord Emelin, snorted as the lad approached and said, far too audibly, 'here comes the boy to ask for the hound's share.' "

Sturm gasped. At the hunt, when the beast was skinned and cleaned, the entrails, the hooves, and all indelicate parts were left for the hounds. Agion's words had not only been insulting, but they were also downright cruel.

"Emelin turned to Agion and said something sharp but inaudible," Boniface said, "but Angriff seemed to pay the big lout no mind. He stood silently before his father until Lord Emelin looked up from the exchange with his cousin. Then Angriff began, his speech soft and mild and overprepared, but as urgent as any words spoken in Castle Brightblade before or since.

" 'My Lord Father knows,' he said, 'that sometimes the Measure and true justice are at odds. He knows also that, regardless of sword and stroke of grace, my spear dealt Lord Grim the mortal blow.'

"It was stilted and awkward, but it made its point. A murmur spread through the room, and Lord Emelin stood up angrily.

" 'Are you saying, Angriff,' he asked, 'that your father . . . that *I* have . . . *stolen* your kill?'

" '*Stolen* is not my word for it,' Angriff replied, his own anger bursting through the calm and politeness. 'I prefer *seized*.'

"It was then that Lord Emelin reached over the table and slapped his son."

"Slapped him?" Sturm asked, his voice rising in outrage.

"Among his fellows at a formal banquet? Why . . . there is no . . . no . . ."

"No answer to such indignity," Boniface replied calmly. "It would seem not. Yet Emelin had overstepped all bounds, had crossed the Measure's decree that 'though honor takes all shapes and forms, the father must honor the son as the son the father.' To strike his father back would be unthinkable, as would words harsh enough to answer the insult. Nor could he stand there and accept the blow and maintain his honor as a man.

"Emelin blushed in the aftermath. He knew he had overstepped, but he couldn't take back the gesture. It would seem that Angriff had no recourse. But listen.

"He stood in front of his father in a smoldering rage, the imprint of old Emelin's hand still pink and flushed on his smooth jaw. Then Angriff turned deliberately and crashed his fist straight into the bridge of Agion's nose.

"It was like the sound of a large limb cracking in a high wind. Agion went over backward and heavily, crashing to the floor, where he lay unconscious, awakening after a good half-hour, babbling about stockings and rhubarb pie."

"My father hit *Agion!*" Sturm exclaimed, shocked and delighted. "But why? And . . . and . . ."

"Listen," Boniface said with a smile. "For what your father said was this: 'Present this to my father the next time you wrangle. It will be as much my blow to him as his was to Lord Grim.' "

Sturm shook his head admiringly. "How did he think of it, Lord Boniface? How did he think of it?"

Boniface opened the bag at his feet and slowly, with some effort, drew forth the breastplate and shield. "It was his way to think of things, Sturm. He thought to leave these with me . . . to give you when the time arrived."

Breathlessly Sturm reached out for the shield.

"I am bound by Oath to give you these," Boniface announced cryptically. "But this sword is . . . *my* gift."

He offered the broadsword lying in his lap. "Your father,

it seems, took the Bright Blade with him or hid it somewhere beyond even the knowledge and eyes of his friends.
But Angriff Brightblade's son *deserves* a sword the likes of
which I am giving you."

He extended the weapon hilt first. It glowed obscurely in
the lamplight of Sturm's quarters.

"Make it your own," Boniface announced mysteriously.
"It is bright and double-edged."

*   *   *   *   *

Boniface left Sturm with the sword resting on his knees.
For an hour, or perhaps two, the lad polished the weapon.
He could see himself in the gleaming blade, the reflection of
his face distorted and foxlike on the angular edges of the
armor. When Lord Gunthar Uth Wistan stepped into the
room, Sturm scarcely heard him.

"You must be more alert in the Southern Darkwoods," the
High Justice observed as the startled lad leapt to his feet, the
sword falling from his lap and clattering against the stone
floor of the chamber.

"I was . . . I . . ."

Lord Gunthar ignored the lad's stammer and seated himself with a rattle and clanking of mail. Carefully he set
down the package he carried—a heavy, cumbersome thing
wrapped in a blanket. Sturm marveled that the man was
walking the halls of the Tower in full battle dress. One
would think that the High Clerist's Tower were under siege.

Now Gunthar extended his gauntleted hand, within
which lay a fresh green cluster of leaves. "Do you know
them?" he asked curtly.

Sturm shook his head.

"Calvian oak," the Knight explained laconically. "You remember the old saying?"

Sturm nodded. He knew rhymes and lore far better than
leaves and trees. " 'Last to green and last to fall,' sir. Or so
they say down in Solace."

"They say the same up here," Gunthar acknowledged. "Which is why it's so odd that I carry these leaves in winter, don't you think?"

He regarded Sturm with a calm, unreadable stare.

"I'm supposed to be going," the lad stated, crouching and picking up the sword. "That's what it means." The room seemed warm about him, and faintly through the window, the smell of flowers reached him on the back of a southeasterly breeze.

Chapter 5

Of Departures and Schemes

That morning, all but the boldest of them averted their eyes.

In the chilly, torchlit corridors, as the night turned and the bell of the third watch tolled deep and lonely, the squires began to stir, preparing their masters' armor and grumbling at the weather and the hour. It was a time that usually bristled with activity and horseplay and gossip, but on this morning, business stopped and conversation hushed as Sturm hastened by on his way to the stables. Silent, almost embarrassed, the Knights and squires averted their gazes. Even the servants, usually indifferent to Solamnic events, murmured as he passed and made signs of warding.

"Faring off a doomed man," Sturm muttered to himself as he stepped into the great central courtyard, into the dark and the flurried last snows of the season. Derek Crownguard, long awake on mysterious business, stood a stone's throw from the stable door, shrouded in misted breath and blankets. A brace of Jeoffreys stood with him, his whey-faced partners in misdeed. Aristocrats all, and first families for generations back, the three of them had no morning duties, and Sturm could only guess what would lift them from warm beds and superior dreams.

As Sturm walked into the stable and reached for his saddle, which hung from its customary peg on the wall, he found it tied and tangled with dried vines, decorated bizarrely with branches of evergreen. He heard the laughter from outside and angrily tugged the saddle from the snarl of greenery. The vines snapped, he staggered with the saddle, and a chorus of young voices arose from the dark and the cold.

"Return this man to Huma's breast," they sang.

> *"Return this man to Huma's breast,*
> *Beyond the wild, impartial skies;*
> *Grant to him a warrior's rest*
> *And set the last spark of his eyes*
> *Free from the smothering clouds of wars*
> *Upon the torches of the stars . . ."*

Sturm stepped from the stable. Despite himself, he couldn't keep from smiling. After all, the boys were singing a Solamnic funeral song.

They finished the verse and stood scornfully in front of him. Derek Crownguard was flushed and breathless with off-key singing, but he loomed substantial in front of his rival, his leather armor pocked and blemished and dirty, his face in much the same shape. Behind him, two pale, bat-faced Jeoffreys wheezed with malicious laughter.

A crazed thought dawned on Sturm. If he were indeed to fulfill Derek Crownguard's wish and never return from this strange and misbegotten journey, why not leave as his father had left his mourning garrison that legendary night when Castle Brightblade fell? Indeed, why not leave them with laughter?

Suddenly, wildly, Sturm joined in the singing.

"Let the last surge of his breath
Take refuge in the cradling air
Above the dreams of ravens where
Only the hawk remembers death.
Then let his shade to Huma rise
Beyond the wild impartial skies . . ."

Louder and louder Sturm sang, drowning out first one Jeoffrey, then the other, then the ringleader Derek himself. Puzzled, a little frightened, the squires backed away from the stable, Sturm following them and singing louder still.

Thoroughly unnerved, the Jeoffreys turned and ran, leaving Derek backing through the courtyard alone. Sturm stepped up to him, singing still louder, until lights flickered and shone in the Tower windows as disgruntled Knights were jostled from their sleep by Derek's strangely backfired joke.

Quickly and more quickly the haughty squire backed up, the laughter all vanished from his face now as he looked into the hard eyes of this obviously mad southerner. So intent was Derek Crownguard on his retreat that he didn't notice the young gardener Jack, who had stopped behind him for a moment's rest in the unpleasant duty of hauling a wheelbarrow of manure away from the stables.

It was a true shame he did not notice.

Backward Derek toppled into the bed of the wheelbarrow, but his fall was cushioned by its rather fresh contents. He lurched from the wheelbarrow, stumbled, and fell, and Sturm finished the funeral song in a loud and exultant voice.

Stephan and Gunthar stood on the battlements above the boys, peering down on them and watching the strange morning music come to pass.

"All Brightblade, that one is," Lord Gunthar said softly to his old friend.

"Not *all* Brightblade," Stephan allowed. "But, the gods willing, he is Brightblade enough."

* * * * *

Sturm smiled again as he saddled his horse. He felt wild and unsettled and strangely free.

Derek had blushed and fumed and backed away, this time very carefully, leaving his first-family arrogance behind him in the snowy courtyard. Lord Boniface had emerged furiously from the steps leading to the Knight's Spur and caught the soiled squire by a clean sleeve.

"How dare you pass the morning in horseplay," Boniface growled, "when I've a hundred tasks remaining for you before sunrise!" They trooped away across the courtyard, the Knight berating his squire and battering him with question after obscure question. The gardener Jack covered a gap-toothed smile and pushed the wheelbarrow off after them, humming Sturm's tune ever so quietly.

Sturm chuckled as he watched the procession. No doubt Derek would be doused and then sent to his carpeted chambers now, angry and flustered, rehearsing what he should have done or said when the upstart from Solace turned on him, roaring with laughter and dirges.

"Give him a day, Luin," Sturm whispered to the mare, who snorted affably in the slowly dispersing dark of the stable. "Give Derek a day, and let me be far away on the road, and there's no telling what the story will be as to what took place this morning in the courtyard."

Already the castle grounds were defined in a pale gray light. The lamps in the tower seemed dim now, and overhead the bats and glowing vespertiles rushed to the safety of cave and lowland barnloft. Deep on the plains, the horizon took shape.

The sun had risen by the time Sturm led Luin into the courtyard and up to the southern gates. Lord Stephan was there to see him off, mist trailing through the white strands of his beard. Gunthar was there, too, and he inspected the young man sternly, making sure his horse was properly saddled and that his inherited armor fit him with Solamnic propriety.

"These ancestral arms are a bit . . . outsized, lad," Gunthar proclaimed in disappointment, staring skeptically at Angriff's breastplate, so wide and swallowing that it looked as if someone had dropped Sturm into a cage. "Perhaps you have a more suitable fit in your quarters?"

Sturm shook his head.

"A closer fit, yes, Lord Gunthar. But more *suitable?* I think not. For I am the Brightblade, called to a challenge by Lord Wilderness. My legacy rides with me to the gods know where." The lad masked a smile. It was a speech he had rehearsed while combing the mare, and he thought it was all resonant and Measured, a fitting exit line and a fitting prologue to his own great adventure.

Pompous little bumpkin, Lord Stephan thought with gentle amusement. Rattling about in that coffin of a breastplate. We'll see how well 'the Brightblade' and his legacy weather the coming news.

"The gods know where, indeed, Sturm Brightblade," Stephan announced aloud as the great oaken gates of the Clerist's Tower opened behind him. "But your first destination is no doubt the Southern Darkwoods, and the way to that place Lord Vertumnus . . . insists on showing you, it seems."

Sturm's eyes widened as he looked over Stephan's shoulder. Inexplicably, vines had grown from the cobblestones at the foot of the Southern Gates, spreading over the huge passageway like an enormous green web. And out on the wings of Habbakuk, tumbling south and east into the rocky foothills, a narrow swath of grass had risen from nowhere. Overnight it had spread from the gates of the castle down onto the Solamnic Plains. As bright as green fire it was, and as flawless as a ribbon or a dignitary's carpet.

"A good host he is, this Vertumnus," Sturm jested weakly, rubbing his shoulder, which all of a sudden had begun to throb. "A good host indeed, to guide me from the Tower to his hold." His words felt thin in the misted air.

"I trust the venture is not as dark as your friend Crownguard makes it," Lord Stephan insisted. "Nonetheless, I cannot lie and say the path will be easy. But may the Dragon and the Mantis guide you also, and may the Gray Book open and show you its wisdom."

Waxing pompous myself, Lord Stephan thought. Must be the hour and the greenery. For it had taken the Knights by surprise, too—Vertumnus's magic leading up to the very gates of the stronghold. A narrow swath of green it was, but powerful. Lord Gunthar had stepped from the gates and touched it, first with his sword, and then with his bare hand. Stephan had followed suit, and the spring grass felt warm and pliant between his fingers, and with the touch had come a strange, undefinable yearning for the depths of the wilderness, for the fastness and green of the forest.

"May the Dragon and the Mantis guide you," he whispered again as Sturm led his horse gingerly through the maze of greenery out onto Vertumnus's magical path. Boniface and Gunthar watched from the walls, too, and to all three of the Knights, the lad seemed frail, forever unprepared. Again Lord Stephan regretted that Oath and Measure prevented the lot of them from taking up arms and following.

Brightblade the lad might be—indeed, Lord Angriff's son he *was*, in image and spirit. But what lay ahead . . .

* * * * *

Boniface dragged his sputtering squire to a secluded spot off the gardens. It was near a shed, where the gardeners' tools lay amid broken statuary and the wreckage of a gnomish irrigation system that had never worked in the first place.

Boniface looked about him and quickly set upon his hapless nephew.

"Is everything in place, Derek?"

"Ev-everything?" the boy stammered nervously.

"Everything, you pampered little fool! The trap at the ford, the mare's malady, the ambush, the surprise at the village, the—"

"Unc—Lord Boniface, please!" Derek urged in a whisper, nodding frantically in the direction of Jack, who was serenely dumping the manure on the pile at the foot of the garden. The gardener wiped his hands and shuffled carefully through a maze of flowers, where he knelt and examined the green bud of a green rose.

"Never mind him!" the Knight ordered, his voice low and menacing. "Only a servant and simpleton he is, but perhaps even *he* would have done better in preparing the surprises for that fool of a Brightblade."

"You may rest assured, sir," Derek replied coldly, his anger and dignity rising. "By Paladine and all the gods of good, you may know that everything you planned for Sturm Brightblade is in place and awaits only his . . . his *honorable* presence."

At those words, the great Solamnic swordsman relaxed and loosened his grip on the squire. With a curious smile, he regarded the lad in front of him.

"Those are strange gods for your oath, Derek Crownguard. Strange gods indeed."

* * * * *

Sturm marveled at how the green strand followed the route he had chosen and planned.

Down through the Wings of Habbakuk it fared, skirting the Hart's Forest, that small thicket that housed, among evergreens and maples, the only vallenwoods in the Vingaard foothills. Southward it glittered, fading from sight in the morning mists but undeniably leading toward the river, toward the provinces of Lemish beyond, and toward the heart of that troubled country where the Southern Darkwoods lay.

It was almost as though his journey had been mapped for him. Yet even though the Green Man had charted his way, the Plains of Solamnia no longer permitted a safe and simple passage, for the times had changed since the great heroic ages of Vinas Solamnus, Bedal Brightblade, and Huma Dragonbane—ages when the country was righteous and just, defended from its enemies by strong lance and stronger beliefs.

Now it was nearly impossible to imagine those ancient times. The countryside had turned in violence and anger against the Knights. Peasants rebelled, Nerakan bandits raided the eastern borders, and darker things still were rumored to have settled in the heartlands—gibbering, scaled things, reptilian and sly, that snatched babies and slaughtered livestock, things that passed through the villages of a night like a cold wind, fingering thatch and masonry, rattling doors. . . .

Sturm shuddered. Before him, the plains stretched to the edge of sight, mist-covered and flecked with the rust of dead heather, over which the green swath stretched like a glittering sash. It was a faceless landscape and harsh, where the country could lose him for days if the path failed or he wandered unwarily. The place had a peculiar silence to it, as if the wind had no voice here.

Beneath him, Luin whickered serenely and stopped to graze on Vertumnus's bright pathway. Sturm turned in the saddle and looked back into the Vingaard Mountains, where the great spire of the High Clerist's Tower glistened in the midmorning sunlight. Though the road back was scarcely a three-hour journey, the tower seemed remote, as though it sat firmly in the heart of another age.

He turned once again to the green way. It stretched ahead

of him, over an imagined route that seemed suddenly hostile. Over the swiftly flowing Vingaard River, down into the hobgoblin strongholds of Throt—and all of this only a prelude to the Darkwoods themselves and to whatever Vertumnus had in mind.

"Why, the getting there *alone* could kill me," Sturm whispered uneasily.

Indeed the getting there for some had been perilous. Stories of danger on the Solamnic roads were plentiful and grim. There was the caravan from Caergoth, missing for days, whose wagons were found still rolling along the road to Thelgaard Keep, the horses still in the traces, though their drivers and passengers had vanished entirely. There were also the dozen pilgrims from Kaolyn, bound for the shrines at Palanthus, whose bodies, noosed and dangling from the low limbs of vallenwoods, were scarcely more than husks by the time Lord Gunthar's search party discovered them.

Sturm rubbed his eyes and wrapped his cloak more tightly about his shoulders. Twice he had imagined someone was following him, but when he looked behind him, he saw only pale sunlight, only wind through the high grass.

The dwarves told even darker stories, he knew, his imagination still racing. How in order to lure kindhearted victims into a lonely and treacherous spot, hobgoblins had learned to mimic the cry of a human infant, so that in the thick recesses of a fog . . .

Fog! Sturm stood upright in the stirrups. While he was wool-gathering, the mare had stopped on the greenway, serenely eating the path in front of them.

Tendrils of mist, unnaturally pale, rose like spirits out of the plains around him. The sun was oblique and muted. The air was white, gray at the greater distances where the rising mist blocked the sunlight altogether.

Sturm leaned forward and squinted, his hand on his sword. So it wasn't evening, after all, but a deep fog. He clucked his tongue at the mare, and warily Luin began to move again, placing one foot cautiously before the other as though she walked through a swamp or along an unsteady precipice.

Then music rose out of nowhere, an old hornpipe in a minor key. Sturm drew his sword and wheeled about in the saddle, but everywhere was mist and music, and nothing more than that. At once he felt foolish, as if he had drawn his sword to fight the air.

"Come out, Vertumnus!" Sturm muttered, his voice rising with his anger. "Get out from behind your fog and nonsense, and let's settle this. Sword to sword, knight to knight, man to man!"

But the music continued serenely, perpetually, the tune varying and doubling back on itself, always recognizable and yet never the same. The fog began to dance to the music, swirling and shifting in a mad, encircling reel. Now Sturm could no longer see the ground. It was as though Luin waded through shallow, indefinite waters.

Cautiously the lad dismounted and walked beside his mare, each step light and doubtful. He could no longer feel the newly grown grass, and he was beginning to wonder if the ground itself had turned to mist.

"The keep . . . is Vingaard Keep to the left? The setting sun . . ." Sturm muttered. Directions were useless now, even if he could remember them in the midst of this infernal, confusing music. The rules of the road were changing rapidly, and he hated himself for being already lost.

For an hour or so, Sturm trudged on through the murk, his path winding hopelessly and his thoughts slipping from bewilderment into alarm.

Quite abruptly, the music stopped. The silence that followed was again breathless and hostile, as though the plains themselves were hushed in the expectation of some terrible crime. Sturm felt his sword shake in his hand.

For a few minutes, he continued his wandering, his steps even more tentative. The hooting of an owl in a blasted oak sounded like a call from the land of the dead, and once or twice the lad thought he heard a baby crying nearby. The sounds brought him dangerously close to panic. Twice he set foot to stirrup but both times gathered his wits and thought better of it.

" 'Tis all you'd need!" he whispered angrily. "A nasty fall from a horse in a deep fog! Crack your skull and drive out what little brains you have left!"

Finally, suspecting that he might even be headed back toward the Tower, Sturm decided to stop and wait out the fog. "For wouldn't it please Derek Crownguard," he asked Luin, "if I were simply to walk out of the mist in front of the great southern gate, having turned myself entirely about in a terror?"

He gritted his teeth. "By Huma!" he swore, "I'd rather *die* than give that scoundrel a moment's triumph!"

Luin rolled her long nose over the lad's shoulder and nibbled his hair thoughtfully.

Together the two of them waited, old mare and young rider. They dozed, startling awake now and then at the wingbeat of quails, at the chittering sound of squirrels in the distant trees. Finally the evening approached, and the country fell hushed and settled around them.

* * * * *

Sturm awoke with a start. For a moment, he thought he was back in the Clerist's Tower, safe in the squires' barracks. But he was armed and cloaked, and his bed was open ground. He turned over and blinked stupidly, remembering at once where he was.

"Luin!" he whispered. The mare had wandered off, but she was somewhere nearby. Through the early morning darkness, he heard her, sniffing and pawing the earth. Sturm struggled to his feet, his father's breastplate unwieldy and too heavy to balance. Reeling one last time, the lad righted himself and stalked off in the direction of the sound.

Suddenly there was a gentle rustling on the breeze, a

sound he would remember at once when he heard it years later in the ruins of Xak Tsaroth. At first he thought it was a storm wind coursing through the leaves, but the air was still. Sturm thought of Vertumnus, of the unnatural change of the seasons. . . .

He stumbled forward as a hot breeze passed over him, carrying upon it a smell of sulfur and ash and anger. At first it seemed as if the plains were burning, that the mist was igniting around him. He was choking.

Sturm spun about, whistling frantically for Luin. The mare emerged calmly out of the mist and the curling smoke, stopping only to browse lazily at a low clump of clover. He scrambled to her side, hoisted himself onto her back . . .

And held on for dear life as Luin caught wind of something beneath the sharp smell of the air, a greater, more sinister terror. She kicked out instantly, hysterically, and galloped into the mist.

Sturm clung to the reins, his ankle tangled in a stirrup. Vainly he tried to wrestle up into the saddle, but Luin's wild and headlong path through the fog carried both of them over rough terrain, and it was all he could do to hold on. Behind him, the rustling sound faded, then resurged, this time far louder. It sounded like nothing the lad had heard before. He thought of cyclones, of the fierce Aferian wind that rides through mountain passes, leveling tree and house as it rushes onto the plains. Faster Luin galloped, her chestnut coat slick and flecked with foam now, and still the great noise closed on them, louder and swifter and more urgent.

Sturm thought of reaching for his sword, of turning to face whatever it was that Vertumnus had sent after him. But Luin kept galloping like a wind herself over the Solamnic Plains. To remove one hand from the reins would risk a broken neck or back, a fatal dragging over the hard ground. He hung on, then, slinging his leg over the saddle once, twice, a third time, but the speed of the horse and the weight of his armor kept him dangling and struggling, unable to recover his balance. The mist behind him began to glow with a menacing, blood-red light, and in the heart of the light, a huge dark shape swooped toward him on leathery batwings, and the air was hot and hotter still until the heat was intolerable.

And suddenly, unexpectedly, the music returned, the fog closed around them, and the light bent away from him, taking with it the sound and the heat. Coughing, gasping, halfway atop the mare, Sturm watched the mist open up and swallow the hulking, leathery form of the pursuer. The heat and the roaring subsided.

And the music echoed in the rocks around them. A different tune this time—a quickstep filled with deception and comedy, so contagious that the nightingales perched in the darkened boughs of oak and vallenwood began to trill and mimic in answer. Luin slowed to a canter, to a walk, and Sturm, winded and baffled, finally settled himself on her back.

"By Branchala, that was a strange thing!" the young man muttered. He looked around him as the mist scattered, falling like rain back into the hard, spare ground. Above him, the stars appeared in the Solamnic night sky—first the moons, then bright Sirion and Reorx. By their reckoning, he was miles south of where he had been.

"What . . . what *was* it, Luin?" he asked. "And . . . where *are* we?"

The mist had subsided now, and from horseback, Sturm could see some distance across the level plains. A village lay in the distance to the west, its faint lights twinkling in the clear winter night. It was an inviting prospect—warmth and shelter for whatever time remained before sunrise.

But Sturm knew peasants, knew the abiding hatred they nurtured for the Order. Whatever the village, however kindly its lights, the Kingfisher, Crown, and Rose were unlikely to be welcomed in its dwellings.

Sighing, the lad turned his gaze east, to where, faint in the sunrise and the fading white light of Solinari, the two towers of a large castle jutted on the horizon. It was not

Castle Brightblade, that was certain, but it *was* a castle, and castles in these parts spelled refuge to those of the Oath and Measure.

Slowly, leisurely, Sturm guided his mount eastward toward the towers, which seemed to rise like mist from the ground in front of him. It was nearly dawn when the battlements heaved into view, and in the faint gray of earliest sunlight, he made out the faded standard of the castle, emblazoned on an enormous shield above the western gates.

The standard was weathered, the paint chipping and peeling, but Sturm knew enough of his own family history to make out its lineaments—a red flower of light on a white cloud on a blue field.

"Di Caela!" Sturm breathed. "The ancient house of my grandmothers! We are far south of where we should be, good Luin. But in a way, I suppose, we are home."

The mare snorted again at the prospect of approaching shelter. Slowly her walk became a trot, then a canter, and with redoubled energy, she carried Sturm Brightblade toward the worn gates of his ancestors.

Chapter 6

The Darkwoods

Deep in the Southern Darkwoods, lying in a hammock of vine and leaves, Lord Wilderness closed his eyes and set down his flute. Around him, the light was distorted, green and amber, as though the woods themselves were a dark and curving glass.

The hammock was suspended between two ancient oaks above the foundation of a ruin even more ancient. Moss-covered stones dotted the clearing like worn teeth, outlining faintly the foundation of a small building, perhaps a moat house or monastery, no doubt abandoned and left to fall apart some time back in the Age of Might.

Vertumnus's eyes flickered open suddenly. Perched above him in the branches of an ancient oak, two dryads stared down at him in perplexity.

"You *could* have killed him!" hissed the smaller of the pair, her black hair knotted in a long coil. Her voice was rich and sinister, like the rush of wind over dried leaves.

Vertumnus did not answer. Slowly he folded his hands on his chest, and for a moment, he looked like the statue of an entombed king, still and regal and unfathomable. The dryads stirred uneasily above him, the tall one scrambling down the side of the hammock as nimbly as a spider down a web until she came to rest by the side of the Green Man and nestled against him, her face buried in the green thicket of his beard.

"I know ye're not for killing him," she whispered seductively, her voice flute music and her touch the light flutter of a bird's wing. "And it makes no difference to us. But daunt him and confuse him and send him addled back to his creed-bound brothers. *Do* it! Do it *now!*"

Vertumnus chuckled, and the wind whistled through his laughter.

"You're as bloodthirsty as stirges, the whole oak-dwelling lot of you," he rumbled. "And as foolish and insistent as magpies."

The leaves rustled as he waved away the dryads.

"Begone with the both of you! 'Tis morning and time for me to sleep."

He stretched, and the dryad at his side scrambled out of the hammock and onto the dried leaves of the forest floor. Pouting, she stared at the green prodigy half-drowsing in the branches above her, his voice filled with alien wonder and magic.

"Not one of us, are ye," she accused. "Not yet. And no longer one of them, though ye may yearn for the days gone by."

Vertumnus only laughed and turned in the hammock. He shook his head, and acorns rained through the netted vines, and for a moment, the air shimmered with a thousand swirling samaras. With glittering black eyes, he regarded the dryad, his gaze warm and amused but unreadable.

"Who are you to say, little Evanthe, whither I yearn or aspire?"

From somewhere amid the thick, spreading branches of juniper, a great owl descended, alighting on the clews of the hammock, a sprig of sharp blue berries in its beak. Vertumnus winked at the owl, ironically regarding the sulking nymphs below him.

"As for now," he yawned, "get ye to an oak tree, and my companion and I will drowse and dream the dreams of the nocturnal and wise." Vertumnus arched an eyebrow, turned to the owl, and waved away the nymphs once again—this time more impatiently.

Angrily the dryads glided toward the center of the woods, looking back over their shoulders once, then a second time, at this unmanageable green mystery in their midst.

"Ye'll *never* be one of us!" the little one shouted tauntingly. "Though ye're green as a sapling, as a summer leek, ye'll never be like us, Lord Wilderness!" Then both of them vanished into the dappled light of the forest depths.

Vertumnus smiled and closed his eyes.

"Diona," he whispered, raising the flute to his lips, "you will never imagine how little that troubles me."

Serenely the Green Man looked into the dark vault of the forest. He touched his lips to the flute, then lowered it, spoke a few soothing words to the owl in a language of whistles and coos and of wind through the high branches, and the great bird nestled in the spreading thicket of his hair. Vertumnus raised the flute again, and the rest of them came from the shadows—nightingale and tiercel, elk and squirrel and bat, and a single amber-eyed lynx.

Slowly Lord Wilderness began to play, in the stately ninth mode that the bards call Branchalan. The startled owl took to wing as the hammock in which the man lay bristled with a fresh growth of leaves. Though the world and the weather around him was still in the tag end of winter, it was suddenly high summer.

Vertumnus played, and flowers budded and blossomed about him, entwining their thin, hollow stems in his beard and hair. Quickly he shifted to the tenth mode, the serene and lilting Matherian, and the air about him wafted with sweet fragrances. On the branches above him, the songbirds nodded, lulled by the lovely smells, and gradually they began to sing along, as they had in the fog on the Plains of Solamnia.

The Green Man's eyes twinkled with delight. For the eleventh mode was next—the Solinian, the Song of the White Moon, the Granter of Visions. Throughout Ansalon, ears were turning, lifting to the air where, soft and almost undetectable, the melody arising from the Southern Darkwoods would fall upon them.

Swiftly the green fingers danced over the body of the flute, flashing and blurring as the music quickened. Vertumnus looked to the gray patch of morning sky above him, visible through the opaque net of branches, and slowly watched it fill with the white face of Solinari.

The eyes of Vertumnus flashed and widened. The dance was beginning. The branches no longer obscured the sky but, caught in the music and the light, they seemed to shrink into a netting of scars on the surface of a glorious moon.

The shimmering surface of the orb turned green as Vertumnus played, clouding with a distant celestial storm. The clouds swirled and boiled silently, and from the midst of their turmoil, images arose, peopling the surface of the moon.

It was like a mirage, like a scene more vivid than memory but less vivid than sight. Crossing the surface of Solinari as though moving across the face of an orb, a party of a dozen dwarves trudged from rock to insubstantial rock.

Vertumnus squinted and continued to play.

Two of the dwarves stopped in their ghostly passage, shadows poised on the lip of the moon. They looked at one another, sniffed, and shook their heads curiously, as though trying to dislodge something from their ears.

Vertumnus smiled, his lips above the embouchure of the flute. It was like this always: The music reached them as a strange disturbance of thought, an elusive thing they wouldn't remember a moment after it tumbled away from their hearing. Yet the Solinian mode was the song of changes. Those within hearing would be changed by the music—that is, if they chose to listen. Some changed subtly, some profoundly, but all who had ears to hear would be touched somewhere in their deepest, most inward heart, and afterward the song would never leave them.

The dwarves vanished as quickly as they had risen from the clouds on the moon, and in their stead, three Knights rode by on horseback, scarves wrapped about their faces against a driving winter wind.

One of them, bareheaded, his dark hair flecked with gray, reined in his horse beneath a snow-covered stand of juniper. Half hidden in the shadow of evergreens and in the dodging light of the moon, he turned his face heavenward, listening to the music with controlled focus.

Something about his bearing seemed familiar . . . familiar indeed. . . .

But he was gone before Vertumnus could look more closely, vanished into the green roil of clouds about the moon. At his vanishing, Vertumnus lowered the flute, and suddenly, as though a levelling wind had passed across its surface, Solinari blazed forth with a silver light. . . .

Then suddenly, inexplicably, it began to wane.

Vertumnus shook his head sadly, his long green locks dripping with dew. Now he would locate the lad again, before the moon was a crescent, a sliver, before it was gone entirely into newness and dark. He would find the one who would occupy his time until the first of spring. Briskly, amusingly, he played a simple eighth-mode jig, so simple that it was scarcely magic. The dryads, hearing the song from their bowers deep in the woods, stepped from the trees and approached him, trailing oak leaves and a strange sil-

---

ver light.

"There are other dancers far more promising, Vertumnus," Diona urged.

"One of the Knights," Evanthe suggested. "Even a brace of dwarves would be more entertaining."

Vertumnus played on as though he did not hear them. Indeed Sturm looked like a plodding prospect, a singularly unimaginative young man bound by custom and convention. What the nymphs did not know was how this Brightblade concerned him—how the quarrel at Yule had warred with Vertumnus over the months. It was time for the lad to learn difficult instruction, about blood and forbearance and the shimmering fraud at the heart of his beloved Order. In the absence of a father, Vertumnus had taken it upon himself to provide the lessons.

Evanthe had been right before. Vertumnus could have killed Sturm Brightblade once, twice, perhaps many times. For the dark thing that followed the lad on the fog-littered plains, a thing that answered to no man and to few gods, danced to the music of Vertumnus. It had neared the boy, had almost overtaken him, but at the last moment, the Green Man had piped it northward toward Kalaman and the bay beyond.

It was too soon for dark things, too soon to test the boy so strongly. There would be perils enough and eventual death. But not now, for the dance was young. And spring was still a fortnight away.

Quickly, in mist and the swelling moon, Vertumnus searched for Brightblade. Over the plains the music swept like a wind, circling about Vingaard Keep, down the great river as far as Thelgaard Keep and still searching, searching all of Solamnia until . . .

With the last solemn notes of the tune, the fog dissolved before an ancient castle, ruinous and abandoned. Vertumnus's dark eyes widened.

The dryads exchanged unreadable glances.

"He is there, Evanthe," Vertumnus whispered. The last of

the fog fell away, and there sat Brightblade, unsteady on his lathered mare. Shaken by fog and fire and a breakneck ride, he seemed diminished, small inside that absurd Solamnic armor.

"It almost makes for pity," Diona said, her dark hand resting on the Green Man's shoulder.

"Not mine," Vertumnus replied, in his voice a last hint of winter. "My branches are bare of pity."

So he and the owl and the dryads watched as the lad rode through the dilapidated gates of Castle di Caela.

"A place that you know, Lord Wilderness?" Evanthe whispered teasingly, her lips at the Green Man's ear. Vertumnus smiled, but he did not answer.

Sturm dismounted and walked the mare across the moss-covered stones of the courtyard, past booths and buildings in disrepair to the mahogany gates of the castle keep, weathered but still intact. The lad tried the door, and with some wrestling managed to yank it open.

"He's a strong one, your dancer!" taunted Diona. Vertumnus raised a long green finger to her lips, pressing playfully until the dryad winced and turned away.

Now the boy stepped inside, and the midday light shone briefly, fitfully into the darkness of the keep.

"He is in the great anteroom now," Vertumnus murmured, "with its tapestries, and its golden birds, and its marble banisters."

"Tell us about it," Evanthe whispered. "Tell us, Vertumnus."

Lord Wilderness closed his eyes and raised the flute to his lips. Something serene, perhaps, in a more magical mode, or something piercing and light . . .

"Vertumnus! Look!" hissed Diona. He opened his eyes as a shadowy figure crossed the distant courtyard like an unwelcome specter in a dream. From shadow to shadow flitted the man, caped and hooded and low against the walls. To the great mahogany door of the keep he came, set hand to the door . . .

. . . and closed it, violently and suddenly, wedging it shut with a dagger. As quickly as it had come, the figure slipped away, and from inside the keep came the muffled sound of the lad beating frantically, helplessly against the jammed door.

Vertumnus lay back in his hammock, the flute silent as his fingers danced across it aimlessly.

"That one," he mused. "That . . . *hooded* one."

With a delighted smile, he turned to Evanthe.

"I know him! I know him by his gait, his every movement."

With a laugh, he rumpled the hair of the dryads, pushing them playfully from the hammock.

"Go to the lady, Evanthe! Diona! Tell her the dance has become more interesting by far!"

And as the nymphs rushed off through the thick evergreens, Vertumnus leapt from the hammock and shook the mist from his long green locks. He slipped the flute into his belt and scrambled from the tree. A long journey lay ahead of him, but it was short compared to the road he had traveled for six years.

"Boniface!" he breathed. "By all the stars unfortunate and fortunate, Lord Boniface Crownguard of Foghaven! He's onto something. Now the music moves more quickly."

* * * * *

Boniface turned from the door of the keep, shaking his head to banish the strange humming noise in his ears.

He was content now. Surpassingly content. For now, the inquisitive lad was locked within the fastness of the tower.

It had taken all his riding and knowledge of geography to arrive at the castle before Sturm Brightblade. He had dismounted in the dark of the stables and slipped across the bailey, having barely the time to secure all the doors from the keep so that once the lad entered, it would be impossible for him to leave. All along the ground floor of the thousand-year-old tower, the doors were wedged impossibly shut. The sheer drop from the upper window was further assurance.

Boniface sighed, leading Luin to a rain-filled trough, from which the little mare drank loudly, the noise drowning out the hammering and shouting at the thick door, the unnatural gnat song in the winter air.

It was not the most pleasant of tasks, this locking of boys in towers. Sturm would most likely starve, and even if great good fortune let him escape, he would be delayed long enough from his forest appointment that his honor would be . . .

What was the Green Man's phrase? "Forever forfeit."

It had to be done, though, Boniface told himself as he led Luin toward the shadowy stable. It had to be done, because in asking after his father, Sturm might uncover the truth about the siege of Castle Brightblade.

He was too young to understand that truth, or how Angriff had threatened the very life of the Order.

Boniface rested his forehead against the warm flank of the mare, remembering. He remembered how Angriff Brightblade had returned from Neraka with visions, with extraordinary danger in his soul. At once they all had noticed the change in the man, how his swordsmanship flowered, how he had become more skilled and reckless and inventive.

Somehow it was a little . . . disturbing. After all, Angriff was newly wed at the time, and his father, Lord Emelin, had only recently passed into Huma's breast, leaving Castle Brightblade to the care of his son. It just seemed that Angriff would have been more . . . conservative.

Boniface shrugged and leaned against the trough.

Angriff had been a puzzle. Always a puzzle. Like that time in the garden, shortly after he returned, when the two of them had walked a narrow path lined with flowers, Boniface a dozen steps behind him and the air loud with finches and sparrows.

Boniface had come around a stand of larick and found his friend bent on the path, gloved hand lightly touching the petals of a green and silver rose. It was as if Angriff was . . . *absent* for a moment, that the flower held something he was desperately trying to remember or recover.

Boniface stood there, with his friend lost in thoughts of rare gentleness, with the sunlight of May slanting through the leaves of the Calvian oak so that all of them—Knight, trail, and silver flower—were cast in a curious green. Hardly the place for ill musings, it was.

But Boniface had thought, although idly and no more than tactically, that here would be a fitting place for ambush, if evil intent were to meet with a secluded spot in a garden and a great swordsman for once unwary.

He shuddered and dismissed such a dark musing.

Boniface smiled to recall it now. He had indeed been young that day in the garden.

Nonetheless, his thoughts had moved elsewhere, to the rose that Lord Angriff cupped in his hand and to other, tamer thoughts beyond that. But Angriff suddenly drew sword and rose quickly. He looked down a bend in the garden pathway, under an aeterna bush, then whirled about and made for the delicate wrought iron gazebo in the terraced center of the garden. He acted unsettled, distracted. He leaned against the scrolled gateway of the little building, as if he had been overtaken by some strange and sudden malady.

It was then that Boniface called the servants, thinking he would need help in carrying Angriff to the infirmary.

The servants arrived, flushed and breathless, but by that time Angriff was composed, thoroughly alert. He brushed aside Boniface's bracing hand and ordered the men to search the garden. They came back soon, assuring the Knights that the premises were secure.

Then Angriff had turned to him wearily.

"I am sorry for this immoderate display, Bonano," he said, using the childhood name Boniface hated but endured from his capable friend. "But when I stooped to admire this silver rose, there suddenly came upon me a change in the . . . energies of the garden. It is what you learn in Neraka, in the face of bandit swordsmen, when your heart and sword hand must learn to sense the intention and impulse of your enemy.

"I felt it just now, here in the garden," he said. "And I saw no one except you. Not even a squirrel or dog."

Angriff grinned and brushed back his dark hair wearily. "I must be more tired than I had imagined," he confessed, and it was hours before Boniface could set aside his own astonishment long enough to tell him that the "change in energy" was his own.

Even more than insubordination, more than irreverence at tournament and in the councils of the mighty, it had been that moment, remembered and magnified over the passage of years, that sealed Angriff's future for Boniface. It was why the Brightblades had to vanish forever.

And why, by simple logic, the boy had to vanish, too.

Chapter 7

Castle di Caela

Sturm sat in the half-dark, rubbing his bruised shoulder.

He was living the bad fable told to frighten children, to steer them away from ruins and ill-kept cellars. Sturm had ventured inside, and someone—Vertumnus, he figured, for lack of a better explanation—had closed the door solidly behind him. He heard the footsteps walking away. And then, of course, the door had refused to open, whether by force or wit.

Sturm looked around. A faint light from a single high clerestory window kept the great di Caela anteroom from sinking into total darkness. And yet the hall was oppressively gloomy, paneled in mahogany or some other dark wood, its polish and glow surrendered to six years of neglect.

For Castle di Caela had fallen to the peasants in the very year that Castle Brightblade fell and Lord Angriff vanished. Agion Pathwarden was a blustery but capable steward who had kept the holdings well, but when he met betrayal and death on the Wings of Habbakuk, he left behind him a thin larder and a scant garrison of a dozen men. The garrison was starved out by the peasants in the late summer of 326, around the time of Sturm's twelfth birthday.

"Starved out," Sturm said to himself disconsolately.

Slowly and a little painfully, the lad stood and made his way toward the unhinged double doors of the great dining hall. The mahogany tables, once the pride of generations of di Caelas and then of the Brightblades that followed them, lay shattered and strewn throughout the dusty room.

Grandfather Emelin was born here, Sturm thought. Father was but a month shy of being born here himself, for when Grandmother was heavy with child, old Emelin took her north, to Castle Brightblade, where Bayard his father . . .

On the lad mused, seating himself in a high-backed chair, tracing his history amid dust and cobweb and wreckage. There was more light in here, the clerestory bright with a dozen windows, through which the wind plunged, stirring the dust and the rotting curtains. A marble frieze, chipped and defaced by peasant hands, spanned the balcony above the hall. Upon it, scarcely recognizable from the vandalism and neglect, the story of Huma played itself out in seven sculpted scenes from the life of the great Solamnic hero.

Sturm sat upright, carefully regarding the frieze. He had a penchant for things old and marbled and historical, and after all, these carvings had been in the family nearly a thousand years. He admired the vine scroll, the magnificently carved mountains, the terrible likeness of Takhisis, the Mother of Night.

" 'Out of the heart of nothing,' " Sturm recited. " 'Aswirl in a blankness of color.' "

Then he looked at Huma himself, whose face seemed to be his own face.

"By Paladine!" the lad whispered. "My face on the face of Huma?" He walked closer through the splinters and rubble, eyes intent on the damaged frieze.

No. He was mistaken. The head of Huma had been chiseled away, no doubt when the castle was taken. What he had seen was but a trick of light, a sudden and unexplainable bedazzlement.

"Light will be dear soon," he told himself. "It's on into the rest of the castle while the sun through the windows can still guide me about and out." With a deep, courageous breath, he climbed the great stairs into the upper chambers of Castle di Caela.

* * * * *

The halls were lined with statuary and rusting mechanical birds.

Sturm had heard of the cuckoos of Castle di Caela—that his great-great-grandfather, Sir Robert, had collected all manner of chiming and whirring machinery, none of which worked, at least as it was intended to work, and all of which annoyed and menaced the visitors. Great-grandmother Enid had stored all of these novelties in the Cat Tower, the smaller of the two castle turrets, but Sir Robert and Sir Galen Pathwarden, an erratic friend of great-grandfather Bayard's, had restored the aviary in all of its irritating glory, sure that the whistling "would soothe baby Emelin."

They were gone now, the lot of them. Robert had drowned when his wheeled contraption of gnomish make, designed to render the horse obsolete, had careened off the drawbridge into the brimming di Caela moat. Great-grandmother Enid had passed away peacefully, quietly, at the age of one hundred and twelve, having lived long enough to see the infant Sturm in his cradle. As for Sir Bayard and Sir Galen, nobody knew. Some time before the century turned, when both men were white-haired and a bit gone in the faculties and were happy grandfathers of their respective broods, the eccentric pair took off on yet another quest, bound for Karthay in the farthest regions of the Courrain Ocean. They were accompanied only by Sir Galen's brother, a mad hermit who talked with birds and vegetables, and none of them had returned.

Sturm fingered the brass bill of one of the comical birds. The bronze head came off in his hand, chirping one last, demented time.

So much for the di Caelas and those who consorted with them. It was a side of the family that was overgrown and wild: Sturm's mother had cautioned against their inheritance, telling the lad he must continually marshall his best Brightblade demeanor or he would be like the whole lot of them, climbing towers and living with lizards and cats.

Sturm drew his sword from its sheath as he ascended to the still brighter second floor, past servants' markers where the great geysers of Two Thirty One had shot through the floors and drenched even the upper stories. Dozens of statues lined the room, stretching back to times before the Cataclysm itself, when both Brightblade and di Caela had walked in uncommon heroism, among the first Knights at the side of Vinas Solamnus. They were all here, forever valiant if somewhat dusty.

Sturm moved by them, inspecting and exploring, his surprise and dismay growing. For here was a statue of Lucero di Caela, Wing Commander in the Great Ogre Wars, his sword drawn, stepping forth into battle. And there the statue of Bedal Brightblade, who singlehandedly fought the desert nomads, holding a pass into Solamnia until help came. There, indeed, was Roderick di Caela, who put down a hobgoblin invasion from Throt at the cost of his own life.

And the last of the statues was of Bayard Brightblade, erected, no doubt, by the Lady Enid in memory of her vanished husband. He, too, was drawing his sword and stepping forth.

Sturm rubbed at his eyes, not believing what he suddenly

saw. For what had seemed a fanciful mistake down in the great hall was unsettling and real here in the upper reaches of the keep.

Each hero now had Sturm's face, down to the boyhood scar upon the chin. From one to another he quickly moved, looking, looking again, looking away. This time there was no trick of light. Vertumnus again?

For a while, he sat by the statue of Sir Robert di Caela, his thoughts wandering. It was some time before he came to himself, and at once he scrambled to his feet, intent that night not overtake him in an abandoned castle. Swiftly he ranged from room to room, chamber to chamber, the sunlight as low as his hopes. All of the windows overlooked sheer and no doubt lethal plunges onto the stone pavement of the bailey.

Desperately looking for trellis or vine or mysterious stairwell, Sturm took the steps three at a time, finding himself in the solar on the topmost floor of the keep. The solar was the spacious chamber in which innumerable di Caela lords and ladies had slept away thousands of nights, and after them, two generations of Brightblades. Heir to much of that tradition, Sturm felt a little drowsy the moment he entered the room.

If anything, things looked even more hopeless from here. Above the solar were the battlements, but the lone ladder leading to a trapdoor in the ceiling lay in pieces no larger than his forearm. True, there were windows aplenty—stained glass, for that matter, in rich and various greens—but they were set high in yet another clerestory, to which not even a squirrel could climb.

Sturm seated himself dejectedly on the huge canopied bed, wrapping himself in what remained of the tattered curtains.

"Tomorrow," he told himself, his eyelids heavy, the curtains musty but warm. "There are cellars in this place, no doubt, out of which . . . I surely . . . can . . ."

He ran out of words and wakefulness, there amid the evening's green light and floating dust. Twice, maybe three times, he sneezed in his sleep, but he did not awaken.

And so on his very first night on the road, Sturm Brightblade slept like a seedy lord in the ruins of the castle. He was trapped, with no prospect of escape, and a weariness so great that he slept undisturbed until the morning sun was visible through the trapdoor to the battlements.

*   *   *   *   *

The new day, however, was no better. The locks to the cellar broke easily enough, but whatever passages or tunnels once led from the cellars were now blocked. The same earthquake that had unleashed the water on the upper regions of the house had sealed off its lower regions, Sturm concluded. Sadly he rummaged amid empty barrels, bottles, and wine racks, looking for secret doors, hidden corridors, and anything edible. He leaned against the moist wall, flushed with exertion and anger.

"If I ever find Lord Wilderness, or whoever locked me in this place," he swore, beating his fists against the hardpacked earth of the cellar floor, "I shall make him pay dearly! I shall . . . I shall . . . well, I shall do *something*, and it will be *terrible!*"

He closed his eyes and seethed. He felt silly and helpless, unworthy of his knightly inheritance. Before dire vengeance could be visited, before he cornered the scoundrel and exacted fierce, Solamnic justice, he would have to find his way out of his father's father's house.

*   *   *   *   *

It looked no better by afternoon. Sturm wandered the halls of the castle, growing more and more familiar with each turn and alcove.

Slowly his anger gave way to rising hunger and fear. The well in the keep and the cistern in the solar provided a trickle of water, but one could starve as easily in a castle, it seemed, as in the wilderness or the desert. That night hunger kept him awake, and he slept fitfully, awakening no more rested than when he had first closed his eyes.

Sluggish and weary, he found himself in midmorning back in the statuary room, drawn to the place and its history. He paced from one end of the hall to the other, passing from one marbled generation to the next with an increasing grogginess, until he reached the statue of Robert di Caela, fixed in the same martial pose as his ancestors and descendants, head strangely askew, as though the long-dead sculptor had sought to preserve his subject's eccentricity through an oddness in the carving.

With a sigh, the lad settled back against the dusty marble of the statue, only to slip from the pedestal onto the floor. In the statuary room, where a score of his ancestors stood enshrined, Sturm Brightblade sat and laughed alone—laughed at his own clumsiness, his unreadiness for all that lay ahead of him. Whimsically he stood, leapt onto the pedestal, and twisted the statue's head in his hands, seeking to right Sir Robert for once in the old man's spotty history.

Sturm laughed and tugged at the marble head, laughed and tugged again, his laughter ringing through the cavernous hall and the sunlight swimming around him. So dizzy he was, so faint and famished, that he never even noticed as the statue tilted, reeled, and tumbled on top of him. His head hit the floor and his breath escaped him.

Sturm awoke to music—the plaintive, solitary sound of the flute and a curious, elusive light among the statues. At first he thought it was a reflection in one of the numerous di Caela mirrors, a flash of moonlight from the window, his own movement caught in burnished bronze. But there was the music he could not explain, and it lent to the light a further, compelling mystery.

He followed the light from the room into the corridor, and the music accompanied him, echoing in the dusty corridors. Standing absolutely still on the landing of the stairwell leading down to the anteroom, Sturm saw the light shift and alter, drifting like mist toward the double doors of the lower great hall. Slowly, his sword drawn, he followed as the light drifted to the center of the large vaulted hall and vanished.

Unnerved, sure that what he had just seen was the first madness of starvation, Sturm seated himself in the high-backed mahogany chair from which he had first observed this forsaken room. Weaker now, his forehead and temples throbbing, he was no longer sure whether he could rise from it again.

"So *this* is the end of the Brightblade line," he announced ironically, wearily. "Starved to death in the feast hall of a castle!"

"If it *is* the end, then the line has descended to fools and schoolmasters!" a voice, gruff and barely substantial, proclaimed from somewhere in the rafters above the lad.

Startled, Sturm tried to rise, stumbling in weakness and fright.

"Which is not to say that didn't show up before in the bloodline," the voice continued. Sturm squinted toward the shadowy rafters.

"Who are you?" he asked nervously, "and . . . and . . . *where* are you?"

"In the balcony," the voice replied tersely. "With the rest of the commemorated."

Then slowly a strange yellow-green light spread from the balcony across the gloomy expanse, and the astonished Sturm marked that the light rose from a helmeted, armored figure astraddle the balcony railing, a pale old man, his face unbearably bright, his features blurred and distant, as though seen through the globe of a lantern.

"Who . . . who are you?" the lad stammered.

The man was silent, leaning over the balcony like a burning masthead or fox fire, that green, gaseous light in the midst of the marshes. His clothing was dancing with fire-light, dripping with an incandescent dew that tumbled to the floor into glittering pools like molten gold. Sturm held his breath at the man's strange menace and beauty.

"Are you the one who . . . imprisoned me here?" he asked, this time more softly.

"No," the man answered finally. His voice was resonant and deep and polished like old wood, and the dark mahogany paneling of the hall glowed greenly as he spoke. "No, I am no jailer. And you are the first to call this palace a prison."

"Who are you?" Sturm asked again. The man stood motionless, a pillar of fire above him.

"Look into your shield, lad, and tell me what you see."

"I see burnished bronze," Sturm said, "and my face in the reflection."

"Hold it up toward *me*, you fool! *Then* look at the reflection! Great Paladine's Beard! You Brightblades were never quick on the uptake! If Brightblade you are, as your shield and your self-pity tell me."

As the man glowed and blustered, Sturm raised the shield, tilting it so that the bright reflection seemed to rest in the boss. With the green light gone, the man looked more pale, positively ancient, and Sturm could make out his features, his mustache, the coat of arms on his breastplate.

Red flower of light on a white cloud on a blue field. The sign of di Caela, of a vanished name in a vanished house.

"Old grandfather," Sturm proclaimed, kneeling on the rubble-strewn floor of the hall, "or grandfather of grandfathers, whoever you may be. Or *whatever*—whether apparition or saint or memory, I salute you as di Caela and ancestor!"

Bravely, ceremonially, the lad extended his sword. Now the man in the balcony moved for the first time, his thin arm waving dismissively.

"Get to your feet, boy, or whatever it is that we used to say when the Measure was measured and I had to put up with legions of your kind. This is a *dining* hall, not a shrine, and I'm Robert di Caela, not Huma or Vinas Solamnus or whoever else you're proffering swords to in this day and time."

Robert di Caela sank through the stone balcony as if through dark water. First his glowing boots appeared on the underside of the platform, then his green leggings and sun-struck breastplate. Luminous and colorful as a great tropical bird, he floated gently to the floor of the hall. The oaken doors, Sturm's sole escape from the room, lay behind Robert, open and visible through the wavering transparency of his body. Phosphorescent weeds and mosses dripped from him as he approached, spangling the dark floor behind him.

Instinctually Sturm backed away.

"A simple back-country knight, I am," Sir Robert said. "Made even more simple by the fact I am no longer living. Though you've stirred the dust and rustled the curtains around here, I mean you no harm, boy—only curious to see you, to find out what brings a Brightblade back after all these years."

Sturm backed into the chair and sat down with a thump. He knew his family tree well enough not to be surprised that a Di Caela lord was hungry for gossip and news.

Sure enough, the ghost leaned forward, white face framed in a well-kept, elegant white beard. Robert's countenance was a pantomime mask, the dark mahogany paneling visible in the vacant sockets of the eyes.

"A quest, Lord Robert—" the unnerved boy stammered.

"*Sir* Robert," the ghost corrected. "Time was when we didn't priss and petticoat with conflated titles. 'Sir' was good enough for the likes of your great-granddad and for the likes of men every bit his equal."

Sir Robert seated himself on a rickety bench, passing somewhat through it as he spoke, and settling with a puff of dust.

" 'Twas a time when a quest was a great thing, lad! We went after enchanters! After lost civilizations and worms encircling the continent itself!"

The ghost closed his eyes, as though he dreamt of those days as he spoke.

"And what," Sir Robert asked bluntly, as his pale eyes flew open, "is the quest on which you're bound, little Brightblade?"

As though he were charmed, enchanted, or starved past lie or even concealment, Sturm told the ghost the whole story, from the night at the banquet through his own foggy wanderings and his time of entrapment here in Castle di Caela. It struck him as he told it—how long and venturesome it had seemed in the doing, and yet how weak and simple and even foolish to recount.

At the beginning of the story, Sir Robert listened intently, but his ardor didn't last long. His expression changed from intent to politely attentive, then abstracted and drowsy, then nodding on the edge of sleep.

"Is that all?" he asked. "You've set out to meet an opponent no doubt your superior in strength and craft, and you've managed to get yourself locked into my estate before you're even halfway there?"

Sturm flushed and nodded as Sir Robert laughed, a low thin chuckle.

"Well?" the ghost asked, standing and hovering not twenty feet from the lad.

"Sir?"

"Look to your ghost lore, boy! What revenge have I asked for?"

"None, sir."

"And what unfinished business have I asked you to complete?"

"Indeed, none."

"Absolutely. As I see it, you've enough unfinished business for a lifetime of your own. What treasure do I have?"

"Sir?"

"What *treasure*, damn it! You've combed the premises from battlements to cellar. What am I hiding?"

"Nothing, sir." The lad was weary of interrogation. He

was hungry and tired.

"Then what is left?" Sir Robert prodded.

"Sir?"

"What *else* do we ghosts do?"

Sturm stood in silence. Sir Robert approached him, green and yellow and red.

"We answer questions. I have returned to answer a question. No, I shall answer *two* questions."

Arms outstretched, the ghost of Sir Robert di Caela hovered scarcely an arm's length from Sturm's chair. Hunger racing through him like fever, Sturm peered at the ghost intently.

"I had always thought," the young knight ventured, "there was something magical and right in the answering of *three* questions."

"Don't bargain with me, boy!" Sir Robert snapped. "It will be two questions or none. We stand on no foolish traditions here. Two questions."

A thousand questions flashed through Sturm's mind as he stared at the ghost, questions historical, metaphysical, theological . . .

But *which* questions?

"Why you, of all the ghosts that might visit me?"

"That is your first question?"

"It is." Sturm regarded the ghost cautiously. Sir Robert hovered a good three feet off the ground, as though he were floating in water.

"Why me?"

" 'Tis what I ask," Sturm replied.

"Damned if I know," Robert replied. "Next question."

"*That* was your answer?" Sturm exclaimed.

"Is that your second question?" Sir Robert asked.

"What? Well . . . no . . ." Sturm muttered. He fell silent, and the green light in the great hall shifted and deepened. Now the shadows of bench, throne, and rubble lengthened along the dusty stone floor until it seemed that the furnishings themselves had grown beyond human proportion.

"I . . . I'm not sure what to ask," Sturm said finally. His mind lodged against the ancient stories of captured mages, bound to grant wishes—how they tricked their captors into asking for a sausage breakfast rather than immortality or infinite wisdom. Whatever the nature and design of the ghost before him, he was not about to let it trick him.

"I think that the question is evident," Sir Robert said with a curious smile.

Sturm gaped at the ghost and settled back into the chair. Sir Robert stood above him now, thin arms folded over his ethereal breastplate, eyes fixed on a ghostly distance. Slowly he lowered his gaze to the high-backed throne and to the young man, baffled and trembling, who sat upon it.

"The question is evident," Sir Robert repeated. "I think you need to ask how to get out of here."

Chapter 8

Encounter by Moonlight

"Very well. How do I get out?" Sturm asked.

"I thought you'd never ask," Sir Robert replied with a chuckle.

He should have known all along, Sturm told himself, for the ghost turned suddenly in stagnant air. Behind him, watery pools of light dripped from his locks and clothing, green and iridescent, as he made a path from the center of the hall, out the doors, and into the anteroom. Sword drawn and at the ready, Sturm rose from the chair and followed.

The footsteps led, to his surprise, back to the cellars of Castle di Caela, where Sir Robert, floating ethereally ahead of him, rushed back beneath the stairway.

"Bradley the engineer's work," he muttered. "So we could

get the wine out after the worm tore up the cellars."

The ghost flitted past a capsized wine barrel, headlong into the far wall, where he vanished entirely, leaving the stone surface shimmering with green light.

"Follow!" a voice urged from the other side of the wall, and when Sturm set hand to the glowing stones, they pivoted suddenly, and he was bathed with fresh air and moonlight. He stepped from the cellar into the castle bailey, bright in the silver glow of Solinari.

Sturm looked behind him. Surely enough, Sir Robert had vanished. Again he wondered why *this* ghost, of all possible ghosts in a castle long abandoned and no doubt richly haunted.

Luin trotted across the courtyard from the stables, apparently no worse for her time left alone. She looked cared for, even well fed, though she was still saddled and bridled as he had left her when he thought his stay in the castle would be a matter of minutes.

Sturm rifled through his packs, coming up with some jerky, some quith-pa, and some stale bread, all of which he wolfed down with no regard for manners or health. As he ate, Luin nuzzled his shoulder contentedly, and after a while, Sturm stroked her long nose and spoke to her, ashamed that she had been so long from his thoughts.

"And how, old girl, did you keep yourself so well over these days? How did—"

It was then he looked around and saw that the castle gardens were green, that grass sprouted up thickly between the stones of the courtyard. The grazing had been plentiful. Bright green the foliage was, not the pale of new leaf.

He had been in the castle for a week. He was sure of it. The first day of spring had no doubt come, or was at best a day or two away. Sturm thought back to the Yule banquet, to the Green Man's stern warning that he keep the time of their appointment, and his thoughts spun with the dire possibilities.

He would miss the time. And the tidings of his father,

promised by Lord Wilderness, would go unheard, would remain unlearned . . . perhaps forever.

At the thought of forever, a dull pain coursed through the lad's shoulder, and with it a sudden panic. For had not Vertumnus promised even more deadly things if Sturm did not keep the appointment?

"The wound would blossom, and its bloom would be deadly."

With no more thought of his comfort or of Luin's, Sturm Brightblade leapt into the saddle. Through the courtyard he clattered, reining and coaxing the horse beneath him, and out into the Solamnic countryside, where the moon tricked the landscape and the guideposts for travelers were confusing.

Over his shoulder, he cast one last look at Castle di Caela, the maternal house of his ancestry. Somehow it seemed insubstantial, a part of the mist that had brought him to its gates. As he rode farther, he could see the two large turrets. The largest one had housed the keep and the hall and the ghost of Sir Robert di Caela—about that one he was no longer curious. But behind that tower lay the other, the Cat Tower, in which his great-grandmother's family had housed their eccentrics—sometimes their truly insane.

A light burned in the topmost window of the Cat Tower, and holding the torch was a pale and elderly man, clad in ceremonial armor. Even at this distance, Sturm could make out the arms that adorned his breastplate.

Red flower of light on a white cloud on a blue field.

*　*　*　*　*

Boniface was not far behind him. Sturm's escape from the keep had taken him by surprise as he nodded atop the southwestern bartizan, his pale eyes fixed idly upon the pale moon. He cursed softly, then cursed himself for cursing, as the lad climbed into the saddle and galloped off through the northern gate before he could descend from the walls and get to the stable himself.

He hadn't expected the resourcefulness of the lad, who must indeed bear Brightblade ingenuity, for how else could he have escaped a castle so tightly locked and sealed?

Lord Boniface Crownguard smiled to himself, leading his horse from the stables and into the bailey. Gracefully he mounted, with the thoughtless skill of a cavalry officer, and blazed out after Sturm and Luin, the stallion beneath him dark and fluid on the moonlit plain.

Soon, however, he slowed his horse to a canter. It was only a matter of time. After all, he had seen to the contingencies. From here to the Southern Darkwoods, it was a gauntlet of traps and snares. In fact, the next surprise was fast approaching.

*   *   *   *   *

At a full gallop, Sturm and Luin charged north and east—or what Sturm thought was north and east—across the Solamnic Plains. The lad's hopes sank further with every swell and irregularity on the horizon: Who would have thought Solamnia was so wide, so incomprehensibly vast?

Sturm closed his eyes as the wind rushed by him. He would never belong to the Order now.

Downcast, his panic at last subsiding, he slowed Luin to a canter. It was then a breeze passed over them from his left, carrying upon it the faint, muddy smell of the river.

Encountering the castle had spun about his sense of direction. He had been traveling south, away from the ford and the road to Lemish. The edged green of the Solamnic grasslands had swallowed the green of Vertumnus's road, and the lad had galloped for an hour, directionless across a directionless plain.

Quickly Sturm reined Luin to a stop, stood up in the stirrups, and looked despairingly across the landscape ahead of him, bleak and featureless in all directions, save for a copse of evergreen here, a solitary vallenwood there.

He thought of how, in this desolate spot, his failure and delay—perhaps even his death—would disappoint the Lords Gunthar and Boniface. He thought of Derek Crownguard's gloating and mean joy. The other pages and squires would squawk and crow like a flock of ravens. . . .

Where are the birds? That was it! Where are the birds?

Sturm whirled and looked about him, his bafflement turning to a strange, rising hope. For *this* Solamnic spring, despite its warmth and greenery, was empty of birdsong. The plains were silent—as quiet as the death of winter.

Sturm rose once more in the stirrups. At the edge of his sight, eastward toward the smell of the river, he saw more winter, and strangely more promise. For the green of the plains turned suddenly brown, and the mist hanging over the land was a winter's mist that sunlight could not disperse.

"It's . . . it's still *winter!*" Sturm exclaimed, slipping back into the saddle. Suddenly the music rose in front of him, brisk and alluring and drawing him on across the wintry plains. Jubilant, he spurred the mare beneath him, and off they went, barreling eastward at a full gallop.

He smiled to himself. The adventure was only beginning.

Luin surged beneath him, hurdling an ancient downed fence as they galloped through farmlands, through fallow pastures. Always the music lay before them, coaxing them onward, and behind them, the greens of spring returned suddenly to winter's brown and ice-crusted landscape.

Sturm laughed. It was easy from here. And so he was thinking when he felt the horse dip and stagger beneath him.

* * * * *

They were lucky not to be injured, even killed. It was some alertness in Sturm that caused him to rein in quickly, with such authority that the mare slowed to a walk at once, then stopped. He scrambled down to her right rear hoof and examined the damage.

It had been no accident. Experienced beyond his years at horsemanship, he could tell at once that someone had loosened a nail, perhaps more, so that any sustained gallop could throw the shoe.

"Why not earlier?" he asked aloud as he walked the mare toward a copse of evergreen, looking for shelter from a wind that once again had become fierce and wintry. "We raced through fog together, away from . . . from whatever it was. Over far rougher ground than this. Why didn't you throw the shoe *then*, Luin?"

Unless . . .

The lad shook his head. Someone had loosened the shoe at Castle di Caela. The same someone who had locked him in. Someone who was following him and trying to make him late.

Sturm walked away the afternoon, grasping at possibilities, traveling vaguely eastward. Luin stepped gingerly behind him on a long tether, stopping occasionally to browse the dried grass. Just how the two of them would get to the Southern Darkwoods remained to be seen.

The music that evening was almost a relief, rising from the emerald gloom of the copse ahead of them. Leading the mare at a walk behind him, Sturm drew his sword and trudged toward the stand of juniper and aeterna, his mind fixed on the solid and possible.

*   *   *   *   *

It was not Vertumnus who played, as Sturm had hoped. Nevertheless, the girl who held the flute seemed almost as wild and gifted. Her almond eyes and slanted ears marked her as clearly elven, and the painted designs on her body were those of the Kagonesti.

It was all Sturm knew of that elusive woodland people. For of all elves, the Kagonesti were the most secretive, and nowadays the most rare. Less organized, with a much less complex civilization than their Silvanesti and Qualinesti cousins, the Wild Elves lived in small bands or traveled alone through the forests and glades of Krynn. Sturm was surprised to see that one of them had settled herself long enough to play. He lowered his sword, crouched behind an aeterna bush, and watched her in wonder.

The elf maiden sat in a clearing in the middle of the copse, cross-legged on the thatched roof of a little cabin, her dark hair awash in moonlight. She was wrapped in fur against the wind and the cold, but one leg stretched forth, bare of white fox or ermine, painted with green swirls and helixes, brown and provocative. A silver flute was lifted to her lips, and she played a slow, stately melody.

Hypnotized by green on brown, by the centripetal swirl of the paint, Sturm felt himself grow short of breath.

Above the girl, the branches of evergreens swayed in the wind, then bent away gracefully, as though allowing the moonlight to shine on her for some mysterious, intricate purpose.

Soon enough, as though she had called it there with her song, the moon appeared in the gap between the trees, shining directly down on her—or two moons, rather, for white Solinari in its radiant fullness sat overhead, awaiting Lunitari, its red sister, to join it at the sky's absolute zenith. Slowly the red moon sailed into view as the girl played and the music filled the grove.

Sturm found himself strangely touched in spite of the day's hardship and accidents. There was a fathomless peace to this scene, as though all good things—beauty and health and virtue and purity—danced for a moment to the flute's measure. There was something sad about it, too. Though he had only chanced upon the moment, Sturm knew that it would pass too suddenly and too soon, and that somehow he was not meant to be a part of it in the first place.

Indeed, he was leaving, putting away his sword and turning back to the road ahead of him, when he saw the spiderweb.

The strands were finger-thick and twenty feet long, its

hub the size of Sturm's shield, spoke and spiral stretching from tree to tree like an enormous fishnet draped over the clearing. Sturm lifted his sword. The spider who could spin such a thing must be dog-sized . . . man-sized . . . horse-sized. His shield high and ready, Sturm spun about, looking for the monster, but the web was empty except for dried leaves and the skeletal remains of ravens and squirrels. Crouching, the lad moved toward the clearing, bent on warning the girl.

He was almost too late. There was the spider, bulbous and huge and mottled gray and white, its front legs arched above the heedless elf-maiden, who continued to play, her eyes closed, her dark hair swaying. Sturm cried out and sprang into the clearing.

The music stopped at once. The girl looked at him with alarm. The spider leapt back, scuttling down the side of the cabin, its movements abrupt and blindingly quick. In an instant, it stood between Sturm and the girl, its forelegs raised as though ready to pounce, its long black fangs flashing and clacking.

The thing was at least seven feet tall. Sturm didn't tarry to measure. Deftly the lad rolled out of the way, crashing into a blue aeterna bush and losing his shield in the process. The spider leapt vainly behind him, its wicked fangs slashing at empty air.

Behind the monster, the elf maiden leapt from the roof of the cottage and, scrambling and scuttling like a spider herself, vanished into the shadowy door of the hut.

Bursting through to the other side of the bush, Sturm lifted his sword over his head, then slashed at the hurtling spider. The creature chittered wildly and sprang out of the way, grappling up a bare vallenwood to crouch in the low branches above the dodging boy. Down the spider leapt, and Sturm would have been crushed immediately had he not plunged forward, somersaulted into the side of the vallenwood trunk and, dazed and breathless, scrambled to his feet to paw the underbrush for his dropped sword. The spider approached, rocked back on its hind legs, and pounced forward viciously. But its fangs closed upon Angriff Bright-blade's breastplate, clashing harmlessly against the ornate bronze.

With a cry, Sturm broke free of the spider's grasp and, looking about him, noticed his sword lying only ten feet or so away. He raced for the sword, scooped it up in a swift, acrobatic movement, and rolled over the ground, springing at last to his feet with the blade leveled, pointed toward the spider . . .

. . . who was no longer where he pointed. For in the midst of Sturm's gymnastics, the spider had moved, clambered to a higher branch of the vallenwood, then hurtled out toward a leaning juniper, which it grasped, apelike, in its front two legs, then darted along a thick, extended branch, and dropped unceremoniously back on the roof of the cabin.

With a cry, Sturm raced toward the cottage, slipping on undergrowth, stumbling over root and bush and bramble. The spider leapt over his head, landing lightly behind him, a thick viscid spiral raveling from its spinnerets. The lad was quick enough this time, stepping from the path of the silk and lunging toward the creature, sword extended.

But again the spider was no longer there. Sturm looked about stupidly, then above, barely in time to dodge the monster as it dropped twenty feet in a murderous pounce. Running toward the juniper, the great net of the spider shimmering above him, Sturm raised his sword and slashed once, twice, a third time into the thick ropes of the web un-til a long strand fell, smooth and tough, into his gloved hand.

"Now," he muttered, turning to face the charging crea-ture, "since sword and strength will not help me . . ."

He turned and dove among the twitching legs of the spi-der, dragging the webbing with him. The fangs clacked over his head, and then he was out beyond the creature, two of its legs entangled in Sturm's weaving. Immediately the lad drew the cord taut around a tree and turned again, scrambling beneath the monster once more. A fang brushed his back harmlessly, and he rolled clear of the spider, tugging the web strand taut behind him.

Five of its legs mired and tied now, the spider toppled on-to the forest floor, scattering dust and leaves as it thrashed angrily. Its cry was like the whir of cicadas, deafening and shrill. Sturm slipped out of his glove, leaving it stuck to the filament, raised his sword, and marched over to the snared beast. Triumphantly he raised the blade . . .

. . . and the elf maiden poked her head out of the door of the cottage and shrieked in horror.

"No!" she shouted. "Stay your hand, human!"

Dumbstruck, Sturm stepped back from the creature, lowering the sword. In fury, the girl slipped from the hut and rushed across the clearing, her dark almond eyes ablaze.

"Untie the poor thing, you scoundrel!"

Sturm couldn't believe what he was hearing.

"Untie him, I said! Or by Branchala . . ."

She drew her knife. Instinctively Sturm raised his shield, but she was by him in a breath, kneeling by the monster, whittling frantically at the web strands that bound it.

"I . . . I don't . . ." Sturm began, but the elf flashed him a look of such withering rage and hatred that he stopped try-ing to explain. He stood above her awkwardly, watching her hack and saw at the web. Finally, reluctantly, he knelt beside her, setting the blade of his broadsword against the coarse and stringy cords.

After a minute or so, the spider was free. Wobbily it stood, as though just awakening or just being born. Sturm watched it cautiously, sword low and shield raised, but the thing staggered, gibbered, and raced off into the copse, a strange, gulping sound in its cry, almost as if it were weep-ing. Completely confused, Sturm watched as the creature vanished into the cedars and pines and laricks, trailing one damaged leg.

"What—" he began, but he never finished the sentence.

The elf maiden's slap caught him utterly, completely off guard.

"How *dare* you burst into my clearing with sword and mayhem!" she exclaimed, then raised her hand to strike the lad again. Sturm staggered back from her.

"I thought you were in danger," he explained, flinching as again the girl moved suddenly. This time, however, she merely brushed back her dark hair, and sorrow vied with anger in her face.

"You fool of a boy," she said quietly. "You had no idea what you were doing, did you?"

Sturm said nothing. With a weak, melancholy smile, the elf maiden pointed to the heavens.

"Look above you," she said. "What do you see?"

"A gap in the trees," Sturm replied uncertainly. "The night sky. The two moons . . ."

His head reeled as she slapped him again.

" 'The two moons' is right, you dolt! You rash, callow, dwarf-brained excuse for a swordsman!"

The elf reeled, clutching against the bark of a vallenwood for support.

"Two moons," she said more calmly, "who join in the winter sky under the sign of Mishakal . . . how often, would you say?"

"I am no astronomer, lady," Sturm confessed. "I know not how often."

"Oh, only every five years or so," the girl said, her teeth clenched and her glittering eyes fixed on the lad in scarcely controllable anger. "Every five years, at which time a specific tune, in the ninth mode of Branchalan harmonies, played by a musician three years in the learning of its intricacies, may be used to undo the magic of druids and wizards."

"I don't understand," Sturm said, backing away as the girl took one aggressive stride toward him.

"You don't understand," she repeated coldly, flipping the knife in her hand, blade to hilt to blade. "The song undoes enchantment, lifts curses, restores the transmogrified."

"Transmogrified?"

"Those who have been changed into spiders!" the girl bellowed and launched the knife past Sturm's ear. He stood
confounded, motionless, the dagger trembling in a bare oak
some twenty feet behind him. Strands of hair, neatly sliced
from below his ear, settled on his shoulder.

"At the one worst moment in five years," the elf said,
"you came upon this clearing. And in doing so, you have
assured that Cyren of the House Royal in Silvanost, descen-
dant of kings and lord of my heart, shall scramble alone in
webs, eight-legged and six-eyed, eating vermin and offal for
the next half a decade until white Solinari and red Lunitari,
each on its separate path, sail through the whole forsaken
sky, past fixed and movable stars, and converge again!"

"I'm . . . I'm . . ." Sturm began, but the words had fled to
the treetops.

"No apologies," the girl said, her smile glittering and
crooked as Solinari drifted behind the swaying junipers and
the clearing was left in the red, ominous light of Lunitari.
"No apologies, please, for I've still half a mind to kill you."

Chapter 9

Of Mara and the Spider

Sturm settled the elf maiden after a few minutes, plying her with apologies and admitting that, yes, he was the most foolish boy on the continent and that to find a greater fool one would have to venture among the goblins in Throt. That apparently satisfied her for the moment. She sighed and nodded, then looked about her in dismay, as though the clearing in which she had lived for two months awaiting the convergence of the moons had suddenly become a real nest of spiders.

"I can't stay here," she announced and ducked into the cabin. Sturm stood outside, shifting his weight from foot to foot, trying to appear useful. Off among the larick bushes, there was a slight movement, a shift in the underbrush, but when he turned to inspect it, whatever was moving and shifting had vanished.

"Spiders," he muttered. "I'll wager everything turns to spiders, the girl and myself as well."

But she emerged most unspiderlike a moment later, her belongings bundled in a packet of cloth and vine and cobweb almost twice her size and slung across her shoulders like something unwieldy and wounded.

"Well, you'll be taking us home, then," she asserted, her knees buckling beneath the weight of the bundle. Sturm reached out to help her, but she waved him away with a stagger.

"Never you mind. I'll set this upon the horse," she ordered with a nod toward Luin, who stood cautiously at the edge of the clearing, still skittish from the commotion with the spider.

"B-But you can't, m'lady. You simply can't," Sturm protested. "She's thrown a shoe and I can't burden her."

In dismay, the elf girl dropped her bundle.

"You mean we shall have to travel to Silvanost on foot?"

Sturm swallowed hard. Though his bearings were none too good, he knew the larger geographies of the continent. Silvanost was five hundred miles away if it was a stone's throw, and such a journey seemed impossibly long and arduous.

"But I am bound only for the Southern Darkwoods," he protested.

She shook her head. "No longer. Now we are bound for Silvanost, to throw myself on the mercies of Master Calotte."

Sturm frowned in puzzlement.

"The enchanter," she explained dryly. "As you may recall, boy, my true love is still a spider."

They stood and stared at one another.

"I'm . . . I'm sorry, m'lady," Sturm muttered. "And more sorry still, in that my path lies only to the Southern Darkwoods. The far reaches of Silvanost are, I fear, beyond my . . . my resources. I have not the time. I may even be followed."

He coughed and cleared his throat.

"Nonsense," she said, her voice cold and flat. "Silvanost could be across the world, and you would still have to take me there. So your honor tells you. What is it your people say? *'Est Sularus oth Mithas'*?"

Sturm nodded reluctantly. " 'My honor is my life.' But how did you know—"

She laughed bitterly. "That you were of the Order? When it comes to the sword, nobody is as heedless as a Solamnic youngling. You may go to your Darkwoods and do what you will, but I shall be with you. And afterward, you will take me to Silvanost. It is that simple. You are bound by your silly Oath and Measure."

'Tis a test! Sturm thought, with a rising fear. The elf maiden glared at him, angrily but innocently. After all, if Lord Wilderness can play so readily with the seasons and their changes, why would he not have allies—outlandish folk among the elves and the gods know what other folk— who would do his bidding readily?

Doesn't this creature also play a flute?

And how would an elf know of the Solamnic Oath, which the Measure interprets in the light of helping the weak and the helpless?

He glanced balefully at the girl, whose stare had not wavered. She seemed anything but weak and helpless.

And yet Vertumnus would know, would hold me to the Oath and my honor, would test me further. . . .

He shook his head. After all, what did Lord Wilderness know or care of honor? It was ridiculous to think such entangled thoughts, to see a green design behind this accident.

"I'm sorry," Sturm began.

And his shoulder exploded in a ragged, knifing pain, next to which all of the other pains had been a slight twinge, a tingle.

This is dying, he thought again, falling to his knees in front of the elf maiden, this is my delay, my cowardice, my dishonor. . . .

And he thought nothing more.

* * * * *

The elf maiden rousted him none too gently, shaking him until he wakened.

Blearily Sturm looked up at the girl and remembered it all: the fight with the spider, the girl's outrage, her story and plea, his refusal . . .

And the pain that had followed, lancing and riveting and white-hot in his damaged shoulder.

"Very well," he muttered, his mouth dry and his throat prickling. "To Silvanost it is. But *after* the Southern Darkwoods, mind you!"

Before the girl could reply, Sturm was on his feet, and with a swift, athletic turn, he had hoisted her bundled belongings onto his back.

The pain in his shoulder had vanished, mysteriously and entirely. He wasn't surprised. The hand of Vertumnus had touched everything about this wooded encounter, this evening of battle and music and promises and moonlight.

Sturm grunted uncomfortably at the weight of the bundle. All of a sudden, his burden was five times as heavy, the road five times as long. He thought of Silvanost, there in the midst of the evergreen grove. He thought of the long trek over the Khalkist Mountains, through the Doom Range to Sanction along the Nerakan border, then down into Blode and south to the great forest. A passage through bandits and ogres, he had heard. Sturm almost hoped that Vertumnus would slay him on the first day of spring.

* * * * *

Mara was her name, and the story she told was pure Kagonesti, full of magic and forbidden love and doom.

"It started four years ago," she explained, framing her answer to Sturm's question as the two of them emerged from the evergreen copse. It was early morning, and the sun peeking over the eastern horizon was their guidepost.

Sturm shifted the weight of the baggage on his back. Though it was barely sunrise, he was already weary, having wandered the groves all night, burdened by the gods knew what belongings. Mara followed him, leading Luin by the reins, and once or twice in the near distance, he had heard the unsettling sound of the spider, clambering from branch to branch.

"Four years ago?" he asked idly. Fatigue warred with politeness. It was hard to attend to another story.

"Down in Silvanost," Mara continued, "where the High Elves rule, with their fairness and hazel eyes. Cyren was of the Calamons, scion to the noblest of families, while I was but a handmaiden to his cousin."

"I see," Sturm said. He wasn't sure he *did* see.

"Obstacles right from the start. The course that never runs straight," Mara explained.

She paused, as though remembering. Sturm heard birds rising from the junipers behind him, rousted by the approach of something—no doubt the scion in question.

"We first saw each other," Mara continued, "at the Great Festival of Peace commemorating the signing of the Swordsheath Scroll. It happens every year, the festival, and every year it seems altogether new. The forest fills with lights beyond imagining, and torches lit in Qualinost and Ergoth mingle amid the trees."

Mara sighed. "It's a glorious evening. As you might imagine, the females of the House Royal, daughters and servants all, are kept from the sight of the lads because . . . well, because it might make someone *untoward.*"

She blushed and tugged thoughtlessly at Luin's reins. The mare nickered and bowed her head in protest.

"This time was the most glorious of festivals," Mara said dreamily. "I remember his eyes—Cyren's, that is. He stepped from the coracle, steadied himself on the soft banks of the Thon-Thalas, and with scarcely a pause, he entered the Dance of Dreams, the fifth and greatest dance of the festival evening. You could tell by his dancing that he was highborn Qualinesti, but I studied his eyes as the cellos sounded. Brown they were, and as deep as the woods, his gaze so direct you would think that he never closed his eyes, never even blinked when he stared into the midday sun. Though I have seen them only three times since, I remember them as clearly as I do the lights in the forest or the tilting stars of Mishakal—the stars that I watched for months, waiting for the one night in five years. . . ."

Sturm winced. The road to the Darkwoods looked longer and longer as Mara spoke.

"But enough of that," Mara declared. "You asked how we came to last night and this pass."

Sturm shifted the bundle again. The eggs of spiders? Rocks? Houses? What was bound in the blankets and leaves and webbing?

"Immediately Lord Cyren took a liking to me," Mara said. "He paid court with his eyes in the altering light, in the song of the harp and the deep cello. But I was a servingmaid, my family a trophy of war. And though Cyren was handsome, I set aside thoughts of those eyes and those songs, for ours was a match too farfetched to imagine. And more than that, he was a strange and exotic one—almost without history, he was, from the far reaches of the forest, and of his many cousins, none had met him and few had heard of him."

She traveled on in silence, and it was a while before she spoke again.

"Notes he sent me in the days that followed—notes borne on small leaf-boats such as a child makes as a plaything. He floated his messages downstream on the slow-moving Thon-Thalas as I stood in the current, thigh-deep in water, washing the clothing of my mistress. His words would scorn and tease and inveigle, luring me away with him.

"There was a bridge, wrote Cyren, at the westernmost

edge of the forest. If I were to consent to go away with him, I should meet him at the bridge by moonlight, and we would ride away together out of Silvanesti, over the Plains of Dust to a land where Kagonesti and Silvanesti are indistinguishable, where folk couldn't tell High Elf from Wild Elf."

"There are such lands," Sturm offered. "I do believe Solamnia is one of them."

"Even the Knights can tell elf from spider," Mara retorted bitterly. "But that comes later in the story.

"Let it be said now that Cyren Calamon of the House Royal sent his green fleet down the Thon-Thalas daily, and each night I would return to my mistress's tower, leaving his notes unanswered. It is improper for a maiden to be so . . . forward. He persisted and persisted, until I knew that, had his intentions been dishonorable, he would have left off long ago. It was then I consented to meet with him—not at his bridge where the wood ended and the lands beyond our borders beckoned in freedom and wildness, but at a safer place, at the ferry west of Silvanost. It was a place out of sight from the marble fastness of the great encampment, where King Lorac and his daughter Alhana live in the Tower of Stars, and yet it was a place less . . . venturesome and hidden than the ones my new friend proposed to me.

"We were foolish in our eagerness. Though our meetings were cautious, even proper, someone saw and someone disapproved. Perhaps," she added ominously, "someone was jealous. And someone spread the story of our tryst through the House Royal. My duties were changed, the quarters of my mistress moved to the high chambers of the Tower of Stars. 'Twas an honor for *her*—an emptyheaded little fluff who thought her stature raised with her altitude, never quite aware that her newfound position at court had anything to do with her servantry. But it was torment for me.

"So we suffered the months, both of us lonely, both of us yearning for escape and reunion, for a midnight flight to a place where lineage and ancestry mattered not at all."

"There is no such place!" Sturm exclaimed, then fell silent immediately, surprised at his vehemence. Mara didn't seem to notice, her mind on the rest of her story.

"The tale turns even darker here, Solamnic. For Cyren was barred from the Tower, and the high windows were beyond his reach unless he had the wings of a bird or could climb . . ."

"Like a spider?" Sturm asked.

"Like a spider indeed," Mara said with a nod. "You see the plan, do you not? Well, know it for what it was—a foolhardy risk. As it has done for thousands of years, love sent the unwise heart to sorcerers. To Master Calotte went Cyren, in the darkest part of the forest, where Waylorn's Tower lies gray and windowless, its shadow mingling with the shades of willow and aspen until all light, whether moon or sun, is blocked by leaf and branch and turret. They say the butterflies are black there, and that the squirrels have gone blind because it is so dark that they steer by smell and hearing alone, their eyes grown useless through the generations."

Sturm hid a smile. It sounded fanciful to him, this dark place of the mage. But he listened as Mara unfolded the sad end of the story.

Under the guise of helpfulness, it seems, Master Calotte had hidden his own passion for Mara. An old elf, and to hear the girl tell it, unspeakably hideous, he held no more hope of winning her than she had in the sincerity of Cyren's courtship. Nor would enchantment avail for old Calotte, for the House of Mystics had ways to tell when a creature was charmed or drawn or otherwise magicked, and the Silvanesti refused to honor a conjured marriage. But all things seemed possible if the old mage were crafty and circumspect.

"It was simple," Mara explained angrily as she and Sturm settled for the afternoon on a rocky knoll in the midst of the grasslands. "Simple to fool a trusting Cyren, who came to him in desperation. Simple, when someone is ready and willing, to transform him into any creature the mind can fancy or memory bring forth. Simple for Cyren it was to clamber up the side of the Tower of Stars, to the window where I sat waiting."

Mara smiled, stretching her legs on the hard ground. Sturm stood above her, staring out over the Solamnic plains, where deep in the eastern distances, he thought he saw the haze and shimmer of water. Were they near the Vingaard, or were these the mirages travelers reported from Thelgaard Keep to the City of Lost Names?

"I was startled at first. If a spider twice your size perched on your windowsill, gibbering and beckoning you outside, you would be cautious, too."

Sturm nodded. "Cautious" hadn't been the word that occurred to him.

"But quickly Cyren made it known to me that he was no ordinary spider, but my true love transformed."

"How did he do *that?*" Sturm asked with a muffled smile, imagining the creature serenading in its shrill, inhuman voice, or weaving Mara's name into the strands of its web.

"Spun a ladder of sorts, he did. A scaffolding web, the druids call it, for upon it, the creatures raise web from tree to tree, the intricate spokes and spirals that draw down their quarry from the air. But it was only a ladder, this scaffolding. It dropped down the side of the tower sixty, seventy feet, from my window down into the dark of the branches below it.

"By Branchala, I was frightened!" she laughed. "The moons were dark that night, so I could descend unseen, but it made me unseeing as well. Set one foot below the next as if I was wading into vipers, I did, but the next thing I know, my feet touch the grass of the forest floor and Cyren is rushing west toward Waylorn's Tower, and stopping, and turning about, and spinning a strand of web behind him that I take up and follow like . . . like your mare following the rein.

"So we passed through the woods, and eye saw me not,

nor did ear hear me as we crossed the Thon-Thalas and made our way through a part of the forest I knew not, to a clearing at the foot of the tower."

She shuddered as the memory passed over her.

"The moment I saw that the spellcraft was the doing of Master Calotte," she said, "I feared for us—especially for poor Cyren. For I had seen this one look at me, too, with a look that made my blood crawl, and I feared that his aid had come at a dreadful cost. Nor was it a moment before we learned what we had to pay."

Mara stood up and, taking Luin's reins, gestured to Sturm that the rest had ended, that the time had come to recommence the journey. Down from the knoll they walked, Luin stepping gingerly behind them, the spider a rustling, muttering presence in the high grass as the elf maiden unveiled the last and darkest part of the story.

"As you can certainly guess, Solamnic, the wizard refused to restore Cyren. He sat there, lodged in the notch of a forked oak, black and rotten and shadowed as his own heart.

" 'Mara,' he says, 'sweet Mara. You know well how Prince Cyren can recover that form in which you so delight, and you know full well the cost.' "

"Scoundrel," Sturm muttered.

"Cyren would have attacked him then and there!" Mara exclaimed. "Would have torn him apart and dripped cold poison into his wounds, had I not restrained him. But the death of Master Calotte, as far as we knew, would imprison poor Cyren forever in the form in which you see him today."

Sturm looked back at the elf maiden skeptically. Having grappled with Cyren himself, having seen the creature blubber and slink off into the woods, he wondered how truly difficult it had been for Mara to restrain the avenging creature.

"Now," Mara said, "we know better. But then we left Silvanesti as a place no longer safe for either of us: I, after all, had defied the will of the House Royal. So had poor

Cyren, and his lot was worse, for his newfound form would make him prey to any hunter from the Hedge to the Bay of Balifor.

"We wandered a year and another, in search of a way to lift the spell of Master Calotte. To sorcerers and shamans we traveled, as far south as the Icewall, west to the Tower of Wayreth in Qualinesti, then back again along a different and difficult path, through Bloten and Zhakar and Khurikhan, where elves are as unwelcome as spiders. Our third year found us on the plains of Abanasinia, where we took up for a while with a band of Plainsmen, whose seeress was a mere girl, a chieftain's daughter of the Que-Shu tribe, subject to the falling sickness and deep trances, in which the grasslands sang to her and the stars reconfigured above her in the shapes of helix and harp."

"True prophecies, then," Sturm observed.

Mara nodded. "This . . . this Goldmoon," she continued, "told us that the spell could be lifted only through music and the convergence of the moons above this very spot in the midst of the Plains of Solamnia.

"So we dwelt here awaiting, Cyren and I. A year and more passed, while I learned to play on the flute the girl had given me, and the moons passed through the sign of Hiddukel, of Kiri-Jolith, of dark Morgion—all pointing to the single night, the crowning night of a five-year cycle, on which the moons converged in the hub of Mishakal and healing and change were possible."

Mara stopped on the downward path. Sturm paced on for a few heavy steps, the bundle on his shoulders again growing wearisome. He stopped finally and turned about when he could hear neither her voice nor her footsteps.

She stood above him, angry and diminished by the sunlight of the early afternoon. Despair contorted her face, and though her anger at Sturm had somehow passed in the telling of the story, she looked at him again with rising irritation.

"That night," she said coldly, "that most auspicious night,

when the moons converge and the music plays and the spell is lifted—that night was *last* night!"

Briskly, her thoughts obviously elsewhere, the elf maiden tugged at the reins and resumed her path down the hill. Luin, jarred from drowsiness, snorted and followed her. Ahead of them, Sturm turned back to the journey with an inward grumble.

"Again and again I am visited with my accident," he muttered. "It was . . . it was a *reasonable* mistake!"

He looked back at Mara, who seemed not to hear him.

"Rocky plains on foot," the lad whispered through clenched teeth, "with a two-ton burden and a whining companion, my horse hobbled and a giant poisonous spider lurking somewhere behind us. 'Tis not a quest for heroes, I'll wager, but at least the going can get no worse from here."

The clouds rushed in before anyone noticed, as though a god had stirred the air with a quick wave of his hand. Suddenly the country was heavy and tense, the smell of the wind faint and metallic. Then the first drop struck the bundle on Sturm's back, and another splashed against the bridge of his nose. Luin whinnied apprehensively, and the skies opened up from the Clerist's Tower all the way to the Vingaard River, which tilted and boiled in the fierce downpour of rain.

Chapter 10

A Change in the Weather

In the Southern Darkwoods, kneeling above the clear green pool in the midst of the clearing, Vertumnus stirred the waters playfully. His fingers skimmed the surface of the pool, showering droplets over the image of Sturm and Mara trapped in a rainstorm miles away. Evanthe and Diona watched delightedly as the image shivered and dispersed and formed again.

"Drown them!" Evanthe hissed wickedly, her pale hands brushing a lock of hair from the Green Man's brow.

"Drench and douse them!" urged Diona.

"Only a rain," Vertumnus laughed and stirred the waters again. "The grass needs watering."

"Only a rain?" Evanthe whispered. "Only a rain, when you could do such marvels . . ."

"As the winds would rumor for ages," Diona coaxed, finishing her sister's sentence. "The things you could do, Lord Wilderness, had you the mind and the imaginings and . . . and the *gumption!*"

Vertumnus ignored the dryads, crouched, and breathed on the surface of the waters.

In the pool's misty reflection, seen from afar, as though they appeared in a crystal ball or a Dragonorb, the young man and the elf maiden huddled together, gray shapes in the driving rain. Suddenly, from the bundled shadows an arm lifted, pointing toward a hillside, a distant shelter. They hastened toward it, their shapes dwindling into the net of rain. Behind them, scuttling and gibbering to itself, a drenched spider followed tamely.

"Rain falls on the just," Vertumnus murmured, and waved his hand over the pool, "and the unjust."

The mists parted on the surface of the water, revealing an encampment in a copse—a tattered web between two junipers, and a thatch-covered cabin only recently abandoned. The waters of the pool stilled and settled, and at the edge of the image, a hooded light bobbed from reflected tree to reflected tree—a lantern in the hand of a dark, caped figure.

"Ah," sighed Lord Wilderness and leaned forward until his face nearly touched the surface of the water. Quietly he whistled something in the magical tenth mode, which the old bards used to look through rock and over distance and sometimes into the future.

The image shivered, and the dark man in the copse lifted the lantern to his own inscrutable face.

"Boniface!" Vertumnus exclaimed. "Of course!"

Quietly, efficiently, the finest swordsman in Solamnia inspected the clearing and encampment. He stepped into the cabin and emerged, almost in one breath, frowning and looking about. Stroking his long, dark mustache, he stood beneath the broken web, apparently lost in thought, and then, as if he had known all along the direction in which his search would take him, wheeled about and vanished from the clearing, the blue evergreens closing behind him like the water's surface over a diver.

"Who is he?" Evanthe breathed.

"Yes," Diona echoed. "Who *is* he? And why does he follow them?"

""Just a shadow in the snow," Vertumnus replied. "But where is the mistress? For her path will cross with his."

The dryads looked at one another in disappointment.

"That hag?" Diona asked scornfully. "What would you with her, when the likes of us are here?"

"That old carrion bird," Evanthe said. "She smells of dark earth and death. No herbs in creation can cover those smells."

"Where is she?" Vertumnus repeated.

And as he awaited her arrival, he stared at the settling surface of the pool and lifted the flute to his lips.

* * * * *

"This will make a lean-to of sorts," Sturm sputtered as he spread his cloak between outstretched branches of oak and water maple. A makeshift tent, it was, but already the cloth sagged with the downpour.

"Of sorts, it will," Mara said. "But not a good one. The rock is limestone here. Cave country, I'll wager."

"Then you have my blessing to search for caves," Sturm said curtly. The long trek and the rain had worn away his patience. Silently he knotted the last corner of his cape to a maple limb, then stood back to admire his handiwork.

Eagerly, water beading and flickering on his bulbous black abdomen, Cyren scurried into the patchwork shelter. He crouched, obscured behind a thicket of his own legs, and rumbled contentedly as Mara, standing outside in the rain, turned impatiently to face her Solamnic companion.

"You're no woodsman, are you?" she asked, as the cape bellied with water and the branches leaned together.

Sturm watched glumly as his encampment collapsed,

sending a sputtering, chittering Cyren out into the rain and halfway up a nearby oak. It was then that the music rose again, weaving through the rain and rising loudly above Cyren's scolding and the intermittent crashes of thunder. Mara looked at Sturm in astonishment.

In turn, he looked back at her, masking his own considerable surprise.

"We'll follow the sound," he said. "And if there are caves we are meant to find . . . well, we will find them."

The elf opened her mouth to protest, but her odd escort with his serious demeanor and ill-fitting armor had turned away from her, plunging into the sheeted rain.

Mara couldn't see Sturm's smile of amusement, for this magical music might inveigle and distract him, might lead him astray or dump him in a swamp somewhere. But this one evening, Vertumnus had done him two favors: The music led him *somewhere*, at least. And it had stopped the infernal elven complaining.

*   *   *   *   *

The nearest cave was less than a mile from the copse. Cyren spotted it first from above. Rumbling excitedly, he motioned his companions toward the small, bramble-covered mouth of the cave. But his enthusiasm cooled when Sturm made it clear that Cyren should precede them into the darkness. The idea, of course, was that a giant spider made a more formidable entrance than young man or elf maiden, but Cyren moved cautiously, extending one leg, then another, then a third, as though he walked over coals. Clicking nervously and startling at his own echo, he poked his head into the cavern, then backed out again, staring at Sturm so dolefully that he might have been pathetic had he not been so ugly.

Sturm waved the spider back toward the cave once, twice, a third time—each time less patiently than the first. Finally, when Cyren balked again, the lad drew his sword and quietly but firmly waved once more.

Muttering, the creature entered the darkness and crouched in terror at the cavern entrance. Assured at last that the place was empty and safe, the transformed prince spun a web in its farthest corner and went to sleep contentedly, dreaming strange dreams in which elven towers and beautiful girls stood side by side with bats and swallows and flying squirrels—countless winged and succulent animals entangled in sticky thread. Luin entered next and stood, warm and dripping in the center of the cave, until Luin, too, fell asleep and dreamed the fathomless dreams of horses.

Mara and Sturm sat together by a smoldering fire near the mouth of the cave, too wet and miserable to sleep. Sturm had taken off his breastplate and set it by Cyren's web, giving the spider more than one cautious glance as he did so. Carefully, almost daintily, he had removed his boots, poured the water from them, and set them to dry by the fire. Mara was much less fastidious. Shivering in her sodden furs, her dark hair matted to her forehead, she seemed to be courting pneumonia.

She could have done the sensible, indeed the healthy thing, by drying herself and slipping out of the furs into a warm blanket. Indeed, Sturm's promise that he would look the other way gave her pause for a moment, until she looked closely into his eyes and decided she didn't believe him. Instead, dripping and trembling, Mara lifted her flute and began to play. It was a pensive little folk melody Sturm recognized as Que-Shu Plainsman in origin. It haunted him, casting his memories back to his growing years beside the Crystalmir Lake, far to the south in Abanasinia.

Now, beside his other miseries, the music was making him homesick.

"I've had enough of piping for this season," Sturm protested gruffly, stretching his hands toward the warmth of the fire. Between wet fur and wet horse and the smoke from an ill-made fire, the smell in the cave was getting to be unbearable, and all things, weather and company and situation alike, seemed to conspire against him.

"Enough of piping?" Mara asked with a wretched little smile as she lowered the flute. "Afraid I'll turn you into another spider?"

"Turn if you will," Sturm offered glumly. "Cyren over there seems happy in his webbing. Or if you must pipe, pipe in the mode of Chislev so that somewhere in the midst of us there is harmony at least."

"So you know a little of the bardic modes," Mara observed. She wasn't especially impressed.

"No more than a standard Solamnic schooling," Sturm replied. "Seven modes, established in the Age of Dreams. One for each of the neutral gods. Philosophers claim that music and the spirits of man are interwoven as subtly as . . . Cyren's web over there. Dangerous stuff, though. The red gods are tricky servitors."

"No more than standard Solamnic schooling indeed," chided Mara, and Sturm frowned. "The red modes are no more treacherous than penny whistle tunes. They lift your spirits because you're taught to be happy when you hear a lilting piece in a major key, and thoughtful and a little melancholy when the song is slow and minor. Now, the white modes are another matter. . . ."

She lifted the flute to her lips.

"The white modes?" Sturm asked, and again Mara began to play the little Plainsman tune, her fingers blurring this time as they raced along the flute. Though the melody was the same and the elf maiden played it as quietly and as slowly as she had before, there was something different in the feel of the music, as though somehow it had been filled with a sudden depth and direction. Cyren's web shivered and hummed in response, and the rain shrank from the mouth of the cave, forming a small rainbow on the damp ground as it receded.

"Did you do that?" Sturm asked skeptically, then gasped as he looked at the elf. For her robes were thoroughly dry, and her hair as well, as though the music were a hot, dry wind that had passed over and through her, until now, comfortable, even toasty, Mara lay back, nodding toward sleep.

She looked at Sturm with heavy-lidded eyes. For a moment, she didn't speak, and the filaments of the spider's web hummed on, echoing the vanished music, repeating the melody once more before they, too, stilled and were silent.

"What do *you* think?" she asked, her voice remote and echoing as though she spoke to Sturm from somewhere deep in the recesses of the cave. "It was the white mode you heard, the martial Kiri-Jolith combined with a Que-Shu rain hymn to drive back the waters from our threshold."

"But I heard nothing—I mean, nothing really different than when you played before."

"How sad for you," Mara said, holding the flute up to the firelight, examining it idly. "How sad . . . and how odd."

"Odd?" Sturm asked. "Why odd? It was the same melody, was it not?"

"*One* was," Mara agreed. "But the other, the white mode, took its place in the absences of the red, in the space between the notes of the Plainsman song. You didn't hear it because you weren't expecting to hear it. Some people can't hear it even when they're listening for it. They seem to be born not to hear it. Perhaps you are one of those."

"What do you mean by that?" Sturm asked testily. He fancied himself a good deal better than tone-deaf. Yet on this rainy afternoon, one tune had seemed identical to the other, and yet the second one had all the magic.

"What do you mean?" he repeated, but suddenly the girl was standing, alert as a wild animal when something foreign and dangerous crosses into its territory.

"Shhh!" she breathed. "Did you hear it?"

"Hear *what?*" Sturm asked angrily. Time and again, it seemed, his senses were called into question. Mara motioned him to be silent, then crept to the mouth of the cave, dagger in hand. Behind them, Luin stirred uneasily, and

Cyren clicked and whistled somewhere back in the darkness.

"Something is out there," Mara whispered. "Something besides the wind and the rain is moving through the high grass over on the other side of that rise."

They looked at one another uncertainly.

"Stand back, Lady Mara," Sturm ordered, his confidence none too strong. "I expect that tending to something besides wind and rain is more my kind of duty than yours."

Drawing his sword, he stepped out into the rain, impressed by his own bravado. Mara looked at him skeptically, but he barely noticed. It was only after he was halfway to the rise in question that he realized he had left behind helmet, breastplate, and shield.

"So much for dash and daring," he sputtered as the rain ran in rivulets down his forehead. "There's no going back now."

Low to the ground, he skirted the rise to the south. For a moment, he passed beneath a lone blue aeterna tree, and all about him was dry and fragrant and loud with the spattering rain in the branches. Then quickly out of the shadows he burst, his sword at the ready and a fierce, boar-hunting cry on his lips.

Not twenty yards away, something dark crossed from tree to tree and scurried behind a large, moss-covered boulder. Sturm didn't break stride. Sensing that he had the advantage of surprise, he loped across the clearing and scaled the boulder with a single, athletic bound, hurtling down upon the caped figure below him before whoever it was had a chance to raise weapon, dodge, or even move.

A tangle of limbs and robes and water, the two tumbled and slid down the hillside, churning the sopping ground as they fell and wrestled. Somewhere amid a wrenching somersault, Sturm dropped his sword. He opened his mouth to cry out, his face plowed into the mud, and he came up stunned and sputtering.

Almost at once the caped man threw Sturm back against

the boulder and staggered to his feet. Groping almost blindly in the mud for his sword, for a rock or a sizable limb, Sturm came up with nothing but a handful of grass and gravel and roots, which he hurled at his adversary with a shout.

The caped man dodged gracefully—a dancer's move, or an acrobat's—and Sturm's humble missile sailed by harmlessly. Staggering from the force of his throw and slipping on the slick, rain-soaked hillside, Sturm managed to right himself and, for the first time, get a good look at his adversary.

Dripping with mud and soil, his cloak interwoven with grass and dried vines, the man looked like an effigy fashioned of forests and night. Slowly, indignantly, he brushed his cloak, and the soil and greenery tumbled from his arms and shoulders.

Sturm gasped, his eyes flickering over boulder and bush, over sloping ground in a desperate search for the sword. Off to his left, in the midst of crushed high grass, he caught a faint glimmer of metal.

The man was silent, his face muffled by hood and rain, but his movements were unsettlingly familiar. Sturm, however, had no time for guesswork. Slipping in the mud, bracing himself once more against the boulder, he lunged up the hill, reaching the sword just before the caped man closed with him. A gloved hand grasped his wrist in a fierce and powerful grip, and Sturm went flying again into the side of the boulder, his vision flashing white as the air rushed from him.

Sturm stood slowly, astonished that he had managed to hold on to the sword. Painfully he raised it and, true to the form of combat dictated by the Measure, waited for his opponent to draw blade. But the opponent stood motionless, a dark silhouette in the driving rain. Sturm waved the sword over his head, yet still the man did nothing.

Then unexplainably, as though it rose from the water-logged earth about them, the sound of the flute bubbled through the rainy air.

Sturm shouted again, his fear and anger warring for mastery. "By Paladine, I challenge you!"

He stopped short, stupefied by the words that had rushed from him before he had time to consider them. In anger and in fear, he had sworn by the highest of gods. Oath and Measure bound him. There was no going back.

Reluctantly, almost as if he could read the thoughts of the lad in front of him, the caped man drew his sword. Sturm's blade flicked out in a clumsy arc. The caped man's sword turned the blow with a quick, feline grace. Again Sturm lunged at his opponent, this time with a forceful thrust, but the caped man parried it easily, almost thoughtlessly. Sturm stumbled forward, caught off balance by the sheer recklessness of his own attack. He fell to one knee and skidded over the wet ground, scrambling to his feet at the sound of the caped man's laughter.

Spinning about in rage, Sturm raised his sword above his head and brought it whistling down in a sudden, blindingly quick movement. It was all the caped man could do to raise his sword. Blade crashed against blade, and the rainy hillside echoed with the sound.

Both men staggered back, each surprised at the force of the blow. Quietly they regarded one another through the dwindling rain, on a hillside furrowed and torn by their awkward battle.

The caped man rubbed his shoulder and transferred his sword to his left hand. Slowly, confidently, he pointed the blade at Sturm, who looked down at his own blade, shattered and useless in his hand.

In desperation, Sturm drew his knife, stepped back, and stared into the glittering eyes of his enemy, who closed with him confidently, preparing for the final blow.

Chapter 11

The Surprising Visitor

The caped man was on him at once, all quickness and slippery dark strength. Sturm felt a hand snake to his wrist and then, with a quick and violent shake, send his knife flying into the tall grass. He struggled desperately, but the man was too strong for him, pinning his shoulders and pushing him onto his back.

Dazed, Sturm felt the sword's blade at his throat.

"Be still!" the caped man shouted. Suddenly he looked around him, alertly and uneasily, as if his words had echoed across the plains, across the continent itself. He sprang to his feet and sheathed the sword, brushing back his hood in the same crisp, athletic movement.

"You . . ." Sturm began, but the surprise stole his words.

"Jack Derry it is, sir!" the young man whispered with a

fleeting smile. "You remember me from the Tower? The gardener? With the barrow in the courtyard?"

"Y-Yes," Sturm replied, as the name and the face came together in his memory. Here in the dividing moonlight, Jack Derry looked unnaturally youthful, his face smooth and beardless like that of a small boy. On closer look, though, the soft brown eyes were weatherworn with hard travel, the black hair matted and tangled, and his leather breastplate was tattered and cracked, its ornamental green roses faded but still recognizable.

It was Jack Derry, all right. But something about him was different—different beyond weather and attire.

"But how . . . how did you . . . and why?" Sturm sputtered, struggling for words.

"Questions go better in a dry spot, somewhere out of the rain," Jack replied softly. "When you show me that spot, you can ask and I can answer."

Sturm's eyes narrowed. The water coursed off his muddy face. "How do I know that this isn't a trap?" he asked.

"By the Seven!" Jack Derry swore, reaching out and grabbing Sturm's arm, "What need had I for traps a moment ago, when my blade's edge rested on your throat?"

It was a convincing argument. Convincing, that is, unless this Jack planned a greater crime, needing only a guide to the elf maiden, who suddenly seemed smaller, more vulnerable than Sturm had thought her before.

"No," Jack said quietly, his face close to Sturm's now, so that the lad saw only the gardener's sharp, black eyes and smelled only the deep odors of root and moist earth. "I mean *none* of you harm. Lead on, Sturm Brightblade. It's best we get out of the cold."

*   *   *   *   *

Panic-stricken, Cyren had wrapped himself up in webbing. He dangled helplessly from a single thick filament in the back of the cave, a struggling cocoon of gray silk.

Mara was at work on disentangling Cyren, her knife sawing at the webbing as Sturm and Jack entered the cave, behind them Jack's squat little mare, whom they had collected on their way to the shelter.

"I need your help," Mara urged, looking over her shoulder.

Sturm set down his broken sword and started to her side, but Jack passed him by, crouched beside Mara, and freed the spider with an effortless turn of his sword. Cyren scrambled to the topmost strands of the web, where he clung and shivered.

"It is the spider in him that . . . that frightens him so," Mara explained unconvincingly.

"I wondered why neither of you came to my aid," Sturm replied.

Mara looked at him, then at Jack, and shrugged. "I said there was something out there besides wind and rain," she said impatiently. "I do not recall telling you to attack it."

"But . . ." Sturm began and, looking from elf to spider to gardener and back again, seated himself abruptly on the floor of the cave.

"Never mind what might have been, Master Sturm," Jack said, crouching by the fire and extending his muddy hands to its warmth. "There are other questions you have, and rightful they are, and I shall do my utmost to answer them now."

* * * * *

Jack had followed Sturm's pursuer, it seems, and in following had uncovered a conspiracy of sorts.

That was the only way Sturm could explain the strange report from the High Clerist's Tower. Jack, it seems, had trundled his wheelbarrow after the Knight and his squire, Derek, and what the gardener heard was a litany of traps and entanglements for Sturm, stretching from the Wings of Habbakuk to the borders of the Darkwoods themselves.

"Snares of all sorts Lord Boniface had planned," Jack said, his gaze alert and unnervingly intent. "From ambush to pitfall to something about the ford I couldn't hear for the distance."

"Perhaps there was more you did not hear, Jack," Sturm suggested. It seemed impossible: Lord Boniface, his father's friend, conspiring with Derek to bring him down on the road to the Southern Darkwoods. Why would he sink to such treachery?

And if it were treachery he fashioned, why bother with a lad not yet even a squire?

Sturm leaned forward toward the fire. It was all too suspicious. There was something about this messenger that hinted at more than greens and servitude, though what it was he could not quite locate. And Jack was hardly the simpleton he played in the Tower.

There was trickery somewhere in the midst of this, he feared. And yet . . .

"Distant it might have been, sir," Jack continued, not at all disturbed at Sturm's disbelief. "So distant a fox might not have heard it—that I'll give you."

He looked at Sturm, and his black eyes narrowed. For a moment, there in the firelight as rainy afternoon passed into rainy evening, the gardener looked like a rough carving wrought from oak or alder by some ancient forest people.

"I'll give you distance," Jack Derry murmured ominously. "But what do you make of your stay in the castle? And poor Luin's shoe—who loosened the nails, I ask you?

"And last, who was it that gave you the marred sword? For it shows plainly here where the break was begun before our fight. . . ." He pointed to a tiny, perfectly straight notch running all around the broken blade's snapped edge.

"Coincidences, all of them," Sturm replied, the edge of a question in his voice.

" 'Coincidence' is Old Solamnic for 'I don't know,' " Jack said to Mara with a wink. "Now, now, Master Sturm," he added hastily. "There's no need for challenge and fisticuffs, for you can believe me or believe me not; it's no concern of my own."

"And yet you have followed us for days now," Sturm said, staring angrily across the fire at this unexpected visitor.

"Followed you? I think not!" Jack replied merrily. "I'm bound for your part of the world, I'll grant, to visit my mother. But our paths divide there, if you're asking me. Or even now, if you'd rather."

"You mean to tell me you didn't come all this way to warn me?" Sturm asked. "That our meeting here on the plains in the middle of a downpour is just . . ."

"Coincidence?" Jack asked with a curious half-grin, and he and Mara burst into laughter.

Sturm blushed angrily.

"So be it, then, Jack Derry," he pronounced, mustering his most Solamnic demeanor. "If what you say of Boniface and other matters are true, then we've no choice but to hole up here and wait for him. If he's planning to undo me, for whatever reason, he'll have to come here to find me."

The gardener only smiled. "We can't have that, Master Sturm, if what I've heard bandied about the Tower has any truth to it. You've an appointed time, they tell me— something about the first day of spring. You might have noticed last night that the moons, great Solin and Luin, crossed in the sky."

Sturm dared not look at Mara.

"If you've aught of astronomy," Jack continued, "you'd know that 'tis a rarity, occurring only every five years or so, and this year it falls a week before the first night of spring."

A week! Thank Paladine and all the gods of good that I've a week left! Sturm rose and turned from the fire.

"Boniface could be a month in coming. A year," Jack Derry went on. "It would stand him well to wait, for you to miss your . . . . assignation with the Green Man."

"You're no gardener, are you?" Sturm's hand moved slowly toward his broken sword. You're a trap, Jack Derry.

You're the doing of Lord Wilderness . . . or an apparition . . . or . . . or . . .

"How can you say that, Sturm Brightblade? Did you not see how well I kept the Tower gardens?"

A dull pain laced through Sturm's shoulder—nothing as sharp as he had felt at his wounding, as he had felt in Castle di Caela or the copse on the plains, but a heavy, deadening soreness that spread to the tips of his fingers.

He couldn't grasp the sword.

"No . . . no, Master Sturm," Jack continued. "I'm as much a gardener as aught else, and little I care for this involved Solamnic schemery." His eyes darted to the pommel of Sturm's sword, then directly, disarmingly back to the lad's face.

"Though you're a fine one and of a proud heritage, or so they tell me, I didn't travel these miles just to warn you or be in your august presence. Bound to the edge of the self-same Southern Darkwoods, I am, to a little village called Dun Ringhill where my ancient mother awaits me with an ancient mother's excitement and yearning for her long-lost boy gone north to make something out of himself in the court of the Knights."

"Dun Ringhill?" Sturm asked.

"Still two days' ride from here," Jack said. "In your boots, it's a walk of four or five days, through plains and riverbeds down along the borders of Throt, where the goblins camp. And in Lemish, where the village is, you'll find no friend of the Knights, either."

Jack rose from the fire and walked over to his squat little mare. He stroked her gently on the muzzle and muttered something to her, something lost in the downpour outside and the crackle of the nearby fire. The mare raised her head, snorted, and turned toward the mouth of the cave.

"I expect, then, I shall be taking my leave of you," Jack offered, leading the mare toward the outside and the loud, rushing shower. He paused at the cave mouth, foot in the stirrup, preparing to mount and ride into the rain.

Mara elbowed Sturm, who spoke up despite his pride and anger.

"Jack Derry?"

Jack stood at the cave entrance, still and expectant.

"Jack . . . do you know any blacksmith in . . . Dun Ringhill, is it?"

"Indeed I do, Master Sturm," the young gardener said, his face still turned. "My cousin Weyland, 'twould be. A fine smith he is, too."

"Fine he must be," Sturm replied, his eyes on the heart of the flame, "for shoeing old Luin here is apprentice work, but reforging a sword . . ."

Jack turned about and stared hard and levelly at the young man by the fire.

"Weyland Derry can forge a sword to your liking, Master Sturm Brightblade," the gardener said quietly. "And your welcome in Dun Ringhill will be such as fits the Order. All according to the Measure, 'twill be, and such as you'll come to expect of my people."

* * * * *

Boniface huddled against the rain, watching the wavering light in the distant cave.

There were too many around the boy. First the elf maiden and her spider—unpredictable at best, and therefore dangerous. Then the simpleminded gardener, if simpleminded he was, or if even a gardener, who had wandered to these parts for the gods knew what reason. To waylay Sturm Brightblade now would involve too many innocent lives. Too many blades. Too many chances for at least one to escape and tell others.

Who would not understand.

Once before, Lord Boniface Crownguard had dealt with witnesses. That time it had been an awkward Knight from Lemish, new to the Order and the Measure.

He had not understood, either, and what had befallen

then was entangled, messy, nearly disastrous.

So there ought to be no witnesses, Boniface thought, and smiled. There would be other chances later. At the ford and in the village . . .

He rose and mounted, riding east, the hoofbeats of his black stallion muffled in the driving rain.

* * * * *

They departed the next morning when the rain lifted. Sturm and Jack walked ahead, leading the horses. Mara rode atop Acorn, Jack's stocky chestnut, who also bore the weight of the elf's belongings easily if not cheerfully. Behind the party, scurrying along from high grass to rocks and back to the high grass, avoiding sun and open spaces, Cyren the spider kept pace unevenly.

At Jack's advice, Sturm traveled no longer toward the famous ford near the Vingaard Keep. If there were, as he was coming to suspect, good truth in Jack's warning about the snares of Lord Boniface, then all major fords would be perilous.

Instead, the party turned due east, straight toward a narrow passage of the river where Jack claimed that the swimming was as safe as the fording. High above them, the kingfishers darted and dove, and had he been looking for omens, Sturm could have taken great courage from the ancient Solamnic symbols on the wing.

He trudged gloomily beside the young gardener. It wasn't enough, it seemed, that he was doomed to certain failure against one as resourceful and skilled as Vertumnus, for now the best swordsman in Solamnia was also laying for him if, by some miracle, he survived his brush with the Green Man.

That is, if he could believe Jack Derry. It seemed preposterous—like something out of an ancient story of blood and dark oath and revenge. Boniface was his father's friend. Angriff had saved him from Lord Grim, had grown up beside him. They had fought together, had studied and suffered and blossomed in wisdom . . . and . . .

Finally there was the Oath and Measure.

It could not be true. Boniface could not be a traitor.

Sturm brushed his gloved hand softly over Luin's neck. Slowly, gradually, sensation returned to his fingers, and he turned his mind to other things—to the dwindling days and the long road ahead of him.

*   *   *   *   *

The new path took the party through rich pastureland north of the ancient stronghold of Solanthus. In some spots, the ground was greening, expectant, and the first migratory birds had returned from their winter stay in the sunny north. Amid the signs of spring, Sturm could look to the south across the level miles and see the fabled fortress, gray and hazed at the farthest reaches of sight. It was fertile in history and lore, the very kind of place he dreamed of visiting. Yet he dared draw no nearer after what Jack Derry had told him. Boniface could be anywhere on the plains, and assuredly his allies could be found in all places.

Sturm sighed and tugged at Luin's rein.

"Why so gloomy, Master Sturm?" Jack inquired, steering Acorn gracefully around pooling waters that might well mark dangerous ground. "Rejoice that we have left the rains behind!"

"It rushes toward spring, Jack Derry," Sturm replied. "Too swiftly, I fear, for my liking. A week only remains until I have to show myself in the Darkwoods, ready for a reckoning with Lord Wilderness himself."

"Look about you, Master Sturm," Jack observed quietly. "Where is Vertumnus, and where is the hook and line with which he draws you east?"

"You don't understand," Sturm protested. "First there's the wound. I know they laugh about that at the Tower. They say I imagined my wounding, but it *is* there, by Paladine! But more importantly, it's the honor of the challenge. I cannot do otherwise. You don't know, Jack. There is no Measure for gardeners."

Jack smiled curiously and rubbed his chin.

"No Measure but the sun and the moons and the seasons," he replied. "I'm *grateful* for those."

"And I for the Measure," Sturm said, much too quickly. "And . . . and of course for this lovely day." He looked around, trying to wear a mask of cheeriness. "A mild tag end of winter it is, Jack. No frost, and the birds returning. Mild as the spring of 'thirty-five, I'll wager."

When the farmers talked of mild springs, they talked of the year 335. Sturm remembered it well, though he was but ten: the thaws of winter and the flowers starting to bloom in the gardens of Castle Brightblade.

"Mild it is, sir, though I don't know about no three thirty-five," Jack said and pointed to the east. "Best that we stop in these parts for the night," he suggested. "We're safer this close to the stronghold, what with the bandits and raiders about."

Jack looked at Sturm solemnly.

"I'd rather Master Brightblade wasn't surprised," he warned, "when he finds out how the folk in the countryside take to his Oath and his Measure."

*   *   *   *   *

The evening was quiet, an enormous relief to Mara, but especially to Sturm. For the first night in almost a week, the lad slept the healthy sleep of a young man, secure in the knowledge that Jack Derry watched over the encampment.

There was something about the gardener that called for a sort of wild reliance. Sturm had felt it in the long day's journey as Jack read the shifts in the wind as a swordsman reads the feints and thrusts of his opponent. Jack was a reliable, even an inspired woodsman, but so, no doubt, was the dangerous man Sturm rode forth to challenge.

Sturm watched Jack tend the low fire, watched the muffled red light cast shadows on his hands and face. In that light, the gardener looked unsettlingly familiar, as if they had known one another through a lifetime.

*   *   *   *   *

"Look close enough, Master Sturm and Lady Mara, and you'll see the southernmost fork of the Vingaard," Jack said.

Sturm stood on tiptoe, bracing himself against Luin and squinting east to where the air seemed to waver at the farthest reach of sight. Mara, seated atop Acorn and looking eastward with the sharp eyes of an elf, nodded at once when Jack pointed out the landmark.

"A child's river it is at this juncture," the gardener continued, with a mischievous grin. "Your spider could send across a hundred letters in his green boats."

Mara was coldly silent behind them. Sturm hid a smile. Surely she regretted the telling and retelling of her story, especially to ears as sharp and satiric as the gardener's.

"As I told you both when we decided on this path, swimming's as good as fording in these parts. The river is slow here, and the ground is level both sides of it. An hour or so will have us into Lemish, and it's only another day to Dun Ringhill, if the weather fancies us and the bandits don't."

He looked disapprovingly at Sturm.

"I expect, Master Sturm Brightblade," Jack said, brushing his brown hair from his forehead, "it would be wiser if you took off some of that armor. Swimming a river, even a slow one, works better without forty pounds of mail."

Blushing at his own fogheadedness, Sturm removed the breastplate, setting it, along with his shield, on Luin's lightly burdened back. Jack looked at him with wry amusement.

"Hard to tell Solamnics from servants now, isn't it, Master Sturm?"

"Follow me," Sturm muttered, and stalked toward the riverbank. Jack, however, moved deftly in front of him.

"If I might be so bold, sir," he suggested, "let's not stand on pomp and protocol. Let someone who knows the river lead the crossing."

Eye to eye the two young men stood, not a hair's difference in height and weight. It was as though Sturm looked into a cloudy mirror, in which the face staring back at him resembled his in age and countenace, but was certainly not his own.

"I'm with the gardener," Mara offered. "A river's treacherous enough with even the best guidance."

"I don't recall asking your opinion," Sturm said icily, giving scarcely a sidelong glance to the elf.

Sturm looked out over the waters. Indeed, they did not look that hard to cross. The river was no more than thirty yards wide at this point, and enormous trees overhung its banks—evergreens, of course, and bare sycamore and vallenwood. The branches of one linked with those of another, forming a thin latticework over the river, almost like a trellis or . . .

. . . or a web.

"Cyren!" Sturm declared jubilantly. Mara looked at him perplexedly, but Jack caught on at once, herding the reluctant spider to the wide bole of one of the more promising vallenwoods.

"Now, Lady Mara," Jack said, his dark eyes dancing intently. "If you'd be so kind, coax your spider across the river there, and see to it that he webs a path for the rest of us. I suppose you can lead this party, Master Sturm, if there's stout cording to hold onto and a clear path through the Vingaard Drift."

"The Vingaard Drift?" Sturm asked. "I—I thought that was east of here." He had heard many stories of the deceptive, switching current in the easternmost fork of the river. Indeed, his own great-grandfather had almost been swept away by the Drift himself, thereby erasing the whole Brightblade line that would follow him. Brightblades and midstreams didn't mix altogether well, and Jack's talk of the

Drift made him terribly uneasy.

"It's not as bad in these parts," Jack explained, "but a river is always deceptive. Perhaps, since I am more familiar with the Drift and its tendencies, we should proceed as we first considered, with me at the head of the party."

"Very well," Sturm agreed, jumping at the chivalrous offer. "Since, after all, you *are* Lemish born, Jack. . . ."

"Done, then!" Jack exclaimed, his mischievous smile spreading broadly as Cyren, prodded by Mara's urgings and a slight nudge from her boot, clambered from vallenwood to sycamore to vallenwood and down safely on the other side of the river. "You'll be a good Knight, Sturm Brightblade."

A strong, viscous cord extended from bank to bank, and hand over hand, the party began its crossing in the slow-moving waters.

* * * * *

The waters were indeed tamer than elsewhere where Jack had chosen to cross. Sturm clung to the cord with one hand and to Luin's reins with the other; Mara followed behind him, leading little Acorn gently and skillfully through the sliding waters. Ahead of them, Jack clambered and bobbed in the river, surfacing and sputtering in delight, as graceful as a seal.

"Not far now!" he whispered as his head emerged from a swirl of waters, dark locks dripping on his forehead. "You can tell all the other Knights and all the little Brightblades to come about this journey—you crossed a river on a spider's dare!"

Jack's eyes widened in mock surprise. It was the first time Sturm had smiled at him.

"My, my, Master Brightblade!" he declared aloud. "I do believe there's someone of substance beneath those Orders and Measures."

Grinning, Sturm brushed his wet hair from his eyes. At

that moment, the crossing seemed adventurous and bright, the waters of the Vingaard loud about him.

So loud was the rush of the current that none of them— not even the horses—heard the bandits approach. The first arrow fell when Jack had passed midcurrent.

Chapter 12

Not Far From the Tree

It was a strange, ragtag group that attacked them.
Humans and hobgoblins milled together in the underbrush, masked and unmasked, in chain and leather and
cuir-bouilli and in no armor at all. Shouting and hooting,
they launched arrow after arrow at the hapless party. Fortu-
nately for the travelers, the attackers were not the best of
archers. Most of the arrows passed harmlessly overhead,
though one managed to strike Luin's saddle with a sharp
whack, startling the poor mare far worse than it hurt her.
But gradually the arrows came closer and closer as the bandits began to find their range.

Jack looked back at Sturm, calmly but intently. He
winked, and his black eyes took in the surroundings—the
overhang of branches, the dozen or so of the enemy waiting

on the banks ahead of them.

"Are you ready to take 'em, Sturm Brightblade?" Jack whispered, the rustle of oak leaves fluting in his voice as out of the water rose his sword blade, dripping and bright.

"I—I haven't a weapon, Jack," Sturm said. Instantly he regretted his words. His voice sounded shrill, thin, even trembling amid the outcry of the bandits and the nearby *whick*, *whick* of the passing arrows.

"Nonsense!" Jack exclaimed with a smile. "Follow me, and I'll arm you in a trice!"

Before Sturm could speak, Jack scrambled up onto the webbing. Like a spider himself, or rather like a tightrope walker, he raced across the strand in a rain of arrows, leaping onto the opposite shore, where a quick, wheeling slash of his sword sent a hobgoblin tumbling to the ground, spattering the red bank with a cascade of bright black blood.

Casually Jack picked up the monster's sword and tossed it, hilt over blade, to Sturm, who raised his hand for it, closed his eyes, and prayed to Paladine that the hilt would reach him first. The cool, reassuring smack of cylindrical metal in his hand told him that his prayers had been answered, and with his bravest war cry, he pulled himself along the cord through the water until his feet touched solid ground and he could rush up the bank to join his comrade.

Puffing and shouting, trailing mud and water, Sturm climbed to dry ground and spun about, the hobgoblin sword heavy in his hand. Five bandits had closed with Jack while Sturm was making his way up the banks. Whirling, ducking, and leaping, the air around him blurred with knife and dagger, Jack Derry looked to be more than a match for the five, but already there were three others bursting from the underbrush, two burly hobgoblins and a lanky man with a long scar on his lip.

Sturm turned to face the ugly trio. Their movements were low, shifting, the prowl of pub fighters rather than the sharp demeanor of soldiers. It should be easy enough, the lad thought, and raising his sword in a time-honored Solamnic salute, he stepped forth into the unfolding battle.

Within moments, he had a healthy respect for pub fighters. The hobgoblins were stocky and strong and surprisingly quick, but even more menacing was Scarlip, the lean bandit who hung back, his throwing dagger at the ready, waiting for the slightest opening. Sturm yearned for the ancestral shield as he danced to his left, keeping the hobgoblins between him and the tall deadly man.

The smaller of the hobgoblins, a snag-toothed, yellow-green rascal that smelled of carrion, lunged at Sturm once, twice, a third time. Each time the lad parried the thrusts, and each time he was forced back farther, farther still, until he felt his heels slide in the mud of the riverbank. Desperately he lurched forward, sliding quickly past the outstretched sword of the creature, and thrust his sword under its leather breastplate as his face pressed against that of the hobgoblin. The thing's yellow eyes widened and glazed over as Sturm pushed it aside, yanked his sword from its middle, and turned to face its larger comrade.

The big goblin, wielding a club the size of Sturm's leg, brought it crashing down in the high grass as Sturm slipped neatly out of the way. For a moment, he was in Scarlip's sight, and the lanky man stepped forward, preparing to throw. But Sturm leapt quickly to the other side of the big hobgoblin, which by this time had raised its club again.

Down the monster brought the weapon, and down again, but each time Sturm was much too quick, his movements too elusive. Behind this strange and deadly dance, Scarlip grew more and more impatient. Watching the tall bandit whenever he could flicker his eyes away from the charging hobgoblin, Sturm saw the man step forward, feint, then stomp angrily when once again his target jumped to safety.

So it could have continued until Sturm grew tired and goblin club or hurtling dagger found its mark, had not Scarlip grown too impatient. With a cry of frustration, the tall bandit hurled the first of his daggers.

It lodged in the back of the goblin, who fell facefirst into the river. Smiling, Scarlip readied a second dagger and launched it toward Sturm, who stood panting and riveted by surprise and fatigue.

Sturm saw the bandit's arm rise and whip forward, the dagger flashing through the air like a meteor. Then something struck him from the side and he toppled, the knife buzzing by his ear.

Jack Derry knelt over him, sword in hand.

"Stay down, Jack!" the young gardener shouted, then spun to face Scarlip.

Dazed, winded, Sturm tried to get to his feet but failed.

Jack? he thought. Why did he call me Jack?

But there was no time for answers. Jack Derry raced toward Scarlip, who drew another dagger and hurled it straight at his midsection. Jack brought his own blade across his body with almost unnatural quickness, deflecting the missile neatly. Scarlip turned and started to run, but he reeled suddenly as a dagger passed over Sturm's head and lodged at the base of the tall bandit's spine. Bounding past Sturm with the quickness of a deer, Mara drew a dagger from Jack's belt and took battle station by the gardener.

Blearily Sturm stood up. He looked toward the river, where seven bandits lay dead, victims of Jack's blinding speed and recklessness. But ten, maybe twelve more were coming in the distance, waving swords and shouting in the harsh accents of Neraka.

"Get out of here, Jack!" Jack shouted to Sturm, who staggered toward him, alarmed and bewildered.

"And take her with you," he said, with a gesture at Mara. "The gods know what they'd do to her!"

"B-But—" Sturm began, and was cut short. Jack would hear none of it.

"Go, Jack!" the gardener cried in his loudest voice, shaking his dark hair for emphasis. "Protect this woman—and don't forget, an acorn doesn't drop far from the tree!"

He took a threatening step toward Sturm, brandishing

his sword. Sturm, convinced that his comrade had gone mad, stepped back as Mara rushed to him, seized him by the arm, and pulled him southward down the riverbank.

"Hurry up, Sturm!" she whispered, dragging him bodily over a vallenwood root. "Now's your chance to rescue me!"

Completely baffled, Sturm gave a last look toward the courageous gardener and turned away.

Though hardly a hero, Cyren had been resourceful enough to herd the horses up the bank. Nervously they pawed the high grass, their big, rolling eyes returning again and again to the dodging spider. Sturm mounted Acorn and pulled Mara up in the saddle by him; she in turn had grabbed Luin's reins and brought the big Solamnic mare in tow behind her. As though the whole escape had been planned for months, Acorn's squat legs moved with quick purpose as she trotted them out of bow range and finally out of earshot.

Sturm looked back one last time before the limbs and undergrowth blocked his view of the river. Jack stood smiling bravely, framed in needles and branches and new leaves. He was taunting the bandits, waving his sword and dancing in a peculiar bawdy fashion Sturm thought he remembered from some lost and cloudy time.

The bandits held back for now. Jack had shown them his skill with the weapon, and none of them wanted to be the next to test his swordsmanship.

But it wouldn't be long. Sturm shook his head, and a great sadness overtook him as he turned to the trail ahead of him, leaving Jack Derry behind. If it weren't for Mara, he would be side by side with the gardener, braving the Nerakans and hobgoblins until victory or death. But she was helpless and frail and . . .

"Keep your eyes on the trail, Solamnic!" the helpless, frail little thing commanded as she grabbed his ear and jerked him back to proper attention. "I won't have Jack Derry risk his fool neck so that you can break ours!"

*   *   *   *   *

They traveled an hour, silent and lost in their lonely thoughts. Though he scarcely knew the gardener, Sturm mourned fiercely, his face hidden in the dark folds of his hood. Yet there was puzzlement equal to the grief.

"Jack," he said to Mara at last, as the two of them rode south through the rising night. "Why did he call me Jack?"

The elf maiden reached into the layers of fur that covered her. The moonlight splashed on the silver flute in her hand.

"So they would come at *him* and not at *you*, simpleton," she replied, and she lifted the flute to her lips.

"I don't understand, Mara," Sturm said, interrupting the first notes of the music.

"Remember the snares and ambushes Jack told you about? The ones this Bonito—"

"Boniface," Sturm interrupted. "Lord Boniface of Foghaven."

"Boniface, Bonito . . ." Mara said dismissively. "Whoever was trying to trap or dismantle you. As I see it, Jack figured the bandits to be one of the snares."

"And calling me Jack . . ." Sturm began, the idea dawning on him.

"Meant that the other young human male was the one they were looking for," Mara said. "The one who would do something foolish and Solamnic like hold them all off while we escaped."

"So Jack was . . . was masking as *me!*" Sturm exclaimed, trying in vain to turn Acorn back on the path.

"Are all the Brightblades this nimble-witted?" Mara asked ironically. "Get hold of your mare, Master Sturm, before she takes us all the way to Neraka!"

*   *   *   *   *

The dark came suddenly and swiftly, as it often does near the end of winter. Sturm had roamed through high grass and farmland, searching fruitlessly for the path to Dun Ringhill. Western Lemish, it seemed, was as featureless as the face of a moon, and just about as hospitable.

As far as Sturm could see, there was no lantern or lamp, no smell of woodsmoke in the air, no sound of herd or watchdog. It was an uninhabited country and a place without landmark.

Sturm dismounted from the mare. The countryside rolled ahead of him, and the clouds blocked the stars so thoroughly that he couldn't tell north from west, much less tell direction by the heavens.

"So much for Lemish," he said disgustedly. "Nothing but a pasture, this is."

Mara stayed in the saddle, squinting as her sharp elf eyes scanned all possible horizons.

"Dun Ringhill is somewhere around here," she said. "Of that much I'm certain."

The grass stirred behind them, and Cyren scrambled into the open, trailing a single white strand of webbing.

"I thought you had been in these parts before," Sturm said, looking up at the girl.

"True enough," Mara said quietly, "I met Jack Derry once—not far from here."

"What? How did you come to meet him? And who really is Jack Derry?" Sturm asked, stretching Solamnic politeness out of curiosity. For after all, there might be something the elf could tell him, something to lead them to the village, to Weyland the Smith and to eventual safety.

"My money has it he's awaiting us in Dun Ringhill. The first step in finding this village is to know west from east. Sunrise will tell us that quick enough."

She peered at him through the furs, her dark eyes intent and questioning.

"You know well that it will not," Sturm grumbled. "Not quick enough, that is. The countryside is filled with bandits, and we'd best not camp in the midst of them."

"Then we steer by starlight," Mara proclaimed and lifted

the flute to her lips again.

"Starlight?" Sturm asked skeptically. "M'lady, look at the clouds. . . ."

But the elf had closed her eyes, an eerie music rising from her instrument. It was a Qualinesti plainsong, sacred to Gilean the Book. Crisp and staccato, the notes filled the moist air around them, and Sturm looked about uneasily, sure that the music would give them away to the bandits.

Mara played, and a silver light shone in her hair. For a moment, Sturm thought she was glowing, then gradually he noticed the same light spreading over his arms and shoulders, over Acorn's neck and the chestnut flanks of Luin behind them. White Solinari had broken through the thick mask of clouds, and the road behind him and before him was as clear and dazzling as midday.

"As I feared," Mara said, the song over and the clouds returning. "We've listed a bit to the south. We'll strike the river again if we keep on as we're going."

"How . . . how did you do that?" Sturm asked, turning Acorn forcefully from the trail that the stubborn little mare insisted on following.

"Gilean mode," Mara said quietly, "with the High Mode of Paladine placed in its silences. When you combine them, it's a song . . . of revealing. It dispels clouds and night, stills waters so you can look to the bottom of pond and river. In the hands of the great bards, it unmasks the dissembling heart."

She smiled at Sturm, who caught his breath at the depths of her hazel eyes.

"But I am no great bard," the elf concluded quietly. "With my music, we are lucky to see a momentary change in the weather."

Sturm blushed and nodded, yanking once more at Acorn's reins.

"Well, the clouds parted long enough," Mara said, pointing due east. "There's our direction. That way lies the Darkwoods."

"But where on the woods' edge can we find Dun Ringhill?" Sturm asked. "The stars don't tell us that. If only we had Jack Derry here!"

"Ah, but Jack is lost or upriver or . . . elsewhere," Mara said. "Leaving us alive if no wiser."

"He believed I could find the way," Sturm muttered disconsolately. "He trusted that I was my father's son, that I am more resourceful than I feel."

"My dear boy," Mara said with a crooked smile, "what in the name of the Seven makes you think *that?*"

"He told me," Sturm said, "that the acorn doesn't fall far from the tree. What else could that be but talk of fathers and sons?"

"Perhaps something a bit more . . . arboreal?" Mara asked. "Or a simple riddle that your thoughts of fathers have kept covered? After all, Jack couldn't give you directions to Dun Ringhill. Bandits have ears, after all, and would follow us like hounds."

Sturm nodded. It made sense. Jack was, after all, a man of concealments and riddles. Seated on the increasingly unruly mare, Sturm mined his knowledge of tree lore, of gardening, of the mythical ancient calendar of the dryads that supposedly followed a symbolism of trees. None of it helped. He felt as though he were back in the maze of Castle di Caela or in the thickest reaches of the Green Man's fog.

The mare wrenched once more, and he tugged furiously at her reins. "By the gods, Acorn!" he snapped. "If you don't—"

He paused at the sound of Mara's laughter.

"*Now* what?" he exclaimed, but the elf laughed even more.

"Let go of the reins, Sturm Brightblade," she said, recovering her breath.

"I beg your pardon?"

"Think about it, Sturm. Who among us knows the way to the village of Dun Ringhill?"

Slowly, reluctantly, Sturm opened his hand. The reins

dropped limply over Acorn's withers, and sensing the new freedom, the little mare turned about and walked steadily east, then south, then east again. Mara resumed the music, this time singing the old song from Qualinost, adding to it equally ancient words.

> "The sun,
> the splendid eye
> of all our heavens,
> dives from the day
>
> "and leaves
> the dozing sky
> spangled with fireflies,
> deepening in gray.
>
> "The leaves
> give off cold fire,
> they blaze into ash
> at the end of the year,
>
> "and birds
> coast on the winds
> and wheel to the north
> when autumn ends.
>
> "The day grows dark,
> the seasons bare,
> but we
> await the sun's
> green fire upon
> the trees."

Ahead of them, green footprints sprouted and grew among the dingy ground cover. Acorn leaned forward, grazed softly on one of them, and began her slow progress on the new trail. Luin followed, browsing at the footprints, too, eating the trail behind them. At a farther distance, the high bushes tilted and switched, a sign that the spider Cyren followed, as always obscurely and furtively.

They hadn't traveled twenty yards before the music arose in front of them, too. A fluid, beautiful descant joined with Mara's singing, and Sturm closed his eyes and saw liquid silver passing like a magical stream before his inner vision.

So Vertumnus had joined in the music again. Sturm sat back in the saddle, resigning himself to Acorn's direction and the melody all around him. Though the Green Man's song invariably led to . . . challenges, it also led toward the Southern Darkwoods. And despite the challenge and the peril, that was the goal of his journey.

On they traveled, and even though the night was thick about them, Sturm's heart was much lighter. Jack Derry's riddle had been a little thing, not much compared to the mysteries that lay ahead. But solving one thing gave hope to solving another. The road ahead of him looked less daunting now, and as the lights of Dun Ringhill shone dimly before him, Sturm imagined the smithy, the sword reforged, Vertumnus faced down and beaten on the first day of spring.

It all seemed possible, even likely. He felt the crisp exhilaration of adventure, of swords and riding and mystery and beautiful females. He sat back in the saddle, brushing against the sleeping Mara, who mumbled and tightened her grip about his waist. For a moment, the journey seemed something he was born to do.

He didn't notice the men until they rose like fog from the high grass, sudden and quick and quietly efficient. The man in the forefront, a brown, wizened little character, smiled and raised his hand.

"Good even, Sturm Brightblade!" he called out, his common speech fluent but thick with the accents of Lemish.

Good old Jack Derry, Sturm thought admiringly. As quick in travel as he is with the sword. "Ho, there!" he called out, dismounting from the horse. And then, more formally and Solamnically: "Whom have I the honor of addressing?"

"Captain Duir of the Dun Ringhill Militia, sir!" the weathered little man announced, standing at comical attention. "Assigned to protect the western approaches."

Sturm looked back in amusement at Mara, who was rubbing her eyes and straightening herself in the saddle.

Sturm stepped forward, removed his glove, and offered his hand in the traditional Solamnic gesture. Shyly, awkwardly, Captain Duir extended his own hand, and the two men exchanged greetings as equals.

Sturm nodded and smiled at the peasant soldier, who slowly smiled back, his blue eyes narrowed now with a new and strange amusement.

"Master Sturm Brightblade of Solamnia," the captain announced, his grip tightening on the young man's hand, "I arrest you as an invader, in the name of the Druidess Ragnell!"

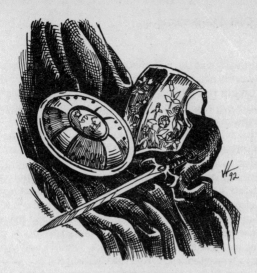

Chapter 13

A Ride Back in Memory

He could return to the Tower now.

Boniface watched Sturm's arrest from the topmost branches of a distant vallenwood. The spyglass he carried with him was cloudy but good. He saw the boy offer his hand, saw the captain take it, saw the gestures of friendship stiffen and sour, and saw the militia take them all—the horses, the elven mistress, and Brightblade—off toward the town of Dun Ringhill, where the old druidess sat at the head of an angry tribunal.

The finest swordsman in Solamnia wrapped his dark cloak about him tightly and shivered with pleasure. From a distance, framed in the menacing red moonlight, he looked like a huge raven or some unspeakable bat-winged creature, huddled in the height of the enormous tree. The spring wind

died at the foot of the vallenwood, and in the upper branches, it was ultimate winter, dead and still, the steam of Boniface's breath rising like a specter into the midnight air.

Let the old witch have the boy, he thought. He shinnied
down the tree like a spider.

Let them hang him, or boil him, or do whatever they do
in the barbaric villages of Lemish. In its own way, it would
be perfectly legal.

Why, it might even jog the council from their notorious
sleep back in the Tower, where the Oath and Measure rust
in the closets. The death of his ward might be enough to stir
Gunthar Uth Wistan southward to invasions long overdue.
Then the people of Dun Ringhill, of the Darkwoods, of all
of Lemish and later Throt and Neraka, would know what it
meant to transgress the Order and Measure.

But even if Lord Gunthar did not budge from the Tower,
if the boy went unavenged and Lemish untouched, if this
night marked the end of the matter, Boniface was still satisfied. For the long wars of a decade would be over at last.

Lord Boniface of Foghaven leapt into the saddle of his
black stallion. Swiftly, with the grace born of fighting from
horseback at close quarters, he wheeled the beast about and
rode toward the Vingaard River at full gallop, his mind rehearsing the oldest of his pains.

* * * * *

They had grown up together, Angriff and Boniface. In
sword and book, in horsemanship and cunning, in their
first raids against the ogres of Blode through the border
wars with the men of Neraka, there was scarcely a hairs-
breadth of difference between one and the other. Only in
their allegiance to the Oath and Measure did the two show
differences.

For Boniface, the Order was life, and its rules and rituals
the breath of that living. Book after book of the Measure,
with its elaborate chapters and lists and qualifications and

exceptions, he had memorized with reverence, so that his fellows had smiled at him, called him "the next High Justice."

They smiled because they had admired him. Of that, young Boniface had been sure, and through squirehood and the first lists of knighthood, his assurance had come from the letter, from the laws and restrictions the Order had established since the days that Vinas Solamnus first set pen to paper.

He didn't understand his friend Angriff, for whom both Code and Measure were more of a game. Sometimes Boniface ached and worried that the time would come when he would have to leave Angriff behind, when his own study and seriousness would blossom in the Rose of true knighthood, and Angriff would be a laughingstock, a cautionary tale for young aspirants that gifts and good looks and a generous spirit did not make you a Knight. He expected it to happen, but Angriff became a squire as well, and then a Knight of the Crown, serving with brilliance in the Fourth Nerakan Campaign.

It would have angered a lesser friend to see that brilliance, those talents, wasted on games and music and poetry, on anything but duty and honor. It would have angered that lesser friend, but Boniface bore with Angriff, hoping against the rising evidence that the heir to the noble Brightblade line, the son of Emelin and grandson of Bayard Brightblade, would turn to discipline and find his joy in fulfilling every action in accordance to the unbending law of the Measure.

Against all evidence, Boniface hoped. That is, until his friend had come back from the east.

Newly wed, Angriff was missing for a month in the wastes of Estwilde, and all but his young bride Ilys gave him up for lost. Boniface himself had stood on the Knight's Spur with the lovely girl, her eyes red and swollen with a week's crying, and told her to hold back her tears and assume the green mantle of Solamnic widowhood.

He hadn't urged her hatefully, of course. It was, after all, a hard time for the Order, and hostile forces assembled far and near. He had simply figured the chances, which were not at all good.

She had nodded dutifully, had ordered the weaving of the mantle. The season had turned from winter to spring as the seamstress rendered the final embroidery, the ancestral sign of the phoenix. Two nights before Ilys donned the ceremonial mantle and became a widow by Code and by Measure, Angriff Brightblade came out of the Plains of Solamnia, riding slowly up the Wings of Habbakuk toward the gates of the High Clerist's Tower, so muddy and wet that horse and rider were indistinguishable and the first sentries almost drew bow against him, fancying him a centaur.

Ilys hid the mantle at the bottom of her bridal chest—shrouded in cedar, to be drawn forth and worn fifteen years later—and they all rushed to the foregates to greet her husband. The heart of Boniface had been as light as any, his joy as pure and surprising and unlimited . . .

Until he took the reins from his weary friend and saw the change in his eyes.

Something had happened in the wastes of Estwilde. Angriff never spoke of it, nor of his journey home, but the flippant way in which he treated Oath and Measure horrified Boniface. Law and life, it seemed, were toys to the frivolous Angriff, who from that day forward abided by only the most basic allegiances. He disobeyed superiors when he found their commands foolhardy or merciless, he forgave disobedience readily in his foot soldiers, discouraged trial by combat, and avoided all ceremony because it "no longer interested him."

Even more, it horrified Boniface that Angriff Brightblade answered neither to authority nor fate. The council turned their head to his misbehavior because his swordsmanship had blossomed. It was the only word for it. Angriff Brightblade did things with a sword that no man had dreamt before him, or since, for that matter. Both he and Boniface had learned from the same master. The movements of their swords were essentially the same, but something happened to a weapon in the hands of Angriff Brightblade. It was as though the sword dictated its own path and Angriff followed it. Something reckless and free had entered his swordplay, and none of Boniface's time-honored rules and classical movements could answer for it.

Boniface watched, and envied, and looked for a time and place to match his skills with that of his old friend.

He found it in the Midsummer Tournament, in the three hundred and twenty-third year since the Cataclysm. Two hundred Knights had assembled at Thelgaard Keep, and for the first time, Angriff and Boniface found themselves in the Barriers of the Sword, the contest in swordsmanship that traditionally occurs on the tournament's second day.

Always before, only one of the three great Solamnic swordsmen would enter the Barriers of the Sword—Angriff one year, Boniface the next, and Gunthar Uth Wistan the third. It was an unspoken agreement, giving a sporting chance to the other Knights and avoiding the rancorous rivalry that can be found at the top level of many endeavors.

Three twenty-three was Angriff's year. Though many a Knight was surprised, and some outraged, to see Boniface's name placed in the Barriers, he was entitled by the Measure and as welcome as any man. So protest was silent, and though Gunthar Uth Wistan refused to speak to Boniface at the banquet the night before, Angriff was generous and friendly and joked about the possibility of their meeting in the Barriers on the morrow.

Boniface remained silent. Through the night he slept fitfully, his dreams a flashing of blade and sunlight, and he woke the next morning with his arms already weary, having fought through the night in those dreams.

Angriff, it seemed, slept soundly and strongly, as a great tree slumbers in the depth of winter. He awoke cheerfully, singing an old song about broadswords and beasts, and promptly invited Boniface to his tent to share breakfast. All through the meal, Boniface couldn't look at Angriff. The movement of his old friend's hand for a piece of fruit or bread startled him like the sudden rustle of an adder in dried leaves, and that morning, his meditations were shallow and fruitless.

The arena was exactly as tradition described it. The circle in the garden was twenty feet in diameter and free of obstacle and impediment, though the setting itself was overgrown, and a huge olive tree extended its branches over the grounds. It was a peaceful spot, quiet before the afternoon's clashing of swords, and yet, to Boniface's ears, the place hummed like a hive, filled with anticipation and an undefined menace.

The first rounds of the Barriers were routine and amiable. Expert swordsmen were mismatched with beginners, who left thankful that the tournament rules called for *arms courteous*, the blunted, light swords of the summer games.

Boniface's first opponent almost caught the great Knight napping, scoring a point and then another while his famous adversary scanned the crowd anxiously.

Could it be for Angriff Brightblade? So was the rumor. The Tower was abuzz in the belief that the two would cross swords in the afternoon, and speculation and wagers flew. Would Angriff's gifts or Boniface's study prevail? Would the wild inspiration of the mystic win out over the beautiful precision and schooled control of the master?

Boniface returned his attention to the matter at hand, the first of his opponents. With a swift, almost mathematical efficiency, he brought the young man to the ground, the rounded tip of his sword at his helpless opponent's throat. Swiftly Boniface turned away, dismissing again his thoughts of Angriff Brightblade as he stalked toward a rest he did not need and a wait for his second opponent in the contest.

Ten minutes late for the next match, Gunthar Uth Wistan, Lord Brightblade's second, waded through the murmuring crowd followed by Angriff himself, who took longer to reach the circle than he did to dispatch his opponent, young Medoc Inverno of Zeriak. It was a maneuver so swift and unexpected it bordered on the foolish. Instead of parrying Sir Medoc's first, inexpert thrust, Angriff simply stepped to his right out of the path of the blundering lad, shifted his blade to the left hand, and disarmed, tripped, and pinned Medoc in one effortless move.

Angriff stood back and saluted his opponent, who lay on his back, scowling fiercely. Suddenly, overwhelmed by the sheer ease and quickness of it all, Medoc laughed despite himself.

" 'Tis not the usual Knight," he said, "so roundly beaten by a master swordsman, who lives to enjoy and tell of it! I have been an uncommon match for you, Lord Angriff!"

Angriff laughed along with him, and with a gesture both gracious and respectful, leaned forward and helped the young Knight to his feet. All around the Circle of the Sword there was murmuring and polite, baffled applause.

Boniface seethed quietly, his fingers itching on the hilt of his sword. The man had ridiculed the Oath and Measure long enough, and to judge from Medoc's laughter, that ridicule was like a disease, spreading and infecting the young and impressionable.

Eight Knights were left after the first round of the Barriers. Again the lots were dropped into the helmet and shaken, and this time a groan of dismay passed through the loges and balconies where the eager crowd was seated. For Boniface and Angriff were to fight in the next match. It was a meeting all had hoped to prolong; they had wanted to savor the possibility all the long midsummer day, until at evening, under lantern light amid fireflies and crickets, the best swordsman of Solamnia would emerge victorious in the final contest. But the real suspense of the tournament would be over soon, and all the rest of the trials would be superfluous, a soft rain after the thunder and tumult and lightning.

But a storm was approaching nonetheless, and the air crackled as the two men prepared for the contest—Angriff with his second, Gunthar Uth Wistan, and Boniface with his, the dark young warrior Tiberio Uth Matar, whose family would vanish, crest and all, from the face of Solamnia within ten years. The storm was approaching as the four men stepped within the circle of earth, and the two combatants donned the leather helmets and linen armor of the Barriers.

The long quiet prelude ended, the men moved to the edge of the circle—Angriff and Gunthar to its easternmost point, Boniface and Tiberio to the west—and all stood still until the trumpet sounded to signal the beginning of the melee.

Angriff moved like a wind through the light and shade of the circle. Boniface wheeled and reeled and lunged for him twice, but Angriff seemed to be everywhere except at swordpoint. Twice they locked blades, and both times Boniface staggered back on his heels, doing everything he could to fend off the attack that followed.

Within only seconds, Boniface knew he was beaten. He had been a swordsman too long not to know when he was overmatched, when his opponent was more skillful and quick and strong and daring than he could even imagine. From its beginning, the match was only a question of time. If Boniface surpassed himself, fighting with an intensity and bravado he had never known until this moment, he might prolong defeat three minutes or four.

Oh, let me not seem a fool! he told himself desperately, frantically. Whatever befalls me, let me not seem foolish! Then he charged his opponent in a last, hopeless assault, sword extended like a lance in the lists.

It was as if his prayers to himself were answered in the moment that followed. For some reason—whether exuberance or sportsmanship or simple mercy, Boniface never understood—Angriff leapt in the air, grabbed a low-hanging branch of the olive tree, and swung gracefully out of the way, landing after a neat somersault some ten feet away from where he had been standing. A few of the younger Knights applauded and cheered, but the gallery was mostly silent as surprise mingled with bafflement and wonder.

But Boniface, standing at the edge of the circle, felt he had been delivered by his old friend's foolishness.

"Point of order to the council!" he declared, sword lifted in the time-honored gesture of truce.

"Point addressed, Lord Boniface," Lord Alfred MarKenin replied in puzzlement, leaning from the red-bannered balcony that marked the vantage point of the tournament judges. Raising a point of order in the midst of tournament was acceptable behavior, but rare. Usually it was done to address a violation of the rules of fair combat.

This was no exception. Boniface raced through his considerable memory of the Measure, ransacking his years of legal study for one phrase, one ruling in the Measure of Tournaments that would . . .

Of course. The thirty-fifth volume, was it?

"Bring to me, if you would, the . . . thirty-fifth volume of the Encoded Measure."

Frowning, Lord Alfred sent a squire after the volume. Combat was suspended while the observing Knights milled and speculated, awaiting whatever dusty rule Lord Boniface of Foghaven had up his scholarly sleeve. Angriff leapt to the branch again and climbed between two notched limbs of the great tree, where he seated himself to await the return of the squire.

The volume was brought to the balcony, escorted by two red-robed sages. Lord Stephan took the book, handling it as if it were glass, and passed it to Lord Alfred who, setting it in his lap, looked down at Boniface expectantly.

By my Oath and Measure, let it be there as I remember, the swordsman thought. Let it be there; oh, let it be let it be . . .

"There is," Boniface began, "if I remember . . . some reference in the Measure of Tournaments . . ."

He paused, nodding tellingly at the surrounding Knights.

" . . . the entirety of which is found at the end of the thirty-fifth volume of the Solamnic Measure, extending through the first seventy pages of the thirty-sixth volume . . . some reference to preserving the integrity of the circle in the Barriers of Swords."

"There is indeed," one of the sages replied, his bald head nodding in agreement. "Volume thirty-five, page two seventy-eight, seventh article, second subarticle."

Lord Alfred bent over the book, thumbing through the pages swiftly. Angriff slid from the fork of the tree and sat in the center of the circle, head cocked like a hawk, listening attentively.

" 'In the midst of the Barriers of Swords,' " he read, " 'whether at midsummer or solstice or at the festival of Yule, any Knight who leaves the circle in the midst of trial or contest shall forfeit his sword.' "

Alfred MarKenin looked up and blinked in bafflement.

" 'Tis talk of the circle, in sooth," he agreed, "but its import here I do not understand."

"Simple," Lord Boniface explained, more confident now, striding to the center of the circle. "When Lord Angriff Brightblade lifted himself from the ground in . . . in avoidance of my onslaught, he in effect removed himself from the circle and thereby incurred the penalty of the Measure."

The last words fell in the midst of silence. Gunthar Uth Wistan stepped forward angrily, but Angriff restrained him, a look of perplexed amusement in his eyes.

"You can't beat him in a fair tilt," Gunthar muttered, "so you're at him with . . . with *arithmetic!*"

Boniface's gaze never wavered from Lord Alfred MarKenin. After all, advised by the deliberation of the sages, he and the council would decide on the issue. Alfred stared one long last time at each of the contestants, then drew the red curtain across the front of the balcony.

They were less than an hour in deciding. When the curtains opened, Boniface saw the troubled countenance of Lord Stephan Peres. Lord Boniface smiled, expecting the good news.

Angriff sat on the ground, calm and abstracted, staring

up into the canopy of leaves and beyond those leaves at the dusk and the first evening stars.

"The council is . . . undecided on the matter at hand," Lord Alfred proclaimed, to an intake of breath among the encircling Knights. "But never fear. For when council is undecided, judgment in the Measure of Tournaments reverts to the Scholars of the Measure, according to volume two, page thirty-seven, article two, subarticle three."

"Subarticle two," corrected the balding sage, closing his eyes reverently.

Alfred sighed and nodded, his voice resigned and thin. "Subarticle *two* of the aforesaid Solamnic Measures . . ."

"Thereby and therein," continued the second sage, a small gray-haired man whose beard billowed over his red robes, "the Solamnic Academy rules in favor of Lord Boniface of Foghaven. Let Lord Angriff Brightblade forego the use of his sword in the contest in question."

He knew it was complicated, that it smacked of skulduggery and legalism, but he had won. Lord Boniface hid his exultation, staring solemnly across the ring at his opponent. Tiberio Uth Matar was not so sly. He began to chuckle, to gloat, and even a cold glance from Lord Alfred himself failed to silence him.

Angriff smiled and dropped his sword. Tiberio stepped to the center of the circle where, according to the Measure, he picked up the discarded blade. Serenely, haughtily, Tiberio scrambled onto the limb himself and, breaking off a branch no more than a foot long, no wider than a finger, dropped it rudely into the lap of Angriff Brightblade.

"Here is your sword, Brightblade," he called out mockingly. "The tree that took your weapon should give one back again!"

Boniface snapped at his insolent second, but Angriff only laughed. Slowly, confidently, Lord Brightblade stood in the center of the Barriers and held forth the olive branch.

"So be it, Tiberio," he declared quietly. "As I heard the Measure, it said nothing of ending the contest. My sword is surrendered, but not myself."

He turned calmly to Lord Boniface, a look of infinite mischief deep in his dark eyes.

"Well, well, Bonano," he said, using a childhood nickname discarded when the two of them had become squires. "Shall we finish this? Man to man and sword to branch?"

"Don't be a fool, Angriff," Boniface protested hotly, and turned to walk from the ring and the contest.

"If you step from the ring, you forfeit your sword," Angriff taunted. "Volume something-or-other, some page, some article, and so forth."

Boniface wheeled about, wrestling with his own anger. Angriff made him feel small, foolish, like a boy punished with a switch. Coldly he stepped forward, sword at the point of address.

"Point of order," he said, in his voice an urgency, a plea. "Does the contest continue in accordance with the Measure?"

Completely bewildered by now, Lord Alfred turned to the scholars. Two heads, one bald and the other gray, bent together for the shortest of moments, and they turned to address the council, a unified front of two.

"We find for Lord Angriff," they said in unison.

"Think twice, Angriff," Alfred urged, but Boniface had closed at once, seeking to break the paltry weapon with a single, powerful swipe of the sword. Angriff stepped aside, deflecting the terrible downstroke with the slightest brush of the olive branch. Following the momentum of his sword, Boniface tumbled to his knees. His helmet slipped down over his eyes, and from somewhere deep in one of the loges, a faint, muffled laugh burst forth.

Furious, Boniface righted himself and slashed out at Angriff, blade whistling through the evening air. Angriff ducked under the attack and rose quickly, flicking the branch in the face of his opponent. Boniface lurched forward, enraged, off balance, but his blade slid by the dodging Lord Brightblade. Laughing, Angriff brought the branch down with blinding speed on the bare wrist of his old friend's sword hand. With a crack, the limb broke in two, and crying out, Boniface dropped the sword. Angriff scooped up the blade and, in less time than it took those watching to blink, pressed its blunt point against the hollow of Boniface's throat.

"I believe I win, Bonano," he announced. "Even by the Measure."

* * * * *

That was why Boniface had to kill Angriff. It had taken twelve years for the chance to arise, when Castle Brightblade had undergone siege and relief of the garrison hinged on the arrival of Agion Pathwarden and the reinforcements from Castle di Caela.

It was Boniface who had sent word to the bandits as to the road Sir Agion would follow, as to the strength of the party and to the place where terrain and surprise and vantage point would leave the Knights most vulnerable to ambush. His words had cut off the hope of Angriff Brightblade, and it was his belief that Angriff would draw in the garrison and fight the peasantry to the last man.

Covering his tracks had been simple. They had departed from Castle Brightblade in the middle of the night and were back before sunrise the next morning. Boniface had taken only one Knight with him, a whey-faced novice from Lemish whose name he could not even remember. In addition, there had been an escort of three, perhaps four foot soldiers. The soldiers were disposable: He handed them over to the bandits, and their bodies were lost amid the carnage when the bandits waylaid Agion. The Knight was a handy scapegoat in the weeks that followed.

But most importantly, Angriff Brightblade had been undone.

Twelve years can quicken a thirst for revenge, even to the point that you will risk all to gain it. Boniface himself was ready to be that last man, to fall in the siege of the castle, if that fall meant he would see the death of Lord Angriff Brightblade.

Even at the last, Angriff played by no Measure. Where a true Solamnic commander would have fallen with the castle, Lord Angriff traded his life for the garrison, giving himself to the peasantry and thereby ransoming all of them.

Including Boniface.

Even now, he remembered—six long years after Angriff had walked out into the snow toward the distant lights, the two loyal foot soldiers following him like mad retainers, like hounds.

Eighteen years after that sunlit midsummer day in the Barriers, Boniface remembered both his defeats keenly.

It was why the boy Sturm had to die. For the line of Angriff Brightblade must end without issue, so that whatever wildness lay in that line could be stilled, whatever defiance of Measure and Code laid to rest before such treachery found its way into the Order once more.

Boniface thought on these things. As his black stallion erased the miles from the Vingaard River to the High Clerist's Tower, he dwelt on them deeply and long, his thoughts enraptured by the intricate laws of his heart.

Chapter 14

Dun Ringhill

The village was no more than twoscore huts and a large central lodge, huddled together at the very edge of the Southern Darkwoods. It seemed to grow out of the forest rather than border it, as though it would be hard to tell where village left off and wilderness began.

Dun Ringhill was brightly lit for the dead of night—candles in every window, townspeople on the steps and in the streets, carrying torches and lanterns. Under other circumstances and in other company, Sturm might have found it inviting, festive—even lovely, in a rural sort of way. But not tonight: The whole village had turned out to see the prisoners, and the welcome was not friendly.

Sturm trudged before the militia, through a gauntlet of wintry stares. The children were too thin. That was the first thing he noticed. One of them, then another stepped forward, hands outstretched in the time-honored gesture of beggars, but adults drew them away, scolding them with cold, flickering phrases of Lemish.

Sturm frowned, straining to catch words of Solamnic or Common in the midst of the talk. He heard nothing but Lemish, its streams of long vowels and silences, like the distant sound of voices on another floor of a house.

Occasionally someone would hurl things at him. Dried mud, dung, and overripe fruit sailed from the midst of the crowd and skidded along the hard dirt path, but the attacks were halfhearted, and none of the projectiles came all that close to their mark.

Mara walked quietly behind him, in the surprisingly gentle custody of a big rough peasant whom Captain Duir called Oron. Duir himself escorted Sturm, his company cautious and firm but not harsh.

"What are they saying, Captain?" Sturm asked on more than one occasion, but Duir did not reply. His sharp eyes remained fixed on the village hall ahead of them, where a bonfire burned in the midst of the square. As they approached the blaze, two of the guards led Acorn and Luin off through the crowd toward the village stables. Sturm watched them for as far as he could see in the darkness and deceptive light. Wherever the stable lay, the smithy would be nearby.

"Keep your eyes ahead of you," Captain Duir ordered. "What're ya gawkin' after, anyway?"

"The smithy," Sturm answered, turning to the square ahead of him, where the bonfire danced and roared. "I've business with your Weyland."

"A confident lad, y'are," the captain observed, "that your business with *us* will be over soon."

"And confident are your people," Sturm replied, "whose thin children throw ripe fruit at visitors. Where does your village get apples in March, Captain Duir?"

The guardsman's hand tightened on his wrist.

"You'll be taking all things up with herself, I'd reckon," he replied.

"That would be the druidess?" Sturm asked.

But Captain Duir did not reply. With a gesture that could have been polite or mocking, he led Sturm and Mara across the square to the bonfire, where a wicker throne sat empty, surrounded by a dozen guards.

*　*　*　*　*

Sturm had grown used to the shape and feel of a storybook rural village, having spent a good part of his life on the outskirts of Solace, a place obscure in that time, though famous scarcely a decade later. When Jack Derry spoke of Dun Ringhill, Sturm had looked forward to a cozy little hamlet, the houses fashioned neatly of wood or wattle and daub, each roof freshly thatched and each fence tidy and in good repair.

But Lemish was unkempt, and its people completely unabashed by rough living quarters. The houses were large and circular, built of planks and wickerwork, their roofs of heavy, sodden thatch. Smoke trailed through a large hole in the middle of each roof, so Sturm guessed that the houses were warmed by a crude central fire.

It was to be expected, Sturm thought. He had heard that the Lemish people still lived in the Age of Darkness, the homes of their most powerful rulers scarcely hovels by Solamnic standards.

But what he had not expected was the square—the blossom and the green of it. In the midst of a drab and forbidding village, the houses on the square were sprouting, leaves and vines burgeoning from their walls as though the planks were still alive, still sending forth shoots and branches.

There, in the midst of a man-made forest, Sturm and Mara awaited the Druidess Ragnell.

She stepped from beneath a canopy of leaves, three beautiful girls strewing her pathway with lavender and lilac. The old woman was bent practically double, her face wrinkled and dark like the shell of a walnut and her white hair tangled and thin. Sturm thought of the sea effigies, the spindly, life-sized dolls made of mud and wood that dotted the coasts of Kothas and Mithas, put there to create the illusion from afar that the coastlines were garrisoned and watched.

The old woman wobbled to the wicker throne and, assisted by the young girls, seated herself with a long, expressive sigh. As quickly and silently as birds, the girls hastened away, their olive skin lost in the forest and dwindling torchlight, until at a great distance, Sturm could barely see their white robes flitting among the trees like wraiths.

"What d'you bring me, Captain Duir?" the druidess asked, drawing Sturm's attention suddenly and swiftly back to the square and the light and the hideous old creature perched on the wicker throne.

"A Solamnic, Lady Ragnell," the captain announced. "A Solamnic and his companion, an elf."

"The Kagonesti are welcome among us," Ragnell announced. "Give the girl the freedom of the village."

Guardsman Oron stepped politely, even shyly, away from Mara. The elf maiden stood in the midst of the militia and milling, begging children, uncertain what to do or where to go. Questioningly, she looked at Sturm, who mouthed the simple word "Go!" Almost reluctantly, she pushed through the crowd to the edge of the firelight and the edge of village square, where she stood for a moment, then backed into the shadows.

Left alone to face the druidess, Sturm turned uneasily toward the wicker throne. What lay ahead of him was uncertain now, made cloudier still by the strange stories he had heard of the druids in these parts. Sturm hated uncertainty, and he steeled himself for whatever surprises the ancient woman had in mind.

Druidism was only a rumor to most Solamnic Knights. Existing at the pale outskirts of the other religions, it seemed purposefully to go against them all, so that druids were called "pagans" and "heretics" by the Solamnic clergy. In some parts of Ansalon, they were said to worship trees; others practiced a strange and changeable magic, one that waxed and waned with the seasons rather than the mages' moons. There were darker things the lad had heard, but standing by the village bonfire, he pushed those frightening stories to the back of his mind.

He blinked nervously at the ugly old woman—hooknosed, a livid scar snaking down her right cheek. Only the gods knew where she had earned that badge of honor, and perhaps even they didn't know the customs of druids in Lemish.

This Lady Ragnell, wrinkled and scarred, was apparently the chief druidess, whatever that meant. The village folk and the guardsmen treated her with reverence and respect, much as the Knights would treat a noblewoman, but they also listened to her opinions and followed her decrees. Now Sturm had no choice but to listen. The old woman leaned forward on the throne, her black eyes aglitter.

"Solamnics are trespassers in these parts, lad. Or didn't you know?"

"I am bound on a journey to the woods beyond you," Sturm declared in his best knightly manner. He strode forward and squared his shoulders, for the first time aware of the weeds and mud from the river fight. He wished he had the authority, the confidence of a Lord Alfred or Gunthar. His voice, new to challenge and proclamation, seemed frail and cracking in the midst of this rustic assembly.

Ragnell shrugged and folded her hands almost daintily in her lap. For a brief moment, more fleeting than a rising tongue of flame, Sturm imagined how she must have looked when she was young. She must have been striking then; perhaps she had even been beautiful. But a century had passed, and slowly she had receded into the wood around her, becoming gnarled and arboreal.

"Y'are bound nowhere, boy," she replied. There was no

unkindness in her voice, no menace. "Y'are bound nowhere but here, until we figure on . . . your *unriddling*. Until that time, there's a place for you in the roundhouse, in a room we've prepared for your visit."

"Perhaps there is better welcome for me," Sturm suggested, "at the house of Jack Derry."

The druidess blinked. "When Jack Derry left here," she replied, "the path brushed over with leaves and snow behind him. There's not a huntsman in Lemish could track him where he went, and none in my employ would want to."

Sturm swallowed uncomfortably, averting his stare from the angular face of the druidess.

"Years have passed," she maintained. "No longer do I know of Jack Derry."

Traitor! Sturm thought angrily, his face flushed and heated. He opened his mouth, but he could find no words.

"But I know your Order," Ragnell continued, "and I know history. And neither makes you a good introduction. Our country is still no friend of yours, our people no friend of the Order."

"Which does not mean that I intend you harm," Sturm replied.

"But it is more likely that you intend us harm than good," the druidess answered, leaning back in the throne and looking off into the fire, as though she divined the future or gathered the past.

"It has always been so," she continued quietly. "Your Knights have ridden across this land like a plague of winds, scattering villages and hopes in the relentless pursuit of something you call lawful and good. But there was a time, only a few years ago, when the menace of your righteousness was swept back, almost swept away."

"The Rebellion?" Sturm asked, remembering his flight through the snowy mountain pass in the care of Soren Vardis.

"The Outcrying, we call it," Ragnell answered solemnly.

"When the peoples of Lemish and Southlund and Solamnia rose against a grim, self-righteous Order."

She paused, revealing a crooked, gap-toothed smile.

"We just about broke the backs of your horsemen, too," she proclaimed. "I am Ragnell of the Sieges, you know."

"I . . . I'm afraid our history does not . . . record that name," Sturm replied, tactfully and haltingly. The old hag laughed and waved her knobby hand through the smoky air as though she brushed aside his history as well as his words.

"The Vingaard Keep fell to my forces, as did Castles Brightblade, di Caela, and Jochanan. But it's the fall of the Vingaard Keep that earned me my name."

Dumbstruck, Sturm gaped at the cackling old woman. Instinctively he reached to his belt, but his shoulder wrenched and his hand groped the air aimlessly.

Little did it matter, Sturm thought bitterly as he gathered himself and locked gazes with the woman seated before him. For after all, his sword lay broken, wrapped in a blanket on Luin's saddle. He wished for a dagger, for garrote or poison—for anything to cut short the monstrous life that sat and gloated before him.

For this was the druidess of whom Lord Stephan Peres had spoken that day in the High Clerist's Tower when he had given Sturm the shield of Angriff Brightblade. This was the woman who had laid siege to Castle Brightblade—the woman who, if the darkest prospects were indeed true, had killed his father.

* * * * *

Through the dark, muddy back streets Mara wandered, the sounds of the gathering dropping away behind her, replaced by an odd, expectant silence—by the calls of nightingales and owls and, now and again, the faint and restless sound of a horse in a stable.

She followed the sound of the neighing to a barn at the

edge of town. Luin was there, sure enough, and in the stall beside her was Acorn, tranquil with hay and home. For a moment, Mara hesitated before the animals, thoughts of escape seductive in her imaginings. Silvanost was an easy fortnight's ride from Dun Ringhill, and astride a healthy horse, she could be at the foot of the Tower of the Stars within ten days.

But there was Cyren to think of: Cyren, who had scurried away at the first sign of trouble and who no doubt roamed the nearby plains, building his web and mourning her capture and starting at noises in the night. Until she found him, she could not hope to leave.

Then there was Sturm Brightblade. He was clumsy, yes, and his fool's honor had cost her reunion and years and, back at the Vingaard River, almost her life. But a fool's honor is a kind of honor nonetheless. Whatever disaster Sturm had courted, he had done so with the best of intentions.

There in the hay-smelling stable, Mara leaned her face against the warm flank of Jack Derry's little mare. Acorn snorted drowsily, her thoughts no doubt on a well-earned sleep after a well-earned supper.

"I couldn't ride off and leave the simpleton, now, could I?" Mara asked nobody in particular, her chin resting on Acorn's back. "Someone has to stay with him and protect him. The Lemish don't take kindly to his sort, and here he is in a hostile town, under guard and . . ."

She paused. Alertly she listened, her elven ears sharp and discerning, but it was only a mouse in the loft she heard.

" . . . and weaponless," she whispered, completing her thought. "But for that there is remedy at hand!"

Swiftly the elf maiden retrieved the broken sword, still wrapped in its blanket, and set out to find the smithy.

*　*　*　*　*

Weyland the smith was large even for his trade—large and ruddy, his forearms as big around as her waist. Though he was friendly enough and mild mannered, the mere physical presence of the man was enough to daunt her, and Mara lingered in the doorway of the smithy as the prodigious blacksmith seated himself on a bench and unwrapped the sword.

"This one, is it?" he asked, his voice like the rumble of rockslides in the mountains.

" '*This* one'?" Mara asked. "D'you mean you've seen it before?"

"Indeed I have, m'lady," the smith replied, turning the gorgeous Solamnic hilt in his enormous, soot-blackened hand. "I'm good at the remembering of an heirloom blade, on account of in Dun Ringhill, we seldom pass down anything more than poverty. This one I saw . . . oh, six weeks back or so. Middle of winter, it was, when Lunitari began her approach. . . ."

"Into the same part of the sky as the white moon," Mara said. She was surprised that the smith was a stargazer. "The boy that brought it to you . . ."

"No boy, m'lady, but a full-grown bearded man," the smith corrected, still examining the sword. "From the north, he was, by the sound of him, but I'm not the kind to ask 'em their origins."

He laid the broken sword—first the blade and then the severed hilt—on the bench in front of him, a look of shrewd speculation on his face. His finger traced awkwardly over the runes that lined the blood gutter of the sword.

"Should have asked him, though," Weyland observed, "seeing as his request was so odd and all. For he wanted me to flaw this sword."

"Flaw it?" Mara asked.

"A hairline crack. A stress point in the metal," the smith replied. He raised one huge hand and gestured. He could have gone on and on, listing numerous ways he was able to render a blade defective.

Able, it seemed, but not willing. A disgusted sneer touched the corner of his lip, and he spat unceremoniously into the furnace. "Don't do that kind of work, though," he explained. "Scoundrel's work, to mar a weapon."

He looked at the blade lovingly and picked it up once more. "Barbarian's work," he said, "to mar a blade such as this. But the man was a gentleman, on a fine black horse with a mounted servant and all, so you'd think he was on procession through the country. Wanted me to ruin the sword, and flaw it so's it would break beyond reforging— shatter like porcelain into a score of pieces that never quite fit together again."

Mara nodded. "His name?" she asked.

"Oh, I couldn't tell you that, m'lady. He never gave it, nor were we even on speaking terms after I refused his business. Just rode out of town in a huff, saying he could find the man who would do the job better. I wondered then why he'd come so far south for a smith if he could find as good a one in his own parts."

Weyland squinted and examined the sword's edge.

"Don't think he did, though. My master might have done it—leastwise he, of all the smiths I know, had the skills to do so."

"Your master?" Mara asked. The confidence and assurance of the big man in front of her hinted at no master. She couldn't imagine Weyland's apprenticeship.

"Oh, yes, indeed," Weyland agreed. "Solamnic, he was, and he heard voices in the metal. But treachery was no more his practice than it is mine, and he's the only other smith I know could cause or mend what you see before you."

Mara gazed at him wonderingly, and Weyland nodded.

"Yes," he said. "I can fix this sword, m'lady, and would gladly do so."

"Thank you," Mara said quietly. Now she had to figure how to get the blade to the prisoner. With a quick bow, she backed from the room, turned and raced back toward the stable. Among the contents of her bundle, wrapped and placed upon Sturm's back for most of their journey, she had hidden a bow and arrows.

The pack lay open over two bales of hay. For the life of her, Mara could have sworn that it had been tightly bound and gathered when she had taken the sword from the stable. But the building was dark, and her duties had been rushed and urgent. No doubt she remembered cloudily, if she really remembered at all.

Whatever the case, it was open now. Spilling into the faint moonlight were her belongings: a bronze harp and three penny whistles, two robes and a pouch wherein lay her childhood collection of shells, Cyren's brooch, his ring with the green dragon seal of Family Calamon . . .

The bow was nowhere to be found. She knelt above the blanket, above her treasures and the baled hay, a rising uneasiness plaguing her thoughts.

"Is this what you're looking for, m'lady?" a rough voice asked from behind her.

Mara wheeled about. Captain Duir stood over her, holding her bow and the quiver of arrows. Beside the captain stood the enormous Guardsman Oron, a dim look of disappointment on his face.

"Oh, we are sorry to have found this arsenal," the captain proclaimed with a crooked smile. "And we are even more sorry that, bearing the trust and goodwill of the Druidess Ragnell, you have come back to retrieve your weapons. I suppose that your next intention was . . . to depart?"

"No," Mara replied, and the captain's eyes narrowed.

"Well . . . if you intended to bear arms in our gentle village, then to what purpose?"

"I . . . I . . ." Mara began, but she knew that Duir had trapped her.

"I see no choice," the captain said slowly, as Oron walked toward her, his big hand extended, "but to prepare your quarters as well in the roundhouse. The freedom of Dun Ringhill was a privilege gladly granted by herself, but you have shown to be more Solamnic than Kagonesti."

They escorted her by the smithy. Weyland filled the doorway, blocking the light of the forge behind him. He watched them take her back toward the green, toward the round-house and the cell beside that of the captured Solamnic.

Weyland shook his head, his thoughts opaque and distant. Then he turned to the forge, closing the door behind him, but not before he picked up the long blade lying on his bench, shining silver and red by the light of the fire.

Had he not been working the bellows, he might have heard yet another party pass as the night turned and the village folk retired to their circular huts and beds of straw. For outside the smithy, something scurried by, stepping lightly and carefully through a nearby alley, whirring softly like a cricket. Yet somewhere within its strange, inhuman language lay human words and human fears and mourning.

Chapter 15

What the Druidess Knew

FOR THREE DAYS, STURM SAT ALONE IN HIS VAULTED CELL.
The cubicle in which they placed him was little more than
a windowless stall. Its side walls were flush with the ceiling,
which sloped to the back of the room, where an old straw
mattress lay. The front wall was a dozen feet high, over
which he could see only ceiling and the gaping hole above
the building's central fire. By night, an occasional star
shone through the opening, and very early one morning,
Sturm thought he saw the silver edge of Solinari at its border. For the most part, the opening was featureless, though,
like the walls that surrounded him, gated and guarded by a
pair of burly militiamen.

The soldiers spoke only Lemish and regarded their Solamnic captive with suspicion. Twice daily one of them

would stick his head in the door, shove a dirty clay bowl at Sturm, then shut the door rapidly, leaving him alone with his porridge and his thoughts.

The whole Jack Derry business troubled him no end. It seemed passing strange that none of the village folk, from the druidess herself down to the cell guards, knew aught of the gardener.

More urgent than this was the question of Mara. Sturm assumed she was safe, but at night, once or twice, he thought he heard her voice from somewhere nearby. On the second night, he could have sworn he heard a thin, plaintive flute song rising from the room adjoining his.

On the third night of his captivity, he heard once more the sound of the flute. Then, as once before on the plains, he heard the old elven hymn, and clearly and mournfully the words filled the air of the lodge, riding the smoke out into the spangled night.

> *"The wind*
> *dives through the days.*
> *By season, by moon,*
> *great kingdoms arise.*
>
> *"The breath*
> *of firefly, or bird,*
> *of trees, of mankind,*
> *fades in a word.*
>
> *"Now Sleep,*
> *our oldest friend,*
> *lulls in the trees*
> *and calls*
> *us in.*
>
> *"The Age,*
> *the thousand lives*
> *of men and their stories,*

> *go to their graves.*
>
> *"But we,*
> *the people long*
> *in poem and glory,*
> *fade from the song."*

Sturm closed his eyes and listened deeply, his thoughts and senses free from all distraction. Mara had spoken of the song concealed in the silences, of the magic wrought by the white mode hidden from most ears. Could some message lie beneath the words she was singing?

He listened long and hard to the sounds and the silences and to the rests between verses. But he could uncover nothing in the quiet. "Nothing," he murmured, and he turned on his mattress of straw. "Only wishful thinking and elven poetry."

As the night progressed, the melody slipped to the back of his thoughts. A third time, in the small hours of the morning when he hovered in that strange, expectant state between sleep and waking, he heard Mara begin the song again.

And on the third time, he heard something: wishful thinking, perhaps, or poetry, but *something* nonetheless that crept into the last verses of the song.

> *"The Age,*
>   *no fear no fear*
> *the thousand lives*
> *of men and their stories*
> *go to their graves.*
>   I am here past the edge of despair.
>
> *"But we,*
>   *hear o hear*
> *the people long*
> *in poem and glory*

> *fade from the song.*
> The magic is free in the air."

In the music of those silences was sweetness and safety and an assuring sense that the dark was not bottomless.

Sturm's eyes filled with tears, and the melodies, both heard and unheard, died into the smoky night air. He sat upright on the bed. In the real silence that followed the end of the song, he strained to hear words, to gather direction or advice or encouragement. But nothing was there except the snoring of a distant guard and the crackle of the central fire.

Intent and wide awake now, he settled back on the mattress and willed himself to sleep, but it was hours before he closed his eyes. When he did, he slipped suddenly from waking to slumber as though he had fallen atop a steep and sheer battlement.

* * * * *

On the fourth morning, the door opened as usual. Sturm sat up, a little hungrier than usual after a restless night, hoping that the porridge might somehow taste better this morning. It wasn't breakfast that greeted him, though, but the Druidess Ragnell.

The old woman walked through the door, escorted by Guardsman Oron. With a swift wave of her hand, she dismissed the big man, who looked after her reluctantly as he closed the door behind her.

"You realize that you will be here for a long time," she said.

Sturm did not speak. How could he address his father's murderess? Angrily he lay back on the mattress, turning his face to the back wall.

Behind him, he heard the druidess shuffle and cough. It was hard to imagine her at the head of an army.

"And this is your greeting?" she asked. "This is that fabled Solamnic politeness?"

Sturm rolled over, regarding her from across the room with a withering stare of hatred.

"I thank you, m'lady," he replied, his politeness wintry, "but I would prefer my porridge to your presence."

The druidess smiled, and with a creaking of her ancient bones, she seated herself in front of him. From the folds of her robe, she drew a branch—of willow, perhaps, though Sturm's botany was weak, and he could scarcely tell. With a practiced, assured gesture, she traced a circle in the dirt on the floor.

"Your trespass is a deep one, child," she observed. "A deep one and dire."

"Trespass? To be brought into your presence under armed guard?"

The druidess ignored him, her eyes on the swirl of dust in the circle she had drawn. Soon, in spite of himself, Sturm found his eyes following the rapid, switching movements of the stick in her hand.

"It is trespass," she explained, "because the people of Lemish fear the Solamnic legions, their bright swords and their horses and their righteous eyes."

"Perhaps their fear is their own doing, Lady Ragnell!" Sturm shot back. "Perhaps some crime of Lemish cries out for justice! Perhaps there are abandoned castles north of here that can attest—"

"Attest to what?" the druidess interrupted, her voice calm and unwavering. Deep in her eyes, Sturm saw a flicker. Rage? Amusement? He could not tell.

"Perhaps there is one reason, Sturm Brightblade," soothed the Lady Ragnell. "Young people say so, which is why we ask them to take up the sword."

Sturm barely heard her, his eyes affixed once more to the circle of dust that was widening now, widening like the ripples on the surface of a placid pond when something is dropped in the water.

"But I am not here for policy, young man," Ragnell said.

She was chanting now, the dust rising around her. "Nor for solemnities of country or court, neither to praise nor punish, but to show only . . ."

Her voice was rising steadily into singing. Sturm heard the notes of one of the ancient modes and struggled to place it. Then, deep in the pause of the notes and the breathing, deep in the space between words, he thought he heard another melody, a song below words and thought.

"I shall show you a handful of dust," Ragnell chanted, the stick moving more and more swiftly, "A handful of dust I shall show you. . . ."

* * * * *

A snowy country, level and treeless, stretched before him, so real that he shivered to look upon it.

Throt. Something told him that these were the steppes of Throt before him. He was looking back into winter, back over months to thick ice and the turn of the year.

Once upon a time, a voice began ironically, the words insinuating into the cold wind he heard and felt. Startled, Sturm shook his head. He couldn't tell if this voice was Mara's doing or rose from the chant of the druidess.

About the time of Yule, in the goblin country, the voice went on. Now there was a village in the vision, a dozen squat huts half-buried in the snow. Smoke curled from a large central fire, and short, stocky shapes, bent and furclad, moved in and out of the shadows.

A squalid place, isolated in the winter desert of Throt. Sturm bristled at the mere sight of it, remembering stories of goblin raids, the hordes as swift and merciless as wolves.

When the Solamnic host rode out of the snow, as swift as a storm over the winter desert, Sturm was exhilarated, breathless. There were twenty Knights, perhaps twenty-five, cloaked and armored, their swords already drawn and thick, dark hides draped across the faces of their shields.

It was the sign of no quarter, the dark shields—when the

evil against them was too great, too unrepentant.

"Why are you showing me this, Ragnell?" he asked. "Are my people going to lose the struggle?"

Wait, the wind said in his ears. *Wait and attend.*

At the head of the column, a tall horseman raised his hand. Behind him, the Knights spurred their horses to a gallop, and the war cry burst from them in unison.

"Est Mithas oth Sularis!"

Like unstoppable wildfire, they rushed through the goblin encampment. The tall commander brought his sword crashing through the nearest of the snow-covered yurts, and the air exploded with the sound of fracturing wood, of tearing hides, of the shrieks of the surprised inhabitants.

At once the encampment was a shambles. Blades flickered like the wings of swarming bees, and the air was loud with the crash of metal against metal, metal against stone and bone. The goblin spears rattled harmlessly against the shields of the Knights, whose swords struck home with wild efficiency. Horses reared and plunged, and the goblins fell in waves before the onslaught.

Sturm shook his head. His hands were sweaty and clenched, and he knelt on all fours above the vision's swirling dust, his breath short and his long hair matted and dripping. For a moment, he saw only dirt and planking. He heard only the chanting of Ragnell in the vast silences of the Dun Ringhill lodge.

Then the scene returned, in sharp and brutal detail. A large, rough-looking man—Sturm recognized him as Lord Joseph Uth Matar, head of the vanished family—emerged from a yurt, two goblin younglings in tow. Filthy little creatures, they were, biting and scratching and fouling themselves in their anger and fear.

Without word or expression, Lord Joseph shoved the yammering little creatures to their knees. He spoke with them shortly, softly, laughing at their threats and curses. The audience over, a young Knight—Sturm guessed it was one of the numerous Jeoffreys—wrestled manfully with the squirming, spitting little monsters. Though his face emerged from the struggle a bit worse for wear after the scoring of their sharp nails, he managed to loop a tight new rope around their wrists and waists.

The huts burned like kindling, like dried grass. Soon the site was ablaze, the black smoke billowing in the subsiding snow. Lord Joseph stood over the goblin younglings, while his lieutenants drew what shabby salvage they could from the tents before setting them to torch.

In the middle of a dozen bonfires, three Knights gathered together over the shrieking little monsters. Lord Joseph squinted, as if he were trying to see beyond the rising smoke. In all directions he turned, now shielding his eyes, as if he were looking for something remote or irretrievably lost.

He nodded, satisfied. Quickly he mounted and muttered something at the two younger Knights, then galloped off at the head of the column. The two waited until the hoofbeats were muffled by snow and distance, until the only sound was the crackle of flame, the screaming and cursing of the young goblins.

. Then they drew their swords, and with an elegance born of years in the Barriers, of fencing school and tournament and careful, expensive instruction in the ways of the Measure, they raised the blades on high and brought them down on the little monsters in a graceful, almost beautiful arc.

Sturm lifted his eyes, startled by the imagined screams. Ragnell was staring at him, her face expressionless.

"Well, then," she said. "I've enough of . . . showing for this day, Sturm Brightblade."

She rose to her feet, and the dust slowed and settled. Heavily, as though the morning had wearied her, she trudged to the door and knocked. Oron lifted the latch and stood aside as the druidess passed by, never looking back at Sturm.

The young knight sat on the mattress, lost in thought, troubled and unsettled by what he had just seen. Mara began to sing again somewhere nearby, and her voice was clear and consoling. But Sturm's thoughts strayed at once from her singing, lost in the Oath and the Measure and the things he had just seen.

*   *   *   *   *

Weyland the smith slept in the room off the forge, the fire safely turfed and banked. At this time of year, he was grateful for the warmth, for the cold nights at the edge of spring were uncomfortable for most of the villagers.

By the early hours of the morning, his sleep became restless. He was accustomed to rising at dawn, and over the years, his body had come to anticipate sunrise, stirring and slipping in and out of wakefulness during the last watch of the night.

He thought he heard something astir in the forge—a faint scuttling sound, as though something in the furnace had shifted. He closed his eyes. Not unusual, such sounds, and especially when an uncommon draft of wind found its way down his baffled chimney, stirring the peat with which the fire was covered. Nothing out there worth stealing anyway, he told himself, and drifted back to sleep, in his drowsiness forgetting the Solamnic sword he had reforged two nights ago.

The sword hung by a cord from a nail in the wall. The work the smith had done was nearly perfect. The blade was sharp and strong and resilient, "ready for a hundred battles," as Weyland had said proudly, holding the weapon up to the afternoon sunlight. And yet from this time forth, it would be two swords: the heirloom of fifty generations of Brightblades, its lineage stretching back to Bedal Brightblade in the shadowy Age of Might; and a new sword, one to which no lineage mattered, born anew and fresh.

This night was the first adventure for the new sword. While Weyland slept, a small hairy tendril reached out and encircled the hilt. Then another and another.

Cyren had barely the strength to carry the weapon. He spun about, staggering backward over the smithy floor, the sword balanced on his back. Suspended between fear and hunger, the sword heavy in his clutches, the spider turned, teetering under the weight, and scrambled for the door to the outside.

Unfortunately, between the dark and the fear and the turning, he rushed for the bedroom door instead. The blade struck the doorframe, and wakened by the sound, Weyland sat upright, bleary-eyed and bleary-headed.

As large an eight-legged vermin as he had ever seen stared at him, wide-eyed, from across the room.

It would be hard to say who was more frightened. Smith and spider screamed together; Weyland leapt through the open window and Cyren clambered about, rattled the sword against the doorframe again, and streaked across the forge and out into the night. Racing around the side of the house, the spider collided with the hysterical smith, and the two of them, screaming louder still, careened off one another and fled into the darkness.

In the center of the village, Sturm awakened to the shriek and the outcry. The guards stirred restlessly outside the door of his cubicle, and someone called out "What's 'at?" from somewhere near the central fire. A beery, deep voice rumbled "Hush!" and the lodge was suddenly still again.

Sturm lay back and looked up through the opening in the roof of the roundhouse. The sky was bright, the clouds distinct and edged with red, as though Lunitari had passed into splendid fullness.

He had been dreaming something about Knights and swords and goblins in a dark battle, and somewhere distant martial music—not a flute this time, nor a voice, but a trumpet.

On the other side of the cubicle wall, he heard Mara muttering. Sturm smiled wearily.

"Can't even stop talking when she sleeps," he whispered.

The scene the druidess had shown Sturm puzzled and unsettled him. The burning houses, the youngling goblins, the hunt in the driving snow . . .

He lifted his eyes just in time to see a long white thread tumble down from the opening, and above it Sturm saw a hideous, segmented face with ten huge eyes.

Chapter 16

Into the Darkwoods

Cyren had come for Mara first. It had taken every bit of his bravery to scale the roof and stand above a large fire, much less to dangle silk into the midst of the village guards. His grotesque, segmented face framed by stars and moonlight, he beckoned frantically, chattering and whirring.

Mara was up the cord like a spider herself. Once, twice, she braced her feet against the concave ceiling, springing and pushing off athletically so that she swung over the lodge like an acrobat. Finally she vanished into the opening in the roof, her brown legs kicking. She peered back into the room and tossed the cord over the other side of the wall to Sturm.

Sturm rocked back on his ankles and took a deep breath.

The escape looked reckless, even foolish, but it was, after all, an escape.

Struggling hand over hand, favoring his shoulder, which had again begun to grieve him, Sturm pulled himself up the webbing until his feet balanced delicately atop the front wall of his cell. Below him, the guardsmen lay sleeping, their backs propped against the outside of his cell. A half-dozen more snored by the banked fire, and at the far entrance, two more slept standing, bowed over their spears.

Sturm smiled, a little more confident, and tied the strand of webbing about his waist. From here, it was only a short leap to the opening in the roof and out to freedom. Bracing himself against the top of the wall, he jumped out, extending his arms . . .

. . . and sailed a good three feet short.

He turned in the air, trying a last desperate grasp, and lost what little balance he had left. His feet flew above him and tangled in the webbing. Stifling a cry of panic, Sturm dropped precipitously headfirst toward the glowing, peat-covered center of the fire. The webbing brought him up a few feet short of combustion, and he swung slowly, silently, like a pendulum above the sleeping guardsmen.

The fall had jerked the breath from him. Panting, he reached up for his ankles, and on the third try, he managed to grab them. Wrestling himself to a better position, he grabbed the cord again and pulled straight up into the opening, where Mara helped him slide onto the roof.

It had seemed like an hour in the doing, and yet another to untangle him. When Sturm looked up, Mara was crouched over him, Cyren looming over her like some canopy transformed by a perverse enchanter.

"Here," the elf whispered, handing Sturm his sword. "Reforged by the very smith Jack Derry told us to find, so I'd venture the work is good."

"The smith!" Sturm hissed. "You found him, then?" Kicking the last spider's strand from his ankle, he crawled toward the edge of the roof.

"He's over by the far stables. We'll be in danger of patrols and discovery there! Why, even a barking dog . . ."

"Show me the way," Sturm demanded. "I'm bound for the smithy no matter what."

He turned to Mara, grasping her hand urgently. "Jack Derry owes me explaining."

Sturm slipped the reforged sword into his belt and slid down the roof of the roundhouse. He caught himself at its edge, where new ivy formed a green latticework down the walls to the green of the village square. Mara sighed and followed behind him, the spider clinging to her back and chattering nervously. When they both stood on solid ground, the elf maiden pointed toward the stables, and beyond them the smithy, and through the shadowy alleys of Dun Ringhill they crept, avoiding the tangling light of the moon, until they stood at the edge of the village.

Where a lone light flickered in Weyland's window.

Sturm heard the music when the smithy came into sight. Remote and insinuating, it recalled the young knight to Vertumnus, to the journey ahead of him and the awaiting challenge. He raised his cloak against the rain and motioned Mara to hang back in the shelter and shadows. In a low crouch, he crossed the last stretch of open ground to the forge. Quietly he crept to the window and, standing on tiptoe, peered inside.

Two men stood at the banked furnace, with rakes removing the peat so that the blacksmith's day could begin.

They were talking about spiders.

"As big around as my head, I tell ye!" the larger of the men exclaimed, holding forth two blackened hands, measuring the creature in question.

The other man remained silent, his back to the window. Sturm couldn't see him for the glow from the fire and the tricks of shadows, but he was strong and agile enough, and he seemed to know the uses of a rake.

"Starting at spiders," he finally said, his voice muffled by movement and the soft tugging sounds of rake over moss.

"What would that celebrated master of yours have to say about that?"

"The same your celebrated father would say," the big man replied with a curious smile, standing upright and wiping his brow. Sturm drew even closer to the window, feeling the hot air from the forge.

"Reckon what a monster like that would eat?" the big man asked, taking up his rake again and resuming work. "Well, do ye?" he pursued.

"Smith," the other man replied curtly. Sturm strained to hear more, but no more came.

"Beggin' your pardon, Jack?" the big man asked, and the other turned, his face clear now in the lantern and forge light.

"Spiders that size'll eat a smith before anything," Jack Derry teased, his expression sober and fathomless.

" 'Less it's a *gardener!*" the smith laughed, raising his rake in mock menace.

Sturm vaulted through the window, sword in hand. He clattered noisily against a workbench, then reeled into Weyland's anvil, coming to rest in a dazed, weaving crouch, his sword raised unsteadily.

It startled everyone, not the least Sturm himself, and for a breath, the three men looked at one another, their thoughts confused and racing. Then Sturm lunged toward Jack, and the forge erupted with shouts and weaponry.

Around the furnace Sturm chased Jack Derry, the gardener scooping up a pair of tongs in his flight and bursting toward the bedroom, where atop the mattress of Weyland the smith, he stood his ground, tongs waving menacingly like a cook gone suddenly mad. Steel clashed with iron, and the iron gave way, the tongs flying apart in Jack's hand.

"That blade will stand up to the best of tools," Weyland proclaimed, a peculiar note of pride in his voice. He grabbed Sturm by the back of the tunic and, with one hand, lifted him cleanly into the air. Sturm struggled like a pup in the gentle jaws of its mother, and the smith reached around him, plucking the sword from his grasp.

Jack Derry scrambled from the bed, picked up a chamber pot, and prepared to hurl it at Sturm. Weyland pushed the lad behind him and loomed as large as an ogre between the young combatants.

"That will be the end of it," he announced sternly. An amiable smile broke across Jack Derry's face, and he set down the chamber pot gently, casually, as though his intention all along had been merely to change its whereabouts.

Sturm's rage had left him. Indeed, he was glad that Weyland had plucked the blade from his hand, and he was surprised at his own sudden ungovernable anger.

Mara appeared at the window, swinging her leg over the sill and stepping inside.

"There's a door in the smithy through which I prefer my guests to enter," Weyland suggested politely, one hand still resting none too gently on Sturm's shoulder.

"I . . . I heard shouting," the elf explained, slipping her dagger back into her belt.

"It was a certain . . . difference 'twixt Master Jack and the Solamnic lad," Weyland explained. "A difference I hope they will settle afore they unsettle my premises."

Sturm broke free of Weyland's grasp and seated himself with great dignity on a footstool by the doorway. Jack squatted on the floor. Around a muscular wall of smith, Sturm glared at his erstwhile friend, who smiled back amiably, maddeningly.

Slowly Jack broke into a bright, mischievous laughter. He rose and somehow seemed much larger than Sturm remembered.

"You surprise me, Sturm Brightblade," Jack chuckled, folding his arms. "And surprises are good for the balance."

"That is '*Master* Sturm Brightblade,' gardener!" Sturm replied angrily.

Jack's smile turned brittle.

"You left 'master' and 'gardener' behind at the river," he said quietly. "You have crossed into my country, where the trees have eyes and the dance is to quite another tune."

Sturm frowned. It *was* a different man who stood before him. Gone was the gardener's bow and grovel, the simple good humor and the affable modesty.

The man before him was confident and firm and generous. He was a prince, an heir of wood and wilderness. Sturm caught a faint odor of rain and leaves, and something else undefinable and faintly familiar.

Sitting on the bench in the forge room, Jack rested his chin in his hands, regarding Sturm with the dark, bright scrutiny of a raptor. "As I was saying before you interrupted," he said, "you have surprised me."

"Where were you?" Sturm asked coldly. "I have been three days locked among druids, and the first day of spring is upon me, with no time to think or prepare. . . ."

His words trailed off under Jack Derry's even stare.

"You might recall," the gardener said, "that I cleared your trail of a few bandits back there at the Vingaard."

"But where . . ." Sturm began to ask again. Jack raised his hand.

"But there were *twelve* of them," Sturm insisted. "Perhaps more."

"Fourteen, by my count," Jack corrected. "Where were *you?*"

"But you *made* me . . . you *told* me to . . ." The words sounded frail to Sturm, and the eyes on him felt heavy, condemning.

"What is it, Sturm Brightblade?" Jack asked softly. "Why this hunt for treachery and betrayal where there's none to find? Nobody's leaving *you* at a snowy castle, your troops huddled and starved."

Sturm had no answer. He rose wearily from the low stool, teetering a little as he gained his feet. Mara moved swiftly to help him recover his balance.

"Where were you?" Sturm asked again weakly, no longer caring about the answer.

The smile crept back to Jack's face. "Why, clearing your

trail, as usual," he replied. "You have broken your prison, Sturm Brightblade, and it took skill and wit and where-withal to do it. The new season is upon us, and the woods are a bowshot away. If you will again accept my guidance, I shall lead you to Lord Wilderness."

* * * * *

Jack said no more in the presence of the smith. He ig-nored Sturm's eager questioning and paused in the doorway of the smithy, the moonlight at his back and a curious un-readable look in the shadows of his face.

"Come with me," he said. "Bring the elf if you must. Come by foot or on horse, it makes no difference. You must come with me, though. The first hour of spring approach-es."

The rain subsided as they stepped from the smithy. Cyren crouched outside the stable, wet and shivering and thor-oughly ill-tempered; Sturm wagged his sword at the spider, and the creature backed away, letting them bring out the horses to be saddled and mounted.

From there, the path into the forest was smooth, almost suspiciously so. No alarm had sounded, there had been no warning bell or crier's proclamation, and the village seemed asleep and unaware.

"You don't suppose Lord Boniface is . . . waiting in the forest, Jack?"

Jack shrugged, leaning forward in the saddle atop dura-ble little Acorn. "Like as not," he said, "Boniface is on his way back to Solamnia. If he knew you were taken to Dun Ringhill, he'd amuse himself on the road home with dire imaginings as to what a pack of druids might do to a Solam-nic prisoner."

"What *would* they have done, Jack?" Sturm asked.

Jack snorted. "Nothing, perhaps. Unless the Order paid them."

"The Order? *Paid* them?"

Jack Derry looked over his shoulder, regarding Sturm with a brief, ironic smile.

"I happened to explore the belongings of the bandit dead," he explained. "For clues, you might say, as to where they came from and who sent 'em."

"And?"

"And each of them carried Solamnic coin."

* * * * *

The Darkwoods seemed to open and receive them. In single file, they rode down the narrow forest trail just north of the town. Several yards into the forest, the lights of the village seemed to wink out, abruptly and completely, as the dense foliage engulfed the party.

Sturm drew his sword at once. The newly reforged blade caught the last white hint of moonlight over his shoulder as Solinari vanished behind a thick stand of juniper. On the blade, for the briefest of moments, a face seemed to appear—a face not his own but familiar nevertheless, as though someone had been watching through his eyes and was suddenly, unexpectedly, caught in the reflected light. Sturm shook his head and sheathed the blade again.

Jack led the way atop Acorn, a hooded lantern in his hand. A slow, stately music seemed to rise from the trees before them, and confidently the gardener urged on his little horse, who traveled the trail surefootedly, as though she had walked it numerous times before. It was all Sturm could do to keep up with Jack. Luin still moved gingerly, uncertain of her footing, and the extra burden of Mara on her back made the going even slower. Time and again Jack would stop ahead of them and hold the light aloft; through the green darkness they followed, the air about them sweet-smelling and close.

The forest was quiet and expectant. Now and again, a bird would call and another would answer, but the country around the travelers lay hushed, and even the early insects of spring were still and silent.

"Jack," Sturm whispered. The gardener reined in his mare to allow him to move alongside. "How is it that you know—"

Something in the underbrush rustled and snapped. A brown dove hurtled overhead with a soft, skidding cry of panic. At once both men reached for their swords, and suddenly, as if he had been one of the trees themselves, a green knight stood on the path ahead of them.

"Vertumnus," Sturm breathed.

"Hardly," Jack Derry hissed. "And if you've aught of your wits about you, you'll steer widely of him."

The enormous knight did not move. A visor of bright enameled ivy concealed his face, and his hauberk was woven of thick green vines instead of mail. The shield he carried was as large as the hay door of a barn, and indeed resembled just that, its thick oak boarding hammered and pegged together.

It was the weapon, though, that captured the young men's attention. A club, every bit as large as Sturm's leg, lay at rest over the big man's shoulder. If the shield was rough-hewn, the club was almost fresh from the forest, a limb still bearing the scars of its severing, the smaller branches that once were its outshoots trimmed and honed into vicious-looking spikes.

"I expect there's a better path into these woods," Jack suggested, and with a deft turn of the reins, he took Acorn off in search of it. After a nudge from Mara, Sturm followed, casting a last look back at the knight, who hadn't moved from his station on the pathway.

"I don't like it," Sturm muttered. "That man before us . . . and to refuse the challenge . . . why, according to the Measure, a Knight is supposed to accept the challenge of combat—"

"To defend the honor of the Order," the elf interrupted, wrapping her arms firmly about Sturm's waist, gripping him so hard that for a moment he lost his breath. "We all know by now, Sturm. We know what the Measure has to say regarding everything from grammar to table manners to the etiquette of swordplay. You've defended the Order against phantasms and innocent spiders and bandits so far, and I've yet to hear any of them slander things Solamnic."

"What *was* he?" Sturm asked. Jack turned to him, his face lost in leafy shadow.

" 'Tis a treant, Sturm—an old race of giants, older than the oldest vallenwood in the forest, older than the age itself. They were here when Huma was a pup, they say, and they ward the forest, protecting its greenery and secrets. Some things there are in this forest that are beyond your fathoming, or mine either."

"How do you *know* these things, Jack Derry?" Sturm asked.

Jack said nothing, but motioned them around a low-spreading vallenwood. Sturm ducked his head dutifully to pass beneath an overhanging branch, halfway hoping that Mara was too busy lecturing to avoid being knocked from the saddle. But she bobbed alertly and kept on babbling about insults and chivalry and Oath and Measure.

"Nor did I hear the man behind us speak ill of your precious Order," she said. "You're taking offense where there's none to take and reading challenges in the wind and the rain."

Her grip loosened, and she sank back into silence. But she couldn't resist a last word. Reaching up and tweaking Sturm's ear, she pulled his head back and whispered.

"Your greatest danger is always with you."

* * * * *

Skirting thick bramble until he found passage, Jack Derry guided the party onto another trail. By this time, dawn was breaking in the woods, and shafts of sunlight streaked into the shadows, dappling the forest floor with pale and various green. They found a small woodland pool, dismounted, and watered the horses.

Mara offered sleepy attendance to Cyren, who had begun to spin a web in an alder some distance away. Since they had left Dun Ringhill, the spider had seemed confident, almost brave: no longer trailing behind the party, half-hidden in leaf and branch and bramble, he had walked resolutely beside Luin, rumbling happily and mysteriously to himself.

The faint baying of dogs arose from somewhere to the west.

Sturm knelt beside Jack Derry, and the two of them bent over the water and drank deeply, each using his hand as a ladle. As the water settled back to its customary stillness, Sturm looked at their reflections, side by side, framed in a canopy of leaves.

Again he saw a sharp resemblance, then quickly cast a stone into the pool.

Jack looked up at him, water still dripping from his chin. He regarded Sturm with a bright, unwavering stare, and again the mysterious smile crept over his face.

"The sound of the dogs is the sound of a hunt, fanning out from Dun Ringhill way, as near as I can tell it. I expect that by now old Ragnell has wind of your going, and if I know her, she's sending forth the search to bring you back."

"What can we do, Jack?" Sturm asked imploringly, the Solamnic swagger gone from his voice entirely.

Jack looked at him thoughtfully, then nodded.

"I expect I can . . . see to something at the western borders, Sturm Brightblade," he said cryptically. "I can brush away our tracks with branches, scatter the scent with rosewater and gin. I can purchase an hour with craft. Perhaps two hours, or even to midday before the dogs take up your scent again."

He squinted into the woods behind them.

"Use the time wisely," he whispered.

Sturm nodded thankfully and bent to the water for another drink. When he looked up, Jack Derry was gone. The woods had swallowed the wild lad readily. Branch and leaf and blade of grass were still in the windless morning, and there was no sign of his passing.

Sturm rose to his feet and signaled to Mara.

"We'd best be off," he urged, lifting the elf maiden into the saddle and climbing up after her. "The heart of the woods is no doubt a good ride from here, and to hear Jack tell it, half of Dun Ringhill is at our heels. . . ."

His voice trailed into silence as every other sound fled the clearing. The chattering of the birds ceased, and the pond into which the two of them looked grew suddenly tranquil and clear. Sturm didn't dare to look up. He searched the reflections on the surface of the pond, the wide netting of leaves, the filtering light.

There, on the opposite shore of the pool, stood the treant, the monstrous warrior, heavy astride his enormous stallion. Slowly and resolutely he lifted his club.

Chapter 17

A Battle in the Clearing

Sturm gripped the reins, turning Luin slowly and clicking his tongue reassuringly at the unnerved little mare. He paced her along the bank of the pond for a better look at the wooden warrior, but constantly his eyes were drawn to the fastness beyond the giant, seeking out a pathway, a trail that would lead around this towering menace.

But Cyren chose the worst of times to find new courage. Suddenly, in one of those awful moments when events move past control and recall, the spider leapt from his web with a shrill, skittering cry and loped across the clearing, his ten eyes fixed on the stolid giant. Through the water he plunged, brash and disruptive, arching his back, his forelegs poised and daunting.

Cyren scrambled up the bank, sidling crabwise toward

the giant warrior. Mara cried out and urged the pony forward, but Acorn stood serenely and safely on the banks of the pond. Meanwhile, the towering knight stopped for no courtesy but raised the enormous club in pure and furious menace. With a quick, sweeping motion as indifferent as wind or the sudden movement of seasons, the weapon descended on the spider's back with the sound of wet branches breaking.

Cyren's legs buckled beneath him. Dazed, he staggered away from his terrible combat, his legs waving absently, thin strands of web scattering from his pulsing spinnerets. He spun about with a shriek, rolled on the ground in agony, and then hobbled frantically from the clearing.

Mara was out of the saddle in an instant. Racing across the branch-littered forest floor, she dodged between trees and shadows in desperate pursuit of her transformed lover. In a moment, both spider and girl had vanished, the clearing reverted to silence, and once, maybe twice, her clear voice called for him in the leafy distance.

Sturm sat back in the saddle. He drew his weapon.

"Who you are," he shouted, lifting his sword, "is no longer a concern of mine. Nor is your lineage, your country, or intent."

The knight across the water stood still in the saddle.

"For now," Sturm continued, his assurance rising, "past all word and thought, you have laid harmful hand upon a companion of mine. And though I have been uncertain, by Paladine and by Huma and by Vinas Solamnus, I am uncertain no longer!

"For I know not of woodcraft or travel, but I know the Code and Measure. And the Order of the Rose takes its Measure from deeds of wisdom and justice. And a Knight of the Rose shall see, through word and deed and sword, if it comes to sword, that no life is wasted or sacrificed in vain."

The giant said nothing but dismounted slowly, heavily. The stallion, free from its monumental rider, snorted and thrashed into the woods as again the warrior settled into a stillness, his enormous club raised on high. At the very head of the club, three long black thorns glinted menacingly in the veiled sunlight.

Sturm dismounted as well, his movements swift and businesslike. He reached over Luin's back and grappled the heavy bundle of shield and breastplate to the forest ground. Under the masked gaze of the giant, he donned the armor of his forefathers and, bowed a little by the unaccustomed weight, through the water he waded, his sword drawn. The reforged blade shone in the forest light, and surging out of the pond, Sturm extended the blade in the time-honored Solamnic salute to the looming figure before him.

It was all Sturm could do to raise his shield.

The impact of the club sent the lad to his knees, and for a moment, his senses wobbled as well. He fancied himself in the Inn of the Last Home, and the eyes of Caramon and Raistlin and his mother sparkled in the green recesses of the leaves around him. Dazed, Sturm shook his head. The eyes winked out, and the lad lifted his shield again as the second blow plummeted home.

Sliding in mud, his armor creaking and rattling, Sturm backed unsteadily toward the water, his enemy anchored firmly before him, speaking in a strange and gibbering language that was not words so much as the sighing of wind through the branches, the crackle and whisper of dried leaves.

"Failed," the giant seemed to be saying. "These miles and these years and these ventures into the hollow and poisonous dark, and you have failed, yes, beyond your worst fears and because of those fears."

The visor of its helmet fell back in its sudden movement, and beneath that visor was no face but instead a deep, featureless plane of wood and oak bark. Then, out of the gorget, the elbows and greaves snaked a dozen, then two dozen branches, twining and tangling and lashing Sturm with their switching movements in the sudden rush of growth. The crown of the tree burst forth from the crest of the helmet, which shattered with the shrill, rending sound of torn metal. Sturm leapt backward, gasping, catching his balance in ankle-deep water. The tree began to move.

"You will never defeat me," its voice said, clearly now as the warrior rose and stretched, his feet rooted fast in the soil but his forty limbs stretching and moving. "You will never defeat me because I am what the sword comes to in the last battle."

Cruelly, almost gleefully, the thing poked its club into the center of Sturm's shield, forcing him back on his heels. Its limbs creaked as it pushed and pushed again, and staggering backward, Sturm felt the water lap at his knees. The thing continued to speak, to gibber at him, but the words and finally the sounds were lost in the rush of water and his own thunderous fear.

Nervously Sturm lunged with his sword, his movements tentative and short. The first thrust struck the armor of the monster and turned aside, and with a casual flick of its club, the thing parried the next blow, and the next.

"Is it always the sword and the lance that settles things for you?" the oak creature taunted, waving the club above its head. Sturm watched, groggy with fear, as the enormous weapon blurred in the forest light, whipping through the air with the whirring of a thousand cicadas, of a hundred thousand bees.

Desperately Sturm scrambled from the water and lunged again, his movements more reckless, more unschooled. Under the flickering movement of the club his blade passed, beneath the breastplate and into the heart of the wood. Quickly, as though it had been stung, the creature cried out, its shriek like the tearing of branches, and the club flashed blindingly into the armhole of the breastplate, sharp upon flesh and muscle and bone, sending Sturm's sword end over end into the undergrowth.

White pain danced through Sturm's left hand as the black thorn lodged in his shoulder, directly in the spot where Vertumnus had wounded him at Yuletide. Stifling a cry, he dropped his shield, spun and scrambled after the blade, the oak creature's club crashing on the ground behind him, sending loud tremors through the earth. Jarred into fearful waking, the forest around them erupted with the deafening quarrels of squirrels, the loud insistent shrieks of hawk and jay.

With his right hand, Sturm clutched the handle of the weapon and turned to face his adversary. In the shadowy clearing the creature looked distant, veiled, as though it had summoned the forest to surround it. Weaving on his feet, his left hand throbbing and useless, his shoulder impaled by a broken black thorn, Sturm leveled his sword and awaited the onslaught of his enemy.

But the oak creature stood still, its weapon motionless and lifted. In the shadows, it looked like an enormous, many-armed spider, its bristling limbs unmoving now in the windless clearing. Puzzled, Sturm stepped once toward the thing as the noise of the forest around him settled and subsided. Slowly he raised the sword, his eyes on the crown and leaves of the tree. Another step he took, and then another . . .

And up through the ground surged the roots, whipping about his ankles, binding him to the spot. Then slowly the limbs approached and descended, the dry leaves shaking like a death rattle.

Sturm slashed at the roots with his sword, but right-handed, he was awkward and scarcely as strong. As one root snapped, another shot up to take its place, and Sturm's blows became more hurried, more frantic and dangerous. Panic-stricken, he raised his sword yet again and tangled it in the web of branches that had covered him. He pulled his hand away, leaving the sword in the thick, coiling branches and, pushed beyond himself by fear, tore at the enveloping roots with his bare hands.

Just as the branches and roots were about to cover him, as one green branch wrapped itself around his neck and tightened, Sturm reached desperately for the blade above him. As he felt the air and the life leaving him, his hand clutched the pommel of the sword, and with the strength that propels a drowning man, Sturm wrenched the weapon from the branches and, gasping, shouting, plunged it to the hilt in the dark heart of the treant.

The creature let forth a dry, rasping shriek, and the limbs that held and tangled Sturm shuddered for an instant. But the heart of the monster was rotten and hollow, and the branches began to tighten again, encircling Sturm's neck and chest with renewed and redoubled energy. The wound in his shoulder throbbed, his will dissolved, and his thoughts passed from fear through a great and drowning weariness and into a black and dreamless sleep.

Before he lost all consciousness, he smiled at the foolishness of it all. It is like some old wooden myth, he thought. I have come this far to be undone by a thorn in the flesh.

Then suddenly the world exploded and crackled around him, incandescent and charged with silver and green light, and he saw and felt no more. They would find him lying at the foot of the blasted tree like an ancient and unexplainable sacrifice.

* * * * *

Mara rushed blindly through the thickening forest, heedless of obstacle or danger. Three times she saw a flash of brilliant black amid the trees ahead of her, heard the clear and familiar whistle and chatter, its accents dire and urgent. Each time she turned toward the source of the sound and rushed toward it, only to find that the spider, made frantic by pain, had scurried elsewhere, leaving her alone with her deepest fears.

On she raced, her thoughts darkening as the foliage closed around her. Ahead, the cry arose again, this time shrill and different. She saw him finally, thrashing in the leaves of a sunlit clearing, a deep, tattered wound on his back. Two legs held at a grotesque, broken angle, he was screeching in pain and trying to burrow at the base of a blasted oak. Mara raced to the spider and touched him. Frantically Cyren spun about, arching his shattered back in desperate, witless self-defense.

When he saw it was Mara, something in the spider surrendered to the darker thing that had chased him for a mile through the midday forest. Slowly, as though he were trying to remember something deep in the years of a memory as old as his species, Cyren folded quietly, the leaves around them stirring as he trembled and twitched.

"Cyren," Mara said vaguely, again extending her hand toward the creature. She was no healer, no scholar, but she was woodwise and acquainted with winter, and she knew the seasons of death. Bravely fighting back tears, she draped her cloak about the thorax of the spider, unsure if such was even a comfort to his kind.

The creature looked at her in its ugly innocence, and for a moment, she almost thought she saw a more soothing face amid the fangs, pedipalpi, and the multiple eyes—the vanished face of Cyren the elf, stolen by magic from her eyes these three years and soon to be lost forever, as death approached with its cold forgetfulness.

"All will be well," Mara soothed desperately, wrapping her thin arms about the creature's savaged midsection. "Sturm will destroy that . . . that *thing* back there, and we will finish our business in the Southern Darkwoods. All will be well, Cyren Calamon, and to us the night of the moons will come."

She didn't know what else to say. She sat beneath the oak in a daze, and it was a goodly while before she noticed that the body she held was not that of a spider but of a mortally wounded elf.

"Mara," Cyren breathed, in his voice still the dry, clicking sound of the spider's call. She turned to him, her eyes widened, and a brief, momentary joy flickered in the depths of her heartbreak.

"Oh, Cyren," she marveled. "You have . . . you have *returned*. Even if—"

She stopped herself at once, deploring her grief-loosened words. But Cyren smiled and touched her face gently with his damaged hand.

"Even if only for a while? Yes, Mara. There is a certain . . . rightness in this form. There is naught I would rather be but Cyren the elf, though he lies indeed at the threshold of death."

Weeping, Mara cradled his head.

"The last cruelty," she said, "is that you are yourself again, only to die."

Cyren chuckled bitterly, his breathing wet and strained.

"Not the last cruelty, dear Mara, but the last save one. For you see, I am not myself but an enchantment cast over the creature who traveled with you these three years in its natural, accustomed form.

"I was a spider by nature, Mara, a spider at my birth and destined to die a spider, I suppose. But there have been . . . two brief times of otherness: one in Qualinost, three years back, and the other . . .

"The other is now."

Dumbstruck, Mara rested her head against the bole of the tree. The clearing reeled about her, and she struggled for her senses. Meanwhile, the elf—the spider—in her arms continued, a pitiful account of how the sorcerer Calotte had drawn him from his web in the height of a thick, black-leaved oak and imprisoned him until a time when he could work his terrible magic.

"For you see," Cyren explained, his breathing more shallow, his hair matted and dull, "the enchanter gave me this form to draw you to him. He thought that you would . . . surrender to him to free me, and then . . . well, then I should be a spider, and you . . ."

"Left with the sorcerer Calotte as husband, or cast from the people forever, to make my way *alone and unfriended in wilderness and desolation*," Mara concluded weakly, recalling the rigid words of Qualinesti law that enforced the proper behavior of maidens. "But why enchant a spider into *you?* Why not . . . make himself handsome, so that despite his rotten heart, a maiden's eye might . . . incline his way?"

"He wanted you, Mara. And he wanted you to come to the ancient, ugly Calotte, knowing full well the creature who stood before you."

"It was a plan spawned in the Abyss!" Mara muttered, her grief turning slowly to anger.

"And yet . . . it brought me a world of light and connection, no longer ending at the edge of the web, and for a while, days and time and seasons and words sprang into being."

Cyren smiled to think of it, but his eyes seemed to focus on a distant point. His voice grew faint and the words faltered.

Cyren looked at her with surpassing tenderness, and for a moment, the elf maiden recalled the green boats and messages along the River Thon-Thalas.

"Does . . . does it hurt very much, Cyren?" she asked, meeting his golden gaze. And she held him there as that gaze became glassy and distant, as his almond eyes became round, lidless, and segmented, as he died into the shape he knew best, and she was left in the shadowy clearing holding a crumpled spider, her thoughts halfway between wonderment and sorrow.

Chapter 18

Of Shadow and Light

The two of them sat on horseback overlooking the Vingaard Ford.

Eight miles south of Vingaard Keep, the ford was the most common passage from the west of Solamnia to the east. The old caravan routes crossed the river at these rocky shallows, and in the oldest Solamnic instructions of geography and survival, it was said that *all* paths to the mountains, to the castles and towers that guarded the ancient region, passed over the river at this time-honored point.

It was a dated teaching. There were a dozen fords along the Vingaard, some of them veiled, some forbidden by the Measure for reasons lost deep in the Age of Might. Nonetheless, commerce from Kalaman, Nordmaar, and Sanction still crossed the river at the Vingaard Ford, where sharp eyes at the keep stood vigil against bandits and darker things.

They must have blinked, those sharp eyes, or the climbing fog off the river and the special darkness of this moonless night must have obscured all view from the towers of the keep, for the two rode unnoticed down to the banks of the ford, the hooves of their horses wrapped in cloth and muffled.

The smaller of the men leaned forward in the saddle and sneezed, unaccustomed to the long riding and the moist night air.

"Hist!" the taller one warned, reaching for the reins of his companion's horse. "You'll call down a rain of arrows with that racket, Derek Crownguard!"

"I don't understand this, sir," Derek whispered. "Veiled missions far to the east in the middle of a cold night, the servants sworn to silence at our departure, and you've threatened me from the Wings of Habbakuk to this very spot as if we were bound for battle."

"Which we may be," Boniface replied, pushing back his hood. "Which we may be, beyond what you have reckoned."

He was more pale, more furtive than Derek had seen him before, his small eyes haunted and calculating.

It will serve me better not to argue with him, the boy thought, but he kept at it nonetheless.

"You said yourself that he was in the Darkwoods, Uncle. Rotting in a druid prison, you said. That when they tired of keeping him—"

"I know what I said!" Boniface snapped. He rose in the saddle and leaned forward, his breath hot with wine and something animal and fearful.

"But that is not enough, Derek!" he whispered. "We must be safe beyond my imagining. If he were to escape, by wildest circumstance or through some hidden skill it has taken him years and terrible danger to show . . . why, the roads must be ready for him."

"This road was made ready a fortnight back," Derek protested, knowing his words went unheard.

Boniface pushed back his hair nervously.

"But a fortnight is a year in the memories of . . . of those we employ," Boniface explained, his voice high, a little too loud.

Derek frowned and leaned away from him, combing the mist for signs of the mercenaries. It had been like this since midmorning, when Boniface had cornered him in the stables.

"Ready two horses," the Knight had growled, his eyes cold and haunted, his grip tightening on the lad's shoulder.

"As . . . as you wish, sir," Derek had replied, fumbling at once with the tack. He saddled the horses in silence, knowing by instinct that none of his questions would be answered until they were well on the road to whatever destination figured in Boniface's fevered strategies.

The gates of the tower had closed behind them and they were well into the Virkhus Hills before Lord Boniface revealed that destination. Even then, only "Vingaard Ford" had passed his lips. The rest were calls and urgings and cursings as they rode the horses briskly over the plains, through the drowned grass and the unseasonably cold air as mist rose off the flanks of the horses and the tower dipped from sight among the mountains.

Derek shivered. Spring was indeed a long way off, regardless of the calendar and the appointed turn of the season. He would have passed from unkind thoughts to grumbling had he not seen movement by the riverbank, a slight shifting of the shadows.

"Over there, sir!" he whispered, pointing to where the shadows parted from the deep fog about the river. Three squat forms approached them, hooded and crouched, gliding up the banks quickly like gnarled, stunted wraiths.

Boniface breathed deeply. By instinct, his hand moved to the hilt of his sword as the horse twitched nervously under him.

I don't like this, Derek thought, alert for more of them in the tangling mist.

Boniface raised his hand, and one of those approaching—the tallest one, the one in the middle—raised his in response. The other two hung back a moment, half lost in the thickest part of the river fog.

"Lord Grimbane, is it?" the approaching one asked. There was something dry in the voice that hinted at centuries of stone and heat. It seemed out of place in these surroundings, and Derek recoiled from it by instinct, wrestling with the reins to keep his panicking horse from galloping madly away.

Only Boniface held steady. "Grimbane" evidently was the name he had chosen.

"Not so loudly," he whispered. "You are in hostile country."

The assassin—for assassin he was, despite Boniface's softer words for the arrangement—chuckled low and cruelly.

"Is this not Solamnia?" he asked. "And are you not . . . my friend?"

"Do you know what to do?" Boniface asked curtly, raising his hood once more.

"Trust me," the assassin hissed. His hand snaked to the dagger at his belt, and to Derek that hand seemed . . . seemed *scaled*, of all things, like the back of a reptile. Behind the assassin, a cape switched and billowed unnaturally.

Surely not, Derek thought, his hand on the withers of his horse, calming the frantic animal. Surely it is some trick of the mist.

"Trust you?" Boniface asked. "Tell me what you are to do, and in the order you are to do it. *Then* we shall talk of trust. We shall talk of payment then, too—of the gold that comes to the trustworthy and the silent."

"Dam the waters upstream," the assassin began, the monotone of his voice signaling that he repeated memorized instruction. "Post the lookouts. If the occasion comes, it will be one lad—on foot or on horse, no matter—the sign on his shield a red sword against a yellow sun."

Boniface nodded. "And if the occasion comes . . . ?"

"Open the dam when the boy approaches midcurrent," the assassin intoned, shifting from foot to foot with a strange, padding sound. "Let the Vingaard Drift do the rest."

"And then?"

"Let no word pass of our doings, of our dealings," was the answer, and then in Old Solamnic, the ancient tongue surprising and corrupt on the lips of this hooded conspirator, "and dispose of my accomplices."

"Dividing the gold will be far easier," Boniface joked in the time-honored language of ceremony and song, and Derek found himself recoiling from his knightly master as well as the gnarled monstrosities with which he dealt.

What is this? the lad thought, his thickheaded arrogance sliding from him like a layer of dirt under a heavy rain. Where does your honor take you, Lord Boniface of Foghaven?

But he said nothing, and Derek Crownguard sat in the saddle as gold—half of the gold in question—passed between Knight and assassin, with the promise that the rest would follow when the boy's body was fished from the river. In silence, the squire followed his Knight up the sloping rise of the riverbank and north toward the keep, where they would shelter the rest of the night by innocent fires, talking Oath and Measure with the garrison.

"What if . . ." Derek began, but Boniface waved away the words, his arm batlike under the dark canopy of his cape.

"Who would believe them?" he asked, his voice steady and sinister. "Who among honorable folk would trust the likes of them against the word of a Knight of the Sword?"

He turned in the saddle, regarding his squire with a cold and level gaze.

"Be thankful 'tis an orphaned brat, without the uncles

and cousins sniffing the blood of every Crownguard after the deed is done. If that were the case, you'd not be clean of this, *nephew*."

He shot Derek a withering stare. "What is more, I shall trust in your silence on this matter, as you shall trust that, given circumstance and the reason to do so, I am fully capable of dealing with . . . inconvenient witnesses. Indeed, I have done so before."

His gaze became distant, abstract. Derek liked it even less.

Lord Boniface shook his head, suddenly and fiercely, as though wrestling himself away from attending to an obscure music. He rose in the saddle and blinked stupidly.

"Tomorrow we return to the Tower, to gather the last . . . contingencies."

On the plains of Solamnia, the ancient Vingaard Keep in sight, Derek Crownguard received his own instruction. And learned what would befall him if he did not follow the lessons.

* * * * *

In the early evening, Sturm awoke to music, to the touch of soft hands. Two beautiful women hovered over him, perched like tiny impossible birds in the thick branches of the oak. Red-haired and pale they were, and almond-eyed like elves, though smaller by far. Both were dressed in thin silver tunics.

"Dryads!" Sturm gasped, recalling the legends of enchantment and imprisonment. He started to his feet. Quickly and firmly, the two restrained him.

"Hist!" one whispered, pinching his lips with her delicate fingers. She smelled of mint and rosemary. "Tell the Master, Evanthe!"

Vainly Sturm tried to slip away from the dryad, but her grip tightened, as did the grip of the roots about his legs. He couldn't move. Then, awakened by his struggles, the greater pain returned, rushing over his chest and shoulder. He remembered the wound he had taken, the black thorn in his shoulder.

The pain returned, but with it came the music, tumbling from the branches like a sweet and silvery rain. Sturm looked around him for Mara, but in vain. Then softly, melodiously, the bewitching creatures at his side began to sing.

Their voices twined with the sharp descant of the flute, which sported through the words like an otter through silver water. Despite his confusion and precarious balance, Sturm found himself smiling, and he propped himself up on an elbow, searching again for the elf maiden.

Vertumnus mused at the foot of a holly not ten yards away, his leafy face uplifted, a brace of owls at his shoulder.

Sturm groped about for his sword, scattering dryads and roots and fallen leaves. The Green Man continued to play, his expression serious and unfathomable. Slipping, wincing with pain, Sturm touched the hilt of the weapon, but it didn't budge from its home in the fire-blackened heart of the tree, and his fingers slid uselessly over the shining metal.

Meanwhile, an unlikely company had joined with Lord Wilderness. From concealment in the surrounding woods, a deer emerged, then a badger. Three ravens circled about the oak and perched amid the high branches, joined incongruously by a small brown lark, and all around Sturm the branches seemed to blossom with squirrels. Finally, out of the shadows came a white lynx, who curled at Vertumnus's feet and regarded Sturm with gold, translucent eyes.

The lad tried to speak, but words and breath eluded him. The dark pain from his wound passed through him once more, and he saw and felt no more.

* * * * *

"Evanthe. Diona," Vertumnus ordered. "Untie the lad."

"And after, sir?" Evanthe asked. "Set him in the heart of this tree?"

"Water the floor of the forest with his human blood?" Diona asked eagerly.

"No more imprisonment," Vertumnus declared. "And no more death. By the turn of the night, he will have passed through both."

"You'll give him to *her*!" Diona hissed. "To that incanting hag with her roots and potions!"

"She'll *herbalize* him!" Evanthe protested. "No fun for *us* in vegetables!"

Vertumnus smiled mockingly. He held the flute in the outstretched palm of his hand and breathed over it softly. The instrument vanished, and in the face of such quiet and powerful magic, the dryads ceased their clamor.

Luin and Acorn shambled placidly into the clearing, hitched to a green covered wagon, bound to the traces by vine and woven rope. At the reins of the vehicle sat Jack Derry, his eyes intent on the lad in the tree. With a quick, respectful nod and smile, he acknowledged the presence of Vertumnus.

"Welcome back, my son," Vertumnus said. The dryads bowed to Jack, and from the smoldering branches of the oak, the lark descended, alighting on his shoulder.

"How is he, Father?" Jack asked, guiding the wagon to a place beside Vertumnus.

"Ebbing," Diona replied, her hand shifting to Sturm's neck, the white fingers gently searching for his pulse. "He has endured much and suffered the wound. His life is low and dwindling even further."

"Untangle him, Jack," Vertumnus ordered.

"As you wish, Father," Jack replied dutifully, with a theatrical wink at the dryads, who blushed and turned away. "Though I cannot see what you'll make of him. Nobility and idiocy war within him, and I'm pressed to tell you which has the upper hand."

"You move through the two worlds like water, Jack Derry," Vertumnus scolded indulgently. "You know nothing of the divided heart."

"It appears that this . . . *arboreal monster* nearly divided his heart for him," Jack observed dryly, touching the wound at Sturm's shoulder.

"The treant knows neither good intent nor evil, neither human nor elf nor ogre, neither friend nor trespasser," Vertumnus explained impatiently. "And yet it is one of us, no monster. You have known that since your infancy, Jack. It has not changed since you left."

Vertumnus said nothing more. While he watched as Jack lifted Sturm from the charred ground, he gestured idly, almost absently, and the flute reappeared in his hand.

"I suppose," Jack said, hoisting the Solamnic lad to his shoulders, "it would not be too bad having Sturm here among us. There would be much I would have to teach him, though."

Vertumnus snorted. "And much he could teach you, Jack Derry, of things formal and stately and abstruse. You've grown like a weed, boy, but five summers in the growing makes for a green tree and a green lad."

"At five years old in the court of Solamnia," Jack teased, "I would be toddling and toying and weeping at slights, like this one did, no doubt."

"He did no such things," Vertumnus said quietly. "Even at five years old."

"Even then you knew him?" Jack asked. "Then no doubt you knew this . . . celebrated father of his."

"It was another life, another country," Vertumnus replied dreamily, twirling the flute on his finger. The ravens alighted at his feet, hopping alertly and staring curiously at the bright glittering thing in the Green Man's hand. "But I knew Angriff Brightblade. Served under him in Neraka, all the way up to the siege of his castle."

"What happened to Angriff Brightblade?" Jack Derry asked. "Has the boy a prayer of finding him?"

"I don't know and I don't know," Vertumnus said, lifting the flute.

"Then why bring him among us, tugging him by his green

wound?" Jack asked in exasperation. "You've no news of his father, and—"

"But news of his father's undoing I *do* have," Vertumnus said. "Why Agion Pathwarden and the reinforcing army never reached Castle Brightblade is old history to the Solamnics, but who it was that arranged the ambush . . ."

"And you'll help Brightblade plan revenge?" Jack exclaimed.

"Nothing could be further from my intentions," Lord Wilderness replied gravely. And he lifted the flute and played and remembered.

* * * * *

As Vertumnus played, the waters stirred before him. Lost in his thoughts and memories, he recalled a distant winter, a time of arrivals, when Lady Hollis had brought him back from a murky sleep.

He had never been sure what had happened. He remembered the midnight assignation that he and Lord Boniface had kept with the bandits, remembered his shock as money and conspiracy had passed from Knight to brigand. He remembered the aftermath, being accused of betraying the Order, slipping his guard at night, and the winter and the walking. The safety of the walls dwindled behind him and the snow was a curtain ahead of him as, blindly and foolishly, he sought a path to the east, a clear road to Lemish and home.

All about, it was cold, and the snow was relentless and the wind so loud that soon he lost all bearing, all sight and reason.

He remembered the torchlight in the far encampment and how that light swelled in the darkness and snow until it seemed like a moon or a sun ahead of him, instead of the death he feared it was. He remembered stepping into that light, the ragged men on all sides of him, and the curses and the blows to his head, punctuated by the fierce vowels of his native language. He tried to answer amid the battering rain of stick and club and knotty fist, and then there had been the sudden blow to his left shoulder, the sharp black dagger of pain above the heart. The world went suddenly white, then dark. Then away.

Finally he remembered this place. He awoke with an old hag over him, singing a long restorative verse. He remembered all of those many words, for each of them, in the way she sang them, spread warmth through his extremities and breath through his paralyzed body. And with each word, age slipped from the singer's face, and she recovered a lost and incomparable beauty—almond eyes, brown skin, and dark hair shining like the winter sky.

Slowly and painfully he had begun to move—first a finger, then a hand. He clutched at the grass beneath him, plucked a blade, then another. But he was still too weak—he couldn't raise his hand. So he closed his eyes and rested, secure in the woman's song and care. He saw nothing but green, green, and he slept and dreamt of leaves and of springtime and of roots deep in the soil.

It seemed like a hundred years. It seemed like time immemorial. And yet he was here, in the Southern Darkwoods, companion of dryads and owls and of this beautiful, mysterious woman. She had given him life, had made him blossom. She had given him the flute and the knowledge of the modes.

And now there were others—others who threatened his life and his kingdom. He had come to know them all, and he had come to forgive them. But forgiveness was not surrender: The Darkwoods grew in his blood and were irrevocably his.

* * * * *

His song was over, rising through the moonlit branches of the vallenwoods. Slowly, almost lovingly, Vertumnus leaned over the lad in the bed of the wagon, whispering something to Sturm that nobody, not even the dryads, ever heard.

Years later, in the High Clerist's Tower, in the cold of a late February, those words would return to Sturm while he slept. Waking, he would not be able to call them out of the murky country of his dreams, nor would he pause too long in the recollection, for Derek would have led scores of Knights to the slaughter in the dark day before, and the morning would be a rush of arms and preparation.

But the words were simple. "You can choose," Vertumnus said. "To the last of this and anything, you can choose."

"He will live, won't he, Father?" Jack asked anxiously. Evanthe snaked her arm through his and kissed him mischievously, her small lips poised behind his ear.

"One way or the other, he will live," Vertumnus declared. "If all goes well in the Lady's care. Now sing, Evanthe. Diona, sing with your sister. While we carry the lad to Hollis, sing the song of the forest."

He turned to Jack with a sudden, wild-eyed roguishness. "You sing, too, Jack. You have your father's fine tenor voice as well as his sword hand. Or so you must, for his are on the wane."

Jack smiled and scrambled onto the driver's seat of the wagon, leaving his worries at the blackened foot of the oak. It was a fine tenor voice indeed with which he began the song. The wagon began to move, with Jack at the reins, and the dryads, each astraddle the neck of one of the horses, joined in sweetly and quietly, letting Jack carry the burden of the song.

Jack Derry sang, and his father accompanied him, the flute flashing over the notes and over the silences between notes. Had Mara been there, at once she would have recognized Vertumnus's playing for the magic it was by the elaborate technique that filled the pauses in the music, the spaces between words. The wagon departed the clearing, the foliage closed around it, and soon all was silent by the clearing and pool except for the fading singing and the brisk and imaginative sound of the flute.

In one of the silences between verses, Sturm's sword dislodged from the tree and tumbled to earth. The scar it had made in the wood healed instantly, and leaves sprouted in wonderful profusion upon its branches. When the music resumed, this time only faint and at the edge of hearing, two knots on the trunk of the tree darkened, then moistened and glistened as the treant wakened, once again opening its ageless eyes.

Chapter 19

The Dream of the Lark

Sturm slipped in and out of sleep as the wagon moved deeper into the forest. He opened his eyes to a dark green canopy and imagined it was night, that he had slept away the day in travel.

But travel to where? And from where? He could remember the events of that morning only vaguely—something about a moving tree, an armed adversary. Vertumnus was in his memory as well, and despite himself, Sturm kept returning to a recollection, cloudy and fevered, of Jack Derry driving a wicker chariot into a clearing.

Covered by green and fever and clouds, he dozed, his sleep interrupted by snatches of song from somewhere, a distant song without echoes, muted as though it rose from the heart of a lamp or a bottle.

Closing his eyes, he listened for the briefest of whiles. Fitfully, the shape of a copper spider passed over the inside of his eyelid like an afterimage following a flood of light. He thought of Cyren, then of Mara, but the thoughts tunneled back into darkness and sleep, and the afternoon passed in dreams he would never recall.

* * * * *

Suddenly the chariot bed flooded with light. Sturm blinked and gasped, tried to sit up, then tumbled back into a feverish stupor. Strong hands were moving him, of that much he was certain, and the light quickened above him, dodging through leaves and needles, and the air was immediately fresh and pine-scented.

He thought he saw Jack Derry once standing over him, but the brightness of the air was so green and excruciating that he couldn't tell for sure. Twice he overheard parts of a conversation he guessed to be between the dryads, for the voices that spoke were high and pure and musical, like the sound of crystal wind chimes.

"Dying?" one of them asked, and "Not so" the other answered.

Then he started, trying in vain to move. For leaning above him was the Druidess Ragnell, smelling of herb and peat moss, her wrinkled face a mask of riddles.

They have taken me back to Dun Ringhill, Sturm thought, fear and anger rising with the fever. But above him, the face blurred and wavered, as though he saw it reflected in disturbed waters, and when it reappeared, it was beautiful and dark and green-eyed, the face of a woman no older than forty, her black hair crowned with a waxy wreath of holly.

Sturm saw the Lady Ilys in the back of her eyes, but it was not Ilys. Though fevered, he was sure of that. "Let it begin," she whispered, and behind her, a choir of birds burst into song.

* * * * *

The tranquil pool before Sturm shivered with the slightest breeze, and the sides of the tree opened around him, forming a rustic chair of sorts in which he rested, his sleep impenetrable and calm.

Muttering, lifting their thin skirts above their knees, the nymphs danced away into the forest, leaving the wounded Solamnic with the other three. The success or failure of the Lady Hollis's doctoring was of no concern to them, the great theater of battle between Knight and treant having reached its loud and spectacular conclusion.

And they despised the Lady Hollis, the gnarled old druidess who went by the name of Ragnell back at Dun Ringhill and who had become a minor celebrity for her assaults on Solamnic castles some six years earlier. For some unexplainable reason, Lord Wilderness had taken her to bride.

Diona, never quite believing the folly of men, turned back once before they lost Vertumnus entirely behind a thick stand of blue aeterna. Setting her hand to the short evergreen, she parted the branches and peered toward the clearing. For a moment, distressingly, she thought that the druidess looked ever so much younger, that her hair was dark and her back lithe and straight.

Evanthe called for her, and the smaller nymph turned elegantly and raced into the forest, the branches of aeterna she had touched erupting in white and golden blossoms.

Of course, neither Vertumnus nor Jack Derry, who stood in the clearing above the ministering druidess, saw the ancientness of the woman in front of them. Hollis knelt gracefully over the wounded lad, her flawless features knit with concern.

"Can you save him, Mother?" Jack Derry asked, and the woman lifted her eyes.

"You've done well to bring him to me this quickly," she observed. "You have done your part well, Son. Now is your father's part, and my own."

"You have found peace from the lightning, then?" Jack asked, his voice thick with concern.

"There are times," replied the druidess, "when the law bows down to the spirit and the heart. The treant will mend and the law survive."

She smiled at Jack and returned to the lad. Over Sturm she hovered, spreading out her arms so that her cloak encircled him. "Bring forth the owl first," she whispered.

The bird blinked and hopped comically from Vertumnus's shoulder, and spreading its wings, it glided silently through the clearing to a perch in the branches above the unconscious youth.

"Now," Hollis breathed, and Vertumnus lifted the flute to his lips. Carefully at first, then more and more playfully and recklessly, he followed the song of the owl with a tune of his own, his fingers flickering over the stops of the instrument. Hollis lifted a yellow, spongy mass of lichen to the nose of the sleeping lad, and in the air above Vertumnus, a strange swirl of mist and light resolved itself into a blue sign of infinity as the first of the three dreams passed over Sturm, and the healing began.

* * * * *

He dreamt that he lay in the mist-covered branches of an oak.

Sturm breathed deeply and frowned. He looked around for Vertumnus, for Ragnell or Mara or Jack Derry. But he was alone, and even from this lofty vantage point, a good forty feet from the floor of the forest, he could see nothing but green and mist.

Dressed in green, he was, in a tunic woven of leaves and grass.

Something told him this was not the Darkwoods.

"Even more," he whispered, "something tells me I have not wakened."

Quickly he said the Eleventh and Twelfth Devotions,

those that guarded the sayer against ambush in the country of dreams, and descended the tree cautiously, his eyes on the shifting ground below. Halfway down, at a safe but uncomfortable height, he dangled from a thick, sturdy branch, then let himself go, trusting in the odd physical safety of dreams.

He was right. Buoyed by a warm wind, he floated onto dried grass and aeterna needles as though he had descended through water. To his astonishment, he was dressed once more in his hereditary armor, carrying his shield and sword.

"What is the lesson in this?" he asked aloud. For the ancient philosophers said that dreams answered questions. Quickly Sturm looked for omens—for the kingfisher that presages a rise to the Order, for the Sword or the Crown.

"Green," he concluded, sitting heavily at the foot of the oak tree. "Naught but green and green upon green."

He propped his chin in his hands, and suddenly a horse whickered from behind a thick stand of juniper. Instantly alert, his sword drawn against monster and adversary, against all stealers of dreams, Sturm moved like a wind toward the sound . . . and the branches moved past him and through him, and he did not feel them pass.

He stood at the edge of a clearing dominated by a pair of tall hewn rock towers. The walls around the daunting black stone structures formed an equilateral triangle, at each corner of which a small tower sprouted like a menacing black hive.

"Wayreth!" Sturm whispered hoarsely. "The Towers of High Sorcery!" To which, it was written, one could come only if invited.

"But why?" Sturm asked. "Why am I set in this country of wizards?"

He heard the voices then, saw Caramon and Raistlin ride out of the trees and stop unsteadily before the towers, their roan horses dancing skittishly. They were at a distance, and it was impossible to hear them, or to see the looks on their faces, for that matter. But a low, soft voice murmured in Sturm's ear, as though it read from a high romance, from a saga or ancient tale.

He whirled about and faced Lord Wilderness, who pointed back to the Tower, the twins, and continued the story.

"The fabled Towers of High Sorcery," Raistlin said in awe.

The tall stone towers resembled skeletal fingers, clawing out of the grave.

Cautiously, reluctantly, Sturm turned back to the dream scene unfolding to Vertumnus's narration. When Lord Wilderness spoke, Sturm saw Caramon and Raistlin move their mouths to the words of the Green Man.

"We could turn back now," Caramon croaked, his voice breaking.

Raistlin looked at his brother with astonishment.

Raistlin turned to Caramon. Sturm shook his head violently, struggling to clear it of cobwebs and dreams and dark, insinuating words.

For the first time since he could remember, Vertumnus continued, Raistlin saw fear in Caramon. The young conjurer felt an unusual sensation, a warmth spreading over him. He reached out and put a steady hand on his brother's trembling arm. "Do not be afraid, Caramon," Raistlin said. "I am with you."

Caramon looked at Raistlin, then laughed nervously to himself. He urged his horse forward.

Mechanically, as though guided by the words, Caramon and Raistlin turned, spoke, and then, as Vertumnus told the rest of the story, Raistlin stepped inside and vanished, leaving a shivering Caramon behind at the tower gates.

Sturm's heart went out to Caramon, alone at the edge of the mystery. In his twin's absence, half of the big warrior lay buried in shadow, and there was something unsubstantial about those broad shoulders and thick arms.

"He's . . . he's like a worn banner!" Sturm whispered, and beside him, Vertumnus resumed the story. Eventually Raistlin walked from the tower into the dreamlight, and Caramon rose to greet him. It was no longer Raistlin, but a young man twisted and submerged and broken who raised his hands, pointed his thumbs toward his approaching brother . . . and . . .

Magic coursed through his body and flamed from his hands. He watched the fire flare, billow, and engulf Caramon.

Sturm cried out and shielded his eyes. It couldn't be! Nor could it be prophecy! Raistlin and Caramon were in Solace. Nothing would send them to Wayreth, if Wayreth would even have them.

And Raistlin. Raistlin would *never* . . .

Vertumnus's hand rested on his shoulder.

"Do not be afraid, Sturm," Vertumnus whispered, clutching Sturm's arm. "I am with you. Do not hide from me."

Sturm pulled away from Lord Wilderness, whose grip became more insistent, more painful.

"Do you understand, Sturm?" Vertumnus whispered, and his breath smelled of cedar. "Do you understand now?"

Then Sturm felt himself rising. The branches parted at his ascent, and suddenly he was borne on a cool, fresh breeze into the autumn sky, where the blue sign of infinity twinkled above him, and he fell into bright, dreamless slumber.

*   *   *   *   *

"Now we send him the second dream," Hollis urged, brushing her dark hair from her dark face. "For the boy will live now. Of that I am assured. He has risen from the thickets of death, and he will live now. The ravens will decide how he does so."

The ravens had circled overhead throughout the first song and infusion, boding softly. Now the three birds settled ominously on the overhanging branches of an enormous vallenwood. As large as small dogs, they were, and they croaked their song dryly, as though reluctant to sing at all. Hollis lifted another herb, a gray lotus flower this time, to the lips of the lad, and he shivered at the touch and taste of it. For a moment, it seemed that a horned battle-axe hovered above Sturm, preparing to descend with indifference upon the guilty or innocent. In this menacing light, Sturm dreamed the second dream, caught in the ravens' music.

* * * * *

This time he was in the High Clerist's Tower, on the battlements overlooking the courtyard.

Sturm floated above the soldiers in the smoke of the campfires. For there were soldiers camped in the tower, huddled close behind the sheltering walls against winter and snow and something . . . something outside those walls, waiting.

It was all the sieges Sturm had ever imagined. He swallowed nervously and floated from fire to fire, borne on the rising smoke from the flames.

The soldiers were infantry, commoners. Some wore the badges of Uth Wistan, some of MarKenin, some of Crownguard, of all things. All wore the badges of a beaten army. They were soggy from the snow, and their eyes were dull and furtive. The Knights strode through them like herdsmen, and not a word passed between Knight and soldier.

"What is it?" Sturm called down to one of the Knights. "What has . . . has Neraka . . ."

Unhearing, the Knight turned toward him and stared through him. It was Gunthar Uth Wistan, almost unrecognizable beneath gray hair and beard.

Whatever had come to pass, the battle must have aged him ten years. Suddenly the sound fled the courtyard, carrying away the murmur of armies, the crackle of fire, the clank and clatter of readying weapons, and a familiar voice rose beside him.

Vertumnus stood on the battlements—in Brightblade armor, of all things! He was wild and disheveled, almost a leafy version of Angriff Brightblade, and Sturm started at the resemblance. Lord Wilderness pointed to the courtyard and again began to recite, his voice soft and haunted.

As he spoke, a desolate column of troops mustered by the gates. A grizzled sergeant at the head of the column looked up to the battlements, his eyes meeting Sturm's as Vertumnus recited the bleak, inevitable story.

They looked diminished, frail in their armor and swords and pikes as they assembled, stamped the cold from their feet, and fell into line behind the mounted Knights. I could single out Breca in the foremost column, standing a head taller than those around him, and once, I believe, he glanced up to where I was standing, the flatness of his eyes apparent even from a distance, even despite the shadows of the wall and the dark air of the morning. And perhaps because of that darkness, there was no expression I could see on his face, but there is an expression I remember . . .

For if an expression could be featureless, void of fear and of dread and finally of hope, containing if anything only a sort of resignation and resolve, that was Breca's expression and those of his companions, saying 'This is not what I imagined but worse than I expected,' and nothing more than that when the doomed gates opened. . . .

"Do not be afraid, Sturm," Vertumnus whispered, his eyes wheeling like moons struck from orbit. "I am with you. Do you understand, Sturm? Do you understand now?"

"I . . . I think so," Sturm said to the glittering stare of Lord Wilderness. "It is . . . that even the Oath and Measure can be betrayed by . . . by madness."

"No," Vertumnus said, his voice a whisper in Sturm's thoughts. "That's not all of it." He smiled again, this time more wickedly. "You see . . . the Oath and Measure *are* the madness!"

Vertumnus seized Sturm by the shoulders and turned him to face the assembling army below him. "Those are the ones the Measure kills," he whispered insistently as the soldiers stirred uneasily, shifting their weights and weapons. "That is the blood upon which your honor floats, those the bones upon which your Code is raised. This huge Solamnic game is always with us, as simple and poisonous as our own proud hearts!"

Spoken like a madman, Sturm thought, and he fell from the dream into an unsettling blackness. Sturm would never know how long he slept.

* * * * *

"Well enough," the druidess announced.

The afternoon had passed into evening. In the distance, the forest was loud with the call and response of nocturnal animals, and above the clearing, the first stars were shining, green in the harp of Branchala, and red Sirrion floated like a burning galleon into the vault of the sky.

Hollis looked up at Vertumnus, her face even younger than when the healing had begun. "He has survived the first two dreams. The third is easy, if he has the will and the stomach for it."

"None of them is easy, Hollis," Vertumnus replied with a curious smile. "You are not Solamnic, so the Dream of Choosing seems simpler than the others. It is actually the most painful."

In the distance, the lark lifted its voice. Hollis nodded serenely and touched Sturm's eyelids with a double-bloomed rose—one blossom red, the other as green as a leaf. Vertumnus began to play his flute, and as he did, silver Solinari drifted over the clearing, spangling the leaves of the vallenwood and of the oak, the holly in the hair of the druidess, and the green locks of Lord Wilderness.

Chapter 20

The Last of the Dreaming

The birdsong was shrill and insistent about him— jay and sparrow, the tilting sound of the robin, and loud above all the larksong that haunted his ears when he moved and the singing died.

Sturm sat up and looked around. He was where they had carted him, as best he could reconstruct from his fevered, fitful moments of waking. The pool was there, and the oak, and the grassy, sunstruck clearing, but Vertumnus and his party were all gone—no Jack Derry nor dryad nor druidess. Sturm lay alone at the foot of the oak, his armor and sword beside him, neatly arranged, so that it seemed like a husk or abandoned cocoon.

He reached over and touched the breastplate. The bronze kingfisher was unnaturally warm, green with verdigris and neglect, as though the armor had lain there for some time. Pensive, Sturm pulled the shield toward him, blinking at the dust-muted sun on its dented boss.

Suddenly someone coughed behind him. He started at the noise, spinning about.

Ragnell stood at the edge of the clearing, her dark eyes fixed on him.

"Y-You!" Sturm exclaimed, reaching for his sword. He checked himself at once. She was, after all, an old woman, and the Measure forbade—

"My intentions are peaceful," Ragnell announced. "Peaceful but instructive."

"I . . . I must have been wounded," Sturm explained as the light hurt his eyes and the clearing swam and rocked. "I must have . . . must have been . . ."

Ragnell nodded. "Seven nights," she said. "A week you have slumbered. And there were dreams, I trust. Momentous dreams of things to come, which you might call prophecy but I should call augury . . ."

Her words confused him, but her voice was slow and insinuating. It twined into Sturm's thoughts with the subtlety of weeds and overgrowth, until he wasn't sure whether he was thinking the words or she was saying them. He shook his head, trying to dislodge her voice, and when that failed, he tried to stand.

"I'm wounded still," he said, his voice dry and breathless.

"Of course you are, Sturm Brightblade," the druidess replied, her tanned and wrinkled face expressionless. "The thorn is still with you, deep in your shoulder, next to your heart." Ragnell watched him intently. "Look at your hands," she commanded.

Sturm did as she said, and he gasped at the sight. Green raced through his veins. His fingernails, too, were green. His hands were dark and leathery, like those of Lord Wilderness.

"What . . ." he began, but Ragnell's voice rose irresistibly from the back of his head, spreading over his thoughts like thick, entangling vines.

"He awoke . . ." the voice began, and the clearing dissolved in mist, leaving nothing but the woman and the shimmering water and the night. Suddenly the white moon rose behind her, its light a thin corona about her green, billowing robes, reflecting like fox fire over the surface of the pool. Sturm reeled in dismay, knowing at last that he still dreamt.

The wound in his shoulder stained his tunic green, then violet, then a deep and abiding black as the sap streamed and settled. Speechless, he looked at his hands. Instead of paling with the loss of blood or sap or whatever flowed from his shoulder, they now burned with a bright green that passed into iridescence.

Ragnell's countenance changed as she approached him steadily. From a wizened old woman, villainous and sly, she became a creature of great beauty—dark hair and dark skin and dark eyes in a dazzlement of darkness, and she smiled with such gentleness that his heart was touched. He fell to his knees, yearning to be with her, whether to be loved as a child or a man he was not sure.

This is a temptation, he thought, looking at the soft lines of her breasts through the green robes. Sent from the Green Man, it is. A trap. I am supposed to . . . to . . .

I do not know what I am supposed to do, except deny her.

The air smelled of cedar, and somewhere beyond the night and moonlight and reflections, there returned the sound of the flute.

Perhaps this is the last allurement, Sturm thought. Perhaps Vertumnus waits beyond this dream, and at last the search will be over.

The woman stopped and drew back her hand. She folded her arms upon her breasts and her lips moved, mouthing words that passed through Sturm's thoughts and imaginings. But he couldn't say that he *heard* them, nor was it Ragnell's voice that spoke them, but a deeper voice now, a voice familiar and yet just beyond the grasp of his memory.

A man's voice, it was, and it conjured something to do with snow and midnight and urgent departures.

Sturm opened his tunic and looked at the wound in his shoulder. The thorn had worked its way near his breast-bone, deep and barbed and ugly. He saw with a start that it was moving even further. It would soon sink beyond sight and retrieval into his darkest interior, where it would do its last, irreparable damage.

Ragnell leaned forward and touched the gash. Sturm cried out and pushed her hand away.

"No!" he cried out. "This forest has wounded me enough! You have done great damage—to me, to the Order, and to my father in the siege of Castle Brightblade!"

The druidess shook her head slowly and smiled. "Many were the Knights of Solamnia who fell in that . . . 'rebellion,' as you call it. But your father was a decent man and not one of the ones I killed."

"Then . . . then . . ." Sturm tried to answer, but the clearing swam away from him, and he staggered and fell to his knees.

Vaguely Ragnell clutched at the lad's tunic, but he tore himself from her grasp.

Ragnell smiled beautifully, incredulously. "Well, then," she said softly, casting her hand across the roiling waters. "If I am a temptation, let us see the terms of tempting."

At her touch, the pool stilled, and framed in the white moonlight, Sturm saw his reflection strangely transformed to a dark lad all in green, leafed and vined, his hair entangled with dew and crowned with holly and laurel.

"By Huma!" he swore. "It's Jack Derry!"

"Not Jack Derry but you," the druidess proclaimed. " 'Tis your own self translated, Sturm Brightblade. Beyond Oath and Measure, into the depths of your being."

"Another druidic dream!" Sturm replied scornfully, turning his head from the reflection.

The pool still lay in front of him, and his face was still

looking back—serene, sylvan, unchanged. He knelt before the tranquil pool, and the reflection knelt to face him.

"Does . . . does *that* lie in the depths of me?" Sturm asked.

Ragnell set her hand on his shoulder. Her reflection appeared in the water, bent and greatly ancient above his kneeling arboreal image.

"That and much more, Sturm Brightblade," she said. "A great wisdom beneath Measure and Oath. Yours is the choice, however. I can remove the thorn, or . . . I can change it to music."

"To music?"

The druidess nodded. "An inner music that will pierce and unite your divided heart like a tailor's needle, stitching it together to a wholeness past damage. The music will stay with you for the rest of your life, and it will change you utterly. Or I can remove the thorn."

She leaned forward and stirred the waters of the pool. "Either way, the choice is yours," she urged.

Sturm swallowed.

"Choose," the druidess urged. She pointed to the wound in his shoulder. While she had spoken, the thorn had worked its way still deeper into Sturm's flesh. It lay between muscle and bone now; Sturm could barely move his arm. It was green to the elbow now, and the color spread slowly upward.

" 'Twill go deeper and do deadly work," Ragnell announced. "Fear not the music. Soon, Sturm Brightblade, you will be part of the woods and the great green of midsummer."

"No!" Sturm shouted. Around him, he heard the sharp, startled shrieks of rousted birds. "Remove the thorn, Ragnell!"

"If I do," the druidess threatened, "you will never see your father." She turned away from him and walked toward the edge of the clearing.

She is lying, Sturm thought, following her. She is lying, just as Caramon and Raistlin were not at the Tower of High

Sorcery, and Vertumnus was not at the walls of the Knight's Spur. She is a dream, and she is lying, and all this reading of dreams is only foolishness, and what I should do is . . .

"Ragnell!" he shouted. Beyond her, deep in the thick blue aeterna, something scurried and rushed away. "Remove this thorn from my shoulder!"

"No." Her reply was soft, uncertain.

"I can choose," Sturm said triumphantly. The words passed through him surely and swiftly, and they were so certain that for a moment, he thought they were not his own. "To the last of this and anything," he said, "I can choose."

"So you can, Sturm Brightblade," the druidess agreed after a long pause. The flute song gave way to the lonely sound of a solitary lark, and in a moment, that music, too, had faded. "Take your sword then, and your Oath and Measure."

She turned to him, and with a strangely sorrowful look, reached to his shoulder and removed the thorn.

"The strength will return at once," she declared as all of them—thorn and druidess, pool and clearing—began to fade before the lad's astonished eyes.

"And you will never have to choose again."

* * * * *

Mara carried the body of the spider to a little knoll at the edge of the forest, where the trees gave way to grass and stone and moonlight, and where, if you looked west through the rapidly thinning foliage, you could see the village fires of Dun Ringhill.

For such a large and spindle-shanked creature, Cyren was surprisingly light. It was as though the spider's departing life had left a thin, papery husk behind it, like a broken cocoon or a locust shell.

Already his legs were dry and brittle.

Mara scarcely knew where she carried him, and even less

why she did so. Around her, the forest was loud and menacing, a dark landscape of grunts and whistles and snapping underbrush. She climbed over a felled maple, then through a thicket of briars that scratched her and clung to her clothing.

Once in a great while, there was moonlight through the branches, and Mara could look up to unobstructed sky, to the deepening violet of the heavens above her, and the neighborless stars.

It was as though the forest had turned against her, and everything in her elven blood was fearful and poised. Time and again, there were harsh, unfamiliar rumblings in the underbrush, something gobbling and wounded and angry. Then soon after would come a brief silvery outburst of a flute nearby, so beautiful and ominous she thought she had imagined the song. More than once, she longed to leave dead Cyren behind her, to rush toward the open and light and cool breezes, to scale a vallenwood and clamber to the top of the forest, where the sky would reveal itself.

Through all of this, she wept.

"Enchantments!" she muttered bitterly, tugging the creature around a squat outcropping of rocks. "It is not supposed to be this way. Princes and kings are trapped in the guise of frog or bird, or they are turned to stone or doomed to a century of sleep. The old stories lied to us, for a stone or frog or bird can become a prince as well, it seems. I was in love with Calotte's enchantments."

Suddenly the whole thing struck her as funny. Laughing bleakly, she seated herself on one of the stones, looked long into the dull, multiple eyes of the spider, and laughed until the tears fell again.

Then, by incredible chance, she caught a whiff of woodsmoke from somewhere to her right, so faint that she might well have imagined it, and again she hoisted Cyren's body, growing heavier the longer she traveled, and plodded off in the direction of the smell.

The spider hoisted over her shoulders, she scrambled up

a rise, pulling herself the last few steep yards by bracing her feet against the thin trunk of a sapling willow. Then it was light, fresh air, and the windswept clearing above the dwindling forest.

Tenderly she set the spider down. She knelt on the top of the hill and drew forth her knife. Intently, almost reverently, she began to dig a grave in the rocky soil. As she did, she sang a mourning song from the west, learned in her travels with the creature she buried.

> *"Always before, you could explain*
> *The turning darkness of the earth,*
> *And how the dark embraced the rain*
> *And gave the ferns and flowers birth.*
>
> *"Already I forget those things,*
> *And how a vein of gold survives*
> *The mining of a thousand springs,*
> *The seasons of a thousand lives.*
>
> *"Now winter is my memory,*
> *Now autumn, now the summer light—*
> *So every spring from now will be*
> *Another season into night."*

So she dug and sang the song again, until a horse nickered behind her and a shadow passed over her. Jack Derry approached and knelt beside her. Silently, with that healthy confidence she had grown to trust in their travels together, and also with an unaccustomed seriousness, the gardener drew forth his knife and joined in the digging.

By midnight, the creature had been placed solemnly in a bed of leaves, then covered over by Jack as Mara played an ancient elven air, sweet and elegiac in the purple night. She played, and slowly, incredibly, the red moon Lunitari rose from behind a stand of poplars and joined white Solinari overhead.

Astonished, Mara looked beyond the surprising intersection of the moons to the high and cloudless sky above Lemish. There the bright helix of Mishakal shone, blue and white in the earliest morning. Jack smiled.

*   *   *   *. *

It was later that morning, or a morning soon after, when Sturm awoke in the midst of the forest. Dressed in full armor, he lay beside a slow, moss-clogged brook in a strange, solitary place he had never seen. Vines and tendrils and briars grew thick about him, and all around the foliage was undisturbed, as though he had been dropped onto this spot softly from a great height.

He rubbed his eyes and rose up. It was a moment before he noticed the change in his movement, the renewed strength in his arm and the vigor in his legs. Amazed, he looked at his hands, which were ruddy and familiar, rid of the green that had haunted his veins and his dreams.

"Dreams . . ." he murmured, and felt his shoulder. The skin was smooth, unscarred, and his arm was limber, completely restored.

"Where do the dreams leave off?" he asked himself, and crashed clumsily through the thicket.

For a long morning and afternoon, Sturm Brightblade wandered the Southern Darkwoods, his apprehension rising. He remembered the words of Lord Wilderness at Yuletide: "If you fail to meet me at the appointed place, on the appointed night, your honor is forever forfeit." And so he searched for Vertumnus's trail, his eagerness tumbling into bafflement as one path after another emptied him onto the plains of Lemish, north of the smoke and the bunched huts of Dun Ringhill. Like a maze designed by a capricious forester, each trail led him back to the same spot, and each time, Sturm was surprised by his arrival, as the path issuing from the forest appeared to be different.

He spent the night at the wood's edge. The trees seemed

to recoil from his small campfire, and by morning, he discovered that his campsite had moved or the woods had receded, for he lay a good hundred yards from where he had bedded down.

Puzzled, still bleary from sleep, he approached the woods and found that the trail had vanished. Several brief sorties into the borders of the woods led him back to the same spot, and it dawned on him gradually that the forest itself was rejecting him. He could enter the woods forever, but whatever road he took would lead him back out at once.

"The first night of spring has passed," Sturm said to himself, his despair rising as yet another path into the forest led back to the campsite. "I have missed my appointment with Lord Wilderness, or squandered it in dreaming. I have dishonored my vow."

And yet he was still alive. The wound in his shoulder had not "blossomed" in some ominous, fatal way. Indeed, he examined his shoulder and found no trace of a wound—nothing except the faintest flutter of discomfort when his fingers pressed too hard against the spot.

Something told him the struggle was not over, that he would meet Lord Wilderness if he kept to the search a little longer. Shielding his eyes, he stared north and south down the thick, impenetrable border of trees and briars, then turned toward Dun Ringhill.

"Of all the places I have been," he whispered, shouldering his sword like an infantryman's pike, "I expect I am least welcome in that village, but surely the secret lies there."

Chapter 21

The Turning Away

LONG BEFORE HE REACHED THE OUTSKIRTS OF THE VILLAGE, Sturm lost the smoke and flickering light he had seen from the north. He tried to steer himself by memory, hoped desperately for Vertumnus's guiding music, but the edge of the forest was featureless, and the only sounds were the occasional calls of the birds. Just when he thought he would never find Dun Ringhill, he stepped over a rise onto its very outskirts.

The place was grotesquely changed, as though something unnamed and large had taken terrible revenge on its outskirts. Hut and hovel tilted crazily, pushed from their foundations by vines, by sprouting trees, and by the constant pressure of encroaching undergrowth. It was green in Dun Ringhill, green to the very rooftops.

Sturm wandered through the jungle of foliage and houses, the fierce buzz of insects in his ears, his sense of smell distracted by the sharp perfume of evergreens, the attar of flowers. From east to west, the greenery had spread, or so it seemed, and the huge central lodge was covered with vines and lifted neatly from its foundations by the great, spreading roots of a two-hundred-foot hackberry.

Sturm weaved through the alleys and side streets quietly, his sword bare as he made his way in a roundabout path toward Weyland's smithy. Across the overgrown village green he raced, west through a spontaneous surge of grapevines and gourds toward the edge of town where, if his senses had not completely betrayed him, the smithy and the stables lay side by side. His armor clattered through the ivied alleyways, and his hope alternated with fear of discovery.

The streets around Weyland's establishment were silent and empty. It was as though this part of the village had been abandoned, or the villagers had drawn away for an hour because something momentous and private was happening near the forge and the stables. Though the villagers were distant, their things were near: Daggers, torques, awls, and spindles littered the village green, and more than once Sturm stepped on broken crockery, which crunched beneath his boots like the exoskeletons of enormous insects. A bronze mirror leaned crazily against the door of a house, its surface obscured by verdigris. Not far from it, strangely untouched by all this growth and decay and abandonment, lay a golden veil, its edges embroidered with green roses. Sturm knelt and picked up the garment, holding it sadly up to the sunlight.

He tossed it into the air. The garment rocked in the breeze, billowed and settled on the windowsill of an abandoned cottage. At that very moment, the ring of hammer against anvil sounded through the edge of the village.

Sturm broke into a run, his hopes racing wildly. Of any man in the village, Weyland would know the way to Jack

Derry. And Jack would know the way to Vertumnus.

The doors to the stable stood wide open, and though the horse neighed and snorted from the warm, pungent dark, in the window of the smithy was movement and light and an even more welcome noise as a man passed back and forth before the forge, singing softly to himself.

Without hesitating, Sturm paced toward the smithy door and opened it.

Vertumnus stood before him, holding tongs and hammer, smiling expectantly.

He set down his tools and wiped his hands with a rough canvas cloth, while Sturm stood in the doorway, bathed by the forge's heat and struggling with his memory.

Sturm dropped his sword in astonishment. Suddenly it became almost clear. The dreams and choices seemed to make a dark sense, though Sturm was still hard put to explain them. He started to speak, to assail Vertumnus with a hundred questions, but Lord Wilderness paused and raised his hand for silence.

"You look wayworn and weariful," he observed, "and I'd be a poor host without offering you bread and drink."

"No, thank you. I mean, yes. Yes, bread would be good. And water."

Vertumnus stepped toward the back door and the well, ladle in hand. Sturm followed aimlessly, bumping clumsily against the anvil.

"It's a green lad you are, Solamnic," the Green Man said merrily, brushing by Sturm on his way to the pantry and the bread. "Green and stubborn, though there is remedy for both, nor is either altogether bad. Your greenness has kept you from corruption and compromise, and your stubbornness brought you this far."

"It brought me to failure," Sturm said angrily, "for the first day of spring has come and gone. You eluded me, Vertumnus, and you win on technicalities!"

" 'Tis the Solamnic in you that whines at technicalities," Vertumnus replied merrily. "I recall that I said if you did not meet me at the appointed time, your honor would be forever forfeit."

Sturm nodded angrily, seating himself clumsily on the smithy bench and accepting the bread and brimming ladle.

" 'Twas the fault of that druidess," Sturm maintained. "Ragnell imprisoned me for three days and made me sleep for a week after that, else I'd have met you in plenty of time."

Vertumnus seated himself on the floor. "You were safe in that imprisonment. You were followed by a relentless enemy, and when the Lady took you into custody . . . he gave up pursuit."

Sturm sniffed angrily. Again this story of conspiracy and Boniface.

"Well?" Vertumnus asked, folding his hands in his lap. He looked like an ancient eastern statue, a symbol of distant serenity. "Well? Do you feel the wound? The loss? The forfeiture?"

"I . . . I don't understand," Sturm protested.

"I would imagine," Vertumnus persisted, "that your honor is still there, unless you're bound to lose it over a calendar. . . . Oh," he declared, as if he had remembered something suddenly. "I've a gift for you."

Vertumnus rose to his feet and hopped to the smithy shelves, stood on a chair, and brought down a long object wrapped in canvas cloth. Slowly, proudly, he unwrapped the thing and held it before Sturm.

It was a sheath for a sword, the work on its surface intricate and flawless. A dozen faces stared at Sturm, embossed in gleaming silver. Like reflections in a dozen mirrors they were, or like the statuary in Castle di Caela, miles and years away. Each face shared his eyes and expression, and each was bordered in copper leaves and roses intertwined, red and green, so that it seemed on fire—a dozen suns, or sunflowers, or burgeoning plants.

"It's . . . it's magnificent, sir," Sturm said quietly, his manners overcoming his perplexity. He admired the sheath from a distance, almost afraid to touch it. Absently he sat on the anvil, squinting to regard the skill of the craftsman. "I trust it could only be Weyland's work."

"The work of his master," Vertumnus said quietly. "No man alive could do the likes of it, if I do say so." Quietly he crouched by the open forge.

"These amenities, Lord Vertumnus, are most welcome to the traveler," Sturm announced in his most formal and measured manner, turning the scabbard in his hand. "And doubtless they are testament to your honor and breeding, as is this wonderful gift."

Muffled laughter came from the corner of the smithy, where Vertumnus crouched in violet shadow and yellow light, laying peat upon the glowing coals of the forge.

Sturm cleared his throat and plunged on. "But I recall an agreement between the two of us, sealed at a Yuletide banquet. 'Meet me on the first day of spring,' you said, in my stronghold amid the Southern Darkwoods. Come there alone, and we shall settle this—sword to sword, knight to knight, man to man.' You told me I had to defend my father's honor, and you challenged mine."

Vertumnus nodded, his obscure smile fading into a sharp and rigid solemnity.

"So we turn to the business," he whispered. Laying the last square of turf on the fire, he stood to his full, imposing height—a head taller than the lad in front of him.

Sturm gasped. He hadn't remembered the Green Man this tall, this imposing.

"Those were not *all* the words that passed between us," he insisted. "You Solamnics, with your passion for rules and contracts, should remember the whole brittle world of what was said and the very words that said it."

"But I do remember," Sturm replied. " 'For now I owe you a stroke,' you said, 'as you owe me a life.' "

"Then our memories agree," Vertumnus murmured. "Follow me into the smithy yard. There we shall satisfy the terms of this agreement."

Sturm set down the scabbard and stepped from the smithy into the afternoon light. Vertumnus waited for him by the well amid a litter of leaves, flawed artifacts, and half-finished ornaments. At once, a low music rose from the earth around them, and Sturm held his naked sword to the fore with a nervous and intent readiness.

"Arm yourself, Lord Vertumnus!" he challenged, his teeth clenched.

Lazily, catlike, Vertumnus leaned against the stones of the well.

And then, in a blurred and blinding instant, he seized Sturm, his green hand closing over the lad's sword hand with irresistible strength.

"Sword to sword," he muttered, and tightened his grip.

Sturm winced. A sensation—overpowering, almost electrical—coursed through his sword arm. Sturm tried to cry out, to release the blade, but the power was binding, riveting and relentless. In shock, he looked at Vertumnus, who returned his stare with a gaze that was wild and gleeful and yet surprisingly kind. From the lad's heart arose a tremendous sense of sweetness, and around him was music, the flute and the timbrel and the elven cello and somewhere, rising in the midst of these, the faint, crisp call of a trumpet he would hear again and again until that day on the battlements of the Tower, when the Dragonlord approached in the distance and he stood atop the Knight's Spur and heard the song one last time, finally understanding what it meant. . . .

He knelt on the ground amid plowshares and horseshoes and bent swords. Vertumnus stood over him, the sword bright in his hand.

"Knight to knight, and man to man," Lord Wilderness concluded quietly.

Sturm could not look at his victorious opponent. Slowly, abjectly, he crept toward Lord Wilderness.

"The terms are nearly met," the lad said, fearful and beaten. "You may give me the stroke that is my due and take the life owed you."

Kneeling before Vertumnus, Sturm wrestled down his terror. He murmured the Solamnic funeral song in bleak preparedness for the falling sword. . . .

Which touched his left shoulder, then his right, with a stroke that was light and affectionate and playful.

"Arise, Sir Sturm Brightblade, Knight of the Forest," Lord Wilderness chuckled.

In consternation and anger, Sturm glared up at his opponent . . .

Who had mocked him and dismissed his honor and taken his weapon . . .

Who had wrenched the Measure even from chivalrous death . . .

"The life you owe me, lad," Vertumnus said, "is the one you would spend in swordplay and vengeance."

Sturm stared at him, dumbstruck and questioning.

"My son has told you of . . . Lord Boniface Crownguard?" Lord Wilderness began. "And you have seen his handiwork before you on the road to the Darkwoods?"

"I—I cannot say that road has been easy, Lord Vertumnus," Sturm replied haltingly. "But I cannot believe it was Lord Boniface's doing."

"Think!" Vertumnus urged angrily. "Bandits and assassins paid in Solamnic coin from here to the Clerist's Tower, a gauntlet of misfortunes and accidents, the one gift you received from Boniface purposefully flawed . . . Simple *mathematics* could tell you the answer if your Oath and Measure weren't blinding you to the truth!"

"But why?" Sturm asked. "If Lord Boniface Crownguard is capable of such treachery, why waste it on the likes of me?"

"Why?" Vertumnus asked, and suddenly music filled the littered yard, as though somehow the wind passed over the flute at his belt, drawing song out of it. "Listen, and look to the reforged blade of your sword . . ."

He could not help but look, and in the heart of the blade,

Sturm saw a snowy landscape, the metal swirling from silver to white. Sturm squinted and looked closer. . . .

A sinister, shadowy company of men, cloaked and hooded against the driving snow, assembled at a remote pass. At the head of the column, a man was seated on horseback, his hood tilted back despite the weather. Bearded and scarred he was, as if he were carved from rubble and dried branches.

The man was deep in conversation with another, elegantly dressed in Solamnic armor. The Knight had come with scant escort: another Knight, it seemed, and three foot soldiers. His armor beaded with melted snow, the Knight in command slipped a scroll into the rugged man's knotted hand and pointed through the boiling frozen air to a dark passage between rockfaces.

"Through that pass they will come," he said.

Sturm knew the voice. He started to shout, but the music surged about him and silenced him.

"The standard will be that of Agion Pathwarden," the man said. "Red centaur against a black mountain."

The rough man huddled more tightly in his cloak. "And for this such a generous payment, Lord . . ."

"Grimbane," the man replied. "You know me only as Lord Grimbane."

"Illusion!" Sturm shouted, wrenching his eyes from the vision. Vertumnus sat atop the anvil, regarding him curiously and a little sadly. "It . . . it *must* be illusion! It *must* . . ."

"But if it is not . . ."

"I shall wreak such revenge that . . ." Sturm began.

"No." Vertumnus slipped gracefully from the anvil. In two long strides, he was beside Sturm, hand clasped tightly on the lad's shoulder.

Sturm gasped. The pain was gone . . . the wound . . .

"No," Vertumnus repeated. "It is no illusion. For I was the other Knight, Sturm Brightblade. I rode in the snow to that remote pass, where scroll and payment were handed over to the brigands. Along with the infantrymen who accompanied us. And when Agion fell and the castle was doomed, I was the one that Boniface blamed."

Dumbstruck, Sturm dropped the sword. Blinded by tears and anger, he groped for the blade on the smithy grounds, while Lord Wilderness continued serenely.

"I followed him into the mountains and the driving snow, buoyed by my love for the Measure, my delight in the honor Lord Boniface had conferred upon me by asking me to accompany him. The love and delight changed to loathing and rage when I watched him conspire, watched the money pass from Knight to bandit.

"But there was nothing I could say. I returned to Castle Brightblade, where Boniface, doubling over his tracks like an old fox in the snow, used the Code and the Measure and the whole damnable Solamnic machinery to convict *me* of *his* treachery. When I left the ranks and wandered into the risking snow, I knew nothing of Hollis and the change that awaited me. I thought I walked toward death, toward a slow fading into ice and slumber, but I preferred such a death to that exacted by the Order—to the shedding of my blood and my joy beneath the nails of a bloodless, joyless company.

"But I have not brought you this far for a bloodletting. Solamnic revenge is a nasty, entangled thing, as hot and poisonous as spiders coupling. And no to your Oath and Measure, too, and the pride your Order derives from them. For the Measure may be revenge by rules, but still it is revenge, still intricate and vicious."

"Then . . . then *what?*" Sturm almost shouted.

Vertumnus crouched beside the lad.

"Stay in the Darkwoods," he said. "Forgive Boniface . . . the Order . . . your father . . . the lot of them. Forgive them and leave them behind you. Forgive them."

"But there is the Oath and Measure!" Sturm insisted. "A thousand years of law—"

"Have done no good!" Vertumnus interrupted vehemently. "They have made monsters of the Crownguards and the

Jeoffreys, have slaughtered nameless thousands, have cost you a father and wounded you past hope, past recovery, unless . . ."

Fearfully, angrily, the lad scrambled away from the man in front of him, striking his shoulder against the stones of the well. Tripping over a discarded andiron, he lurched to his feet at last, his eyes clenched in pain and desolation and anger, his knuckles white on the hilt of the sword.

Blasphemy. I shall not have it. By Huma and Vinas Solamnus and Paladine himself, I shall not have it!

"My father is the Order now!" Sturm cried out, his voice thin and anguished in the silent yard. "My family is the Order! Go back to your woods and leave me alone!"

*   *   *   *   *

He awoke lying on the anvil, the scabbard in his hands. All about him, the smithy had vanished, and with it the stable. A solitary Luin grazed peacefully amid a nearby vine-covered orchard, and Lord Vertumnus was nowhere to be seen.

The music had stopped. In one direction, then another, Sturm moved, circling about the anvil and facing in all directions, hoping the song would resume, would guide him to Vertumnus. But the whole village was silent—thickly, oppressively quiet.

Luin raised her head and whinnied, but Sturm heard nothing.

He looked above, and the wind was diving silently through the trees. The leaves rustled noiselessly, and overhead a flock of geese moved quickly south in their seasonal migration toward the cooler regions, their wingbeats and cries inaudible.

"What?" Sturm asked aloud, starved for a sound, even that of his own voice. He shouted again, and again a third time.

It was the only sound in creation, and it shivered before it lost itself in the deep and abiding silence around it. Then out of the silence came the dull, regular sound of a drum in the distance. Sturm strained to listen, to follow the sound, but wherever he turned, it was equally faint, and wherever he moved—toward Luin, toward the anvil, back toward the center of town—the sound was unchanging, muffled.

He was in the village green before he recognized it as the sound of his own measured heart. He stopped and drew the sword. In the quiet around him, he heard the scuttle of leaves, a high wind sighing in the branches. . . .

And at once, unexplainable by all of his rules and codes and instructions, he knew that he would never again find the Green Man.

*   *   *   *   *

Vertumnus leaned back in the low notch of the vallenwood limbs, staring intently at the clouded surface of the forest pool below him. At the foot of the tree sat the Lady Hollis, and beside her was their son, Jack Derry.

Weyland the smith crouched nearby amid a dozen of his fellow villagers, his beefy hands involved in an intricate weaving of copper and silver wire. What he was making was not apparent yet, not even to the most clever in that circle, but all watched eagerly, awaiting whatever amazement his touch would reveal in the metal.

They had gathered there, all of them, at the summons of the druidess, eager for news of Lord Wilderness as the morning waxed to a bright midday. Rumors circulated among the villagers: that war was brewing with Solamnia, that Lord Wilderness had been seized by a band of Silvanesti elves, that he had ridden alone to the north, seeking vengeance for some incomprehensible injury. Finally they heard the music carried on a crisp wind from the direction of the town, and they knew he was nearby and would be with them soon.

In late morning, the music had stopped, and Captain

Duir, posted at the outskirts of the woods, was the first to see Vertumnus approaching, downcast and walking slowly, the leaves in his clothing and hair sere and yellow.

Vertumnus told them nothing, nodding abstractly when Jack Derry introduced him to the elf maiden Mara. He ignored the consolations of the Lady Hollis and the bickering of the dryads and climbed to the spot where he now was seated and lost himself in deep meditation.

After a while, the villagers forgot about Lord Wilderness and returned to their various forest tasks, to the gathering of comfrey and foxglove, to the hunt and to fishing in the large brook that ran through the depths of the woods. Mara continued to watch him, to puzzle at his absence and unhappy demeanor. At last she asked Lady Hollis if the meeting with Sturm had taken place.

The druidess nodded, intent on steeping a yarrow tea which Mara's years as a maidservant in Silvanost told her was a cure for melancholia. "Indeed it has," Lady Hollis maintained.

"Then I expect from the look about Lord Wilderness," Mara said, "that young Sturm has bested him."

Hollis looked above, where Lord Wilderness leaned forward in a silent stateliness, his dark eyes troubled.

"*I* expect from the look about him," the druidess replied, "that young Sturm has bested himself."

It was hours before Vertumnus spoke. The day had passed into late afternoon, and the larks were already nested. All about the company, the forest was alive with the quarrels of squirrels and the high, skidding sounds of brown doves returning south to roost in the branches of elm and maple.

"He has departed now," Vertumnus announced. Instantly two hundred pairs of eyes fixed on the limb of the vallenwood where he sat, the yellow leaves falling sadly from his beard and tunic. "Back toward the Vingaard, and no doubt on toward the Tower and the rest of his ponderous Order."

"Where you might have gone yourself," Hollis observed,

"were it not for the good fortune of a winter's night."

Vertumnus smiled down at her. "And the kindness of the forces who besieged Lord Angriff's castle."

Hollis smiled, handing a steaming cup of yarrow tea up to her perched and leafy husband.

Vertumnus looked fondly at Jack Derry below him, still marveling at the rapid maturing of his and the Lady Hollis's sapling son. After all, to be but five years old and grown to maturity, with a fighter's arm and a ranger's eye and . . .

And an interest in a certain recently bereaved elf maiden.

Vertumnus smiled, then frowned. There were other things to see to, and some of them were pressing close at hand.

"I understand," Lord Wilderness announced, "that Mara the elf is skilled in the knowledge of the flute and some of the ancient modes."

Mara blushed, but Hollis laid a reassuring hand on her shoulder.

"I—I have learned a few tunes in my time, Lord Wilderness," she said, her eyes on the leaf-strewn floor of the forest.

"Well and good," Vertumnus said. "And I understand it was love and invention that led you to them."

"I was greatly deceived when I learned them," Mara said bitterly, lifting her face to the Green Man.

"Deceived, perhaps," he agreed, "but not greatly. Love and invention outlast the best of our dreams."

Mara frowned. She had passed, it seemed, from incomprehensible Solamnic rules into this world of leaf and shadow and parable. There was no telling what would come next.

"What do you ask of me? Of my playing?" she questioned.

"Accompaniment," Vertumnus replied, and from the branches of a nearby maple came a vicious, rousing hiss. The dryads poked their heads from behind a cluster of leaves, their little eyes glittering with anger.

"It's not enough," Diona said, "to hitch your wagon to this hag of a druid!"

"You're taking in elves now!" accused Evanthe. "For what sinister purpose, the gods only know."

"Begone with the both of you!" Vertumnus laughed, tossing the teacup at them. He sprang from the vallenwood branch and landed lightly on the ground, scattering a flock of doves. "Else I'll shut you back in the trees where I found you!"

"We don't scare easily!" spat Evanthe, dripping with the lukewarm dregs of the yarrow tea. "You showed your softness when you wouldn't kill that Solamnic or . . . or . . . *ensorcel* him!"

"But you know of no softness in me," Hollis declared flatly. She folded her arms and smiled fiercely at the dryads. "I am the sacker of villages, the razer of castles. And I can ensorcel as well as any."

The dryads cried out as the maple limb upon which they sat burst forth with thick sweet sap. Chagrined and syruped, they made their escape, leaping from branch to branch, leaf and dirt adhering to their sticky garments as they rushed off into the depth of the woods. A wave of laughter followed their departure.

"Would that I had the magic that young Sturm needed," Hollis said, a little more soberly.

"He could choose whether or not to let the thorn be changed to music, and change him in turn," Vertumnus said. "He chose instead to have you remove it, to stay as he was. He chose his sword arm and the Order."

"But the wound will always be with him," Ragnell insisted. "Though the time will come when he does not remember it, the wound will always be there."

"To the last of this and anything," Vertumnus said, drawing forth his flute, "the lad could and can choose. But there is one thing remaining that demands my hand, my *ensorceling* . . ."

Vertumnus scowled, and Jack Derry laughed at his father's dramatics.

"My love and invention," the Green Man concluded quietly, his eyes on Mara. "For there is an ambush prepared at the Vingaard Ford. I must protect the lad from an old blood feud, from the burden of his father's quarrel on the shoulders of the son. And for this, I need the accompaniment of another flute, another music."

Mara bowed nervously. "It would be my honor to assist you, sir. And my honor," she added quickly, "to assist Sturm Brightblade."

Vertumnus nodded happily. It was the best of answers. And briefly he instructed the elf in the strange duet. She would play an old Qualinesti winter song, bracing it with the silent music of the tenth mode, the Matherian—the music of meditation and thought, for only a mind resolved and intent could bring about what Lord Wilderness had planned.

He, in turn, would play a song from the Icewall sung by the barbarous Thanoi, and behind it he would place the intricate dazzlements of the fourteenth and highest mode—the mode of Paladine and changes. And then, when four melodies were rising from the two flutes and the two players, well . . .

Then the changes would come, and winter would return to the Solamnic Plain.

Vertumnus smiled. He would see what he would see.

Chapter 22

At the Ford of the Vingaard

THERE WERE ELEVEN OF THEM NOW, WHERE AT FIRST there had only been three. Crouched by a fire at the banks of the Vingaard they waited, assured by the Solamnics that the lad would soon pass.

There was always safety in numbers. Sturm would be alone.

Tivok, the leader of the band, bundled himself against the brisk spring night. The other eight had joined them without warning, their scales blue and their tails twitching slowly in winter lethargy. He had prepared to undertake the murder with only two henchmen and had devised a clever plan that would see to it that the henchmen did the fighting.

Then the eight surprised him, walking into the campsite after a three-day journey from southern climes, and suddenly the plans had changed.

But that was the way in these times: there were more of his kind—the draconians, born of dragon eggs perverted by a dark and unnamed power—more than Tivok had ever imagined there would be, and he had heard talk that even greater numbers—some of them wielders of magic, some shape-shifters—were traveling north from the hatcheries of the Icewall.

Let that be as it is, the chief assassin thought, turning his lidless eyes to the cloudy sky. None of them need know the *amount* of gold that the Solamnics placed in my hand. Ten swords will do the work with certainty, where two would have been . . . more risky. I shall stay on this hill overlooking the ford until the tenth night after the first of spring, like the Solamnic said.

And I shall oversee. Yes, I shall oversee.

And the bounty, if the lad comes? I will keep my half, and divide the rest ten ways instead of two.

He laughed to himself at the shrewd economics, his laughter the sound of wind over dry leaves. If only this infernal cold would pass, if spring would come beyond the signs of the stars and calendars . . .

*   *   *   *   *

The Solamnics had said that the quarry would come, if he came at all, within the ten days following the equinox. He would be equipped with ancient Solamnic armor, more ornamental than functional. His breastplate would be adorned with an ancient family crest: red sword against the yellow sun.

The lad would be tired, they had said. Perhaps defeated, certainly vulnerable.

The assassins had killed three travelers already, unfortunates who had fit the description, or part of it, or were just ill-fated and alone at the edge of the Vingaard Ford. They had rushed from a thick stand of juniper and pulled the first one from his horse. The weather had been warmer then, and the task was easy.

He was nondescript, that first doomed wayfarer, a thin, gap-toothed boy from the southeast who spoke his last words in Lemish when the barbed swords entered him.

The second had been older, though from a distance, his posture and movements were crisp and forceful and altogether young. Tivok had given the signal to the four upriver, waiting at the makeshift dam, on the off chance that the traveler would elude the first ambush.

It took all six of his remaining henchmen to overcome the old rascal, who fought and kicked until the end, wounding two of them in the process. Ever the tactician, Tivok moved the wounded to posts by the dam, replacing them with fresh fighters.

From Tivok's vantage point, he couldn't tell the third traveler was female, especially since she was bundled against the rapidly falling temperature. She, too, had fought bravely, and she had the advantage of the weather. Indeed, one of the assassins fell to a deft thrust of her sword, but the blade had lodged in him when his body turned to stone, as his kind always did, and her tight grip on the weapon had unhorsed her.

The other five milled over her like enormous brazen flies, their dark wings flickering.

"How long will we waste our time in bad weather?" one of them asked Tivok as they buried the girl's body in a shallow grave by the riverbank.

"Yet a while," Tivok hissed, brushing back his hood to reveal his sloped and crested forehead, his copper scales. "Yet a while still." Setting his shoulder to his slain comrade, he pushed over the hulking stone figure so that to those approaching, the dead assassin would look like a boulder, an innocent brown outcropping of rock.

"Count it as . . . practice, Nashif," Tivok suggested to the questioner, a hint of warning in his voice. "Count it as maneuvers."

Nashif had no answer. Silently the five assassins slipped into the shadows among the evergreens, two of them stopping to lick their blades.

*   *   *   *   *

Sturm was scarcely two miles from the ford as they were burying the girl. He rode atop a rested and strangely unsettled Luin, his cloak wrapped tightly about him against the surprising return of winter.

Already he was forgetting his last encounter with Lord Wilderness.

His final time in Dun Ringhill had been brief. He had wandered the overgrown ruins, looking for more signs of Ragnell, of Mara or Jack Derry, or even of Vertumnus, but the place was desolate, the foliage so thick that he could have sworn it had been abandoned seventy years instead of seven days.

The loss of Mara troubled him the most. Somehow it seemed against the Measure to leave without knowing what had happened to her. And yet in the course of his strange and healing dreams, he thought he had seen her face, seen her move among the throng of villagers that he glimpsed in his fevered and wakeful moments.

Something assured him that Mara was safe, was cared for, though he wondered if he would have felt that assurance had he not been weary and inclined to leave.

By the afternoon, he had given up. Saddling Luin, he rode out of the village and onto the plains of Lemish. By late afternoon, he forded the southeastern branch of the Vingaard River at the very spot where he, Jack, and Mara had been ambushed by the bandits. Emerging from the water onto the opposite bank, he felt unburdened, as though something mysterious and demanding had been lifted from him.

He slept fitfully not far from the sound of the river, and his dreams were of Boniface and snow and knives.

Early the next morning, he was riding again, north and west as his memory took him. Steering by the planets was no use, for while he had been in the Darkwoods, the sky had changed. Chislev, Sirrion, and Reorx had returned to their old provinces of the sky, and you would think it was winter if you reckoned by the planets rather than the calendar.

Indeed, the weather itself had turned brisk, and the springlike prospects of Sturm's first day on the road homeward had bogged down in an icy rain by evening of the next day. He stopped in a copse of oak and alder, this time constructing a lean-to deftly, skillfully, with a breath of thanks to the elf maiden Mara.

It was midmorning on the third day when Sturm Brightblade reached the northernmost stretch of the Vingaard River. The cold had swept out of the east overnight, and he had awakened to a hint of frost on the oak leaves, to the steam of his breath in the air. Two hours' ride had brought him to the famous ford; beyond it, a chill mist lay on the riverbanks, and to the north, the Vingaard Keep was lost in oppressive, icy fog.

Sturm reined in his horse beside a large brown boulder and stood in the saddle, rubbing his hands to warm them. The waters were unnaturally shallow for early spring, when the river usually swelled and overflowed its banks. It seemed a stroke of good fortune. With an easy crossing and a long brisk ride over the Solamnic Plains, he could camp in relatively safe country—maybe even the Virkhus Hills—and be at the Tower by noon tomorrow.

Then would come the explaining, the answers to Gunthar and Alfred and Stephan.

And the meeting with Boniface. He would have to think on that. Think on it, and watch for poison and for daggers in the dark.

Angrily he brushed back his hood. Why Boniface was after him was a mystery still. Something his father had done, no doubt, but how the son figured in was beyond his green fathoming. But the Order was his family, and the Tower was home, despite the dangers that lay therein. He would return quietly, and when the time was right . . .

He would uncover vipers in the midst of the gardens. He would avenge his father.

Nonetheless, he wished he had stayed in the Darkwoods. His wish grew even stronger when, out of the mist in front of him, five squat and shaggy figures approached slowly, their swords drawn and their tails thrashing ponderously.

He had never seen draconians before. Indeed, he had never heard them named except in a kender legend he had heard, ridiculed, and dismissed in the leisurely month before this last momentous Yule. But the first look was enough to judge by, and he drew his sword from its newly forged scabbard.

As he did, the snow began to fall. Lightly it scattered across Luin's sturdy red shoulders and across the bare blade of the weapon. For a moment, Sturm thought he heard music, distant and merry and wild, but he pushed it from his thoughts.

The draconians approached even more slowly, lifting their barbed swords even though they were still a good twenty yards away. Sturm offered a brisk Solamnic salute, and three of them stopped approaching altogether. Crouching, hopping like ravens, they turned to one another and began to whisper, waving their weapons excitedly.

At once, Sturm spurred Luin forward, sword flashing over his head. With the ancient Solamnic cry on his lips— "*Est Sularus oth Mithas!*"he rode toward the two nearest draconians.

He was by the first two before they could raise their shields, sword crashing into the head of one. With a lightning turn in the saddle, Sturm brought the blade down on the other, and then, more quickly than thought, reined Luin toward the next three, who shrieked and moved sluggishly toward the shallow river.

They appeared to be already moving in waist-deep water.

Sturm rode between them and wheeled Luin about at the banks of the Vingaard. Sword upraised dramatically, he faced them with another loud, piercing cry. Terrified, the draconians dropped their weapons and plodded in different directions, their rasping shrieks lost in the music and the rising wind.

Leaning forward hard in the saddle, Sturm watched them scatter. It would be simple to follow them, to hunt each of them down. But into his memory came the vision Ragnell had shown him that night in the great lodge of Dun Ringhill—the wintry landscape of Throt, the ransacking of the goblin village, the cruel swordplay over the wretched, spitting creatures.

"No," he whispered. There might come a time for hunting them down, but not now. Nor was he the man. He watched until they vanished behind rocks and bushes and brambles, then turned to the ford and the crossing.

The water tumbled slowly around him, licking tamely at the hocks of his mare. Over the steady sound of the river, Sturm thought again that he heard the music. He remembered the sound of Mara's flute, and something deep in his memory and imaginings told him that she was safe.

* * * * *

From his vantage point on the knoll above the west bank of the Vingaard, Tivok watched the lad rein his horse into the shallow water. The draconian wrapped himself against the icy east wind and waved to his comrades camped upriver. It was the second squadron. The four of them—little baaz draconians stationed by the makeshift dam—would be watching. They would scatter rock and felled branches until the waters surged through with an unleashed swiftness and power, racing south and swelling the banks of the river. If they timed it right, the first waves would strike the shallows when the rider came to midstream.

Tivok chuckled. We would see how this stripling handled

a horse.

He was sure this was the one. He had heard the Solamnic oath ringing in the brisk air and seen the sword rise and flash overhead like heat lightning in a distant sky.

Nashif would be punished for letting this one pass.

Tivok signaled again to be certain, then licked his sword to poison the blade.

* * * * *

The snow was falling heavily now, and the banks upriver were crazed with a thin film of ice.

Hawode, second-in-command to Captain Tivok, shifted uncomfortably on a clutter of rock and wood. It was downright tiresome watching that little rise for a sign from the commander. Wasn't there an old saying about a watched pot?

His head hurt. He was drowsy. Draconians weren't made for this season and its weather, their cold blood lulling them when the temperature dropped. Already he had wakened one of the wounded ones, pummeling her with the butt of his sword and promising her more dire punishments if she slept again.

She had regarded him balefully from under her black hood. It made him long for the promised summer.

He shook his head, scattering the pain. The hill grew more and more faint as the snow thickened, and twice he had lost sight of it for a panic-stricken moment. He had thought of taking initiative then, of opening the dam and letting the water rush forth, in the desperate hope that Tivok had signaled unseen from the knoll.

It was stupid, he knew. So he hadn't done it. He sat there and sulked until the outline of the hill had formed again out of the blinding white, and his panic had settled back into a dim unease.

If this was spring in Solamnia, pondered Hawode, his thoughts lazy and dwindling, he would hate to see . . .

The thought froze unfinished in the icy air. The draconian dozed, his slumber deepening with the snow as he joined his three companions in the wintry and dreamless sleep of reptiles.

*   *   *   *   *

Tivok was furious when the rider reached the other bank.

He hissed and lumbered down the hillside, sliding through two inches of fresh snow, his cape billowing like the sail of a ramshackle ice-rigger.

They had all failed him—Nashif and the ambush party, Hawode and those on the upriver dam. He had dreaded that it would come to this, but he dreaded worse the loss of Solamnic gold.

He skidded, fell, and righted himself, cursing softly. His sword shot from his hand, leaving a thick green streak on the breast of the snow. It lay on its edge at the bottom of the hill, its barbed blade glinting, washed clean by the melting snow.

After all, thought Tivok, picking up the weapon, he had plans of his own this side of the river. His thoughts on the struggle to come, he sheathed his weapon absently and loped to the western bank of the ford.

*   *   *   *   *

Luin shivered as the wind struck her wet flanks. Sturm dismounted quickly and drew a blanket from the saddle, drying off the mare as best he could.

The crossing had been easy, almost suspiciously so. The music had faded in midriver, but the mare had plodded along complacently and steadily from the east bank to the west. Though the change in the weather promised an uncomfortable ride, the longest part of the journey was behind Sturm now, and no more perils awaited him save the last and most deadly—the confrontation at the Tower with

Boniface.

Again the lad mulled over the past fortnight, sorting evidence from rumor and fact from hearsay. He would have been an easy target, kneeling absently by the flanks of the mare, his hands and mind preoccupied, had not Tivok approached by the water's edge, his footsteps breaking loudly through a thick sheet of ice.

Sturm lurched to his feet at once, drawing his weapon and wheeling to face the large draconian. With a menacing hiss, Tivok drew his blade and brought it whistling down. Sturm raised his sword to block the blow and felt the clash and grating of blades all the way up his arms and into his shoulders.

The draconian was stronger than he. He couldn't hope to match him blow for blow.

Sturm scrambled away from Tivok, dodging a pivoting slash from the creature's barbed sword. Snorting with surprise, Luin trotted down to the riverbank, leaving the two combatants to their business. Holding his sword level and to the fore, Sturm circled the draconian, crouching and ready for the onslaught.

Tivok, however, was no green, untutored fighter. He bided his time, moving steadily with the circling lad, and when the moment came, it was sudden and accurate and almost deadly. Sturm toppled away from the unexpectedly quick rush and thrust, blocking one blow and deflecting another, slipping over the icy ground until he was out of sword's reach. Only the quickness of his youth and the winter sluggishness of his enemy's blade saved him from quick death on a ragged edge.

Nevertheless, the draconian had drawn blood. Sturm rose unsteadily, clutching his leg.

Tivok stepped back, leaning scornfully on his sword.

"That, Solamnic, should be sufficient," he announced.

Sturm said nothing but steadied for another onslaught.

"The blade, you see, was poisoned, as is our practice, dishonorable though your Order may find it."

"What has my Order to do with this?" Sturm asked angrily, lifting his sword.

"Its money has paid for the poisoning," Tivok retorted with a dry laugh. Tauntingly he raised his sword as well, turning the blade slowly.

"Wh-What do you mean by that?" Sturm asked. His leg throbbed and he stumbled.

"Solamnic money paid me and my mates," Tivok explained, his voice halting and sweet, as though he were teaching a young and thick-witted child. "The finest swordsman of your Order offered me gold and ordered me here to await your return."

"Boniface?" Sturm asked, though he already knew the answer. The draconian began to circle, his black tongue flickering.

"Don't anger yourself," Tivok teased, sword changing from hand to hand. "Poison moves all the more swiftly through hot blood." He laughed and took one tentative step toward the lad. "But Boniface it was," he whispered melodramatically, his eyes glittering with wicked merriment. "Called himself Grimbane, he did, as if we hadn't heard of the great Solamnic swordsman, couldn't hear him talkin' to his squire as they approached the Vingaard. 'Tis Boniface indeed, and he'll give me more gold for your head, which I'll take when the poison's through with you."

The draconian approached Sturm confidently, his breath misting the toothed blade of his sword.

"If I am poisoned, then what does the rest matter?" Sturm declared coldly. The thought was reckless, strangely liberating.

Tivok shrugged ironically. Then music erupted all around them.

It was a warlike skirl of flutes, an old funeral song of Solamnia, loud and shrill. Tivok flinched and was startled for only a moment, but Sturm was on him before he could recover, singing as wildly as he sang that icy morning in the courtyard of the Tower.

"Let the last surge of his breath
Take refuge in the cradling air
Above the dreams of ravens where
Only the hawk remembers death.
Then let his shade to Huma rise
Beyond the wild impartial skies. . . ."

Tivok staggered back, his tail thrashing roughly in the ice-encrusted mud. The two swords locked instantly, Solamnic heirloom and saw-toothed draconian saber. Sturm slipped gracefully between the blades, rolled under the draconian's legs, and leapt to his feet on the creature's other side, swatting his tail playfully with the flat of the sword.

"Back here, Your Amphibiousness," Sturm taunted. He wheeled and brought his sword around in a dazzling arc, and it took all of the draconian's quickness to stop the slashing blow.

Back Tivok staggered, the lad before him a prodigy of blade and movement and invention. Wherever Tivok's sword went, Sturm parried it, as though the weapon itself sensed movement and intent. Sturm danced just out of reach of the sword, lunging and darting like a hummingbird, his long blade thrusting and nipping and flickering.

There seemed to be two of him, splashing bravely at the margins of the Vingaard.

Slowly the draconian's fear overtook him. Something had gone awry with the poison, for by now the human should be helpless, paralyzed.

Tivok looked about frantically, searching for high ground, for reinforcements, for avenues of escape. Always his eyes came back to the sword, flashing and turning at his throat, his chest, his face. Sturm danced and sang as he fought, and the air whistled with the sound of wind over metal and the faint descant of a distant flute.

The draconian gathered himself and leapt toward the lad

in desperation. Hurtling through the air, he turned clumsily, his sword waving ineffectually as Sturm stepped aside . . .

And brought his sword down at the base of the creature's skull.

It was all over in a moment. Though the last cry of Tivok the draconian carried upriver to his drowsing cohorts, no one came to his aid to avenge his death upon the lad who vaulted into the saddle and, too wise to wait for further trouble, spurred his little mare to the west across the level, forsaken plains.

Lying on the dam, Hawode stirred at the distant noise, then tumbled into a deeper sleep.

Chapter 23

Always the First of Spring

VERTUMNUS SET DOWN HIS FLUTE AND SIGHED.

Below, the villagers sat transfixed by the song, their faces uplifted. They hadn't seen what the pooled waters of the clearing had shown him—the reflection of Sturm's crossing the Vingaard and the struggle that took place on the western banks.

Jack cleared his throat.

"Not much of your exalted friend left in that son of his," he observed teasingly, his gaze on Lord Wilderness.

"You could have learned much from him, Jack," Vertumnus insisted. "Most of the world out there is like him."

"We wish the lizard had eaten him!" Diona hissed.

"We do *not!*" Evanthe argued, pulling her sister's hair until the smaller dryad squealed with anger and pain. They wrestled like squirrels on a high branch, then stopped suddenly as Evanthe hung precariously from a twig.

"But why, Lord Vertumnus?" they asked in unison. "Why did the lizard's poison fail?"

"Washed by the snow of our music," Vertumnus explained. "And no more scuffles and snicker-snacks from the two of you!" He waved his flute at the dryads, and the wind coursed through it. Instantly the vallenwood sprouted branches all about them, trapping them in a cage of wood.

The Green Man looked into the pool, where leaves floated aimlessly and the waters rippled and swirled. The faint call of birds at the edge of the forest signaled spring's return, and a warm western breeze sailed through the branches.

"He is a noble sort," Jack observed after a long silence in which the villagers, believing the music and drama were over and that what was said now passed only between father and son, dispersed to various tasks in the clearing. "Honorable and brave, and only half tedious. He distinguished himself with sword and honor."

"That is all he chooses to know," Vertumnus observed. "And he may perish for lack of knowledge." As he put away his flute, music again filled the clearing.

Quickly the company in the trees turned toward the source of the melody. The elf maiden Mara stood at the far edge of the pool, clad in a white gown of gossamer and leaves. A wreath of holly was woven into the strands of her dark hair, and her eyes were adorned with the subtle colors of berries.

Hollis stood behind her, grinning at her handiwork and at how Jack Derry's eyes and smile widened at the sight of the girl.

Mara held the flute to her lips and played on, the stately hymn of Branchala, for which only the elves have words. The villagers, sensing something wonderful and beyond their understanding, stopped their tasks to listen. Standing in a ring of children, Weyland the smith turned to face the elf maiden and reverently removed his hat.

"Bitch!" Diona hissed angrily, but she fell into silence at a withering glance from Vertumnus. Jack rose and climbed down the tree, his eyes never leaving the brilliant spectacle of maiden and music, his thoughts adoring and intimate.

Vertumnus turned away, surrendering the privacy of the moment to his son and the girl.

"The first of spring is always approaching," he whispered knowingly.

*   *   *   *   *

Around Sturm the night had settled, and the stars arranged themselves in the winter constellations. It struck him for the first time that perhaps the days had reversed themselves, that the year had sunk back into ice to await the coming of spring.

For a moment, his thoughts turned to the Southern Darkwoods. Perhaps if the spring were postponed, there was still time to turn the horse about, to retrace the path he had taken. . . .

But he was deep into Solamnia now, a scant three hours' ride from the Tower of the High Clerist. He had chosen to return, and now he would do so, regardless of judgment and censure and the threat of Lord Boniface. It was honorable to see this through, to brave the disapproval of Lords Gunthar and Alfred and Stephan for the sake of justice. And for revenge.

Surely the Knights would incline their ear to redress Lord Boniface's misdeeds. For Justice is the heart of the Measure and the soul of the Rose.

On he rode, into the mountainous night, until the faint sentry lights on the battlements of the Knight's Spur shone high in the west like one last constellation.

*   *   *   *   *

They clothed him, and fed him, and put him to bed. Old

Reza attended the Knight's quarters in the early hours of the morning, and it was he who saw to Sturm's comfort, arranging bread and cheese on a table in front of the lad and pouring goblet after goblet of water while he poured Tower gossip into Sturm's inattentive ears.

"And the Jeoffreys feuded with the MarKenins once more, young master, though not as fiercely as they done back in the summer of 'twenty-seven. It all started when young Hieronymus Jeoffrey lit into Alastor MarKenin after some hunting they done in the Hart's Forest. Hieronymus come from it with a black eye and a dented countenance, which makes Darien Jeoffrey decide that Sir Alastor is needin' to be . . . well, adorned likewise. So Darien and a trio of younger Jeoffreys light into Alastor in a dark passage over the Knight's Spur, and he comes out with eye and countenance and a broken left hand to boot. Which Lord Alfred redresses by pushing Darien against a crenel the next morning and grabbing the lad's off hand with a little too much emphasis, if you understand . . ."

Sturm nodded. Reza continued serenely, forgetting his traditional place in the excitement of the story and seating himself by the young man.

"But in that process, Master Sturm, Sir Darien comes away with the additional bruised ribs, which Lord Adamant goes around claiming Lord Alfred has not got and is in sore need of. So Lords Adamant and Alfred came to the edge of dueling and would of passed over into swords or lances had not Lord Stephan stepped in and smoothed down the hackles. . . ."

Sturm nodded and mumbled, his mouth full of bread. The Tower was the same.

"And, of course, like he always does," Reza babbled on serenely, "Lord Boniface says that they should settle it by the sword anyway, though betwixt you and me, young Master, they could settle it if only one of them knew how to let a bygone be and get on with the business of knighthood. Anyway, Lord Boniface says it could be *arms courteous*, the blunted sword or the wicker, but that the Measure said, and so and so . . ."

Sturm was instantly alert at the name of his father's old friend. Slowly he set down the goblet and stared at the ancient servant, trying his best to appear calm, only mildly interested.

"Lord Boniface, you say? Then he . . . is here at the Tower?"

Reza nodded. "Have some more cheese, Master Sturm," he offered, pushing the plate toward the lad. "Yes, indeed, Lord Boniface is here."

"Then I shall have to pay my respects, out of family loyalty," Sturm replied—a little too quickly, he feared. "Yes. I'll call on him and pay my respects."

He smiled at the old servant and accepted another wedge of cheese. His thoughts raced quickly over strategies.

"He'll expect you right away," Reza prodded. "You know how he is about the Measure."

"Indeed he will," Sturm said, grateful for the interfering nature of ancient retainers. "Indeed he will, Reza, and given the hour and my weariness, I should be beholding if you would say nothing of my arrival until a time when I might . . . present myself to him."

Reza nodded, bowed, and backed away from the table. Sturm finished the bread, sure of the old man's confidence. Then he stood quietly, yawned, took the candle from the table, and slipped down a back stairwell to his cubicle. He was tired and already dreaming as he approached the room, oblivious to the hour, the birdsong outside, the soft shuffling on the stairs behind him.

As Sturm closed the door behind him, a faint light appeared on the stairwell landing. Stealthily Derek Crownguard peered around the corner, smiled, and padded up the steps to his uncle's chambers.

*　*　*　*　*

Sturm announced his presence the next morning.

He collared a page in the hall and sent the boy rushing to Lord Alfred MarKenin, bearing the news that Master Sturm Brightblade had returned from parts eastward and south and would be honored to give account of his journey in the presence of the High Council.

When the page returned at noon to escort him to the council room of the Knight's Spur, Sturm followed the child, his armor spotless and buffed, his sword glittering and naked in his hand. For an odd moment in his quarters, he had thought to place the weapon in the sheath that was Vertumnus's gift.

He had decided against it. It was a gleaming reminder of his defeat.

Sturm knew that the High Council was made up of Lords Gunthar, Alfred, and Stephan. Since the council sat privately with each returning Knight, Boniface would not be present. For what Sturm had to say, that absence would be most welcome.

* * * * *

The council room was none other than the great hall in which the Yule banquet had taken place. Stripped of its ornament and restored to its everyday function, it seemed dark and serviceable, an office of state rather than a seat of ceremony, the heart of efficiency rather than elegance.

His first surprise was a rude one. Alfred was there, and Lord Gunthar, but instead of Lord Stephan Peres, Boniface Crownguard of Foghaven sat in the third council seat. When Sturm entered the room, Boniface leaned forward, his face expressionless but his eyes cold and absorbed as an archer's on the target.

Sturm completed the three ceremonial bows distractedly, and in the third of the six formal addresses, he stumbled over the word "impeccable" and blushed deeply.

It was not according to the Measure, this sloppiness. It

had been too long since he attended to ritual, and there was Boniface besides. . . .

"You presume much, Sturm Brightblade," Alfred observed, "to request audience with this council. After all, you are not yet of the Order."

"True enough, Lord Alfred," Sturm agreed. He found it difficult not to look at Boniface. "And yet on Yule night, when Lord Wilderness challenged me and I decided to embark, it was at the urging of the Order and with its blessings. I thought it . . . proper . . . that I should answer in turn to its judgments."

"What you think is . . . 'proper,' Sturm Brightblade, is not necessarily by the Measure," Boniface remarked, his voice dry and cold. He leaned back in his chair, folding his hands elegantly across his chest. "But we of the council have an interest in what came to pass regarding your journey to the Southern Darkwoods. And so, given these extraordinary circumstances, the Council . . . indulges your testimony."

"For that I am most grateful," Sturm replied, recovering in the intricate dance of deference and courtesy. "And I might welcome the Lord Boniface to a place upon the High Council, expressing the hope that his appointment was in . . happy circumstance."

There was a long pause, in which the three council members glanced uneasily at one another.

"Lord Stephan is elsewhere," Alfred replied. "Be seated."

Sturm looked in puzzlement from face to face, waiting for further tidings of his old friend, for the High Justice's explanation. But Lord Alfred averted his glance, leaning to whisper something in the ear of Boniface, who nodded vigorously. Gunthar was the only member of the council who would regard the lad directly. His quick, almost undetectable wink was reassuring, though it revealed nothing.

Sturm cleared his throat. "I suppose," he began, "that I should begin with my news of Vertumnus."

And he told it all, or almost all, trusting in the truth and the judgment of at least two who sat on the council. He told how he had ventured through the maze of a ghostly castle, through bandits and hostile villagers into a wood of illusions, guarded by mythical creatures and mysterious, deceptive paths.

He told his story, scarcely mentioning the various ambushes, snares, and traps he had encountered on his journey to and from the Darkwoods, nor did he speak of Jack Derry or Mara, though he wasn't certain why he kept his friends from the recounting. Three pairs of eyes were fixed on him in the telling, and when he finished, the council hall settled into a thick, uncomfortable silence.

"Well," Lord Boniface began, with a sidelong glance at Lords Alfred and Gunthar. "I suppose a certain honesty lies in any account of failure."

"More than that is revealed in this telling," Lord Gunthar protested, turning to Boniface in irritation. "And if the Lord Boniface were . . . *more seasoned* in matters of the council, he would realize the virtues and merit of the lad's journey."

"Perhaps the Lord Gunthar would care to instruct me," Boniface replied ironically, addressing his words to Sturm as he pivoted in his chair. "The boy was sent to the Southern Darkwoods to meet with Lord Wilderness on the first night of spring, there to resolve a mysterious challenge. By his own admission, Sturm fulfilled only the first of his duties—to reach the Southern Darkwoods. No matter that he might as well have gathered mushrooms or . . . consorted with fairies."

He smiled cruelly, and with a deft swordsman's movement, drew forth his dagger and began to pare his fingernails.

Sturm's jaw dropped. Setting aside the Measure with the same recklessness that had guided his sword against the draconian on the banks of the Vingaard, he turned to his antagonist.

"Mushrooms and fairies are less . . . nightgrown and unbelievable than what I *did* see, m'lords. For I saw one of the Order . . . a renowned Knight of the Sword . . . in dark conspiracy against me, and for reasons that I know not!"

The hall was ominously silent. A servant's broom rustled over the stairwell outside the door, and an incongruous owl hooted in astonishment somewhere in the eaves of the castle. The Solamnic Lords didn't move, and Sturm thought of Castle di Caela, of its marbled monuments to family and folly, as he told the story anew.

This time he left nothing out. Jack Derry emerged in the tale, with all his unstudied know-how, and the elf maiden Mara in her petulance and music and her odd devotion to a cowardly spider. For the first time, Sturm mentioned the druidess, the name Ragnell stirring old memories on the faces of the council.

But through all his story one name returned again and again, from the moment the door of Castle di Caela closed behind him all the way to the last words of Tivok, the draconian assassin.

Boniface it was. "Grimbane." Lord Boniface of Foghaven, Solamnic Knight of the Sword.

Conspirator. Traitor to the Measure.

It was as though the world had stopped. After a minute's silence, in which nothing whatsoever spoke or sounded or even stirred, Lord Alfred cleared his throat.

"These," he intoned, "are the most ominous of charges, Master Sturm Brightblade."

"Charges for which," burst in Lord Boniface, "I shall demand satisfaction!"

Angrily the swordsman pushed away from the table, knocking over his chair and scattering paper and leather-bound volumes of the Measure. He drew his sword and stalked to the center of the room, where he turned and faced them all—his accuser and the council members who had heard the story.

"I believe, Lord Alfred," Boniface announced, his voice quivering with emotion, "that in the sixteenth volume of the encoded Measure, on the twenty-second page in the third article, it is related that the Order of the Sword, which takes its Measure from affairs of courage and heroics, enjoins all members thereof to accept the challenge of combat for the honor of knighthood. I believe, Lord Alfred, that the honor of knighthood has been impugned."

Gunthar stood up and walked calmly to Boniface's abandoned chair. He picked up three of the leatherbound volumes that lay on the floor by the table, thumbing through each of them with a dry, ironic smile.

"Sturm Brightblade impugns no Order," Gunthar corrected, his eyes on the High Justice. "Instead, he accuses a single Knight—Lord Boniface of Foghaven."

"Then trial by combat is enjoined," Boniface argued, turning briskly toward Lord Alfred. "The Lord Alfred should recall from his recent . . . *contentions* with Lord Adamant Jeoffrey that such is the prescribed ruling of the Measure on questions of honor."

"And yet we settled that through reason and goodwill," Gunthar insisted.

"Through the blandishments of an old man who walked off into the woods, leaving the Order behind him!" Boniface snarled. All eyes turned uneasily to the legendary swordsman, who looked to the rafters of the hall, where doves nested and gurgled. He closed his eyes and seemed to gather himself.

"If you will notice the forty-fifth page of the aforesaid sixteenth volume," he said, his voice hushed, almost rapturous, "in the first article, it states unequivocally that trial by combat is the preferable recourse for matters individual between Knight and Knight."

"Have it one way or the other, Boniface!" Gunthar exclaimed angrily. "Is Sturm to be judged as a Knight or an un-Ordered lad?"

Lord Alfred thumbed idly through the volume in front of him, his eyes on the glowing mahogany walls, his thoughts entangled and bottomless. Finally he spoke, and even the doves ceased their noises to listen.

"Boniface is correct," he declared, his voice dry and

shaken. "Trial by combat is the recourse, if but one disputant insists upon it. What remains for Sturm is the choice of *arms extreme* or *arms courteous*, of swords deadly or blunted."

Sturm swallowed hard and shifted on his feet.

"No matter the outcome," Lord Alfred announced, "neither charges nor judgment will ever leave this room. Nor will any of us, until those charges are settled, the judgment given according to Oath and Measure and our sacred tradition."

"*Arms courteous*," Sturm said quietly.

Lord Boniface smiled. "I have won the first pass," he declared.

Lord Gunthar walked to a chest at the far corner of the room and produced the padded wicker swords that would decide the issue. "You have beaten a green boy at the Barriers," he said to Boniface through clenched teeth.

The swordsman's back stiffened.

"I am schooling the lad to a demanding Measure, Gunthar Uth Wistan," Boniface retorted. "As his father would have it, were he alive."

"His father would have more," Lord Gunthar muttered. "And he would exact it from your skin."

"By the Measure, Lord Gunthar," Boniface said, his voice jubilant, taunting. "By the Measure now and always, and let the swords fall as swords will fall."

Chapter 24

ARMS COURTEOUS
AND A JUDGMENT

IN THE CENTER OF THE HALL, THEY SQUARED OFF, the
green lad and the legendary swordsman. Sturm hoisted his
shield, then rolled the weapon in his hand. The wicker
sword was lighter than he had imagined, and it felt assuring, familiar.

The Solamnic trial by combat was an ancient, honorable
practice, sanctioned from the Age of Might and the days of
Vinas Solamnus. When charges were brought against a
Knight of the Order, the man could defend his innocence by
sword. Victory assured innocence in the eyes of those
present and the Order itself, regardless of the evidence
against him; if, however, he were defeated, honor bound
him to confess his crime and accept the exacting punishment of the Measure.

Sturm swallowed nervously. It was serious business against a serious swordsman. And yet for a moment, his hopes sprouted. Stranger things had happened in the Order than an upstart catching a champion off balance or nodding.

Stranger things had happened to Sturm himself.

He rocked on his heels, awaiting his fabled opponent.

Slowly, confidently, Boniface put on his white gloves. He lifted the champion's targe he had won twenty years ago at the Barriers. The crossed blades on the shield's face were faded and chipped with the strokes and thrusts of a thousand unsuccessful weapons. Casually the Knight took up the sword he would use, examined it for flaws, and, testing it for balance, spun it in his hand like a strange and magical toy. Scornfully he turned to Sturm, returning the lad's ceremonial salute brusquely, coldly.

"We await your pleasure, Lord Alfred MarKenin," Boniface announced, and crouched in the ancient Solamnic Address, the stance of swordsmen since the days of Vinas Solamnus. Reluctantly Lord Alfred raised his hand, then lowered it, and in the center of the council hall, the contestants circled one another in ever-decreasing spirals.

Sturm moved first, as everyone knew he would, for patience is slippery in a green hand. He stepped forward and lunged at Boniface, his movements skilled and blindingly quick.

The older Knight snorted, stepped aside, and batted the sword from Sturm's hand, all in a graceful turn as effortless as brushing away a fly. Sturm scrambled after the sword, which came to rest against a dark wall, its hilt extended mockingly toward his hand.

He grabbed the sword and turned about. Boniface laughed and leaned against the long council table, the sword twirling in his hand.

"Angriff Brightblade would be pleased indeed," he taunted, "to see his son spread-eagled and groping in the Barriers."

With a bellow, Sturm rushed at Boniface, charging wildly like some enormous, enraged animal. The Knight waited calmly, and at the last moment, he whirled away, tripping Sturm and slapping him on the backside with the flat of the wicker sword. Tumbling head over ankles, the young man skidded over a dropped volume of the Measure and crashed into a scribe's table, shattering its spindly legs.

"Finish it, Boniface!" Gunthar shouted, his face flushed and his eyes blazing. "By the gods, finish it and leave the boy in peace!"

Boniface nodded dramatically, his smile venomous and merry. He wheeled about and stalked toward a dazed Sturm, who raised his sword uncertainly, unsteadily.

* * * * *

Reeling, his senses jostled and his hands heavy, Sturm watched as Boniface's sword danced around him, beside him, nicking against breastplate and helmet and knees. It was a swarm of hornets, a flock of stirges, and no matter where he raised his shield to block, his sword to parry, Boniface's weapon was under him or over him or around him, biting and slashing and gouging.

Twice they locked blades, the fracturing sound of wicker on wicker echoing in the council hall like the sound of tree limbs breaking. Both times Sturm was pushed back, the second time staggering.

Boniface was not only quicker and more skilled, but he was also twice as strong as the lad in front of him.

Cornered, outmaneuvered, battered and checked and scratched and flustered, Sturm pressed against the farthest wall of the room, his back flush against the double oaken doors that had been locked behind him when the audience began.

There was no place to run, no place to dodge the onslaught. His thoughts in a frantic scramble, drowning in a torrent of swords, Sturm searched for something—

anything—to turn back his enemy.

The draconian, he thought at last.

Now what did I do. . . .

His sword flew out of his hand. Hurled forty feet through the air by a deft turn of Boniface's blade, it clattered and broke on the stone floor of the council hall. Instantly a wicker point rested in the hollow of his throat, and he looked into the eyes of Boniface—as blue and lifeless as a cloudless winter sky.

"Judgment, Lord Alfred," Boniface requested. He wasn't even breathing quickly.

"The council finds for Lord Boniface of Foghaven in trial by combat," Lord Alfred declared, his voice thin and abstracted.

"Pack your belongings, little boy," Boniface hissed. "Solace is quaint in the springtime, I am told."

* * * * *

The four of them emerged from the council hall in silence. In the corridors ahead of them, pages and squires ducked into the alcove, and servants turned too diligently back to their work. Nobody asked the outcome of the trial by combat, nor even why swords had crossed in the first place. The council was sworn to silence in such matters, and neither Alfred nor Gunthar would ever speak of this afternoon.

But everyone would know. If they couldn't tell by Sturm's scarlet face, by the grim satisfaction in the steel-blue eyes of Lord Boniface, they would know from the detailed account of Derek Crownguard, who had peered through the keyhole at everything that had transpired.

And they would hear what Derek and Boniface wanted them to hear. "A real swordsman took Angriff Brightblade's boy behind the woodshed and taught him respect for his elders."

So was the version Sturm thought they were hearing as

he packed his belongings the next morning. He imagined the cruel news dropped at breakfast into the midst of the whey-faced, conspiratorial Jeoffreys, who would laugh behind their bacon to imagine it.

Slowly he wrapped his shield, breastplate, and sword in thick canvas. They had served him better than he had served them. Perhaps at some later time, he would be worthy of them again. As for now, he would take defeat like the Knight he devoutly hoped to be.

All accusations and suspicions were supposed to die in the council hall. According to the laws of trial by combat, Boniface of Foghaven had set them to rest with his sword. Indeed, as Sturm wrapped the last yard of cloth about his sword, he was beginning to believe that Boniface was innocent.

For the draconian's word could well have been slander, simply conjured out of an overheard name and a spiteful heart . . .

. . . and as for Jack Derry . . .

Well, in the past fortnight, dream and imagining had blended so thoroughly with fact and reason that . . .

He shook his head. Boniface was guilty, regardless of Oath and Measure. He knew it in far deeper places than ritual touched. And yet Sturm's own weakness with the sword had assured the freedom of his assailant. The trial was over. Regardless of what he or Alfred or Gunthar thought about the matter, Boniface had been found innocent, acquitted by his sword hand and the ancient Solamnic machinery of statute and tradition.

Hoisting armor to his shoulder, Sturm followed the elaborate maze of corridors from his quarters to the courtyard. It was like the day he had departed for the Southern Darkwoods, shorn of farewells and encouragements and even kindly glances. Everyone hastened to avoid him, to find himself elsewhere when Sturm crossed to the Tower stables.

Gunthar had spoken to him the night before and urged

him halfheartedly to stay on at the Clerist's Tower. He was relieved when Sturm insisted on going and said his good-byes awkwardly, with fumbling words and a brusque hand-shake.

Nor would he tell the lad anything about Lord Stephan Peres.

Lord Stephan would have seen me off in better style, Sturm thought as he inspected old Reza's feeble and dis-tracted efforts at saddling Luin. There would have been jests and windy words from the battlements, and even per-haps some wisdom, though the gods know what wisdom one can find amid all this misdirection and folly. . . .

But Lord Stephan was . . . away. Reza had come to the matter at last, as he fretted with the saddle, and the bizarre story of the old Knight's departure came to slow and scarcely coherent light.

It seems that the very night after Sturm left the Tower for the Darkwoods, Lord Alfred MarKenin had dredged up a band of unlikely hunters for a jaunt after deer in the Wings of Habbakuk. Lord Adamant Jeoffrey's younger twin brothers had volunteered at once, eager to curry favor with the High Justice, and Derek Crownguard, too, when Lord Boniface's sudden duties at Thelgaard Keep had left him un-attended. Given such a triad of young lions, Alfred had in-vited Lord Gunthar as "a steadying influence." Gunthar begged off, seeing no prospects in the group for either hunt-ing or good fellowship, but Lord Stephan overheard the of-fer and imposed himself on the party at once.

"Where did they hunt, Reza?" Sturm asked. "And what does this have to do with Stephan's leave-taking?"

"In due time," Reza said, leaning in the doorway as Sturm gathered his clothes and stuffed them in a saddlebag, his thoughts intent on the Knight's story. "Meanwhile, here's the rest of it: They were a mixed lot, were Lord Alfred's hunting party, and when they decided to take me along as a lyamer of sorts . . . well, they weren't the best at what they were fixin' to do. Lord Alfred decided we would go to the

Hart's Forest, on account of that's forest enough for the likes of the Jeoffreys."

Sturm smiled. The Hart's Forest was a forty-acre deer park not far from where the Wings tapered into the Virkhus Hills. Once he had admired the place and loved to hunt there, but after his journey to the Southern Darkwoods, it seemed rather tame and arranged—a well-planned garden of trees and wildlife.

"Well, we get there about sunup," Reza continued, "and we thrashed around for near three hours, flushing squirrels and gnats and starlings, with nary a trace of deer. It bothered Lord Alfred, I'd wager—them clumsy Jeoffreys, Derek Crownguard's loud voice, Lord Stephan blowing on a beaten-up hunting bugle and tangling his armor in vines. So finally Lord Alfred called off the hunt, and it wasn't even noon yet. We turned about and started out of the park."

Reza leaned forward, hushed and amused.

"And it was then that the woods began to change. Trees sprouted leaves and blossomed, roots burst from the ground, and fruit fell out of the treetops."

"Fruit?" Sturm asked incredulously.

"Oh, the seasons have been in a fix for quite some time, Master Sturm," Reza explained. "No doubt you seen some of it yourself. Anyways, it was like the woods decided to become a forest, a Silvanost or . . . or a Darkwoods, Master Sturm. And it turned against the lot of us—scared the daylights out of the young ones, it did. Young Master Dauntless Jeoffrey got thrown from his horse when this little yellow lizard fell out of the branches of a vallenwood onto the poor creature's nose. The other Jeoffrey twin—Master Balthazar, is it?"

"Beaumont, Reza," Sturm corrected, setting his foot to the stirrup. The saddle shifted somewhat, and he stepped back with a frown.

"Master Beaumont . . . rides through a spiderweb and startles himself, and it gets worse when the spider that built the thing is the size of a thumb and bites him."

Sturm grinned in appreciation.

"So this Master Beaumont turns his filly about and gallops away, and nobody sees him until three days later, and we all think the forest has swallowed him, too. He came back nigh impossible to recognize, what with his face all swollen from the spider bites."

Reza tightened the cinch of the saddle and stepped back to admire his handiwork.

"But what about Lord Stephan, Reza?" Sturm asked.

"There's what happened to Master Derek," Reza urged slyly, winking at Sturm.

"Very well. You know I can't resist. What happened to Derek?"

"Ran into a tree."

"A tree?"

"Thorn tree. Master Derek says it sprung up before he could stop his horse. A low branch caught him in the chin, and the next thing he knows, he's in the Tower infirmary and it's two days later."

Sturm stifled a laugh. It almost lifted the sadness of defeat and leaving.

"But, Reza," he insisted, sobering, loading his belongings onto Luin's back. "What of Lord Stephan? It grieves me that I cannot say good-bye."

"The oddest thing, it was," the servant said, staggering under the weight of the breastplate until Sturm lifted it from him and hoisted it onto the mare. "For in the midst of all of this, there was music playing."

"Music!" Sturm exclaimed in alarm.

"We all heard it, but none of us knew where it came from."

Sturm frowned, started to speak, then remained silent as old Reza prattled on.

"It was all around us. Sound of the flute, it was, and the branches all swaying with the melody, and the birds all chiming in. It weren't but a moment until Lord Stephan answers the notes with that battered old bugle of his, and for the first time, it sounds like a musical instrument, and the birds answer the bugle notes in turn.

"Then a green path opens in the woods. I saw it. It started up not a yard from my feet. Winds between the trees, it does, like a carpet leading up to the dais at a coronation. Lord Stephan starts laughing like the red moon has struck 'im. Then 'At last!' says he. 'At long last, something!' and off down the path he rides, laughing like a madman."

"Did nobody try—" Sturm began, but the old servant was bent on finishing the story.

"He rides off at a gallop, his armor sprouting greenery as he's riding, and he's laughing, his old laugh booming amongst the birdsong and the flutes. Lord Alfred galloped after him, would have cut him off and reined in the horse, too, but Lord Stephan brushes him aside and says 'No,' he says. 'No, I have been about this for years,' and he laughs and goads the horse toward this thick stand of oak, and it was like a stand of trees in front of him opens up to let him in and then closes behind him real nice and quiet, so the forest looks like it always did before we come there. We searched for Lord Stephan until late afternoon, halooing and sending out the dogs, but those of us the woods hadn't swallowed nor run off were a mite skittish about the business, as you might imagine. . . ."

Sturm nodded absently, his thoughts on Lord Stephan. It was a strange tale, but like so many strange tales he had heard, it had a whiff of the familiar to it. He would not mourn the vanishing of Lord Stephan Peres, nor was he even inclined to go look for the old man. There was something sudden and wise in his disappearance, as though Lord Stephan had looked around and discovered he had outlived the Order.

Reza went on for a few minutes more—some involved story about how everyone blamed everyone else for the mishaps in the deer park. He stood back as Sturm climbed into the saddle.

"There's more than a few of us, Master Sturm," the old

man said, patting Luin's flank reassuringly, "that look forward to our own eighty-fifth year and what it brings."

"I hope my own is like that of Lord Stephan Peres," Sturm replied, and he turned Luin's head toward the gate.

* * * * *

Sturm was two days traveling back to Solace, passing through the Virkhus Hills and onto the Solamnic Plains, following the same path he had taken two weeks, a season, a lifetime ago. His only company was a growing sense of loss—of something irrecoverable that lingered at the edge of his thoughts like a half-remembered melody.

Now the Hart's Forest had meaning to him as he passed south of it. It shimmered green and orderly at the edge of his sight, and for a brief moment, Sturm thought of venturing north, of combing its measured recesses in search of the vanished Lord Stephan.

He decided against it. Had not Stephan waved the lot of them away, plunging into green thought and green shade with a willing heart?

To each his own, Sturm thought sourly, but he knew that did not sum it up.

Down through the plains he rode, keeping the river safely to his east. The double towers of Castle di Caela loomed for a while in a foggy eastern distance, but Sturm had no desire to return there. On he galloped, past Thelgaard Keep and over the border to Southlund, where a day's ride brought him to Caergoth and the sea. All the while, he waited expectantly for a music that did not return.

He kept the armor hidden safely away, wrapped in canvas and secrecy, until he was on the Straits of Schallsea. It was as Raistlin had said: The North could eat you alive. Solamnia was dangerous country for Solamnics, more dangerous still for the grim and embattled Order.

He did not look back as he crossed.

After he set foot on dry land at the northernmost reach of

Abanasinia, the travel was easy, the familiar sights rising like fog or music upon a distant plain. There were the mountains—the rounded Eastwalls and the imposing Kharolis Range behind them—and once he caught sight of a tribe of Plainsmen loping soundlessly on the western horizon, framed by sunset and distance and their dark magic.

"Home," he whispered, and he tried to feel something of home: a wistfulness, a burning in the depths of his heart. He felt none of those bookish sentiments. Indeed, he felt nothing at all but a sense of recognition—that these were places he had seen before, and from this point on, he would not be lost on the road.

Nothing was home, he decided. Not Solamnia. Not here.

Homecoming did mean pleasant reunions. Sturm rode into Solace to find Caramon busy with hammer and peg in the village square, putting the finishing touches on a curious scaffolding and stage.

Caramon's greeting was brisk, enthusiastic. Smarting from the big man's bear hug, Sturm rubbed his shoulder and examined the handiwork before him.

"It's for Raist," Caramon maintained proudly, seating himself unceremoniously on the grass and reaching for a jug of water. "To raise us some traveling money."

The big man winked and rubbed his fingers together in an innocent imitation of a worldly merchant.

"How exciting," Sturm said, regarding his old friend soberly. "And where will your travels take you, Caramon?"

"To the Tower of High Sorcery," Caramon whispered, beckoning Sturm closer. "In Wayreth Forest. To the first big test of my brother's magic."

"Don't you . . . have to be *invited*, Caramon?"

"That's just it, Sturm," the big man replied. "Raistlin *has* been invited. He has been tested early and long, and they have found him worthy!"

Caramon beamed and nodded toward the far end of the green. There, in a dazzle of sunlight, a slight red-robed figure pivoted and murmured, dark birds dancing in his hands and at the hem of his garment.

Tested and found worthy? Sturm thought as he watched the young mage at practice. Sleight of hand, I suppose, and perhaps an array of mirrors and smokes. It's not that easy when you venture forth, because the whole green world itself is deceptive and pipes mysteries at you from places beyond your knowing.

It's a music that just about killed me. But despite it all, I still have the Measure and the Oath.

Sturm frowned. The thought did not seem consoling.

But I could have had other things, had I chosen. There are choices out there, Raistlin. And the best part of magic is that you can choose.

To the last of this and of anything, you can choose. I hope you will choose honorably.

Heedless to the arrival of his old friend, the young mage stretched his arms, shivered in the spring wind as a cloud passed over the sun, and climbed the steps of the newly finished scaffold. It looked like party games to Sturm, like a clever child's magic show, as bottles and birds and blue flames whisked through the air and vanished.

Soon a crowd began to gather, villagers from Solace, farmers from the outlying countryside, even a dwarf or two and a curious kender, of all things, standing at the back of the crowd, craning to see the events on the scaffold. Somewhere in the milling and murmuring of all these people, where the guttural remarks of the dwarves mingled with the broad accents of country folk and the melodious southern talk of Haven and Tarsis and far-off Zeriak, the faint sound of a flute arose and lingered, sowing the air with promise.

Epilogue

Of Remembrances and Inns

Once more the year turned, and after it another spring, cold and forbidding. And Lord Gunthar Uth Wistan passed through Solace.

His stay was brief. Sturm's solitary cottage was a bit cramped and humble for a prominent Solamnic Knight, and there was something in Lord Gunthar that balked at the idea of his good friend's son having settled beneath a thatched roof, sleeping on a hard dirt floor.

Gunthar left provisions behind him and enough silver to last the lad comfortably to midsummer. He also left a story, and at his departure, Sturm hastened to the Inn of the Last Home, bearing bread and tidings for his friends.

Raistlin warmed his hands by the fireside as Sturm entered the room. Caramon loomed at a southern window, looking out at a late light snow that fell on the branches of the enormous vallenwood that housed the rustic old inn.

It was as though the twins were lost in separate dreams. Raistlin wore a red robe now, in anticipation of his magian tests at the Tower of High Sorcery in Wayreth. Caramon's misgivings about the journey ahead of his brother had infected Sturm, too, until the sight of the robes made him uneasy and apprehensive.

Raistlin turned toward him, smiled faintly, and seated himself at a cluttered table.

"Something in you speaks of tidings, Sturm Brightblade," he whispered, clearing away crockery and cutlery with a thin pale hand. "That old urgency and Solamnic importance. Seat yourself."

Caramon stayed by the window as Sturm sat and unwrapped the bread. Raistlin ate greedily, feverishly, as Otik moved silently to the table. Sturm handed the innkeeper a coin, and the burly man removed himself to kitchen fires and the teapot.

"I have brought news, Raistlin," Sturm announced, frowning at his friend's incessant hunger. "Lord Gunthar carried the news to me."

Caramon turned from the window and shivered.

"Won't it ever be warm, Raist? The snow gets into your bones by this time, and it's like the first of spring is forever in coming."

Raistlin waved away his brother's comments and smiled ironically, his dark eyes fixed on Sturm. "Enough talk of the weather, Caramon. Our friend Sturm Brightblade has news of high intrigues in the Order, brought to him no doubt by his august visitor."

Sturm shifted in the chair, his gaze bright and intent. "This is the story they are telling in the High Clerist's Tower now. Vertumnus returned at the Yuletide, and what that means is that my long banishment is over."

Caramon pulled up a chair, and Sturm began the marvelous, confusing tale.

"Now this is only one of many versions of that story, mind you. For each man there—Lord Gunthar, Lord Alfred, all of the MarThasals and Jeoffreys and Invernos—remembers it differently now, Lord Gunthar says."

"As before they remembered the Yule and his first visit differently," Caramon prompted.

Raistlin shot his brother an impatient look. "I remember Sturm's account of the first visit, Caramon. Unlike the Knights involved, I need no one to refresh my memory."

The room fell to an uncomfortable silence. Sturm cleared his throat.

"Well, be that as it may, none of them remember it quite the same. But on a few things, most of them agree.

"After I left the High Clerist's Tower and came back here, Gunthar and Alfred watched Boniface rather closely, to hear Lord Gunthar tell it. The issue was supposed to be over and buried, settled in trial by combat, but neither of the two justices could help but think that there was something . . . sour and disturbing about Lord Boniface, about how he had challenged and bullied and taunted me from side to side of the council hall. Nonetheless, they were bound by tradition to accept the outcome of the trial, and of course there were other things to attend to, with spring upon them and wider duties for the Order in the Solamnic countryside."

"In other words," Raistlin interrupted dryly, "they forgot about you."

"I don't mean it that way," Sturm protested, hastily and a little strongly. "It's just that . . . that . . . the Order has other business as well."

The dark twin nodded as his gaze shifted back to the fireplace, to a long, half-dozing abstraction.

Otik bustled out of the kitchen, carrying a tray of steaming crockery. The last of his other guests, a kender and a dwarf Caramon claimed to know, had bundled themselves and waded slowly out the main door of the inn, leaving the common room hushed and virtually empty.

"By the time late spring passed into early summer," Sturm

continued as Otik set the tea in front of him, "it seemed as if Boniface had forgotten the matter, too. Lord Gunthar said he ate better, he slept later, and eventually he lost entirely that haunted, beset look he had carried with him throughout the previous winter, and he was joking again with the squires, hunting with Adamant Jeoffrey, and even managing a lengthy summer trip west to his holdings in Foghaven.

"So the controversy was all over, or seemed to be. Even the approach of Yule failed to bother anyone or remind them of past hard feelings, for they were reasonably sure—from Lord Alfred down to the youngest Knight who remembered—that this holiday would be pleasant and quiet, like the Yules of a simpler time before the Green Man's trespass.

"Boniface, too, was merry enough as the banquet approached, and downright jubilant when it began, seated amid his regular faction of Crownguards and Jeoffreys, and this year with several highborn Jochanans to boot. The hall was brighter than any remembered, strung with new lanterns and abundant with torches, as though even the linkboys had caught the lightness of spirit. The music, Lord Gunthar said, was better than the year before—a kender trio from farthest Hylo, two penny whistles and a timbrel, frantic and bawdy and as loud as a nest of squirrels."

"I'd love to have heard that music!" Caramon exclaimed.

"Hush!" Raistlin snapped, swatting his brother weakly as Sturm smiled and poured the tea.

"Boniface was jubilant, they say, informally propping his booted feet against a long oaken table as if he was at hunt or in the field, not at some formal banquet. Holding court, he was, in the midst of the younger Knights, talking swordsmanship and armor and horses, toasting the hunt and the birth of someone's son . . . a Jochanan, if I recall."

"I am rapt for the particulars," Raistlin observed ironically. "Go on with the *real* story, Sturm."

Sturm sipped the tea. It tasted of apple and faint cinnamon—a winter tea, no doubt the last of Otik's stock.

"As the wine poured," he said, "the talk grew louder and louder, rising over the kender hornpipes until it distracted Lord Gunthar, and believe me, he is not iron when it comes to manners and protocol."

Caramon nodded dimly. Raistlin coughed and lifted the cup in front of him.

"Gunthar said that the young Knights ignored him," Sturm continued, "and that they were only louder and more fierce as the banquet went on. The bluster turned to shouting and jostling, and Lord Gunthar said that it was hard to imagine Boniface in the midst of such horseplay. He said that it was as if something had changed in him, that even his celebrations were . . . desperate. Boniface threatened the sword at the slightest disagreement and called all to task for their lapses in protocol, citing volume and paragraph of the Measure."

"In short, he was typically Solamnic," Raistlin commented, sipping again from his tea.

Sturm ignored his companion. "It was as though Boniface had . . . had clutched the Oath so tightly that he had lost it. Or so Lord Gunthar said. All of a sudden, he heard a flute amid the laughter and penny whistles."

"At last!" Raistlin breathed, setting down the cup. "You have a long way in getting to the point of the story, Sturm."

Sturm ignored him. "The farthest tables fell into silence as the sound of the flute joined with the penny whistles. The new sound delighted the kender musicians, and they began to improvise upon the melody until the sound of the whistles merged with the sound of the flute, and it was hard to tell who was playing what.

"Gunthar looked up, he said, and a thousand roses tumbled from the rafters. Pink and white and red and lavender, they showered the Knights and ladies with a hundred thousand petals. The kender musicians whooped with delight and tossed their instruments into the air, and the flute continued on its own, a solo in the midst of the raining roses."

"Go on," Raistlin urged intently.

Sturm smiled. It was the part of the story he liked the best. "There's not much further to go, my friend. It was then that the doors of the hall burst open. Lord Vertumnus had arrived, at the head of an army.

"Doves flew in front of him, and owls and larks and ravens, scattering to the rafters and singing as they scattered. Squirrels and hares followed them, and foxes stalked in behind them, strutting among the tables like sharp-eared hunting dogs.

"Well, the kender were ecstatic by now, their dances more brisk and disruptive, overflowing onto tables and onto the dais. Gunthar said it became too much for Adamant Jeoffrey, who grabbed two of the little folk by their topknots and held them still."

"There's one I'd like to do the same to," Caramon muttered ominously, looking over his shoulder at the door of the common room. "And I'd like to sling him around while I was at it."

"A dozen elk followed," Sturm said, "and two dozen deer after them. The creatures entered silently, and Derek Crownguard was startled out of ten years by an enormous dark-eyed buck, its long, serious face crowned with a wide rack of antlers, who crept up behind him and nuzzled him."

Sturm laughed at the image. The prospect of Derek Crownguard backing up into yet another surprise amused him no end. Lord Gunthar had told and retold that particular scene, to his young friend's continual delight.

"Then the music arrived," Sturm said when he recovered, "in the wake of the deer and the elk. Three centaurs cantered into the hall, capsizing table and chair and the family banners. Each of the huge creatures played the nillean pipes, and on the back of each rode a green-robed female. Gunthar says it was a human druidess and two dryads, all playing hand drums. I suppose you know who they are from the story I have told you.

"Last of all came the great bear, the grizzly, striding all confident and free right into the midst of the Order. And

Lord Wilderness sat atop the broad shoulders and back of the bear, his flute raised and glittering, playing and playing at a new song. . . .''

Caramon stood up, his impatience rising with him. "This is all well and good, Sturm, all this stuff about processionals and music. But what about the Knight? What about that villain Boniface? I can't stand a story where he doesn't get what's coming to him."

"That is next, Caramon," Sturm replied. "Boniface rose from the table, his hand resting lightly on the hilt of his sword. Gunthar and Alfred stepped down from the dais.

"Vertumnus slid from the back of the bear, and again he pivoted in a full circle, his flute vanishing again somewhere in the leaves that covered him. Centaurs set aside their pipes, the druidess and dryads their hand drums, and the music drifted from the room."

" 'I am Vertumnus,' he announced, his voice as always mild and low. 'And again in the turning seasons, I wish to make a point near and dear to my heart. And to rehearse the legends of druids.' "

"I know of no druidic legends," Caramon declared.

Sturm shrugged. "Neither do I. And neither, it seemed, did Lord Gunthar. He looked around at his cohorts—at Alfred and Boniface and the squadron of Jeoffreys and Jochanans, and he saw the same blank look on each face.

" 'Very well,' Lord Gunthar said. 'Rehearse your legends, Vertumnus.' He laughed about it when he told me. He said that he strutted and blustered as if he could have stopped Vertumnus from saying or doing anything he wished, but I suppose that's all the Measure is sometimes—saying we can control something because we don't want to look at its depths, its prospects. . . ."

"Enough philosophy," Raistlin declared. "It doesn't become you."

Sturm continued, his eyes on the fire. " 'It is a simple legend, Lord Gunthar Uth Wistan,' the Green Man announced, 'one brought to me by the Lady Hollis.'

"Then Hollis, or Ragnell, or whatever name she really goes by, dismounted from the centaur.

"They've a puzzle about the lady, you know," Sturm said, his gaze lost in the depths of the glowing coals. "Some saw a hideous hag descend from the centaur's back; others saw a young and beautiful woman, her dark hair crowned with ivy. Some—very few—saw no druidess at all."

He smiled and shook his head, and the twins glanced at one another curiously.

"But each of them heard Vertumnus, and his next words all remembered clearly.

" 'I have heard,' the Green Man claimed, 'that a druidess can cast a spell so powerful that a treasonous man—a rank betrayer of friend and Order and country—cannot draw his sword from sheath or scabbard. Or so the druids have told me.'

"The council hall was silent, Gunthar said. Not a word passed beneath the banners. Then all of them started at the sweeping noise of a blade drawn from its sheath. As one, they turned toward the source of the sound."

"Boniface!" Raistlin said with a triumphant laugh. "The pompous fool fell for a child's trick!"

"*What* trick?" Caramon asked, reaching across the table for more of the bread. "I thought we were talking about druid spells."

"You're right, Raistlin," Sturm said. "It did discover the villain. Boniface was standing beside his chair, shamefaced and horrified, his sword halfway bared.

"Vertumnus grinned at the prospect. Of course, I do not believe those legends, though some of you may find them convincing,' he said, and he climbed the dais to stand by Lord Gunthar.

"Boniface pulled the remaining length of blade from the scabbard and swaggered to the center of the room. I can imagine the look on his face. I'm sure that I have seen it before. 'Does Lord Wilderness accuse me of dark and treacherous crimes?' he asked loudly, and I would have liked to have been in that hall—been a fox or a raven or even a winter spider—to have seen what came to pass.

"Because Vertumnus only shook his head. 'Your sword hand accuses you, Boniface of Foghaven,' he replied mildly, and I know that the mildness heaped further coals on the heads of the family Crownguard."

Wordlessly Sturm rose from the table and stood by the fireplace, then moved to the window. Outside, the snow had stopped, and the stars peeked out of a low netting of clouds. At the edge of the eastern sky, the white rim of Solinari glittered on the horizon.

The red moon was nowhere in sight.

Sturm took a deep breath and turned to face his companions.

" 'Then my sword shall redeem me from insult and calumny,' Boniface said, and then he raised his sword in the traditional challenge to trial by combat. Vertumnus nodded and extended his sword hand, and they tell me that green fire danced over his fingers. Then he winked at Lord Gunthar, once and mysteriously, and asked in a stage whisper, 'Will no man lend me the use of a sword?'

"Gunthar claims that he doesn't know why he gave Vertumnus his sword. The Crownguards are calling him a traitor. They've called him worse names through the winter and into the spring, and even Lord Alfred says that Gunthar was charmed or ensorcelled.

"Gunthar says it was something else. He says that, despite the commotion and the accusings, he's glad he did it.

"But whatever it was, charm or freewill, he drew his sword and handed it to Vertumnus, who stretched, yawned, and leapt to the center of the room, not a sword's length from Lord Boniface.

" 'Arms extreme,' is it? Lord Wilderness asked.

" 'Arms courteous,' Boniface replied nervously, and he sheathed his sword as Derek Crownguard stepped by the nibblesome elk and made his way to the chest where the wicker swords lay ready.

" 'As you wish,' Vertumnus replied. '*Arms courteous* it shall be, and may truth rest in the sword arm of the victor.'

* * * * *

Caramon leaned forward. It was the part of the story he had awaited.

Otik coughed impatiently behind the bar. Closing time had come, and the three lads had made no motion to their cloaks and belongings, much less toward the door. The innkeeper whistled loudly as he wiped off the empty tables, but making his way across the room, he overheard and paused, caught up like the twins in Sturm's unfolding story.

Sturm closed his eyes. "Three hundred pairs of eyes watched expectantly as the two men circled one another, wicker swords humming in the smoky air. I know what it sounds like. I heard it myself almost a year ago to this night.

"And having faced both of them in the Barriers, I can tell you how it must have begun. Vertumnus handled the weapon deftly and thoughtlessly, like a juggler, while Boniface stalked about him, his movements stronger, more labored. It was a match of equals but of opposites, I would have wagered.

"But Gunthar told me otherwise. He told me that from the outset Lord Wilderness ruled the contest. Once, twice, a third time he parried Lord Boniface's lunges and thrusts, on the third occasion vaulting through the air and landing lightly on the other side of his adversary, slapping his bottom with a sharp stroke from the flat of the wicker blade.

" 'Sauce for the goose!' Vertumnus cried in a honking, mocking voice, and Boniface flushed and charged after him. This time Vertumnus's sword was at the Knight's face, delivering round slaps to each ear before Boniface had the speed or balance to block either blow."

"Such . . . such *insult!*" Caramon exclaimed delightedly, and Sturm nodded, struggling guiltily with his own vengeful delight.

"Gunthar said it was an indignity, said he was tempted to turn his head away, but that he was glad he didn't. He said that, curiously enough, out of the corner of his eye, he noticed the High Justice's shoulders shaking with laughter.

"Playfully Vertumnus backed his opponent around the room, his blade humming and whining. He touched swordpoint to the brooch at Boniface's throat, and with a flick of his wrist, sent the bauble flying and the cape to the floor. Then the Green Man switched his sword to the left hand, shielded his eyes with his right, and fought Solamnia's finest swordsman to a standstill. Even blinded, he made true his parries and thwarted the skill and speed of Lord Boniface's attacks."

Caramon let out a low whistle. Otik coughed again and leaned over the table next to the lads, wet rag in his meaty hand.

Lost in the story, Sturm was beyond attentiveness and courtesy. With a sigh, Otik seated himself behind Caramon and listened to the rest of the tale unfold.

"At the far corners of the council hall, dazzled by Lord Wilderness's display of bravado and skill, some of the younger Knights began to applaud. Lord Wilderness moved with the panther strides of a younger man, and his sword hand, flashing with a reckless brilliance, dodged in and out of the torchlight as the blade whistled and sang like a flute.

"And this is what Lord Gunthar told me, and all of the Knights saw it happen this way: Suddenly the ancient stone walls of the council hall cracked and crumbled and burst forth with branches. Trees lurched from the ancient tiles on the floor, maple and oak and blackthorn springing from the masonry. Vertumnus stalked toward Boniface, waving his wicker sword.

"Then Boniface wheeled toward the nearest door, but there a very old man, white-bearded and garlanded in green, blocked his escape. Boniface wheeled into and out of the shadows. The baffled torchlight glinted off his armor, off his ceremonial targe, as the old man brought forth a trumpet and sounded a hunting call."

"Stephan?" Raistlin asked with an ironic smile.

Sturm nodded. "Gunthar knew him at once. Boniface must have, too, for he clutched at a chair to recover his balance.

"By the door, Lord Stephan bent to a fencer's stance of his own. 'Let foliage become foilage, Lord Wilderness!' he whooped, and nearby a nervous squire tittered and was silent. 'And let the stones of Castle Brightblade cry out against Boniface of Foghaven!' "

"By Paladine, it's shaping into a real *donnybrook!*" Otik cried out from behind the rapt Caramon. All three of the companions turned in surprise to the hefty innkeeper, who flushed and motioned at Sturm. "Go on, young master. The hour is young, though the inn be closed."

Sturm nodded and returned to his story.

"Vertumnus wheeled about, his gaze following his opponent 'with serenity and scorn,' as Lord Gunthar put it. He plucked an olive branch from the dense greenery above and extended it to the Knights on the platform, who moved away as Boniface backed between the chairs, his sword still raised.

"Abandoned and set upon, the Knight glanced toward the shadowy exit behind the dais, covered by a wooden screen. There was somebody standing there, too—somebody green and young and strangely familiar. . . ."

Sturm smiled at the thought of Jack Derry. Silently he wished his young friend well.

"So there was no escape. In the crowded council hall, in the midst of the Order, Boniface Crownguard of Foghaven played his last scene by the Measure.

" 'By the Measure, Lord Vertumnus,' he said, and his voice was loud and assured and battle-seasoned, rising above the murmur of Knights and the bugles and the drumming of the dryads, which had taken up once again in the rafters of the council hall. 'I insist that we fight by the rules of the Solamnic Order.'

" 'Very well,' Vertumnus agreed. 'One measure is as good as another, from where I stand.'

"Then Boniface marched from the dais, and the wicker swords clashed for the last time."

Sturm paused here. He sipped tea and looked dreamily toward the fire.

If you have learned anything, Sturm Brightblade, thought Raistlin, *you have learned how to tell a story.*

"Almost from the beginning," Sturm continued, "the outcome was obvious. Boniface fell twice, stumbling over the very rules he knew so well. His sword seemed heavy, his movements planned, and though the Green Man's weapon also moved slowly at first, it gathered speed and inspiration. Lord Wilderness fought by code and rule, as precise a fencer as one could imagine or fancy, and yet Lord Gunthar told me that Vertumnus found room to frolic, explore, invent.

"Boniface fell the first time when he tripped over the steps of the dais. He slid to the foot of Lord Alfred's chair, scuffing his hands and knees, and the wicker sword flew from his grasp, skidding toward the servants' door, where Jack Derry stepped from the shadows and stopped the weapon with his foot, scooting it back toward Boniface in one quick movement.

"The Knight struggled to his feet, picked up the sword, and wheeled toward Vertumnus, who had hung back politely, awaiting his opponent's recovery. They locked swords once, twice, then Vertumnus attacked with a series of slashes and thrusts, knocked the weapon from Boniface's hand, and, before the Knight could duck or dodge or step aside, set the blunted tip of the sword at the hollow of his throat.

"Be thankful, Boniface," Vertumnus announced, "for though you are a traitor to your Order, you are no skilled murderer. Though your money and intelligence blocked the pass from Castle di Caela to Castle Brightblade, blocked it with four hundred bandits, you are no murderer. Agion

Pathwarden should have seen the ambush coming . . . should have known enough to turn back. It was accident that brought him death that winter night in the midst of rebellion and siege."

"What?" Caramon exclaimed. "Why, Vertumnus—"

"Gave Boniface a way out!" Raistlin exclaimed. "Why, how odd! Don't you see, Brother? The Measure punishes treason by banishment, murder by death!"

Sturm smiled. "For such a . . . critic of the Order, you know its rules well, Raistlin. In one challenge, Vertumnus had secured the punishment of Lord Boniface and forgiven him as well."

"I don't follow," Caramon said.

"Nor I," rumbled Otik, behind him.

Raistlin rolled his eyes. " 'Tis simple, as I understand it. All Boniface had to do was own up to dealing with those bandits, as Sturm told us he had done, then say that he had *no intention* of harming a hair on Agion Pathwarden or any of his Knights. The treason charge would stay, but the capital charge of murder, the Order would . . . would set aside. But it eludes me, as well, why Vertumnus would free his old betrayer to a comfortable exile in a far region."

"Hear the rest of the story, then," Sturm said.

"Indeed, the Green Man's next words to Boniface were a warning: 'You can choose,' he said, raising his flute in the dark hall. 'Choose wisely!'

" 'But treason is worse,' said Boniface, 'though its penalty be only banishment. While the murderer hangs from the rope, treason is far worse. I shall not suffer that living charge. No,' he said, his voice rising, filling the room with his confession. 'I shall abide by the sword and fall where I have lived, in the arms of the Measure. Agion Pathwarden and his garrison are dead, and I killed them all and planned for the killing. Murderer I may be, but I say I have never betrayed the Order.' "

"The fool!" Raistlin exclaimed. "With his freedom before him . . . it was suicide by the rules!"

"Or it was something else," Sturm said. "For the life of me, I am not sure whether it was folly or the most noble end he could make.

"At any rate, Boniface stepped away from the dais calmly and explained to all present his guilt in the murder of Agion Pathwarden. Horrified at what had passed, Gunthar stared at Lord Wilderness, who stared back at him grimly. He said that Vertumnus's eyes were 'opaque and fathomless,' and he suspected that Vertumnus found his the same."

The longest pause of all signaled the end of the story. After a few minutes, Otik arose and returned to his business, and the three companions stared at one another across the table.

They remained quiet, almost reverently so, as Caramon slipped a cloak gently over his brother's shoulders. Together the three of them walked out into the Abanasinian night, and in the morning, the first passersby could tell easily where their paths had parted in the freshly troubled snow.

* * * * *

But there was more to the story that Gunthar did not tell to his old friend's son, more about which he chose to remain silent, suspecting that had he told even Sturm, it would have been the betrayal of a cherished secret.

For the Knights had led Boniface away ceremoniously, to the dying sound of the flute. When the year turned, the gibbet would rise in the courtyard of the Tower, and few outside the council hall would know the reason that Boniface Crownguard of Foghaven would be hanged on the first day of spring. Few would know, but the testimony of the Order was strong against him, and he walked up the steps defiantly, his full Solamnic armor bright and relentless.

But that was yet to be on the Yule night when Vertumnus lingered with the company, an hour after the guards escorted Boniface away. Dismissing dryad and centaur and druid and bear, Lord Wilderness played his flute a last time for the fellowship of the Order. It was a serenade brief and mournful, the Knights and squires and pages and servants all seated and rapt as Lord Wilderness soothed and sustained them with melody.

And there is a story arising from that night regarding what next came to pass. Vertumnus, it is said, launched off on a melody so ancient that new trees, trees unheard of since the Age of Dreams and known only in the songs of bards, sprouted from the floor of the hall, and the Knights knew them by name without asking, prompted by a strange and wild impulse in the music.

Suddenly Gunthar recognized the cadence and began to sing. " 'Out of the village,' " Gunthar sang, and instantly Lord Alfred beside him joined in, their voices a tuneless but powerful duet:

"out of the thatched and clutching shires,
out of the grave and furrow, furrow and grave,
where his sword first tried
the last cruel dances of childhood, and awoke to the
shires forever retreating, his greatness a marshfire,
the banked flight of the kingfisher always above
him . . ."

One by one, the other Knights took part, and the song rose as it always did, but this time more music than chant, this time blessed and informed by a melody not of the Order, a tune beyond Oath and Measure.

Few of the Knights looked to Huma's chair, but three of the pages, their eyes reverently upon the hallowed spot, saw a ghostly helmet and breastplate, a shimmering of red and silver seated at the place of honor, as though the twin moons themselves had converged to issue forth history.

None of the older Knights saw the presence.

Nor did Vertumnus himself, whose thoughts even Gunthar did not know: thoughts that played over the Tower, its spires and battlements, through past and present and a future that would bring the boy back from Solace, swept up in forces he had chosen again—forces that would bring him to the battlements six years from now, when the Tower lay in siege and the War of the Lance raged about him.

You can choose, Sturm Brightblade, Vertumnus thought, lowering the flute for the last time in the great council hall, in the moment before he vanished into a world of leaves and light. The leaves and light and foliage vanished along with him, leaving the council hall shadowy and bare. To the last of this and anything, you can choose.

A single green rose, perfect and wild, graced the seat of Huma's chair.

Bridges of Time Series

This series of novels bridges the thirty-year span between the Chaos War and the Fifth Age DRAGONLANCE® novels.

Spirit of the Wind
Chris Pierson
Riverwind the Plainsman answers a call for help from the besieged kender in their struggle against the great red dragon Malystryx.

Legacy of Steel
Mary H. Herbert
Sara Dunstan, an outcast Knight of Takhisis, risks a perilous journey to Neraka to found a new order of knighthood in the land of Ansalon.

The Silver Stair
Jean Rabe
As the Fifth Age dawns, Goldmoon, Hero of the Lance, searches for a new magic and founds the great Citadel of Light, linked to the heavens by an endless stair.

The Rose and the Skull
Jeff Crook
When Lord Gunthar, head of the Solamnic Knights, dies mysteriously, the order must make an alliance with their deadliest enemy, as a troop of gully dwarves races across Krynn to unmask treachery.

Dezra's Quest
Chris Pierson
The daughter of Caramon Majere brings aid to the centaurs, as they try to escape a terrible pact made with Chaos.

Edited by Margaret Weis and Tracy Hickman

An anthology of short stories from prominent DRAGONLANCE authors, describing the terrible battles and brave exploits of heroes during the first decades of the Fifth Age.

Contributors include Margaret Weis and Don Perrin, Nancy Berberick, Richard A. Knaak, and Douglas Niles.

The Raistlin Chronicles

The story of Raistlin Majere, Ansalon's greatest mage, told by the person who best knows his tale.

The Soulforge

Margaret Weis

A mage's soul is forged in the crucible of magic. Now, at last, Margaret Weis reveals the hidden story of Raistlin Majere's early years, from his first brushes with magic to his Test in the Tower of High Sorcery. His life, and those of the people near to him, will be changed forever.

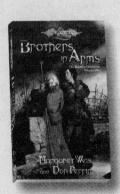

Brothers in Arms

Margaret Weis and Don Perrin

As the shadows of war gather across Krynn, Raistlin and his brother Caramon offer their services to a commander. Half a continent away, their sister Kitiara also enlists in an army and begins her rise to power among the Dark Knights of Takhisis.

*From the pen of **Ed Greenwood** . . .*

Stories of the Seven Sisters

Widespread and many-tentacled is the evil that threatens Faerûn. Before its heart can be found, all of the Seven Sisters, Chosen of the goddess Mystra, will play a part . . . and all too much blood will be spilled.

The Temptation of Elminster

The third book in the epic history of the greatest mage in the history of Faerûn.

The young Elminster finds himself apprentice to a new, human mistress—a mistress with her own plans for her young student. Tempted by power, magic, and arcane knowledge, Elminster fights wizard duels and a battle with his own conscience.

Elminster in Myth Drannor

It is the time of the great elven city of Cormanthor, and the mage Elminster enters where no mortal has gone. Among the elves of this great settlement, he learns magic, and when peril threatens, he helps spin the mythal that transforms Cormanthor into . . . Myth Drannor.

Elminster: The Making of a Mage

From his lowly origins, Elminster rises to become the foremost mage in Faerûn, one who will walk the centuries with elf and dwarf, mage and sorceress alike.